SHATTERED
Memories

HURTFUL LOVE BOOK ONE

VERA HOLLINS

Edited by: Emily Junker
Formatted by: Champagne Book Design
Cover Design by: blankyc.art

For Rasa, the source of my best memories and my twinkling star.

PROLOGUE

A few hours earlier

LIFE COULD BE A KALEIDOSCOPE OF MEMORIES. ALL COLORS mashed together into one, some darker, some lighter. Some you wanted to forget, some you wanted to keep with you forever. This night was a memory I wanted to keep with me forever.

The stars dotted the sky with twinkling intensity, and the glow of the moon blended with the dozen lights peppering the garden. The peaceful burble of the fountain made for the perfect soundtrack to this moment.

A moment that was meant to be filled with kisses and whispered promises.

With love.

I sensed him before he even made a sound. I always did.

I leaned against the back porch railing as I turned to look at him. He was six feet two of ripped muscles and burning desire, dressed all in black. The pounding of my heart grew louder in my ears as he approached me, drowning out the distant sounds of the party. Even after all this time, he was able to transform me into a mushy puddle. He commanded my body and made himself the center of my world—made himself my everything.

His eyes devoured me as his gaze traveled down my body, leaving me feeling naked. His lips twisted with pleasure; he knew well what effect he had on me.

"You're so beautiful," he said in the deep, husky voice I loved.

I raised myself on tiptoes to bring my lips to his ear. "You too."

His body shuddered beneath my whisper. He let out a groan, grasping my upper arm and bringing me closer to him. "I'm tempted to ditch this party and go somewhere where I can be alone with you."

Tingles rushed down my spine as his fingers moved up my shoulder and reached my neck. He gazed into my eyes with a need that matched my own.

"Me too, but it's Prescott's birthday."

He placed his hands on the small of my back and drew me to him. "Do you think he'd notice us gone?" As I chuckled to this, he pressed his forehead to mine and continued, "I need you."

I ran my finger across his inviting lips, imagining them all over my body, every part of me locked in anticipation of it. "I need you, too. So much it scares me sometimes."

He cupped my cheek. "Don't ever be scared of what you feel for me. We belong to each other, and that will never change."

His lips connected with mine, and my nerves buzzed with awakening desire. I felt my head spinning as our tongues clashed, drowning in his taste. His delicious, delicious taste. He tasted like trouble and wicked thoughts. Like fiery lust. Like everything I'd ever wanted.

He was mine. Carter Reese was mine.

We drew apart from each other minutes later, both breathless and dazed. Nothing mattered—no party, no other people. Only he and I.

"I love you."

I smiled and opened my mouth to tell him I loved him too, but the ringing of his phone interrupted me.

Carter groaned. "Someone's timing sucks."

I giggled. "You better answer that. It's probably Prescott wondering where you disappeared to."

His brows drew together as he pulled the phone from his pocket and saw the caller.

"Who is it?"

"It's Jackson." He answered the call. "Yes?" His jaw tightened as he listened. "Now?" He met my gaze. "Fine. I'm coming." He shoved his phone back into his pocket. "He's at the mechanic. His car broke down on the way here, so I have to go pick him up."

"Then go."

"I'll be back soon." He brushed his lips over mine, and a shudder rushed through me. Hungry for more, I grabbed his biceps and leaned into him, prolonging our kiss. He moaned into my mouth and caught my face with both hands, giving me an almost bruising kiss that I felt *everywhere*, but that ended too soon.

With a resigned sigh, he tore away from me and headed down the path leading around Prescott's house.

"Go back to the party," he told me, walking backward. "We'll finish this later." The promise in his gaze burned hotly.

My heartbeat pounding, I touched my swollen lips with my fingers, staring into the darkness. I should get back inside.

Still, something kept me rooted to the spot. Out of nowhere, a feeling flared to life and grew stronger, searing inside my chest and bringing on a wave of panic.

Something bad was going to happen.

I didn't know if this was a product of the few shots I'd taken earlier or not, but that didn't stop me from rushing to the driveway to catch Carter. It felt like my life was at a crossroads and about to take a wrong turn, and I had to persuade him not to go.

I reached the driveway too late; his black Maserati was already tearing down the road. My phone's battery was dead so I couldn't even call him and tell him to turn around.

I shook my head. I was acting silly. Everything was going to be just fine. He would be okay, and when he got back, we would laugh at my reaction.

Rubbing my cold hands together, I returned to the house.

Only hours later did I find out that nothing was going to be fine and my life had indeed taken a wrong turn.

Because nothing remained the same.

And all that Carter and I had was now gone, becoming only a wrecked memory suffused in pain.

CHAPTER ONE

Present

THE FIRST SIGN THAT SOMETHING WAS TERRIBLY WRONG WAS the unanswered calls. Prescott had tried both Carter's and Jackson's phones, but neither of them answered.

I returned home hoping to find Carter there, only to find Mom with her boyfriend, Dominic, in the foyer with a phone pressed against his ear and an expression that stopped my heart.

"I understand," Dominic said into the receiver. "We'll be right there." He ended the call.

I reached him in two quick strides. "What happened?"

"It's Carter. He had an accident and was taken to the hospital."

I slumped, my hand against my mouth. "No, that can't be right."

His grim expression was answer enough.

Mom gnawed on her lip, two vertical lines forming between her brows. "How did it happen?"

Dominic explained as he shrugged on his blazer, "There was a fire in a restaurant downtown. According to her friends, a girl was trapped in the restroom and Carter rushed in to save her. As he was getting her to safety, part of the ceiling collapsed and knocked him out, but firefighters managed to pull them both free."

My heart tightened. "No."

"He's in surgery for TBI now." He reached for his keys. "Let's go."

Cold fear slithered through me at the mention of surgery. Surgeries always gave me a terrifying impression, something that only happened to people in movies, but this was real, and Carter was having one just now. I struggled to breathe evenly, having to consciously draw in breaths as I followed Dominic and Mom to his car. This had to be a nightmare. This couldn't be real. It just couldn't.

Carter was just supposed to pick up Jackson. How did he wind up in that fire? If he died—

No. He couldn't die. I couldn't lose him too.

The drive to the hospital was quick, but to me, it felt like a lifetime had passed. The moment Dominic's car pulled into the parking lot, I bolted from the car on wobbly legs and started for the hospital without waiting for Mom or Dominic.

"Zoe, wait!" Mom called after me. Her purse banged against her hip as she covered the distance between us. She placed her cold hand on my shoulder. "We need to be calm, okay?"

"I can't be calm when I don't know if he's even alive!"

Dominic led the way inside. "Let's not jump to conclusions, alright?"

The trip to the reception desk and then the operating waiting room was nauseating. Other visitors and hospital staff moved in all directions, conveying a sense of urgency. The smell of antiseptic was overwhelming. I wanted to reach Carter as quickly as possible, but I also wanted to prolong the moment because I didn't want to hear it if he hadn't made it. The receptionist could only tell us he was still in surgery. I didn't know whether that was a good sign or not.

The waiting room was empty when we arrived, save for Jackson. Jackson always had a stony face, one that revealed little

SHATTERED MEMORIES | 7

to no emotion, so seeing him pace back and forth with a distraught expression and a hand slicing through his disheveled hair sent my heart down to my toes.

"Jackson!" I darted to him. "Why didn't you answer your phone? Were you with Carter? How did Carter end up in that restaurant? How did he look when they got him out?"

He shifted his stance, his features and gray eyes turning steely. There was some untamed, dark energy in him that only added to my nerves. "Calm down, Zoe."

"Don't tell me to calm down!"

"I assume you were with my son since you're here," Dominic said.

"Yes, sir. I was at the mechanic shop across from that restaurant, waiting for Carter to come pick me up. The fire started just as he arrived. We heard there was a girl trapped inside, and since the firefighters hadn't come yet, Carter rushed inside to save her."

I supposed I should be proud of Carter for being so brave and heroic, but all I felt was regret that there wasn't someone else who could have saved her. If Carter hadn't gone to save her, he would've been okay.

"He was unconscious when the firefighters pulled him out. The paramedics brought him here, and he's been in surgery since."

Knowing we wouldn't get anything more from Jackson, Dominic and I stepped away. Neither Dominic nor I could keep still, so we both began to pace.

As time trickled by, desperation seeped deeper into me, and I sat down next to Mom, seeking her comfort. She took my hand and squeezed it. We didn't say anything.

The nurse finally stepped out of the operating room a while later. Dominic and I rushed toward her.

"How's my son—Carter Reese? We were told he was in surgery."

"Will he be okay?" I asked.

"The doctor will be out soon, and you'll be able to talk with him." Her face revealed nothing, which only made me think the worst.

I dropped back into the chair next to Mom and began to bounce my leg. She pulled me into a hug.

"Trust that he's going to be okay," Mom told me.

"Mm-hmm."

The doctor took his sweet time coming out. It could've been minutes or hours when he finally emerged, and I burst into a laugh when I saw the smile on his face.

"He's out of danger," the doctor said.

"Thank God," Mom said beside me as I squealed, wrapping my arms around her. My chest caved in like a deflated balloon. Carter was alive. He was okay.

I wanted to see him and make sure he was alright. I wanted to hold him and never let go of him. That moment couldn't come soon enough.

The doctor went on to explain the details of the procedure Carted had undergone, but I was only half-listening, bubbling over with joy.

"When can we see him?" I asked.

"Soon, but family members only," he replied, looking between all of us. "He will be transferred to the ICU shortly. He will need to stay there for observation. Now, if you don't have any questions, I'll take my leave."

"Thank you, doctor," Dominic said.

The doctor nodded and left.

Mom went over to hug Dominic. There was a profound relief on their faces as they embraced each other, like the whole weight of the world was taken off their shoulders. Dominic's fingers clutched the back of Mom's shirt, his eyes closed.

"He'll be okay," Mom whispered to him. She sounded as if she was saying that for both their sakes. "He'll be okay."

Filled with restless energy that begged to be released, I started pacing back and forth, until Jackson smiled at me.

"Count on Carter to pull through everything," he said.

I smiled back. "I didn't doubt him for a second. Okay, maybe just a little." It was way more than *a little*, but neither of us said that.

"I'm going to arrange for Carter to get transferred to a private room," Dominic said and left in the same direction as the doctor.

Sometime later, they moved Carter to a private ICU room, but he was still unconscious when they finally allowed us to see him. Some portion of fear slammed back into me as I rushed into the room first and saw his motionless form. He was hooked up to a heart monitor, an IV drip, a nasal cannula, and various other tubes. His face looked pale under the room lights, creased by tired lines. A bandage covered his head.

My gaze ran down his arms—arms that had held me tightly just hours ago. Then his lips that owned me . . . lips that had curved into a gorgeous smile as he'd told me he loved me.

And now he was here, lying in this hospital bed. The doctor said he was out of danger, but if he was out of danger, why wasn't he waking up?

I took a deep breath and covered his hand with mine. "You better be okay. You have to be."

Mom stopped next to me. "He'll be okay, honey," she repeated what she'd told Dominic. "We have to believe in him."

I ran my hand down Carter's cheek, my heart aching in my chest. I wished he would just open his eyes. I wished this wasn't real.

"You two should go home and catch some shuteye," Dominic told Mom and me. "I'll stay with Carter."

I shook my head. "I don't want to go." I wanted to stay by his side no matter how long it took.

"You need to get some rest, Zoe. I'll call you if he wakes up."

"But—"

"No *but*s."

"Come on, honey," Mom said, pulling me by my elbow. "Dominic's right. We'll be back later in the morning."

"Fine," I conceded reluctantly.

I leaned over Carter and placed my hand on the side of his

head. I imagined him waking up and telling me this was just a nightmare that would pass.

I didn't move, waiting for his eyes to open. His eyes remained closed, and I had to take a deep breath against the pain that slashed through my chest. I rubbed at the spot.

"I'll be back soon, I promise," I whispered and left a lingering kiss on his lips.

Tears filled my eyes, but I'd let them spill only once I got home and didn't have an audience. Mom and Dominic whispered something between themselves before he kissed her and gave her the keys of his car. With one last look in Carter's direction, I followed Mom out, despair building in my chest at the distance increasing between Carter and me.

Jackson stood up from a chair. "How is he?"

"He's unconscious, but he's stable," Mom said. "We're hoping he'll wake up soon."

Jackson frowned at my expression. "He's tough, Zoe. He'll wake up before you know it."

"Yeah. Let's keep our fingers crossed."

We all headed out of the hospital together. The whole way home I wondered how the hell I'd ever get any rest knowing Carter was here.

I was already counting hours until I could see him again.

I was right—I barely got any sleep at all. I kept looking at my phone, expecting a call from Dominic, or for Mom to enter my room to update me on Carter's condition. The wait became unbearable, so I took a quick shower, dressed, and jumped into my car, unable to wait on Mom to go to the hospital together.

Carter and I had a complicated history. We met two and a half years ago when Dominic started dating my mom and then brought us to live with him and Carter. To say we'd gotten off to a rocky start was putting it mildly, but once we succumbed to our true feelings . . . every day had been the best day of my life ever since.

Carter was fierce in hate, but he was even fiercer in love, and he never failed to show me how much he loved me. He always put me first. What we had was rare, something I'd never felt with any other guy and was sure I'd never feel with anyone else ever. So, seeing him suffer was a special kind of pain. What hurt even more was that I could do nothing to help him. I was powerless, and I hated it.

My phone rang, almost startling me. My heart jumped at Dominic's ID on the screen.

I hit the answer button. "How is he?"

"Great news, Zoe. He's awake. I'm going to see him now."

Yes, yes, yes!

I fisted the air, releasing a chuckle. "I'm already on my way."

I ended the call and floored the gas pedal, barely staying within speed limits as I navigated the streets. Another laugh burst out of my mouth, joined by a few more. He was awake. I wanted to dance with joy, but that would have to wait.

I rushed into the hospital and made for the stairs. I was filled with too much energy to be able to wait for the elevator. My sneakers thudded against the patterned flooring as I raced up to his floor and then to his room. My heart was in my throat, beating fast— part from exertion, part from excitement.

Just as the door of Carter's room came into view, it opened, and Dominic stepped out.

"Dominic!"

His brows went down when he saw me. I didn't stop, making to step around him to enter the room, but he caught my arm and stopped me. "Zoe, wait."

I gave him a puzzled frown.

"We should talk first."

"Talk? Why?" I craned my neck to see around him and through the cracked door.

Carter was lying awake in his bed. Our eyes met, and my heart jumped in my chest with joy. He looked me over, two lines of confusion settling between his brows.

I moved to join him, but then his eyes frosted over. Dominic stopped me from moving farther.

"We really should talk—"

"What is *she* doing here?" Carter spat out.

My breath stopped in my throat. "Carter?"

"I called the doctor," Dominic told me. "He must be confused, that's all."

I tore my gaze from Carter's angry eyes to look at Dominic. "What do you mean?"

"I said, what's she doing here?"

Dominic caught my shoulder. "Carter isn't feeling quite well. I'm sure it's temporary—"

I pushed past Dominic into Carter's room, confused as to why he was looking at me with hostility. "I came to see you as soon as I could. How are you feeling?"

His eyes grew even icier, and I stopped in my tracks. That look was so familiar. It was exactly how he'd looked at me two and a half years ago, when my mom and I moved into his house.

It was a look of pure hate.

"I don't want you here. Leave."

I didn't understand. Was this really happening?

"Carter, what's going on? Why are you—"

Dominic pulled me by my elbow, taking me to the corner farthest from Carter's bed. "He doesn't remember," he whispered to me.

My breathing halted. "He doesn't remember what?"

"It appears he doesn't remember the last two years of his life. He has amnesia."

CHAPTER TWO

I STARED AT DOMINIC, BLINKING FAST. THAT HAD TO BE A JOKE. "You can't be serious." I turned to face Carter. "Carter? You remember everything, right? You remember *us?*"

"*Us?* What the fuck are you talking about?"

"I think it's best we wait until the doctor comes—"

I left Dominic's side and approached Carter. "Come on, Carter. You're joking, right?"

The doctor stepped in. "Good morning." He wore a smile that felt out of place given the current situation. "It's good to see you awake, Carter. How are you feeling?"

Carter crossed his arms over his chest, glaring at him. "How do you think I'm feeling? I woke up in a hospital and have no fucking idea what's going on."

"Doctor, my son . . . he seems to be having trouble recollecting some things."

The doctor acknowledged that with a nod. "If you two could please step out, I need to have a moment with Carter."

I tried to see anything in Carter's gaze—anything that would tell me this was only a brief moment of confusion—but it was like I was facing a wall. There was nothing even remotely comforting there.

"Carter, you—" I started.

"Let's go, Zoe." Dominic pulled me backward by my shoulders, breaking my eye contact with Carter.

My breathing quickened as we stepped out and Dominic closed the door behind us. The pounding of my heart sounded like thunder to my ears in the silence of the hallway.

"There must be a mistake. He has to remember," I said.

Dominic looked to the side, but he smiled for my benefit. This sent me pacing up and down the hallway as we waited for the doctor to emerge. My heart contracted with pain at the image of Carter looking at me with hate.

When the doctor stepped out of Carter's room, I skidded to a stop.

"How is he?" I asked the doctor before Dominic had the chance to.

"I'm going to have to run some tests. He's feeling confused and tense. He doesn't remember how he got here or any recent events. In fact, it seems there's a huge chunk of his memory missing. The last thing he remembers apparently happened roughly two years ago." He glanced at me. "He commented how you look older, so that only confirms it."

I clamped my hand against my mouth, my legs barely holding me upright.

"Is it permanent?" Dominic asked.

"I can't say for sure. That all depends on Carter. Some people remember after a short period of time, but some never do. But let's stay optimistic."

"This can't be real. It can't be," I told Dominic once the doctor left. If it were true . . . if he forgot we'd ever been together and the last thing he remembered was from a period when he hated me . . .

Dominic's expression was grim. "You saw him."

"Yes, but . . . is it possible that his feelings are gone along with his memory?"

He didn't answer, and my heart gave a painful kick against my ribs.

"I need to see him." I moved to enter Carter's room, but Dominic caught my arm.

"I think you should take it easy first. Come."

"No, I want to—"

"Zoe, you saw the way he was. Right now, we need to process this and see where we can go from here."

I didn't want to *process* this but fighting him on it wouldn't get me far. I dragged my feet as we made our way to the cafeteria, fear twisting my stomach.

We claimed a table overlooking the gardens, and as Dominic went to get us drinks, I studied the flowering bushes and trees planted in visually appealing patterns around the hospital. The sunrays highlighted their colors and created an almost dazzling effect. It was a view deserving to be immortalized in a picture, but I wondered if it was possible to come here and enjoy it with the bleak reality within the hospital.

I couldn't get my mind off that look in Carter's eyes. It was a look I thought I'd never have to see again; it was a look so out of place after all these months of his love. After the way he looked at me last night and the words he said.

"We belong to each other, and that will never change."

I buried my face in my hands, fear coiling sharply in my stomach. Life had thrown me curve balls too often for me to think this was just something minor.

Dominic placed a cup of mocha in front of me and lowered himself into the chair across from me. "He's going to recover."

"How can you be so sure? What if he doesn't? Then what? This is huge. This—"

He placed his hand over mine. "Hey. We're not doing him any favors by panicking."

I clamped my mouth shut. He was right. I *was* panicking, and panicking never did any good. Besides, he'd just gotten out of surgery. He needed time.

Once I was calm enough, Dominic went home for a shower and change of clothes, and I took the stairs to Carter's floor. I was going to talk to him and explain that we were together and loved each other very much.

My nerves danced a tight tune in my belly as I crossed to Carter's room, which was strange to me. The last time I felt so nervous about seeing him was when he intimated the hell out of me, way before we got together.

A girl coming from a different direction stopped in front of Carter's room, and I slowed down. Her long, black hair reached the hem of her high-waist jeans, her tiny waist flaring out into curvy hips and thick thighs.

She ran her hand down her hair to smooth it and knocked on his door.

What the . . .? I didn't know her, and I didn't know what she was doing here. Plus, she wasn't family. She wasn't allowed in his room.

She hadn't closed the door all the way, so I stepped up to it and placed my ear to the small crack.

"Hi. I'm not sure if this is a good time, but I wanted to see you and thank you for saving my life. You entered a burning building to save a stranger . . . That's . . . Wow."

My heart stuttered. She was the girl he'd saved.

I barely dared to breathe as I peered inside. My chest clenched at the small smile on Carter's face. There wasn't an ounce of the hate he'd radiated in my presence earlier.

"I was told what happened, but I don't remember it. I, uh, don't remember a lot of stuff."

"Oh. That's too bad. But at least you're alive. When that beam fell, I thought it killed you. I tried to drag you out, but you were too heavy."

He smirked. "It's not surprising you couldn't move me. You're tiny compared to me."

"True. You're so tall and muscular. You must lift weights." There was an undertone of flirting in her deep voice.

His jaw tightened, but he covered it with a smile. I had a feeling what caused him to react that way. He didn't know if he lifted weights or not since he couldn't remember it.

The girl dropped down on the chair next to his bed. She obviously didn't need an invitation or encouragement to stay. "I tried lifting weights, but they're just so heavy. I prefer lifting my camera instead."

"Your camera?"

"I like taking photos. It's my passion. I take my camera everywhere with me. I almost brought it here." She said it as a joke, and they both laughed, even though it wasn't funny at all.

"I'm Nora, by the way."

"I'm Carter."

With a sickened feeling in my stomach, I watched them relax into the conversation. She was definitely flirting, and he didn't do anything to deflect it. I felt sicker with each passing minute.

"What are you doing?" a nurse asked me from behind, and I spun on my heel.

"Nothing."

Her brow arched. "I need to see the patient, so please step aside."

I did just that because I didn't want Carter and Nora to know I'd been eavesdropping. I stopped at a safe distance so that when Nora came out, she wouldn't know I was there to see Carter.

It didn't take long for her to leave the room after the nurse entered, and I wanted to thank the nurse for choosing this time to stop by. I made sure not to look suspicious as Nora passed me, so she barely even looked in my direction. Her hair swayed as she shimmied, and her walk was all too confident. I felt something twist in my chest as she disappeared around the corner.

She was the type of girl Carter could easily fall for.

I shook my head, chasing that thought away. It didn't matter.

We were together, and he loved *me*. Amnesia or not, those feelings wouldn't disappear just like that. Right?

I waited for the nurse to finish whatever she was doing and leave before I entered Carter's room, but when I did, he was asleep.

I sat down in the chair Nora had vacated and observed him. Some people looked like angels when asleep. Carter looked like the devil himself. The handsome, sharp lines of his face were even more pronounced with his eyes closed, and even after all this time, I couldn't stop admiring them.

And what was there not to admire? Carter was giving a whole new meaning to tall, dark, and handsome. There was nothing ordinary about him. He had the kind of face and body that haunted one's thoughts and produced fantasies. Thanks to basketball and regular workouts in our home gym, every part of his body was sculpted to smooth perfection. His lips were pouty and soft enough for the most languorous kisses. His chin and nose were defined, giving him a more mature look. His jaw was sharp-cut. But what I liked the most about him were his green eyes, which reminded me of dark forests, pine trees, and secrets that could destroy you. Eyes that could look at you piercingly, like there was no single thought you could hide from them. Eyes that I wished would open now and crinkle with a smile.

Soon enough, stress and the lack of sleep caught up to me, and my eyes closed on their own as my head tilted down. I didn't want to sleep. I wanted to keep looking at him, to make sure he was okay, but before I knew it, I was leaning against his bed and closing my eyes.

I dozed off.

"What do you think you're doing?"

I blinked my eyes open at the sound of Carter's voice. I needed a moment to remember where I was.

I raised my head from my arm and met his eyes, cracking a smile. "You're awake." I rubbed my eyes. "How are you holding up?" Forgetting myself, I placed my hand on his.

His gaze widened at the contact. "Don't fucking touch me." He yanked his hand away.

My stomach sank. I fought to keep a smile on my face. "I know you don't remember these past two years, but we're together now. We've been together for a year and a half, and we love each other."

"*Love?*" He said the word as though us loving each other was the most ridiculous thing he'd ever heard. "I don't love you. I hate you."

My head jerked back. This couldn't be happening. "You don't hate me. You—"

"Don't tell me how I feel. I don't know what happened between us before, but it doesn't matter. We're *not* together."

No, no, no. This was all wrong.

"Baby, you suffered a traumatic brain injury. That's why everything is different for you, but you're going to recover."

His eyes flashed with danger, and once more, I was reminded of the old Carter who couldn't even stand to be in the same room as me. Who never wanted to see my face again.

"Don't call me that. And get the fuck out of here." With a hiss, he winced and grabbed his head, his eyes closing.

"Carter?"

"My head is starting to hurt because of you. Leave."

"Carter, listen to me." I reached for him, but he shoved my hand away.

"LEAVE!" he roared, clutching his head.

The nurse rushed in. "What's going on here?" She took one look at Carter before she directed a stern gaze at me. "You're upsetting the patient. Please, leave."

I felt as if I was being yanked out of a Ferris wheel and

about to crash down onto the hard ground. Tears pricked my eyes, begging to be released, as I wrenched myself out of the chair and raced out of Carter's room. I almost ran into Prescott, who had apparently just arrived along with Jackson, Prescott's bodyguard following behind them.

Prescott caught me by my elbows. "You okay, Zoe?"

I couldn't even look at them. If I did, I'd fall apart right there. "I need to go." I broke our contact and darted off, my heart twisted in a cruel fist of pain.

CHAPTER THREE

"**Y**OU TWO LOOK GORGEOUS."
"*The best couple of Silver Raven Academy.*"
"*You're so beautiful together!*"
"*I envy you so much! When can I find my own Carter?*"

I went through the comments on my last Instagram post, my heart clenching harder after each comment I read. The post was a photo of Carter and me, taken at Prescott's party the night before. I was holding a shot in my hand, and Carter was hugging me from behind, both of us grinning.

The contrast between that Carter and the one I saw this morning was nauseating. I'd played our encounter in the hospital over and over in my head, and I still struggled to accept that it was real. That it wasn't a trick of my mind.

I dropped my phone on my bed and went out to the balcony. My room was on the side of the house overlooking the giant pool in the backyard and treetops merging with the clear blue skyline around our property. The landscape could go head-to-head with those of luxurious resorts around the world, and when Mom and I had first arrived here, I'd spent time on the balcony every day, soaking in the view, despite that it had been almost winter. For a couple of weeks the following spring, my Instagram profile had consisted mostly of photos of the trees and flowers around the pool, and sunny skies.

"It never gets old, does it?" Mom came up behind me, her gaze following mine. Her thin lips were curved up in a small smile.

There were absolutely no clouds in the sky, and the sun cast unrelenting warmth on us. I would've been sunbathing by the pool right now had this not happened with Carter.

"It still doesn't feel real either."

She stopped beside me and placed her hand on mine on the railing. "Dominic told me Carter woke up."

"But he doesn't remember the last two years."

Mom sighed. "I was about to go see him, but Dominic told me that might not be a good idea considering that Carter's last memory was of the time he and I didn't have a good relationship."

"It sounds unbelievable. We were so happy. Everything was fine. But now he has amnesia. How's it possible that he forgot us being together?"

Her fingers tightened around mine. "It's really unfortunate, but at least he's alive. To think that he could've died is horrible. He was very lucky."

"Having two years of your life just wiped out doesn't feel like luck."

"I heard the hospital would do tests. It might be something temporary."

Count on Mom to always be the optimistic one.

It had always been that way—just me and Mom against the whole world. I'd lost my dad when I was six, and it had been only Mom and me ever since. No other relatives, no place to permanently call ours, no security or safety. No warm hugs from Dad. Throughout all of that, Mom was a beacon of hope and strength, pushing forward no matter what.

Even now, her lips carried a smile and her eyes were bright, as if to say everything would be alright just with the sheer power of smiles and optimism. As if all previous disappointments didn't matter because if you stayed strong, you'd come out a winner sooner or later.

Sometimes, I had to push myself to believe the world wouldn't crumble around me. That it wouldn't bring me down that easily. I'd been a witness to endless disappointments and difficult choices throughout the years, starting with Dad's death, and after one disaster too many, I'd grown inclined to believe happy endings existed only in movies. But because Mom believed in our happy ending and she was my hero, I had to force myself to stay strong for her and power through when all I wanted was to give up.

I reached for her and wrapped my arms around her, putting my head on her shoulder. She leaned her head against mine, blanketing me with her sweet, cinnamon scent. Her embraces were one of the best things in the world. I'd always loved to sink into her arms and have her hold me whenever I needed comfort.

"You didn't see the way he looked at me, Mom. It was just like before. Like he never loved me."

She ran her hand through my hair, her soft fingers making my eyes close. "Let's wait a few days. We have to believe his amnesia is only temporary. Once he remembers, things will go back to the way they used to be."

"You really think so?"

"I believe so."

And because she believed, I didn't contradict her, sinking deeper into her arms as her caresses eventually quieted the doubts in my head.

Carter had held a lot of resentment and hatred toward my mom and me back then. His mom had died in a car accident when he was only fifteen, and just a few weeks later, Mom and I moved into his house. Suddenly, Carter had to see a new woman in his father's life, along with her kid, while he was still grieving. Before his mom's death could even settle in. It was no wonder he'd seen us as intruders.

From day one, Carter made it known we didn't belong. Dominic was super rich, courtesy of a successful architecture firm passed down through multiple generations of their family, and he owned a breathtaking mansion, along with several other properties. Carter had always enjoyed a lifestyle I'd only dreamed about before we moved in—a lifestyle I'd seen only on TV. He'd never had to worry about going hungry or eating whatever was cheapest. He'd never had to count every cent and fear he wouldn't be able to pay the bills. He hadn't had to live in shabby places or move often because the rent became too high or we were way past due.

So, when Mom and I arrived with only a few belongings and our jaws dropped at all that luxury, Carter used that to support his argument we were here only for the riches. He believed my mom was using his dad, and he pointed it out each time Dominic bought something expensive for Mom, took her to some tropical island, or Mom and I went on a shopping spree.

And as if he already didn't have enough reason to hate us, he'd claimed his dad had *cheated* on his mom with my mom, something both my mom and Dominic had denied.

So, during the first year, we were mostly at each other's throats. Until the annual school ski trip to a resort up north shortly after my sixteenth birthday, when Carter and I got lost together in the woods and ended up breaking into someone's vacation cabin to find shelter. We were stuck there for a day until the rescue team found us, and that time together changed everything. *We* changed. We admitted our feelings for each other and finally gave in, starting a relationship right then and there.

It was then that he admitted to me that even though he'd hated me, he'd been attracted to me from the start but fought against it, finding any reason to push me away.

As I stood in the living room ten days after Carter's accident, waiting for Dominic to bring Carter home any time now, I clung to the fact that no matter if all he could remember was hate, he still had to be attracted to me.

I'd paid close attention to what I would wear when he returned home, going for a look that would leave him unable to resist me. He'd loved when I wore shorts or mini dresses because they revealed my long, toned legs, so I'd settled on ripped denim shorts. The same shorts Carter had once claimed were "clinging to my perfect ass." My full breasts burst forth from a low-cut top that revealed my flat stomach, which was also toned—all thanks to my dance and cheer routines and workouts. I'd spent a good amount of time putting on makeup and curling my hair, which now reached my shoulder blades. And to top it all off, I spritzed on his favorite perfume of mine—a mixture of cherry and rose.

Following a nervous urge, I tugged at my shorts. These last ten days had brought a measure of heightened anxiety, and it showed in my twitchy hands and undereye bags I'd had to cover earlier. After that day, I'd gone to visit him one more time, but it turned out to be another disaster, and I saw there was no point in trying to visit him again. But each day spent away from him was torture on its own.

Carter's neuropsychiatrist told us it would take days or weeks for Carter to feel a semblance of normalcy, and that due to his brain injury, he was prone to headaches, confusion, difficulty concentrating, mood swings, and anxiety, to name a few. He stressed how important it was to be patient with Carter and offer him a calm, secure environment. He explained that Carter had been shoved into something completely new for him—the life of a seventeen-year-old Carter didn't belong to him—and he didn't know how to adapt. In Carter's mind, things were the way they were when he was fifteen, which not only meant that he couldn't know what had changed since then, but it was also up in the air whether he could keep up in school now that we were starting our senior year.

I was getting ready to check the time on my phone for what felt like the thousandth time, when a car's wheels rolled over the concrete of our driveway. I darted to the window and saw Dominic pull in behind Carter's Maserati, which Jackson had brought back the other day.

Carter slid out of Dominic's car, and his gaze went to the black Maserati. He'd received the car from Dominic for his seventeenth birthday. He loved that car very much, and even from here I could see he had difficulty looking away from it now.

He bent back inside the car to say something to Dominic, then slammed shut the door of the Bentley, cutting off whatever reply Dominic was about to make. The action brought back bitter memories.

Carter and Dominic hadn't had a good relationship before Mom and I arrived, and after our arrival, it only got worse. Dominic hadn't tried to mend the relationship with his son, and whatever success Carter had had, it hadn't been impressive enough for Dominic. On top of that, Dominic had wanted Carter to continue his legacy and work at the family firm after he got a degree in architecture, refusing to entertain the notion that Carter might want to choose his own path. Only after Carter and I got lost during that school trip did Dominic realize losing his son would break him, and he tried to do better. Finally, a few months after Carter and I started dating, Carter agreed to patch things up with Dominic and give him a chance.

Seeing Carter's attitude toward Dominic now showed me that the repercussions of Carter's amnesia were far-reaching. It wasn't just my relationship or Mom's relationship with him that suffered.

Carter turned toward the house, and flutters filled my stomach. He didn't move immediately, his gaze darting over the building like he was checking if everything was the same as it had been two years ago.

His fingers tightened around the strap of the duffel bag hanging off his shoulder. When he stepped forward, I rushed to the antique mirror over the fireplace to check my looks for the last time. I readjusted my push-up bra and confirmed my makeup was on point.

I had just about enough time to reach the archway separating the living room from the foyer when Carter appeared in my sight.

I drew up, my pulse leaping. He was still wearing a bandage on his head, and he looked tired, but that didn't make him any less handsome.

He raised his head, and his eyes landed on me. His steps halted.

"Hi, Carter," I said breathlessly.

He blinked in surprise. His gaze dropped down my body, lingering on my cleavage first, then my stomach and legs. My skin warmed under his perusal, my pulse rising even more as he looked back at my breasts. They had been much smaller two years ago, and it was clear he noted the difference.

He lifted his eyes to mine abruptly, clenching his jaw. "What's with the dressing up? You look cheap."

I jerked back, unable to stop my face from grimacing.

Dominic dropped a hand on Carter's shoulder from behind. "Watch your mouth, Carter. That's no way to treat Zoe."

Carter shrugged off Dominic's hand. "Oh yeah? What are you going to do about it? Ground me?"

Dominic opened his mouth to argue, but I raised my hand in the *stop* motion. I didn't want them to fight, especially because the doctors had said he needed our support, and any additional stress could make him regress. "It's okay, Dominic. Really."

Dominic's expression didn't shift. His gray eyes were stormy, and it was a look I'd seen too often before. One of the reasons for their bad relationship stemmed from how badly Carter had treated me. Dominic had wanted us to be a family, but I'd never felt like I fit in, and Carter certainly hadn't considered me his sister. Not even a friend. After we started dating, it took us some time to admit to our parents that we were together and then for Dominic to get over that fact, even though he was glad we weren't fighting anymore.

"I don't need a welcoming committee, so step aside." His body collided with my shoulder as he passed me, the contact sending tingles through me despite its nature. But then he stopped and turned his head in my direction as his nostrils widened around a long sniff of my scent. For a brief second, his eyes glazed over.

I tried to keep breathing evenly as my heart rate accelerated. I burned to know his thoughts. To know if any part of him, no matter how small, remembered.

He jerked his head away and carried on, and I released a shaky breath.

Dominic and I didn't say anything as Carter navigated the living room, taking it in. His gaze snagged on each thing that had been moved or was new, like a sectional sofa overlooking the outdoor pool, or an eighty-five-inch flat-screen TV hanging off the wall separating two French doors, or a few giant potted plants that infused green into the otherwise beige- and white-colored room. His jaw clenched tightly.

I pressed a hand against an ache forming in my chest. He looked as if he felt like a stranger in his own home.

My mom appeared in the doorway with a plate of cookies in her hands, her retro floral dress swishing around her feet. She was smiling at him as if she hadn't taken a day off so she could spend the whole morning making his favorite dishes and welcome-home cookies until she was ready to drop. She'd been that way back then too; no matter how badly Carter treated her, she always gave her all to be as accommodating to him as she could be.

Carter frowned at her, but that didn't thwart her smile. "It's so good to see you, Carter. We were so worried about you. I made you some cookies." She extended the plate toward him.

"I don't want your fucking cookies."

She went rigid, pain flashing in her eyes.

Dominic stepped forward. "Watch your tongue, son. We're going to have a serious problem if you don't drop your attitude."

Carter scoffed. "When have your empty threats ever stopped me?"

Dominic looked ready to raise his voice at Carter, but Mom placed her hand on his shoulder, shaking her head. "Now is not the time to argue."

At her words, Carter's mouth twisted in an ugly sneer, but before he could say anything, he noticed the photos on the fireplace mantel. His jaw went slack. The photos were of the four of us, taken over the last year and a half at birthdays or holidays.

He reached the mantel in two brisk strides. "Where are the photos of Mom?"

"We put them away," Dominic said.

Carter sliced him with a glare. "Why?"

"We thought they were bringing bad memories."

"Bringing bad memories for *who*?" He addressed this to Mom, and the air in the room turned thick with tension. I could recognize when Carter was pushed near his limits, and right now was one of those moments. He looked dangerously close to blowing up.

Carter had never quite agreed to removing his mom's photos. The day Dominic took them down was the day they stopped talking for weeks. Dominic insisted the past should stay in the past and that it was high time to move on. Carter hadn't broached the subject after they'd reconciled, but it had remained a sore point for him. Now, without his recent memories? He would only loathe Dominic more.

Taking a deep breath through his teeth, Carter looked at the photos again. His lip curled at the photo of the four of us together in front of the Christmas tree last Christmas. We were all wearing Christmas hats and smiles. It was a perfect picture of a happy family.

His hands twitched into fists. He spun around to leave, but his leg caught on a small side table Mom had bought a few months ago. The vase atop it holding orchids careened to the edge and stopped only an inch away from the drop that would lead to its demise.

"For fuck's sake! Is there anything that hasn't fucking changed?" He pressed his hand to his temple.

"Son, you better take it easy—"

"Don't *son* me! You never cared about me, so don't pretend you do now."

The muscle in Dominic's jaw pulsed, along with a vein running across his temple. That expression was so like Carter's; it said Dominic was being pushed to his limits as well. "I care about you."

Carter didn't even acknowledge that. "Is my room at least where it used to be?"

"Yes," I said.

He headed out without looking at any of us.

"Wait," Dominic said. "Your phone. You left it in your car before your accident."

My insides coiled as Carter eyed the phone in Dominic's proffered hand. His phone was full of memories of us. Our photos and videos together, photos of me, tons of texts we'd exchanged. Our whole relationship was in there.

He took the phone, fixing me with a look. I shifted my feet. He turned on the screen, but he wasn't able to go farther than that.

He glared at Dominic. "How do you expect me to use it when it's locked?"

"The passcode is one-one-two-five," I said. "My . . . birthday."

His spine went rigid. Hate glimmered in his eyes as he slowly shifted them to me. "Is there anywhere you haven't squirmed your way in?"

My cheeks burned. I couldn't look at either Mom or Dominic.

"I didn't force you to use it as your passcode. In fact, you were the one who wanted to use it."

His hand flexed hard around his phone, and it hurt seeing so much aversion in him. He unlocked his phone, and since I stood to his side, I could see he had dozens of missed calls and messages, most of which were probably from me.

He opened my text thread, and his brows dipped low as he looked through my last texts. A chilling look settled in his gaze when he reached his last message to me. The text read: *"You're going to be the sexiest girl there."*

He turned off the phone abruptly and continued toward the stairs. Dominic and Mom looked between each other, as though unsure whether they should go along with him or not.

"I'll go," I said. He should be alone to process everything on his own, but his room contained even more memories of us. I needed to explain at least some things to him.

"We'll be in the kitchen," Mom said.

I nodded and jogged across the foyer after Carter. The house had two wings, reached by two sets of stairs in the foyer. Carter's and my rooms were in the left wing. Mom and Dominic's bedroom was in the other. On my way up the stairs, I passed the paintings from artists all around the world, and the recent additions caught Carter's attention. Dominic loved art, and the whole house was like a homage to it, with paintings just about everywhere and books filling Dominic's floor-to-ceiling shelves in his office. Books spanning not only decades but centuries.

Tearing his gaze off the paintings, he proceeded to his room, which was right next to mine. He left the door open as he stepped inside, and I stopped at the threshold, watching him warily.

He dropped his bag on the floor, his gaze bouncing off the furniture. His walls were black, and a king-sized bed stood facing a set of windows, as opposed to the previously white walls and double bed he'd used two years ago. His basketball sat close to his walk-in closet, and a pair of Air Jordans were right where he'd left them before Prescott's birthday party. His basketball trophies occupied the shelf flanking the closet, each of them earned in the past year and a half. Basketball had always been his passion, but he only got serious about it during sophomore year. It was at that time that he grew so tall, gaining all those muscles I yearned to touch and kiss.

But none of those changes seemed to register with him; his eyes were on the photo of me from the woods near our town, Pine Hills, on his nightstand. Then on the teddy bear I'd bought him for Valentine's Day this year (which was a joke because he hated stuffed toys, but he'd kept it anyway). Then my shirt hanging off the back of his chair and the steamy romance novel I was reading last on his desk. And then there was my floral scent. It permeated the air, as permanent a resident in this room as his own scent.

I cleared my throat, stepping inside. "You bought that book

for me. It's written by my favorite author." I pointed at my shirt on the chair. "And you love when I wear that shirt. You always ask me to wear it."

"Shut up."

My stomach clenched. "I just—"

"SHUT UP!" He grabbed the book from the desk and threw it in my direction. I flinched as it hit the floor in front of me, its pages now twisted from the impact. "Take your fucking book with you! And your fucking shirt." He snatched it off the chair and flung it at me. I barely managed to catch it before it covered my face.

My fingers gripped my shirt. "Carter, enough! This isn't you!"

"This isn't me? Are you now in my fucking mind too so you know how I feel?" He grabbed my picture from the nightstand and smashed it on the floor. The glass exploded, the shards skittering all around him in an erratic mosaic. "Get out! Get the fuck out of my room!"

For a moment, all I could do was stare in shock at the mess. The mess that was becoming blurrier as tears pricked the backs of my eyes. "You need to calm down, Carter. As much as you don't want me here, we need to talk. You have to understand that—"

"I DON'T HAVE TO DO ANYTHING!" He went over to his shelf and knocked all his trophies off it, then the lamp off his nightstand. "This is not my life! I don't want any of this!"

I cried out, my knees shaking. I'd never seen him this angry. Never.

He spun around and when he saw me standing frozen on the spot, he closed the distance between us and grabbed my arm, getting into my face. "Do you want me to throw you out by force? Because I will if you don't leave right. This. Second."

Dominic rushed in and pushed Carter away from me. "That's enough!"

"Get her out. I don't want to see her. I don't want to see any of you!"

My mom appeared behind me. She took my shaking hand

and nudged me to follow her out. "Let's go, honey. This is all too much for him."

"Yes, both of you, go. Go far away," Carter shouted.

Mom pulled me away, and with my vision completely distorted by tears, I watched the guy I loved get farther and farther away from me.

And I didn't know what the hell I could do.

I hated crying. Crying was a waste of time, and it never solved anything. Even when your life kept fucking you up. Even when you couldn't see a way out, but you kept pushing forward because stopping would mean getting run over.

But the tears kept coming after that argument with Carter. I paced around my room day and night, torn between wanting to make him see reason and giving him time. But patience had never been one of my virtues.

Many times over, I reminded myself of what the doctor had said, that Carter's anger was a normal reaction, considering his condition. To Carter, an important portion of his life was missing—a period of life when he was growing as a person, growing to know who he was and what he wanted—and now he had to adapt and rediscover himself. His past experiences had shaped him into who he'd been before the accident. Take that away, and what did you get? I wasn't giving up hope that he would remember eventually, but then again, what if he didn't?

He'd spent days closed in his room, and he refused to come out even to eat. Since he didn't let my mom come near his room, Dominic or our housekeeper, Mrs. Hopper, delivered him his meals. He only went out to see the doctor and get his bandage taken off.

I'd never seen him so closed off before. There were times when I went to his door and just stood there, wishing I could go in. Wishing that standing by his door wasn't the only way I could stay physically close to him. Wishing I could help.

I had tried to help. I'd written him a list of things, like where he kept his phone charger, what the passcode for his computer was, his usual routine, or what his favorite latest music and restaurants were, and pushed it under his door, my heart pounding as I waited for his reaction. But he never opened the door or acknowledged me otherwise, and I returned to my room without knowing if he even saw it.

But he saw it, alright. I got proof of it the next time I came out of my room and spotted the torn pieces of my list by his door. It rang loud and clear what he thought of my help.

I felt powerless and caged, and the only thing that helped me keep my mind off Carter was my part-time job at a downtown Italian restaurant, Bellezza. I made sure to work extra shifts, because I couldn't torment myself with thoughts of heartache while I was running myself ragged.

The night before we returned to school, I spent a long time in my bath, thinking about the first day of our senior year without Carter by my side. Since it was decided that he could start his senior year normally (Dominic made sure the teachers would pay special attention to him and go at his pace), Carter wouldn't miss school, and I would have to see him there every day.

Carter and I had always gone to school together. We'd shared most of our classes and spent breaks and lunch together. Being there without being able to be with him, talk to him, *touch* him . . . it felt as though I was missing something essential. I was already feeling lonely, and I needed his closeness. I missed sharing with him everything I'd heard. A few times, I'd caught myself reaching for my phone to text him about something I thought would interest him, only to remember I couldn't do that. For a year and a half, I'd had a lover, best friend, my go-to whenever I needed help . . .

And now I'd lost it all.

Fed up with wallowing, I got out of the bathtub. So much for a relaxing bath. I wrapped myself in my bathrobe and tossed a look at the mirror, grimacing at what I saw there. My eyes and nose were red from crying. My face looked leaner, with sharp cheekbones cutting through the valley of my pale cheeks, even though I made sure to eat even when I didn't have an appetite.

I didn't bother blow-drying my hair. Wrapping my arms around myself, I plodded out of my bathroom and changed into my sleeping top and shorts before I dropped face-first into my bed. Carter's scent reached me from the pillow beside mine, still there. It was as if the pillow also refused to let go of him.

I took the pillow and buried my head in it, taking a long sniff. My heart fluttered in my chest. I wanted to go to his room and tell him how much I needed him. How it physically hurt not to have him by my side.

The pillow conjured up the memory of the last time he was in my bed. It was a day before Prescott's party. After he'd made love to me, he spooned me and wrapped his arms tightly around my waist. Carter often had trouble sleeping, but he was able to fall asleep the fastest when he was hugging me.

Right before sleep claimed me, he'd whispered to me how much he loved me.

"You always make me feel so weak next to you. I can never resist you," he'd said then.

"If it's any consolation, you make me feel the same."

My heart aching now, I reached for my phone on my nightstand and opened my messages to read the texts Carter and I had exchanged the morning after.

"You snore when you sleep," he'd messaged me.

"I don't snore, and you know it."

"Want me to record you next time to prove it?"

"Don't you dare."

"And what are you going to do to convince me not to?"

"You're so sly, Carter Reese."

"Just the way you love me."

The door to my room burst open, and I almost dropped my

phone as Carter strode in. I scrambled into a sitting position, hope stretching my heart. He came into my room.

He stopped above my bed, and my hope deflated when I noticed his expression. "Carter?"

He opened his mouth to say something, but then he looked down the length of my body, leaving his words unvoiced. All my nerves buzzed with awareness, waking up under his slow and thorough perusal. He left no inch of me unseen.

Desire pooled low in my stomach when his eyes stopped on my breasts. I was sure he could see my taut nipples, which stretched the thin material of my top. It was all I could do not to combust.

His fingers clenched around, what I saw only now, his phone in one hand and a large bag he carried in the other.

He snapped his eyes to mine. "Just to be clear in case you're still under any illusion, whatever happened between us is history."

He dropped the bag on the floor, and all my belongings that had been in his room spilled out of it.

Icy cold invaded my heart.

He showed me the screen of his phone, which was displaying our text exchange. Horrified, I watched him delete all of it, his eyes locked with mine as he pressed the *delete* button.

It was gone. All our texts. Just like that.

And then . . . then he opened his gallery and deleted all our photos and videos together, twisting the knife deeper into my heart. All our kisses and smiles and happy moments stored only in his phone . . . gone forever.

I wanted to say something, to let out any sound . . . but I couldn't.

"You and I are done. And as far as I'm concerned, you and your gold digger mother can go straight to hell." He turned to leave, but then he said over his shoulder, "And don't even think about talking to me at school. From now on, you and I don't know each other."

He walked out and slammed the door shut. The wood rattled.

For a full minute, I could only stare into space, his venomous words playing on torturous repeat.

"Fuck you, Carter. Just . . . fuck you." My voice caught.

I wrapped my arms around my knees and buried my head in them, starting to sob.

We'd been so happy. Everything had been perfect.

I should've known it wouldn't last. I should've known life would throw another curveball at me.

Because he was gone. My Carter was gone.

And after witnessing so much hate in him, it was hard to believe that this nightmare would ever end.

CHAPTER FOUR

Two and a half years earlier

MOM HAD SAID OUR BETTER LIFE STARTED TODAY. SOON after she began dating her friend Dominic, she announced we were moving in with him. I thought that was quick, but Mom and Dominic wanted us out of poverty. No more missed meals or late rents. No more shady boyfriends or low-paid jobs where her coworkers or customers put her down or she had to work late hours or double shifts. No more worrying if we would get to survive another day. Mom had fallen in love, and this time it seemed as if it was permanent. This time it seemed as if she'd finally got the man of her dreams.

The man in question was a rich, successful business owner, and he was handsome for his age—all prerequisites for a Disney-like ending.

Only, the moment we arrived at Dominic's estate, it turned out that things weren't that simple. My eyes were wide as saucers when Dominic parked the car at the end of a circular driveway and I got my first look of his home. It could easily pass for a house straight out of a Hollywood movie, with countless rooms and a vast expanse of land surrounding it.

Since I didn't own a lot of clothes or a fancy suitcase, I'd stuffed everything into one duffel bag I was perfectly capable of carrying on my own. But Dominic's housekeeper came out, saying she would take care of it, and took it inside, leaving me to stare dumbfounded at her. Was this how people arriving at fancy hotels felt? I didn't know. I'd never been to one.

This really was another world.

I'd like to say I felt like a princess coming home to her castle, but Dominic's house didn't feel like home. I didn't feel like I belonged there or deserved to be there. Any day now, I expected Mom and me to return to our regular lives, because wherever we moved, it didn't last. We didn't have roots. Or purpose, for that matter. Just pure survival.

Mom's face was like the sun peering above a mountain as she took notice of the house. She didn't move away from the car, and Dominic pulled her into a hug, already attuned to her feelings.

I smiled at the sight. This was the first time I saw them hugging, and I had to admit they looked good together. Both were beautiful above average.

Mom and I shared the same chocolate-brown eyes, tall height, and slim body shape. The only difference was that her brown hair was a few shades darker than mine, her nose was long, and her lips were thin.

As for Dominic, he was tall and well-built. I'd only ever seen him in suits, but each suit showcased a strong and muscular body, like he was physically active on the regular. He came across as charming, as someone who knew what he wanted and how to get it.

He tucked Mom's arm into the crook of his elbow, and together they went inside the house. I trailed after them.

The foyer reminded me of a church; it was cavernous and ornate. I couldn't stop gaping at the crystal chandeliers and rows of paintings on the walls. Or the black-and-white checkered floor. Or wrought iron handrails flanking the two flights of stairs. Or the back of the foyer that opened into the backyard and, from here, what appeared to be a pool.

Everything—absolutely everything—looked as if it cost more than what Mom earned for months, if not a year. There was no way this was our address now.

"My son should be here to meet you," Dominic said. "Carter is your age, Zoe." He stopped at the bottom of the left stairway. "Carter! Carter, come down here to meet Erika and your new sister."

I jerked. *His new sister?* Dominic had started dating my mom only recently. It was too soon to say I was anyone's sister. For all we knew, Mom and Dominic could break up next month.

The air changed before I saw him at the top of the stairs. It became cold and thick with tension, and I felt my pulse quickening. Then I saw him, and my mind straight-up blanked. All that computed was the way he looked.

He was tall for his age. His body was lean, and if the muscles peering out of the sleeves of his tee were any indicator, he was already hitting the gym. He was stacked with more muscle than any guy my age I'd ever met. His body wasn't what stole most of my attention, though. It was his face that made my pulse flicker in my neck.

Dominic was handsome, but his son was gorgeous in a way that commanded all eyes on him. In a way that made you think about him even long after he'd left the room. His eyes were dark in color, but I couldn't be sure from here if they were brown. More like green. His hair was cut short, making him look like a rebel, giving prominence to his wickedly full lips. The lines of his face came together to form symmetrical perfection.

I shifted, all too aware I was wearing denim shorts that almost cut into my butt and a tee tied into a knot above my navel. I desperately wanted him to like me.

"Carter, come downstairs," Dominic told him.

Carter's jaw clenched at his dad's subtly veiled command. He didn't take his eyes off me as he descended the stairs, and my body tingled more with each second it was exposed to his searing eyes. I had to remind myself to breathe once he stopped in front of us. He looked me up and down, and my heart twisted at the judgment in his gaze. He shifted his attention to Mom, and his face contorted with so much hatred that my breath fluttered in my throat.

I'd wondered how Dominic's son would treat us, and now here was my answer. There was no love lost between us.

"Carter, this is Erika Saunders and her daughter, Zoe. As I mentioned to you, they'll be living with us from now on."

Carter didn't move an inch, his eyes blasting ice at his dad. There was so much accumulated hostility there, and it begged the question whether it was because of Mom and me moving in or they had some other unresolved issue between them.

"Mom's funeral was only a few weeks ago, and you're moving your mistress in here already?"

I inhaled sharply. His mom had just died? *Mistress?* What was going on here?

"You're out of line. We discussed this, and I told you you're going to treat Erika and her daughter with respect."

"No, we didn't discuss anything—you were *demanding*. And I refuse to accept your gold-digging mistress and her kid. They're intruders."

"Don't insult them, boy! Erika is not a mistress or a gold digger."

Carter snorted. "You two have been fucking each other for months. You strung Mom along and never tried to give your marriage another chance. You didn't even have the decency to show up for her funeral on time. I bet you were late because you were fucking this slut—"

Dominic slapped him before any of us could see it coming, sending Carter's head to the side. Mom and I gasped.

He hit him. He actually hit him.

"I've had enough of you. Go to your room."

Carter's lips pulled back in a snarl, his eyes full of venom and fury. "Gladly," he let out through his teeth. "Anything not to see any of your fucking faces." He started climbing the stairs, but then he turned and smiled with malice. "Though I guess it won't matter. Because you'll get tired of her ass soon, and they'll be back to their gutter, where they belong, in no time." He turned and left.

A heavy silence dropped over us. Only now I realized how hard my heart was pounding.

I looked at Mom. "Is it true? You and Dominic were . . . you were seeing each other for months?"

"That's not true," Mom was quick to say, her eyes pleading with me to trust her. "I told you, we met a couple months ago, but nothing ever happened. We were just friends. I swear."

I nodded, a heavy weight dissipating in my stomach. I believed her. She would never lie to me. And she was the most honorable woman I knew. She would never be with someone else's man. Maybe her relationship with Dominic came too soon after his wife's death, but love worked in mysterious ways, and who were we to judge? Each person grieved in their own way, and if Dominic was happy with my mom and made her happy, I couldn't complain.

This left the only other possible conclusion: Carter was delusional.

But one thing was certain—that thing about our better life starting today?

Mom had been way off her mark.

The house was huge and too empty. Why people owned houses with countless rooms they would never use was beyond me. Everywhere I went, I was reminded of the differences between Carter's world and mine, and I felt like a fish out of water. It didn't help that Carter was going through a rough patch because of his mom's death (I didn't know the guy, but I doubted his MO was constant partying and drinking), and it added more proof that my place wasn't here.

It took me days just to remember where all the bedrooms and

guest rooms were. There were so many empty rooms you could make a hotel out of the place. Everything was so neat, no dust or stains leaving their mark. Dominic was hiring a housekeeper, Mrs. Hopper, to come a few times a week to clean, make meals, and do laundry, but the woman was too efficient, seeing that she was often gone before you even noticed she was there to begin with.

Then there was their kitchen. It looked like all those kitchens in glossy magazines or TV shows, with expensive appliances, built-in cabinets, and a long dining table that could seat a whole presidential delegation. Their fridge wasn't like the ancient, rusty stand-ups that were the hallmark of each of our apartments. It was a side-by-side, all made of stainless steel and with a touch screen, and most importantly of all, it was always stacked with food. From the bottom to the top, the shelves were full of all kinds of food and drinks, some shelves solely dedicated to organic veggies, fruits, milks, you name it. I wondered if they ever stopped taking it for granted.

My room was a story in and of itself. It overlooked the pool and the snow-capped mountains in the distance. A double bed faced the windows and balcony, with a bookshelf spanning the whole wall on its left side. Dominic had heard I loved reading books, but since the only way I could afford reading was to borrow books from the library and didn't own any, he gave me a generous gift card that allowed me to buy about fifty books of my choice that now filled the upper shelves. He said it was a welcome gift—a welcome gift I didn't feel comfortable about.

Everything was decorated in warm tones. There was a chandelier hanging from the ceiling and a vanity table with a large bouquet of flowers on it. An enormous flatscreen TV was mounted to the wall across from the sofa set in the center of the room, diagonally from a desk with a Mac computer (another welcome gift from Dominic). To top it all off, I had my own private bathroom and a walk-in closet, with several floor-to-ceiling shelves for shoes and racks for all kinds of clothes.

As if these changes weren't enough, I couldn't get used to my new bed. It had a super comfortable mattress and pillows, and the strangeness of it all had me tossing and turning until the early morning hours.

The night turned out to be another wakeful one, so I gave up on sleep at four in the morning and dragged myself downstairs to the kitchen.

I'd barely made it there when I heard the front door opening. A minute later, Carter hauled himself into the kitchen, keeping his gaze down. His face was tired, and his eyes were red. He smelled of cigarette smoke. All signs of another night spent partying.

Still, even in this disheveled state, he looked like every girl's dream. I was curious to know if he'd hooked up with someone or if he had a girlfriend. Though why I cared about his love life, I had no idea.

"Aren't you too young for this?"

He stopped and gave me a condescending once-over. "No one asked for your opinion." He pushed me aside to open the fridge.

"Your dad is worried about you. You shouldn't—"

He slammed the fridge shut and glared at me. "You're here like what, a week? And you think you already know this family or have the right to tell me what to do? Fuck off."

I squeezed my hand into a fist. I felt anger, but I also felt pity and understanding because of his mom. Mom had told me his mom Anastacia had died in a car crash involving a truck. The truck driver fell asleep, and the truck drifted into her lane. She avoided the truck but lost control of her car, and she went off the road and crashed into a tree. She died on the spot. It was so sudden and tragic—something I had firsthand experience with as well. My world had been reduced to rubble the day my dad died, and I had no doubt his was now too.

"I'm sorry about your mom. I know how crushing it could be—"

He slammed a hand on the counter on either side of me, caging me in.

My heart took off at a gallop. His hateful eyes moved across my face, making me all too aware of how close he was and his distinctive male scent. There wasn't a single flaw on his face, and I wished he didn't look so beautiful.

"Do us both a favor and stop talking to me. You're nobody. You think you're something special now that you're here? I've got newsflash for you: you're still trash." He pushed away from me. "Now get out of my sight."

I ground my molars. "And you're a piece of shit, Carter. I tried to be nice to you and understanding, but I'm done. You can take out your anger on someone else."

The flash of fury on his face was the last thing I saw before I stepped out of the kitchen, my pulse racing madly with the anger owning all of me. It was directed at him for being such an asshole. And at myself for ever feeling attracted to him.

I slammed shut the door of my room and bit into my fist, screaming. Our whole encounter rattled me. I didn't know what to think about the fact that he could throw me off balance so easily, but I knew one thing with certainty.

I hated Carter Reese.

CHAPTER FIVE

Present

MOM HAD GONE THROUGH A FAIR AMOUNT OF HARDSHIP IN her life, especially as a single mother, doing all she could to keep us afloat. When Dominic came into the picture, it was the first time in a long time I saw Mom truly happy. She blossomed under his attention and care and transformed into a bundle of contagious joy. She fell head over heels for him, and I had no doubt she never cared about his money, not even for a second. She wasn't that kind of a person.

I wasn't either. When we first arrived at Dominic's house, it took me months to get used to not having to worry about surviving, and even today, I couldn't get rid of the habit to save money. Or the urge to work. Both Mom and Dominic tried to convince me to quit because I didn't have to work, and they were also worried it would take away from my studying time, not that it did because I always made sure to study and do my homework even during my busiest weeks. I couldn't quit because I never took our new life with the Reeses for granted. I wanted to depend only on myself, not on others.

Carter's words from the previous night hadn't come as a surprise, but they were a slap to my and mom's dignity, and part of me wanted to hurt him. It wanted me to tell him he hadn't changed at all, even though he wasn't the Carter I'd fallen madly in love with. This wouldn't be happening if it wasn't for his brain injury, and I told myself to keep hoping we would bounce back.

As I started down the stairs, as ready as I could be for the first day of school, I spotted Carter with Dominic by the front door. My heart beat faster as I looked Carter over in his school uniform, noting how effortlessly sexy he was. He'd gained even more muscle over the summer, and it showed in the way the fabric of his shirt stretched over his broad back and his navy pants over his tight ass. His close-fitting shirt was untucked, its sleeves rolled up. He didn't wear a tie or blazer, though both were required. His hair was slicked back, bringing forth his rectangular jaw and broad forehead.

My stomach stirred because this was how he styled his hair and wore his uniform prior to his accident. It appeared that some things hadn't changed in spite of his memory loss. It was a thrilling thought.

"You should ride with Zoe to school," Dominic said to Carter as they stepped outside.

My heart twisted. Carter had always taken me to school, but he wasn't allowed to drive with his injury.

I stopped behind them. Following Dominic's gaze, Carter looked at the red Audi parked beside Dominic's car, and I could sense the shift in him. Cold hostility oozed out of every pore of his body as he looked back at Dominic.

"You bought her a fucking car?"

Dominic ground his jaw. "Yes. It was a birthday present."

Carter's hands balled at his sides. "Why don't you go on and give her the whole house already? So she won't break a sweat getting everything."

Dominic took off his glasses and pinched the spot between his brows. "I'm not going to argue with you about it now, so drop it." He found my gaze over Carter's shoulder. "Zoe, you're going to drive Carter to school."

Carter whipped his furious gaze over his shoulder at me. "No way. I'll ride with Jackson." His eyes flicked down my body before he looked away, and it happened so quickly I would've missed it had I not been looking at him.

Jackson's gray Porsche rolled up in front of us just then, the sun casting a glare off its shiny surface. The car was furiously fast and unapologetic, just like Jackson. He honked the horn.

Without a word, Carter jumped into Jackson's car. Jackson cast a look between Carter and me and said something to Carter. Carter tossed me a glare and shook his head at Jackson. Jackson threw me a "Sorry, nothing I can do" expression before he slammed on the gas, and they left.

"Are you okay?" Dominic asked me.

"I will be."

"He'll come to his senses. I'm sure this is just temporary."

"That's what I keep telling myself too."

But that didn't make it feel any more believable.

With a sigh, I got in my car and cranked up some music as I stepped on the gas. The car moved forward like a knife through butter, so slick and quiet, and I felt some of my bad mood dissipating. I enjoyed driving this car, all the more so since the novelty of owning it hadn't worn off, even to this day.

My best friend, Summer Holmes, was already in the parking lot, leaning against her Volkswagen Beetle as she waited for me. Her long hair, a few shades lighter than mine, billowed in the wind. She straightened up when she saw me and checked her reflection in the window of her car before she met me half-way.

She gave me a wary look. "I saw Carter arrive with Jackson a few minutes ago."

I'd kept Summer in the loop after the accident. I'd texted her countless times, each message more self-pitying than the last.

"He didn't want to come with me. He hates me, Sum."

"He doesn't hate you."

"You didn't see him."

"Maybe he thinks he hates you, but you can't erase what you two had that easily. He'll come to his senses."

"That's what I'm hoping for."

I checked my look in the screen of my phone, making sure one last time that even though I felt like shit, at least I looked good. I was dressed in a school-issued navy pleated skirt and a navy blazer that was open to reveal my buttoned up white blouse with the two top buttons open. My hair was pulled into a ponytail with a few tendrils framing my face, containing a tint of chocolate in this light. My hundreds of dollars' worth of makeup gave my face a luminous look, its sole purpose to capture attention. Judging from Summer's reaction, it'd hit the bullseye.

A group of students waved at me as they passed, and I waved back, wondering what their reaction would be once they found out about Carter and me. Being the captain of our cheer team and the girlfriend of one of the most popular guys in the school had brought me a fair amount of popularity. That meant everyone liked to gossip about me and wanted to know about every detail of my personal life—the juicier, the better. One would think that rich people had class. Or fulfilling lives. Apparently not.

Summer seemed to be reading my mind. "I didn't notice any gossip on social media."

"Me neither, but that doesn't mean it'll remain a secret for much longer. Give it a few hours, and it'll be a hot topic. Hell, I'm being generous. Give it an hour." I flicked invisible lint off my skirt. "Anyway, let's go."

The wind picked up as we made our way to the school. Everything about our school was formidable, and it seemed the weather was acknowledging that too.

Silver Raven Academy was a prestigious private school. The three-story gray stone building rose amid the center of a forest, on a property that spanned acres. The building featured large windows that allowed for plenty of natural light and stretched into three wings, one of which was the sports center and the gym. The kids of some of the richest people across the state attended this school, and whoever went to Silver Raven had a guaranteed spot in an Ivy League school. It was the only reason why I'd enrolled here. I didn't take it for granted either, though; hitting the books would help me get into any good college if the Ivy League plan turned out to be a bust. Connections and power were the currency around here, currency I had *only* because of Dominic and his influence in this town.

Rich kids were never my crowd, which was why I got along with Summer. We could understand and relate to one another. Summer was here on a scholarship, the only way she could've ever attended this place. Her family worked for Jackson's family, and Jackson's mom, being in charge of the scholarship committee, awarded her a fully paid ride. Supposedly, it was a gesture of goodwill, since Summer's family had been working for Jackson's family for two generations now.

The large foyer was swarming with students, and footsteps resounded across the marble floor. A water wall separated two sets of stairs, each set leading into their own wing of the building. Potted plants decorated all the hallways. The lockers were new and shiny. Whoever built and furnished this place spared no expense, because opulence radiated out of every corner. Even the staff were above average—all sophisticated and knowledgeable.

A few more girls waved at me in passing, and a couple of guys openly checked me out. I smiled. Most guys turned their heads when I passed, and although it stroked my ego, I cared only about a certain guy checking me out, and I had yet to see him. I didn't have to wait long for it, though, because our lockers were side by side. We were bound to see each other at some point.

Summer and I headed in the direction of my locker when the girl Carter had saved passed by, and I stopped to gape at her. She was wearing the school uniform, but she wasn't a student here before. She must be a new transfer.

"That's Nora," I told Summer. "The girl Carter saved."

Summer did a double take. "That's her? She's a new student then?"

"Apparently."

Her eyes rounded, and I knew she noticed it too—Nora was breathtakingly beautiful. Some guys were already staring at her and talking amongst themselves about her, and a few girls were openly looking at her with envy. Her uniform hugged her waist and hips like it was made for her. Her long hair was braided, and her face was covered in flawless makeup.

Jealousy and panic twisted my insides because she would probably be near Carter. They could be sharing some classes.

"What's on your mind?" Summer asked.

"I told you about their conversation. It was obvious she was into him. What if she hits on him?"

"There's a chance, yeah, but he'd have to be interested in her."

"She's a knockout. Carter isn't blind."

"But you're also a knockout, so there's that."

Carter was already at his locker when we got there, with Prescott and Jackson standing beside him and, of course, a horde of girls that had gathered around them as if they were royalty. And in their eyes, they might as well be. They were the most popular guys here; they were planets, and we were all satellites orbiting around them. Each one of them was gorgeous.

Jackson was a model. He was over six feet tall, with a lean body and toned muscles. His dirty blond hair almost reached his shoulders, highlighting his gray eyes, a strong, V-shaped jaw, and plump lips that rarely smiled. Although he was always surrounded by people in one way or another, he was aloof and didn't let people in that easily. His eyes always contained a level of emptiness, as though he took little joy in life. His aloofness worked in his favor because he always had a line of girls chasing after him, hoping to finally "tame" him.

As for Prescott, he was a big shot actor. Paving his way in the industry since he was seven years old, he had a number of movies and television shows under his belt. He'd already won several awards, and he had the talent and looks to account for it, with his dark brown eyes and hair, chiseled face, and an overall bad boy appearance. Needless to say, he had an army of girls and paparazzi waiting for him at every corner. The tabloids were full of stories of his partying, reckless driving, property damage, and one-night stands. He was as unattainable as Jackson, refusing to stay with anyone long enough to memorize their name.

Jackson noticed us first, and Summer walked a little straighter. It was her usual reaction whenever she saw him. That and the tell-tale flushing of her cheeks. His gaze almost completely skipped over her and fixed on me, as though she didn't exist, and she released a sharp exhale of breath.

Summer and Jackson were ex-best friends. They had known each other their whole lives, since Summer and her parents lived in a bungalow on Jackson's estate, right behind his mansion. Jackson's mother had made it clear from the start that Jackson and Summer belonged to different worlds and weren't allowed to associate with one another, and I had a feeling it had led to Summer and Jackson's falling-out she still refused to tell me much about. But despite the distance between them, Summer never stopped pining for him.

My attention turned to Carter. He read something from a small piece of paper before he entered the combination of his locker. His back was to me as he opened the door, and I used the moment to feast my eyes on him—on his strong shoulders and forearms, his tapered waist, and his powerful thighs. I knew his body like I knew my own, his every muscle imprinted in my mind. I felt a flicker of sensual awareness deep within me, my heart beating harder.

I wasn't the only one staring. Two girls standing close by didn't take their eyes off him, and fear spread its tendrils through me. What if he found a new girlfriend? Like Nora. Or what if he returned to his old ways and just messed around with girls? My first time was with Carter, but his first time certainly hadn't been with me.

With my chin raised, I reached my locker and met his gaze head-on. His eyes narrowed at me, but then they went to the deep

V of my partially buttoned blouse. Heat spread across my skin, increasing with every second he didn't move his gaze. The hand holding his locker door tightened around the metal.

"I told you not to talk to me at school."

"You think I'm here because I want to talk to you?" I pointed at my locker. "This is my locker. Haven't Prescott and Jackson given you the memo?"

Carter scowled at them.

Prescott shrugged his shoulder. "Didn't cross my mind."

"You've gotta be kidding me," Carter gritted out.

As a way of response, I turned the lock and opened my locker. Carter's gaze burned into the side of my face, knotting up something inside my stomach.

"I can't believe this. It's like you're in every part of my life."

"And what do you expect? That's what happens when you're together with someone for a long time, Carter. Our lives are intertwined."

He clenched his jaw. He slammed his locker shut, and I watched him leave with my lips downturned.

Jackson gave me a glance filled with pity, shrugging.

"He'll get over it," Prescott told me.

"I'm not so sure about that, but thanks."

"You gonna be okay?"

I nodded, my lips forming a tight smile. "Yep."

"We'll put in a good word for you."

A girl stepped out of the crowd surrounding us and cleared her throat. "Um, Prescott, can I get a picture with you?" She blushed all the way to the roots of her hair. "I'm one of your biggest fans."

Prescott smirked at her. "Sure." He leaned toward her and posed for the camera, letting her sling her arm around his waist and press her head against his shoulder.

I had to give it to him. People always asked him for photos, and he never refused, even when it was the last thing he wanted. Maybe he didn't make much effort at being a "good guy" in the public eye, but he treated his fans well.

The girl squealed. "Thank you. You were so hot in *Darkless Nights*! Are you going to be in more action movies?"

"Maybe. You never know."

"You definitely should. You look so sexy when you fight!"

I cringed inwardly. *Okay.*

"Jackson, would you give me your autograph?" Another girl stepped forward, her Sharpie already at the ready.

Jackson's expression was unimpressed as he pushed himself off the locker. He took the Sharpie from her.

"Right here," the girl said, lifting her skirt for him to leave his signature high on her thigh.

Summer released a choked sound. Her face said it all as she watched Jackson sign his name too close to the girl's panties.

Jackson turned to leave, and Summer's face contorted with pain. He hadn't looked at her even once.

"See you around," Prescott told us and followed after Jackson, causing a couple of girls to trail after them not-so-discreetly.

Summer hooked a strand of her hair behind her ear. "I wish he would talk to me."

I wiggled my lips left and right. "What if you tried to speak to him?"

"No. He doesn't even want me near him. Besides, I wouldn't know what to say." She sighed. "Enough about me." She gave me a worried look. "Are you really going to be okay? Carter looked way too tense."

I spun to face my locker, taking a deep breath as pain shot through my heart. "I'm fine. It'll get better. *We* will get better, I'm sure of it."

I made sure to make it sound convincing; I just didn't know whom I was trying to convince.

Her or myself.

CHAPTER SIX

T HEY SAY HOPE DIES LAST. SO, I TOLD MYSELF I WOULD HANdle everything, wait it out until Carter recovered his memories and was himself again. I refused to consider the alternative.

When I entered third period, I found Carter sitting at the back of the classroom, the desks on either side of him already taken. We always sat next to each other in class, not that I'd expected that to be the case now. To my surprise, on his left side was none other than Nora.

She was talking to two girls in front of them, but she had Carter's full attention. My stomach turned over at the half-smile playing over his lips.

"So, it's true? Carter saved you?" one of those girls asked her.

"Yeah. He broke in the restroom where I was stuck and helped me navigate through the fire. It's a miracle we didn't suffocate or catch fire, seeing as it was everywhere. If it hadn't been for Carter, I wouldn't be here today." She looked at him as if he was the world's greatest hero, and for her, he probably was.

I wanted to gag.

"That's so cool," the other girl said, a big smile plastered over her face.

"*Carter* is cool," Nora said in a sugary voice, never taking her gaze off him. "Not many people would've done that."

Carter gave a shrug. "It's not a big deal."

"Not a big deal? You go around saving girls often, then?"

He chuckled, and the sound slashed through my chest. *I* wanted to make him laugh like that. But now I couldn't even talk to him without being on the receiving end of his hate.

"You're in the way," someone told me.

I stepped aside, realizing I'd been standing in the middle of the classroom and staring all this time.

Just then, Carter looked in my direction. His smile disappeared.

Pursing my lips together, I dropped into one of the available seats at the front. I closed my eyes and took a deep breath, feeling his gaze on the back of my neck. Once more, there was a heavy weight in my stomach, and it felt as if this day would never end. As if his hate would never end.

I reached for my phone and opened Instagram to take my mind off Carter, but it didn't help. It was hard to tune out their voices, which carried on until the teacher arrived. Nora's voice was breathy, and she laughed to almost everything he said. It didn't take Einstein to figure out she really liked him. And why wouldn't she? A gorgeous, popular guy had saved her life. Of course she would have a crush on him.

The question was if he would reciprocate.

Chalk screeched against the blackboard, and I whipped my gaze up with a wince. My fingers tightened around my pencil. I hadn't been paying attention to the lecture or taking notes at all. The teacher had filled half the blackboard by now, but the words didn't make any sense to me.

"So, it's true?" the girl next to me asked in a whisper. "You and Carter are done?"

So, the news had already spread. This day kept getting better.

"Keep your nose out of other people's business."

Her eyes turned to slits. "You don't have to be such a bitch about it." She tossed her hair over her shoulder as she faced forward again. "You're not right for each other anyway."

"What's that supposed to mean?"

She arched her brow as she looked me up and down. "You can pretend you're one of us all you want, but we all know you came from the gutter."

My heart kicked against my ribcage. It had been awhile since I'd been insulted for being poor. Since I'd started dating Carter, to be precise.

"At least I'm not a bitch like you," I replied, drawing a gasp from her.

Her reaction was satisfying, and it was enough to make this class bearable, or more precisely, the fact that I could feel Carter's gaze burning into my back the whole time.

I was among the first to rush out when the bell rang, refusing to look back at Carter and Nora even though I was sorely tempted.

Summer met me in front of the cafeteria. "Everyone's talking about you and Carter."

"I got a glimpse of it just now. One girl asked me if it's true Carter and I weren't together anymore. Then she let me know we weren't right for each other."

"Really? Bitch."

I chuckled and pushed open the cafeteria doors. "That's what I said."

My gaze zoomed in on Carter's table. Summer and I had always sat together with Carter, Prescott, Jackson, and some of Carter's basketball buddies, but that was out of the question now. To make matters worse, I saw Nora taking my place beside Carter.

My stomach knotted. Carter looked as though he wanted her there. Jackson and Prescott didn't seem to mind her, not that they paid her that much attention, because Prescott had his gaze set on his phone, and Jackson was busy with some girl sitting on his lap.

Summer tore her gaze away from Jackson, smoothing her perfectly penciled brows as she faced me. "What now?"

"Now we find another table."

We joined the lunch line. I caught quite a few stares from girls around the room, and I hated seeing either glee or pity on their faces.

A senior stopped by my side and leaned uncomfortably close to me. "I heard you're single, so I'm here if you're interested." He smirked.

"I'm not interested."

"Your loss."

Summer shrugged at me, watching the guy leave. "At least you can always count on a rebound."

I eyed the food. "Not funny."

I settled on filet mignon, white asparagus, and cucumber quinoa salad, and with my tray in hand, I turned to scan the room. Denise, one of my cheer squad mates, raised her hand, gesturing for me to join her table. She was sitting with my other squad mates, Trisha and Amalie.

"I think we found our table," I told Summer.

Their table overlooked the outdoor eating area, next to a set of windows soaring from floor to ceiling. Natural light bathed the cafeteria, creating a contrast to the monochrome tables and walls. I might've taken a couple photos of me posing there when I started going here and posted them on Instagram. It was that photogenic.

"Hey, girls. Thanks for inviting us to sit with you." I took the seat across from Trisha, which allowed me to see Carter's table.

"Don't mention it," Amalie said, pausing the application of her mascara to look at me. "We were just discussing the squad this year. It's going to be so exciting." She squealed, bouncing in her seat.

"We can't wait to start practices," Trisha said with a chuckle, playing with a curl of Amalie's hair. They were a couple and so in love it was adorable.

"Are you sure you want that? You know our coach is brutal," I said.

"It beats spending your days on the couch. I was so lazy this summer, I gained three pounds! I need to get back in shape."

"I'll always love you, babe. No matter how many pounds you gain." Amalie smacked a kiss on her lips.

Denise sighed. "I should also get back in shape. My family and I went to see our relatives in France, and I couldn't resist all their food. Like, their dishes are delicious." She licked her lips.

"How about you? What was your summer like?" Amalie asked me.

"We heard about Carter's amnesia," Trisha said. "That sucks."

I pushed my food around the plate. "Yeah. It's been a hard few weeks."

"Is it true you broke up?" Denise asked.

My heart squeezed tight with pain. I'd prepared myself for these questions, but that didn't make this any easier. "Yeah."

"That's too bad," Amalie pouted.

"It's his loss," Trisha said.

Amalie capped her mascara and dropped it into a pink vanity case she carried around with her. "You two were the golden couple. Everyone thought you were going to get married and have babies!"

I rolled my eyes, chuckling. "No way."

"It's true! Like, you two are OTP. There's no doubt about it."

So much for being OTP.

Not knowing what to say, I let my gaze wander around the cafeteria, studying the faces around me. Sometimes, Silver Raven Academy gave me the impression of one giant catwalk, where outer beauty reigned. People here spent thousands and thousands to look as beautiful as possible. Half of the girls had had something done to their faces, whether that was a nose job, a lip filler, or a chin implant. The other half relied on high-end makeup to conceal all their irregularities. Girls with no makeup were like a dying breed—rare to find and extremely fascinating once spotted. Most of the guys were slaves to haircare and skincare products, and some of them succumbed to the lure of plastic surgery as well.

There had always been an air of importance around here, like you'd entered a dimension reserved only for the privileged few, and it was a feeling that could crush you from all sides if you didn't belong.

A familiar pair of dark brown eyes met mine with a smile from across the room, and I smiled back at him. It was Summer's cousin Jacob. He was seated with the rest of our basketball team, and his best friend, Tara, was sitting by his side. She was animatedly telling him something, despite having lost his attention.

Jacob said something to her and stood up. He headed our way, causing a few girls to stare after him, along with Tara.

Jacob never lacked for female company or attention. Tanned, sinewy, and with rich chestnut hair, he was giving Carter a run for his money. He was also one of Carter's biggest rivals, on and off basketball court, starting from even before Carter met me. Jacob had harbored a crush on me ever since the ski trip a year and a half ago, and we almost got together, but then Carter and I happened.

"Hey, Zoe." Jacob dropped into the chair next to Summer. "Cuz."

"Nice of you to stop by," she said.

"I figured. How's your first day?"

"Teachers are already talking about homework, so what do you think?"

Jacob laughed, a mellifluous sound that had the girls around us turning their heads to look at him. "I thought you loved everything that has to do with studying."

"Even I have limits."

Jacob nudged her shoulder with his, then smiled at me. There was a glow in his eyes that hadn't existed before, and I had an inkling he'd found out I was single. "How was your summer, Zoe?"

Aside from my boyfriend being in an accident, then him forgetting about me and breaking up with me? "Peachy. Summer told me about the summer camp."

"Yeah. It was brutal. It felt like I joined the army."

I chuckled. "That bad?"

"Worse. But it'll be worth it."

Jacob was also a scholarship student and a basketball player, with dreams of going to the NBA one day. He always gave his all to show everyone he was their equal. He didn't miss a single practice, joined every camp he could, and was among the best-scoring players two years in a row.

"You think we'll win this year too?" Our team had won state last year, and everyone heaped praise on Carter's leadership and Jacob's sometimes unpredictable plays.

"The stakes are high. We have East Creek High as our biggest rivals, and they sure as hell can't get over our last game."

East Creek High had a long-standing feud with Silver Raven Academy, but that feud had worsened after we kicked their asses in the first round of the playoffs last year. We won by a mile, and their captain, Brandon Mead, swore we would pay, Carter most of all.

"Are you coming to Strider's party tomorrow night?"

"Definitely."

He flashed his teeth in a smile. "Great. Then I'll get to see you then."

I met Summer's gaze. She'd told me Jacob had hooked up with a few girls over the summer, but nothing was serious. I wasn't sure if he expected something to happen between us now that I was single.

My heart twisted in my chest. It was hard to see myself as single. I belonged to Carter, and part of me refused to accept that we were over. We couldn't be over just like that. Carter's love for me had to be somewhere deep in him, even if he wasn't aware of it. Besides, he could recover his memories any day now.

As if looking for a fix, I sought out Carter with my eyes and stiffened when I found him already looking at me. His gaze shifted to Jacob, charged with intensity.

I felt a pang in my chest. Was it possible he was jealous because I was talking to Jacob?

Yes, it was obvious—he didn't like me talking to Jacob.

Perking up, I breezed through the remainder of lunch and last period, ignoring the continuous whispers and stares thrown my way and Instagram notifications blowing up my phone of people asking if it was true Carter and I were done. I hummed to the song playing on the stereo as I drove home, replaying his look in my head.

Since Mom worked as Dominic's assistant in his office, they both usually worked until five, so the house was empty. The smell of disinfectant hung in the air, indicating that Mrs. Hopper had cleaned recently. Work took up most of my mom's time, so she couldn't take care of the house or cook meals, not that she ever needed to since Dominic had always hired housekeepers. It was nice not having to watch her exhaust herself balancing work and housekeeping for a change. It was the least she deserved.

After I dropped my backpack in my room and changed out of my uniform, I danced my way down to the kitchen, my hips and arms moving as smoothly and naturally as breathing. Dancing had always been my escape, my passion, my natural response when I was happy or sad. Whenever I was dancing, life just wasn't that hard anymore, and right now, I wanted to dance forever.

I opened the fridge and took out a bottle of water, smiling as I compared Carter's look from the cafeteria to his look of possessiveness when we'd been together whenever some guy looked at me. They were similar. Carter had always claimed I was his, staking his claim whenever some guy flirted with me or tried to get my number. His possessiveness was one of the things I loved about him.

I closed the refrigerator door, revealing Carter standing behind it. I drew back with a yelp. *When did he get home?*

"Carter! You scared me."

His eyes blazed into me. Heat zapped through every fiber of my body as he supported himself against the counter and leaned toward me. "You don't waste time, do you? For someone so in love with me, you couldn't wait to get it on with Jacob Myers."

My breathing picked up, and I wanted to smile. That had to be jealousy.

I itched to take the last step between us. He was so close it almost felt impossible not to. "Are you jealous?"

His gaze flitted to my mouth, his brows knitting. "Jealous? I'm *furious*. Furious that I was stupid enough to stick my dick in a slut like you. I'm furious that of all guys, you chose my enemy, which only proves you're a calculating bitch with some ulterior motive. It's too bad he's broke. That and his dick is tiny. He won't be able to satisfy you, but I guess you can't have it all."

Motherfucker. I was livid. I was shaking with how livid I was. I'd never thought it would get this bad again—that he would be this spiteful, nasty asshole—but it was, and I wanted to scream, to pound my fists into him to wake him the fuck up.

But I feigned indifference. "It sounds to me like someone's worried about my pleasure. I'm flattered." I smirked. "But don't worry, I'm sure he'll be able to satisfy me more than you ever could. Because let's face it—you're barely average."

All of that was a lie, but I didn't care—until he winced, and then I immediately regretted my words. What the hell was I doing? I was supposed to be making him see me for who I was, not pushing him away.

"I—I'm sorry, Carter. I didn't mean that."

It didn't make any difference. Without a word, he turned around and left me in the kitchen, the thudding of his feet like spikes of pain right into my heart.

CHAPTER SEVEN

EVERY COUPLE HAD THEIR OWN SPOT. THE ONE PLACE WHERE everything felt right, where they felt they could stay forever. A trove of memories. A sanctuary.

The attic in our wing of the house had been ours. With heavy steps, I entered the place that held some of our best memories together.

If this space could talk, it would speak of a fiery love that threatened to engulf both of us with its flames. Where we hadn't been able to keep our eyes and hands off each other. Where we'd shared so many secrets. Where he'd taken my virginity and showed me just how good life could be.

I closed the door behind me and took a few steps in no particular direction, my hands cold.

The attic had been unused before Carter and I transformed it into what it was today after we started dating. A pile of pillows sat in the alcove looking out onto the forest around the house. Carter's whiteboard that he used for architectural design occupied one corner, along with a tower of books on architecture. My romance books lay in a scattered mess on the wooden nesting tables, right across from the dartboard on the side wall. A bean bag hammock hung in another corner, facing the eighty-inch TV with a PS5 below it.

I sat down on the fluffy carpet in the center of the space, my gaze falling on the open book resting on it. My heart squeezed in my chest. The text was on architectural lighting. It had been the last thing Carter was reading before the accident. For days, he'd been talking about energy-efficient lighting and the right balance between aesthetics and functionality. I hadn't had a clue what he was talking about, but I'd loved listening to him talk and watching his eyes shine with excitement.

A memory unfolded in front of my eyes.

Carter and I were lying next to each other on the carpet, the music from Carter's phone playing softly from the corner. Carter reached out and tickled me under my armpit.

I swatted his hand. "Don't." I burst out laughing when he took that as a signal to tickle me again. "Stop it!"

His laughter joined mine. "Why should I? It's so fun to torture you like this." He tickled me harder, and we ended up wrestling and rolling around on the floor.

"You're a sadist!"

"And you're whining too much."

"I'll stop whining when you stop tickling me."

"I will if you beg me to."

"Never."

"You asked for it."

I yelped as he started tickling me everywhere, and my laughter turned hysterical, tears collecting in the corners of my eyes.

"Okay! Okay! I surrender. Stop, now! Please."

He didn't stop. "What's that, again? Louder, I didn't hear you."

"Please!"

"Not loud or convincing enough."

"Please, please, please!"

He chuckled and kissed the tip of my nose. "Good girl." He got off me. We rolled to our backs, our chests rising and falling around rapid breaths.

I shifted my head to look at him and noticed his expression had turned serious.

"What's that face for?"

He put his arm beneath his head. "There's something I've been thinking."

"Hmm?"

"You're going to think I'm crazy."

"Try me."

"I'm going to work for Dad's company."

I raised myself on my elbow to look at him better. "You are?"

Carter had always refused to follow the path Dominic expected him to follow, saying that hell would freeze over before that happened. But recently, he'd discovered he loved architecture. He thought it was fascinating how you could complement space with a design that reflected that specific community. How special it felt to make your creation a part of a town, one community, a creation that was a product of labor and vision. He wanted to be part of that. However, he didn't want to ride on his dad's coattails. He wanted to be successful on his own.

So, when he started studying buildings and acquiring books on architecture, it had nothing to do with Dominic's plans for Carter. It had everything to do with Carter's passion for building, and I was happy for him, because he'd found something he was passionate about. He'd found something he wanted to do.

Just the way I felt about dancing. The difference was he was going to pursue his passion.

"Not immediately," Carter said. "As you know, I want to build a name for myself first. Work with others and then join his company."

I placed a kiss right over his heart. "I think that's a great idea. I'm so proud of you."

He grinned. "You are?" The way he looked at me told me just how much this meant to him.

"Yes."

"I think this is the first time you've told me that."

"Get ready then, because I'm going to keep telling you that."

With a happy smile, his lips landed on mine, and his body covered mine in one swift movement as his tongue plunged into my mouth. Pleasure sparked deep in my stomach, throbbing with each stroke of his tongue. He drew away to look at me with eyes glazed with lust and adoration.

"Do you have any idea how perfect you are? Thank you."

"Don't thank me. I'm just telling the truth. You're going to be a great architect. And I can't wait to see your buildings."

He smirked. "And I can't wait to start. But first, I want to start something else . . ." He lowered his head down my body past my stomach, and then there was no more room for talking.

I blinked away the memory, my chest aching. What was going to happen to Carter's dream? Would he feel passion for architecture again even though he had no memory of ever choosing it as his career?

I reached out to close the book, but then I stopped myself, my fingers curling above the open page. No, if I closed it, then . . . then it would be like cementing the possibility that he would never remember. That things wouldn't be as they used to be. If it was open, then there was at least a kernel of illusion that not everything was lost. That he was still here.

I retracted my hand.

It was going to wait for him. Just like me.

I grabbed one of the novels from the nesting tables and sat in the alcove to read, pretending Carter was on the other side of the attic, drawing on his whiteboard.

And if I closed my eyes, I could see him there, his expression focused as he created with precision, effort, and devotion.

I gasped at the wave of anguish that memory brought, and I willed myself to start reading. I needed to lose myself in a fictional love story before I lost myself in this painful longing that plagued me each day.

I wanted to spend all day Saturday in my room before I headed to the party, but Dominic had other plans. He wanted us four to have a BBQ beside the pool.

Just a few weekends ago, we'd had an amazing Saturday lunch together. Mom and Carter had finally reached the point where he always asked for her advice and opinion on everything, and she was fussing around him like a real mom. I took a photo of us posing in the pool with my phone, with Mom and me lying on floating mattresses while Carter and Dominic stood behind us with bottles of beer in their hands.

I looked at the photo now, and my chest tightened. Memories were like glass—pretty on the outside but could be deadly if everything broke apart. It was hard to believe that something that had brought me so much happiness was what fueled my misery now, and I wished it didn't hurt so much. I was torn between deleting the photo and keeping it like the precious thing it was.

I could hear Mom and Dominic setting things up by the pool, so I stepped into my closet to get dressed. Things were bad between Carter and me, but that didn't mean I had to stop caring about what I wore in front of him. So, I made an effort, choosing a mid-length flowery dress that had been a birthday gift from him. He'd loved me wearing this dress the most. He'd said it made me look like an angel and a tease at the same time.

New Instagram notifications popped up on my phone just as I headed downstairs, and I stared at them. I was on the fence whether I should open them or not. I'd purposely avoided checking social media so I wouldn't see people talk about me, and I was sure my DMs were full of questions about me and Carter.

Curiosity won out, and I pulled up my Instagram. My gaze flicked over the newest message requests.

"It sucks you split with Carter. I'm sure you'll be back together in no time. Hang in there."

"Aww, I'm sorry you and Carter didn't work out, babe. If you need someone to talk to, I'm here."

"Hey, gorgeous. I was thinking you and I should go out sometime. Text me if you're interested."

"Hi! Did you know you're absolutely beautiful? How about we meet for coffee this weekend?"

"Good riddance! You were never good enough for him. I'm so glad he dumped your ass."

"Hahaha you got what you deserve, bitch!"

"I just knew you two would break up. It was just a matter of time. How does it feel to be dumped?"

My hand had started shaking around my phone, and I barely stopped myself from chucking it across the room. What had I been thinking? It was as if I were asking for more drama.

No, I couldn't deal with this now.

Pushing all those messages out of my mind, I logged out of Instagram and stepped outside. My blood began pumping hard when I saw Carter lounging in the deck chair beside the pool. It was clear he didn't give a damn about helping Mom and Dominic. He was on his phone, and music was blaring from his earbuds.

My mouth went dry as my gaze swept over him. He was dressed in shorts and a tank top that brought attention to his defined arms, and I stared a second too long at his powerful biceps as it flexed when he shifted his phone to his other hand. My body warmed with the need to wrap myself around him. It physically hurt having to rip my gaze away from him and dull that urge.

Dominic was currently flipping burgers on the grill. Mom was setting the table, and I went to help her. Her sad gaze cut toward Carter, and I didn't need to ask her to know she was hurt because things had regressed between them.

It wasn't fair that all that progress she'd made with Carter was now gone. He'd accepted her as part of his family and never brought up the past, and that had meant so much to her. Her happiness couldn't be complete without Carter's approval.

I reached for the cutlery and nodded toward Dominic. "That smells delicious."

He deposited a fresh batch of sausages and burgers on a plate. "Wait until you taste them."

"I don't doubt it for a second. You always make tasty burgers."

Carter glanced up from his phone to look between us. It was the same look of judgement he gave me and Mom when we'd had our first family meals after we'd moved in. It had made me feel alienated then, and a portion of that feeling swirled in my chest now.

"So, what's the occasion?" I asked Mom, motioning with my hands at the table.

She shrugged. "Oh, you know, we just wanted to spend some time together. We've spent time together so rarely lately since we've gotten so busy at work with all the new clients and projects."

It was true we hadn't had enough family time recently because they were busy at work, but I caught the undertone in her words.

I leaned closer to her. "No, what's the real reason?" I whispered, although I could still hear music coming from Carter's earbuds.

She glanced at Carter. "The doctor thought it would be good for Carter to continue with our routine. To show Carter how our family functions and help him ease into it gradually."

"You think this will really help?"

"We have to do whatever we can for him. One step at a time."

I sighed and began placing forks and knives on the table.

"I saw a new dance studio downtown. Apparently, the owner used to work with celebrities and has decades-long experience in the industry," she said after a moment of silence.

A flutter rippled through my belly, followed by an echo of pain from the past. Like always, I suppressed it before it led me to grim thoughts.

"Really? Cool."

"That's it? I thought you'd be more interested in it."

"Why would I be interested?"

"You know why. You love dancing."

"That doesn't mean I should apply."

She held my gaze for a long moment. "You should think carefully about what you'd like to do for the rest of your life, honey."

"No, I should think about getting into a good college. We talked about this already, Mom." Quite a few times, actually.

"Would that make you happy?" Her tone suggested she thought I definitely wouldn't be as happy as I would if I had my dream job.

I glanced away. Since Mom hadn't been able to realize her dreams, too busy with surviving to have that luxury, she'd made it her mission to impart to me how important it was to make your dream a reality. She'd counted on me to realize mine. And, sure, dancing had always been part of my dream.

But dreams didn't feed empty bellies. It wasn't as if I'd just work hard at making it happen and things would magically come my way. And the past had taught me well that fairytales didn't exist—only cruel, harsh reality. So, I wasn't going to waste my life chasing some fantasy and put myself through more disappointments. The dance industry was too volatile and competitive as it was, and I was too scared to even consider trying. The imperative goal was to get into a good college. Mom hadn't gone to college, and there wasn't a day when that hadn't proved to be a colossal mistake.

Not taking this life with Dominic for granted meant I was prepared for it to be over one day. Life was unpredictable, and it could pull the carpet out from under me at any moment. Carter's amnesia only confirmed that. What if Mom and Dominic broke up and we were back out on the streets?

I needed to pursue a reliable career so I'd have choices. I hated Silver Raven Academy, but it was a necessary evil. It was the most surefire way for me to get not only into college but into an Ivy league college. I didn't care about college, per se, nor did I have a specific career in mind. I just wanted a stable, well-paid job, and if graduating from an Ivy League school led to that, then by all means, I'd go to the best college there was.

"I think doing what you're passionate about will make you the happiest," Mom continued. "You don't want to wake up one day regretting your choices. By then, it might be too late."

"Earning good money will be enough for me."

"But maybe you can allocate some time to join a dancing group and see where it will take you—"

"No, Mom. I told you, no professional dancing for me."

I could see she wanted to argue more, but she didn't push it. Dominic was done with the meat, and he told me to tell Carter to join us as he set the meat on the table.

My heart was fluttering in my chest as I approached Carter. As my shadow covered him, his eyes moved up my legs and the rest of my body, lingering on the deep V of my dress. He took his earbuds out.

"You don't give up, do you?"

"What are you talking about?"

"Dressing up. I've seen better."

I gritted my teeth together. "That's not what you said a few weeks ago."

He tensed up. He averted his gaze, pressing his lips together.

A sense of triumph filled me, but it was short-lived. "Why can't you give me a chance to show you I'm not who you think I am?"

"Because I'm not interested in knowing you. Or being with you."

"Then why did you start dating me in the first place?"

He launched up from the deck chair and straightened to his full size, grabbing my arm. Tingles rushed all the way through me at his nearness and touch. His scent surrounded me, a familiar, overwhelming smell that had me almost swaying. "That Carter is gone. So, you better stop any illusions you have that you and I will ever be together again."

"And what if you remember? Then what? Are you just going to keep ignoring that you loved me?"

His posture went rigid. His eyes shifted back and forth between mine, and I wished, I so wished, I could make a crack in the wall he'd built around himself.

"Is everything alright, you two?" Dominic asked.

Carter muttered a curse and released me, striding away to the table. Why did he have to be so stubborn? How could I ever get him back when I couldn't even speak to him without it becoming an argument?

"Help me serve the meat," Dominic told him.

I expected Carter to refuse, but he complied without objection.

Once we were all seated at the table, the atmosphere between us turned thick with tension. Mom and Dominic glanced at each other, as if seeking support from one another.

"How was your first day of school?" Dominic asked us.

Carter only snorted and took a bite of his burger.

"It was fine," I said.

"How about yours, Carter? Were you able to catch up?"

A muscle ticked in Carter's cheek. "I'm not a two-year-old. I can handle myself."

"You forgot two years of your life, son. It will take time to adapt."

"You don't say. But don't worry, you're making it easy for me— you're the same douchebag I recognize from back then."

"Carter!" Mom gasped.

Carter turned his attention to her. "And you. Have you already spent his hard-earned millions? The last thing I remember, he got you a black card. These last two years must've been good to you."

Dominic smacked his hand down on the table. "You're way out of line, Carter. Enough."

"Why? I'm just telling the truth. We're a family, right? Family always tells the truth."

"I won't hold this against you because of your condition but know that I won't let you tear our family down. Things have changed between us. *You've* changed. I won't let you destroy all that progress."

Carter's gaze was all fury and hatred as he watched all of us. His mouth curled with spite. "Maybe I don't remember your 'happy' times, but I do remember Mom crying day after day, begging you to remember that you have a wife. I also remember her body in that casket. And I especially remember that you didn't wait for her body to grow cold before you brought this woman and her daughter into our house. You lied that you didn't cheat on Mom—"

"I didn't lie!"

"You lied that you didn't cheat on Mom," Carter repeated. "And you expected me to be okay with it. You expected me to accept this woman as my *mother*"—he spit out the word—"and her conniving daughter as my *sister*. And never, not even once, did you ask me how I felt or what I wanted. My mom died, and I needed my dad. I needed someone to care about me. But you were never there."

"I apologized to you, son. You don't remember, but I apologized, and I told you I was going to do everything in my power to make things right between us."

Carter's lip twisted wryly. "And look how that's turning out for you."

Dominic's face paled. Mom's eyes filled with tears, and my stomach twisted. I hated seeing her upset.

"Carter—" Dominic started in a dangerous voice, but Mom placed her hand on his chest.

"No, remember what the doctor said." She cast a sympathetic smile at Carter. "Carter, we understand this is a difficult situation for you. We won't pressure you. Just know we're always here to support you."

"I don't need your fucking support, whore."

Dominic jumped to his feet and slammed his hands on the table, causing the plates to rattle. "That's it. Go to your room."

Carter's face contorted with such animosity it tore through me like a knife. "You don't have to tell me twice. I never wanted to be here anyway." His chair screeched as he pushed to his feet and rushed inside.

I got up too and sprinted after him, catching up to him in the foyer. I grabbed his arm to stop him. "Insult me all you want, but don't bring Mom into this."

"Bring her into this? She's right at the center of it!"

"Is it so hard for you to believe that we're good people? That we love both you and your dad and mean you no harm?"

"You think that would matter to the woman whose husband replaced her with another woman? Who never stopped loving him, unlike him, who at the first sign his marriage was in trouble decided to step out on her?"

I'd never doubted Mom was telling the truth when she said she hadn't had an affair with Dominic, but then why did I get an uncomfortable feeling just now?

I swallowed hard. "Even if what you say is true, even if they were together while your mom was alive, they're both human. Like all of us. We all make mistakes and selfish choices, but that doesn't mean we shouldn't be forgiven."

With my every word, his eyes filled with more disgust, and I got the feeling this was the absolute worst thing I could've said to him.

"Do you even fucking hear yourself?"

"Carter, I—"

Dominic and Mom started laughing outside.

Carter swung his gaze in their direction. His face scrunched up in unexpected pain, and it was like someone had kicked me in the gut.

"Carter—"

"No, I'm done talking."

My heart ached as I watched him climb the stairs. I fisted my hands. I hated that I couldn't get through to him.

Feeling the bitter taste of defeat in my mouth, I returned to Mom and Dominic. They were leaning in to one another, speaking in hushed tones until they saw me.

"Has Carter calmed down?" Dominic asked.

"What do you think?" I sat back down on my chair.

He took off his glasses and rubbed the spot between his brows. "I don't know what we're going to do with him."

Mom caressed his shoulder. "You heard his doctor. He needs

our support and a calm environment. We have to keep trying to reach out to him."

"I'm trying, but I can't allow him to insult you or Zoe."

"We can't deny there was bad blood between us, darling. Maybe we patched things up, but with his amnesia, we're back to square one. It's stressful for all of us, but it's the hardest for him. We just have to be patient."

"I understand, but that doesn't make it right, honey. Especially now that . . . you know."

I looked between them. "Know what?"

They exchanged a quick look. "It's just that we're so busy at the firm," Dominic said. "This has come at the worst possible time."

I wanted to tell him there was never a right time to get amnesia, but I kept my mouth shut.

"I was also told he doesn't want to go to counseling. I don't know how I can help him if he doesn't want help."

"He needs time," Mom said. "Zoe and I will be okay. Isn't that right, Zoe?"

I wasn't sure what to say. I couldn't tell if things would escalate from here. It was already bad enough as it was. "I just wish he wasn't so difficult."

"I think his reactions are understandable. Imagine waking up one day with no memory of your last two years. You'd feel like a stranger in your own life, right?"

"Maybe. But I wouldn't take it on the people I cared about."

"We're all different, Zoe. I'm not justifying his behavior, but you have to remember we all have different ways of dealing with a situation. Then there are his mood swings and frustration. He's suffered a brain injury, and we have to take that into account. He's bound to be all over the place."

"Even so, we don't have to tolerate bad behavior." Dominic gave me a steady look. "If he ever bothers you, you're to come straight to me to tell me about it. Alright?"

I'd never complained to Dominic about Carter, because their

relationship had been damaged enough without me contributing to it. I didn't see a point in starting now.

I gave him a terse nod, looking at my plate.

Mom reached across the table to cover my hand. "Be patient with him. Let him get used to his new reality, but in the meantime, show him you're his ally. Show him how much you know him, how much you *understand* him. That ought to help."

My gaze flicked up to hers. Maybe she was right. I'd convinced myself to wait for him to recover his memories, but what if that was a mistake? What if I could use our past as a way to his heart?

"If you think so."

She smiled at me. "Oh, I'm sure of it." She gestured at my dress. "And I'm sure Carter liked seeing you in that dress. You look fantastic, dear."

"He said he's seen better."

Dominic ran his hand down his face.

Mom chuckled. "I don't think so. You're the most beautiful girl in the world." She patted my hand. "Remember that he's going to recover eventually."

I just nodded.

Unlike Mom, I was a pessimist. It was hard to keep believing our relationship was reparable, but if I buckled under doubts, that would be turning my back on our love.

No, I wasn't going to give up on Carter just yet. I had to get him to see he loved me, and if not? I'd just have to make him fall for me again.

CHAPTER EIGHT

CARTER AND I HAD ALWAYS GONE TO PARTIES TOGETHER, SO going to a party without him didn't feel natural. I dressed to impress, knowing he would be there too, but without his lips and hands on me, it wouldn't be the same. That didn't mean I couldn't get drunk and dance my ass off, though, so I threw a smile on my face and entered Strider's house with my head held high.

As a basketball player, Strider enjoyed a certain amount of popularity, and as such, he was one of the main sources of parties around here. It didn't surprise me that his house was already too crowded. Some indie alternative music was playing from the built-in speakers around the house, and everywhere I looked, some couple was kissing, using whatever available surface they could find.

Guys turned as Summer and I passed, and I noticed one of them eyeing Summer up. I bumped her shoulder and motioned with my head at the guy checking her out.

"He likes you," I told her.

She broke his stare and fussed with her purse. "Are you sure he wasn't checking you out?"

I gave her a narrowed gaze, placing my hand on my hip. "Tell me, Sum. When are you going to stop waiting and start living?"

She averted her eyes. "I'm not waiting for anything."

"Oh yeah? Then why don't you give any of these guys a chance?"

"As if they're interested in me."

Sometimes, she frustrated the hell out of me. Summer lacked confidence, big time. She was convinced no guy could want her and there was nothing I could say to bring her around. She didn't like her face, claiming it was too average, and she preferred to hide herself and stay in the background even with a full face of makeup.

The thing was, she didn't have the "in your face" kind of beauty. Her type of beauty was a quiet one, natural, the kind that hit you right between the eyes when you least expected it. If only she could learn to appreciate it and focus more on what she had instead of what she wanted to have.

With a slow gait that attracted appreciative gazes, Jackson stepped away from a group of guys blocking the entrance to the living room. He wore black jeans and a sleeveless red t-shirt with dropped armhole that offered a clear view of the tattoo sleeve on his right arm. Leather bracelets covered his left wrist. His face was detached, his eyes aimlessly roaming over faces until they found Summer. Almost imperceptibly, he moved his gaze down the length of her mid-thigh navy dress that fit her curves like it was made for them. As quickly as his eyes traveled down her body, they were shifting away, his gaze turning to me.

"Hi, Zoe."

"Hi. Having fun?"

"Ask me after I've had more booze."

I chuckled. "I guess Strider will have to step up his game to impress you."

"You know nothing can impress me."

Summer twisted her hands together. Jackson obviously wore some scars, and I saw the guilt on her face—the guilt that she'd only exacerbated his issues.

According to Summer, Jackson had always been a quiet and reserved kid who didn't trust anyone. It took him a while to warm up to Summer, but once he did, it was like she was his lifeline. He only ever laughed with her. He only ever opened up to her. But then their fallout happened, and he'd spiraled after that, turning into this guy who looked like he was just existing in this world.

I smiled, trying to cover my concern for him. "Is Carter here?"

"Yeah." A line formed between his brows. "It's weird to see him not remembering familiar faces."

"It's even weirder for Carter," I said. "Imagine being forced to interact with people who know at least something about you, and you know nothing about them."

Carter was trying to hide it, but I'd seen it at school yesterday each time a group of people surrounded him—he was barely keeping up appearances. People had been whispering about his memory loss, watching him like he came straight off Dr. Phil's show. They wanted to know what it was like, what he remembered and whatnot, swarming him with questions whenever they got a chance. They didn't get much, because admitting any weakness went against Carter's personality. He was very proud and stubborn, and he would never ask for help even when he needed it. I'd been his only exception.

And now that link between us was gone too.

"Did he tell you how he feels? If he remembered anything?"

Jackson shook his head. "He doesn't remember a thing, and he hasn't said much other than asking us about the time missing from his memory."

"Did he ask about me?"

He looked away. "Yeah."

My heart stuttered in my chest. "And what did he say about me? About us?"

"I don't think you want to hear it."

"Give it to me straight, Jackson. I deserve the truth."

He let his gaze wander somewhere over my shoulder. "He isn't happy about it. He said he wouldn't touch you with a ten-foot pole."

I dug my nails into my palms.

"Prescott and I tried to tell him you two were in love, but he's denying it. So, there's that, I guess."

My throat felt clogged. "Jackson . . . do you think he'll ever remember?"

His eyes held no light as they met mine. "I really don't know."

A redheaded girl in a crop top and tiny skirt came straight up to him. "You're that model, Jackson Monroe." She giggled. "You're so much hotter in person!"

Boredom and annoyance flashed over Jackson's face before he hid it beneath unreadable features. He tucked his thumbs into his pockets, looking down his nose at her.

"Why don't you come with me? I promise I'll show you a good time." She winked at him, running her fingernail down his chest.

He followed her finger closely, his expression remaining unchanged. The finger reached the belt of his jeans, revealing exactly what she had in mind. He glanced at Summer.

Summer was too still next to me, and I could swear she wasn't breathing.

The girl took his silence as agreement and pulled him after her, and he let her.

"See you around," he tossed at me over his shoulder.

I placed my hand on Summer's shoulder. "How are you feeling?"

"Like a fool."

I bit into my lip, feeling for her. "I'm sorry."

"No need to be."

I sighed. "Let's go get drinks."

"Right behind you."

My heart picked up its pace as we started for the kitchen. I just knew Carter was somewhere nearby, and my eyes kept seeking him out.

The kitchen was packed, like the rest of the house, and I navigated the obstacles of drinks and cigarettes in people's hands. Bottles of alcohol and shots took over the whole kitchen island. Trisha, Amalie, and Denise were standing beside it.

"Hi, girls."

"Hey, Zoe. You made it," Trisha said, her cheeks rosier than usual. She had a naturally pale face as a redhead, and it was easy for her to blush, but something told me the empty cup in her hand had something to do with her flushed appearance.

"What are you drinking?"

"There's a delicious punch over there." Denise pointed at the bowl filled with reddish liquid on the dining table, a couple of gold bracelets dangling from her wrist. They matched her gold dress, which complemented her dark brown skin and eyes. "Or if you're up for some Jell-O shots." She motioned at the shots lining the island.

"I prefer tequila."

Amalie giggled. "My kind of girl." She reached for the bottle of tequila and poured me a shot, swaying in the process. "How about you?" she asked Summer.

"Wine is fine."

"Hey, you made a rhyme," Trisha exclaimed and squeaked out a laugh. Yep. She was drunk.

Summer and I grabbed our drinks, and I downed mine. I immediately went for another round, then two more.

Positively tipsy, we all went together to the living room, pushing through the throngs of people and couples grinding against each other to the rhythm of the song. I let the music get me high as we joined others dancing in the middle of the crowd. Trisha and Amalie put their hands on each other's hips and started kissing, while Summer and Denise began swaying against each other.

I turned to face the crowd. My hips and arms followed the sensual bass, my blood pumping with elation. A few guys nearby fixed their eyes on me, intently watching me roll my hips as I moved down, then back up. I couldn't care less about them, yearning to see the guy I loved watching me, but he wasn't here.

Whoops reached us from outside, and I looked through the open French doors at the crowd gathered around the pool.

"Is that Carter?" Summer asked me, pointing at the guy doing a keg stand. It was Carter, alright. Prescott and Strider were holding up his legs, and some girl was holding the keg tap to his mouth.

"Yes." I was already jostling past the crowd of people to get to him. The chanting got louder, and more people gathered as Carter chugged the beer, his arms straining against the beer keg.

The crowd counted to forty seconds. Carter was still going, and it made me remember what a wreck he'd been after his mom's death, with nonstop drinking and stuff like this. He was going to be hammered.

Once everyone counted sixty and Carter finally stopped, he got to his feet, only to stagger and grab Prescott to keep his balance. My stomach dropped. His eyes were glazed, and there was a lazy smile playing on his lips as he pushed past Prescott and headed to the beer cooler.

I shoved aside two guys separating me from him and grabbed his face. "Why are you doing this to yourself?"

His eyes widened at me, then went down my body. Every inch of me went ablaze with awareness. I was wearing a tight black dress with lace running down the sides of my waist. My elongated legs in heels were almost on full display. It felt like he was caressing me with his gaze, so intimate and slow. His pupils dilated.

"*Fuck.*"

"Carter?"

He snapped his gaze up to meet mine, then averted his eyes. "Stay away from me." He pushed my hands off his face.

"I can't stay away when I'm worried about you."

He grabbed a bottle of beer from a cooler. "Save your worry for someone who cares."

"You'd made so much progress, Carter. You stopped drinking and doing shit like this."

He stumbled as he opened the bottle. "This is me starting it again." He tipped the bottle back to drink from it, but I plucked it away.

"No."

"No?" His eyes flared with fury.

"This is for your own good, Carter. I can't watch you self-destruct all over again."

Something slipped through his mask of hatred and anger. It was a hint of vulnerability and loneliness, and my heart twisted for him. He needed help, and no matter how much he didn't want it, I couldn't just let him do this to himself.

"It's my fucking life. I can do whatever I want."

"But this won't help. It won't make you feel any better."

"And what the fuck do you know?" He made a sudden step toward me, and I took a step backward, colliding with the cooler. He leaned toward me and grabbed my shoulder, pinning me between him and the cooler. My insides clenched with desire. "I'm sick of you acting like you know how I feel. You don't know shit about my feelings."

"Then tell me! Talk to me."

His gaze dropped to my lips for the briefest second, and it was all I could do not to grab his shirt and yank him closer to me. Cursing into his chin, he snatched the bottle out of my hand and turned around, downing the whole beer in a couple of gulps.

"Don't do this to yourself. Let me help you."

"No one can help me, least of all you," he whispered, the words laced with hurt that seemed to come from the very depths of him.

"Dude, let's backflip into the pool," Strider said as he passed us.

"Hell, yeah." Carter tossed the empty bottle aside and went to join him.

Was he serious?

"No, Carter, you can't." I grabbed his hand. "You're too drunk for that."

He pushed me aside. "I can, and I will."

I watched with horror as he walked unsteadily to the edge of the pool with Strider. People gathered around them. Prescott joined them, and a few fangirls tagging along behind him squealed and got their phones ready to film.

One by one, the guys backflipped into the pool to the excited shouts of the crowd.

Except Carter miscalculated. He backflipped, but he didn't push himself far enough from the edge, and he started falling face-down toward the tiles. My heart jumped into my throat.

"Carter!" I screamed right before he splayed out his hands against the tiles to prevent from hitting his head and sank into the pool.

I rushed toward the pool, my heart running a hundred miles an hour. I waited for him to come up, but he didn't surface. "Carter! Carter, come up!"

Finally, he surfaced, and I kneeled at the pool's edge, gripping it with my hands like I'd break apart if I didn't. My eyes frantically searched for any proof of injury on his body. "Are you okay? Are you hurt anywhere?"

Suddenly, he threw his head back and burst into peals of laughter. It was the kind of laugh that took something from me, verging on hysterical, and my heart broke as he continued laughing.

He wasn't okay. He wasn't okay at all.

"That's it. We're going home." I scowled at Prescott, who came to stand behind me with Summer. "Help me get him out before he does something even more stupid."

"No, I don't want to go home," Carter said, convulsing with laughter.

"You have to."

Together with Prescott, I got Carter out of the pool and told Summer to call an Uber. Carter could barely stand on his own now, so I had Prescott support him all the way to the Uber parked in the front of the house, a member of Prescott's security detail trailing after us.

Carter didn't say anything during the ride home, sitting with his head pressed against the window. He was staring off into the distance, and it hurt to see him looking so lost. I wished I could do anything to comfort him, to chase away his demons. I wished he would drop his guard and see I wasn't his enemy. I raised my hand to touch his shoulder but then decided against it. It wouldn't make any difference.

The lights were off in the house, but I couldn't count on not coming across Mom or Dominic, so we had to be as quiet as possible. I got out of the Uber and went over to his side to help him, but he refused my help.

"I can walk by myself."

I grimaced as he stumbled out of the car and wobbled into the house. He had trouble with the stairs, so I walked right behind him in case he slipped and fell, trying to ignore the dark all around us and the shivers it gave me. I followed him into his room, glancing around as my chest filled with emotion. I felt like I was entering for the first time, even though this room was as familiar to me as my own.

Carter hadn't bothered to turn on the light, so I didn't either, not that it was necessary, since the moonlight washed over the darkness with bright light. Without taking off his wet clothes or shoes, he fell headfirst onto his bed.

Shaking my head, I reached to take off his shoes. I didn't get past the first one before he rolled to his back and raised his head, scowling at me.

"Leave me alone."

"You can't fall asleep like this. You're all soaked."

He didn't answer, but he also didn't bother to take anything off, dropping his head back down and closing his eyes. I took that as a sign to finish what I'd started. After I dropped the second shoe, I moved to sit on my knees next to him and reached for his shirt.

This time, he grabbed my wrist and stopped me, sitting up. "What are you doing?"

"I told you. Your clothes are all wet. You can't sleep like this."

His eyes shifted between mine then grazed my lips. My breath hitched in my throat.

He yanked me toward him, and I almost ended up sprawled against his lap. I straightened up as much as I could with him holding my wrist, my right knee wedged between his legs. My pulse ratcheted up as his eyes roamed all over my face, studying each inch like a sculptor would their creation.

"Is this what you wanted? To use that I'm drunk to seduce me?"

"I would never do that to you."

He tilted his head. "Why do I think you're lying?"

"Think what you want. If I really wanted to use your condition to seduce you, I would've already been all over you."

He licked his lips. He grabbed my hip with his other hand and pulled me even closer. "So, you mean to tell me if you could kiss me right now, you wouldn't take the opportunity?"

My heart kicked hard against my rib cage. His eyes darkened, taking on a shade of midnight jade, and I couldn't move, hardly daring to breathe . . . until he looked at where he was holding me and finally spotted the ends of the tattoo on the inside of my wrist.

He lowered my arm, his eyes widening. The tattoo was half of a bird, its edge ending in a way that corresponded perfectly with the ending of his own half bird he wore on his left inner wrist. We'd gotten them for our first anniversary.

Holding my arm, he pulled me so that I was sitting next to him and placed his arm beside mine to study our tattoos together. They matched like two pieces of a puzzle. My heart swelled with love and yearning and memories that colored my world.

"You see where the heart of the bird is on my wrist?" I asked breathlessly. "It's right over my artery, where your special spot is."

He swallowed thickly, his eyes flicking to my mouth before meeting my gaze. "My special spot?"

"Kissing spot. You always love—" I cleared my throat. "You always loved to kiss me there. You said you loved to feel my pulse pounding against your lips."

His breath came out in one harsh burst. His eyes studied me with such focus it was as if he was trying to see all of me.

My stomach stirred. It felt like time had stopped, his eyes holding me captive.

But then, as though something suddenly shifted in him, his gaze sharpened, and he dropped my hand. "Get out."

My heart constricted painfully. "Don't fight this, Carter. You—"

"I said, get out!"

I dug my nails into my palms as I stood up so I wouldn't let out a sound. He could've slapped me, and it wouldn't have been as painful. Why? Just . . . why couldn't he give me a chance?

I wanted to scream at him, but I refused to show him any more weakness. I spun on my heel and headed for the door.

"And don't tell Dominic anything about tonight."

I squeezed my hands into fists. "When have I ever broadcasted your 'adventures' to Dominic?"

"Good. Keep it that way."

My nails dug deeper into my palms. I left the room before the first tears came out.

I managed to fall asleep only when the first sunrays appeared, dreaming of Carter and a love that had no limits or expiration date.

CHAPTER NINE

O N MONDAY, I ARRIVED AT MY LOCKER TO FIND CARTER RUM-
maging through his, and my breath caught in my throat
as I stepped beside him to open my locker.

The look on his face when I'd explained to him about our tattoos had told me that despite how much he was fighting me, there
was still hope. My Carter was still somewhere inside him, and it
might just be a matter of time before he was coaxed out.

So, Sunday afternoon, following Mom's advice to show him
I was his ally, I decided to start writing him notes about our past
as a couple, his personality, choices, and dilemmas, along with the
tips I'd found for coping with memory loss. I sat down and wrote
a long note about the feeling of security he'd felt when we got together. How he could finally rely on someone else and share his
burden, and the way it had helped him. How everything was easier
when he didn't have to constantly be on guard. I ended it by telling him he could count on me to listen to him any time he needed
it and left it by his door in the evening. It wasn't much, but it was
something, and I was impatient to see his reaction.

I almost stopped breathing as he closed his locker and turned to look at me. I had to bite into my cheek against the pang I felt deep in my chest.

"What are you trying to accomplish now?"

"What?"

"That note." He narrowed his gaze at me. "Did you think I'd fall to my knees in gratitude once I read it? That I would fully open myself up to you?"

I winced. "I'm just trying to help."

"Bullshit. You're using it to squirm your way back in."

"Carter, you need all the help you can get. Think about it. You lost two years of experiences, information, interactions. I just want to help you get to know your life better."

He slammed his hand against the locker beside me. "I told you; you can't help me."

I jutted out my chin. "I've helped you many times before. So, try me."

His eyes moved between mine once, twice, and something in my chest caved at the hesitation I found in them. It showed me he only needed someone to care.

A muscle ticked in his jaw, and he pushed himself off the locker, pivoting around and leaving for his class without a word. I released a shuddering breath after he turned the corner. *Keep pushing, Zoe.*

I saw him again in third period. He was in the back row, and I grimaced when I noticed he was seated between Jackson and Kim Winters. Kim was my squad mate and the biggest gossip in the school. She was so into everyone's business, people said if Kim didn't know about it, it didn't happen. She was one of my least favorite people around here.

Her beady little eyes sized me up, and it was clear she knew all about me and Carter and was basking in it. To make matters worse, the only two available spots left were in front of Carter and Jackson.

Summer and I shared a look.

"Do we have to?" Summer asked.

"As if we have a choice," I muttered.

Kim's eyes flashed with malicious delight as we approached. Carter raised his eyes from his phone and frowned when he saw there was no other place for me to sit. All the hairs on the back of my neck stood at attention as I dropped into the chair in front of him.

Summer sat behind the desk next to me, and I caught Jackson out of the corner of my eye look up from his phone at her. His gaze trailed down her neck, which was left exposed by her side-braid. His nostrils flared, and he looked back down at his phone.

"Why does she always have to be so goddamn close?" he muttered into his chin.

Summer froze, catching his words. Color suffused her cheeks as her gaze bounced around the room. With clipped moves, she took her things out of her backpack and made it her mission to arrange them neatly on her desk.

"I don't think you can straighten those pencils any more than that," Kim said, leaning over her table.

Summer's fingers froze over her pencils. She retracted her hands as she glared over her shoulder at Kim. "Don't you have something else to look at, Kim? Like your pathetic gossip column?"

"Now that you've reminded me." Kim pulled her phone out of her pocket. "I could write about you in today's post."

I whipped my head around to look at her. She wore a vicious smile that made my stomach twist with disgust.

"Tell me, dear Summer, have you considered plastic surgery? Your face is just so plain. I mean, we can all tell, even with all that makeup you wear. Honestly, the makeup just makes you look like a doll. It's kind of sad."

That was a low blow. Not only because she'd insulted Summer's looks, but also because Summer loved makeup and aspired to be a makeup artist one day. Ever since she learned how to do makeup, she was all about trying out new products and techniques, and she damn sure knew how to accentuate her best features.

I glanced back at Jackson, who was slumped in his chair with a bored look on his face, clearly not giving a damn that his former best friend was being put down. I frowned, looking back at Kim.

"The only thing sad here is you, Kim," I said.

She turned her overly made-up eyes on me. "Ouch. Someone's salty. Breakups will do that to you, I guess."

My heart dropped, and I glanced at Carter. His face was impassive, but his eyes dared me to say anything about our breakup so he would have a reason to lay into me.

Swallowing hard, I forced myself to look back at Kim. "You ought to know. Seems like all the guys you date can't handle you for more than a week. It must suck to have been dumped by half the guys in school."

She snarled at me. "At least I don't keep waiting around for a scrap of attention from them like a desperate skank."

Whoa.

I opened my mouth, then closed it. I couldn't come up with anything to say.

Unable to look at her or Carter, I turned back around and bit my tongue. *Bitch, bitch, bitch.*

"You're so better off without her, Carter," Kim said in her irritating nasal voice. "No one could stand her when you were dating her. She acted like she owned this place. Like she was something special."

My heart lurched in my chest. What the fuck?

"And she *always* flirted with other guys. Like, we get it, sweetheart, you're *so* hot and everybody wants you—"

I spun around in my chair, wanting to gouge out her eyes. "Stop fucking lying! Those are all lies! You're just jealous of me because I'm captain of our cheerleading team and guys don't want you."

Her satisfied smile fell. "Shut your damn mouth."

I knew it wasn't smart to provoke the one person who used gossip as a weapon, but Carter already had a bad enough opinion of me. She didn't need to fill his head with this. "But it's true, and you know it. Just like you know you're making up lies about me right now."

"Is everything alright back there?" the teacher asked, and I turned in my seat to see her standing beside her desk, watching us along with the rest of the classroom. I hadn't even heard her arrive with how worked up I was.

I turned to face forward and crossed my arms over my chest. "Yes. Sorry."

She *tsk*ed, shaking her head in disapproval. "I'm going to have to ask you to leave your differences outside of this classroom. This is school. Act accordingly."

Kim snickered behind me, and it was a challenge not to turn around and pounce on her. I spent the entire class fuming, having to listen to her whisper something to Carter, my name occasionally popping up.

Helplessness spread through me, and I had to count to three every time I breathed in or out so I wouldn't give in to the fear that she was worsening the damaged relationship between me and Carter. Once class was over, Carter was out of his seat and the classroom before anyone else, and he didn't look at me even once.

Kim curled her lip at me as she passed me on her way out.

I grabbed her arm. "What did you tell him?"

Her long, manicured red nails dug into my wrist as she shoved my hand off her. "Nothing he didn't know already—that you're trash who doesn't belong in our world. I guess now that Carter's out of the picture, you'll have to find someone else to leech off of."

"You're a pathetic excuse for a human being, Kim."

"Look who's talking." She flicked her hair over her shoulder and walked out as quickly as her Saint Laurent heels could take her.

"That bitch needs her dirty mouth cleaned out with bleach," Summer said.

"So do you," Jackson said, swinging his backpack over his shoulder.

Summer snapped her gaze at him, all color draining from her face. "What?"

Completely ignoring her, he moved past her and left the classroom.

It took her several seconds to be able to move after that, and she blinked rapidly as she stared after him. Her lips pressed together as she reached for her things blindly and shoved them into her backpack.

"That was so uncalled for," I said, surprised myself by his words. It had been a long time since Jackson had spoken directly to Summer. But now he'd upgraded his silence with an insult.

"It doesn't matter. Let's go." She headed out first.

I gave her a long look as I caught up with her. "You never explained to me what happened between you two to stop being friends. I just know you had a fight but not why."

She bit her lip, her eyes flashing with pain. "I really don't want to go there."

"Maybe I can help you."

"I know, but there's really nothing you can do. I just have to get over it already."

Jackson was walking some distance in front of us, and as we watched him, a girl came up to him and struck up a conversation, moving in step with him. She raised her hand to his shoulder, and I noticed a moment of tension in him before he relaxed into her touch, letting her stay in his personal space.

Summer's features twisted with pain.

"Sum, you don't look like you're going to get over it. You look like you're getting worse."

"It'll pass. Don't worry about it." Her tone told me to let it go, so I stayed quiet.

We entered the cafeteria, and my own features twisted with pain when I saw Nora sitting with Carter at his table again. This time, she had a DSLR camera with her, and she was showing him some pictures on it. I imagined flinging that camera to the floor, then yanking her away from Carter.

My gaze snagged on a couple people staring between me and them, as though expecting a show, and I remembered to school my features.

Summer and I grabbed our food and joined Trisha and the

girls at their table. It didn't take long for Jacob to show up, and Trisha and Amalie smirked between themselves.

"Hey." He dropped down next to me. "I was looking for you at the party, but I couldn't find you."

"Sorry, I had to leave early."

"Did something happen?"

The girls save for Summer were devouring our interaction with round eyes. Amalie even had a fry hanging out of her mouth, having forgotten about it.

"Carter got plastered so I had to get him home."

Jacob's brows raised. "Is he giving you trouble?"

"Let's just say he's currently a piece of work."

He pursed his lips, then ran his hand down his neck. "Do you have practice after school?"

"Yeah. The coach wants us ready before the season starts."

"Great. I have practice then too. I'll see you in the gym, then." Giving me a quick once-over, he stood up and left for his table, drawing lovey-dovey gazes from the girls around us. Even Amalie and Trisha couldn't stop staring after him.

"He so likes you," Denise told me.

Summer raised her hand in the air. "I attest to that."

I shook my head with a smile. At least someone liked me these days. "Anyway, I have news. Coach told me we're going to hold tryouts next week."

"Nice. Can't wait to see who will make it," Denise said.

Trisha raised her hand. "Me too."

I also raised my hand. "Me three." Tryouts were a chance for new talent to get a shot and for our team to get even better, and as captain of our squad, I got to have a say in who made the team, along with our coach.

I loved being in charge of the team and perfecting our choreography, and after I gave up on my dream of becoming a choreographer, I'd put all my energy into cheerleading and making our team as successful as possible. Especially since this was my last year on the team.

"I just hope we'll be able to find good replacements," Trisha said.

"And I hope Nora won't try out," Summer said in a low voice so only I could hear her.

The smile I'd been wearing petered out. I hadn't thought about that.

I glanced at her and Carter. They were laughing together as she took a couple photos of him, and it felt as if she was stealing pieces of him from me. How much closer did this girl need to get to him? They were already sharing classes and lunch. They already looked like best buddies. Was cheerleading even her thing?

I spent the rest of the lunch period trying not to stare at Carter and Nora laughing together or sitting too close to each other. Before I knew it, last period was over, and I was on my way to the girls' locker room.

All summer long, I'd missed having practices, and I was anxious to start working on new routines. I felt amazing when I danced on that court, and after the anxiety of these last few weeks, I needed to have my mind on something else.

As I stepped into the girls' locker room, all the girls turned to look at me. I kept a tight smile on my face, expecting a barrage of questions about me and Carter.

I liked to think I had a good relationship with most of the girls; as their captain, I was supposed to keep them all together and maintain order. But I wasn't naïve—half of them wanted my spot, and the other half either thought I didn't belong or only tolerated me. Trisha, Denise, and Amalie were my only friends here.

I'd just reached my locker when Jenna, Kim's best friend, cornered me against it.

"I heard about you and Carter," she said. "I'm so sorry."

Classic Jenna. Unlike Kim, who was all poison administered directly, Jenna was all smiles and sweet words right until she backstabbed you. Those who fell for her "nice girl" mask lived to regret it sooner or later.

"I bet you are," I muttered. Jenna had run bets on how long

Carter and I would last. She had bet on just two weeks. After losing that bet, she spread a rumor that Carter and I had broken up, the sore loser that she was.

Jenna tilted her head. "What was that?"

"Nothing."

"I can't believe you two broke up." She let out an exasperated sigh. "We all thought you were solid."

I almost rolled my eyes. "I'm not giving up. He'll remember us."

"And if he doesn't?"

"Then I'll just have to make him fall in love with me again."

She shrugged as if she wasn't so sure about that, and I felt a stab of irritation. The whole school knew back then how much we'd hated each other. For weeks after we got together, people kept looking at us as if they were witnessing a miracle.

"Aren't you afraid someone might steal him?"

I glanced around us, shifting on my feet. All the girls were listening in on our conversation, and I didn't like the look on some of their faces. They looked at me as if our breakup had been inevitable. As if we'd been doomed to fail before we even got together.

It reminded me of the time I'd heard someone say how something born out of hate couldn't last. How we were too destructive, and it was bound to happen again and tear us apart sooner or later.

Trisha, Amalie, and Denise flanked me, wearing defiant expressions that caused Jenna to shrink back.

"Why do you ask? Are you planning on stealing him?" Trisha asked her.

Jenna's arms folded over her chest. She glanced away. "Of course not."

Denise cocked her brow. "Why don't you give the girl some space to breathe, huh?"

Jenna scrunched up her nose and moved over to her locker. Kim entered the room and joined her, and Jenna didn't waste any time in relaying our encounter to her in a whisper. Vipers.

"Thank you," I mouthed to the girls.

Amalie winked at me. "We've got your back."

"Let's get ready so we won't be late. You don't want Coach to give us grief already," Trisha said.

I chuckled. "Yeah, we definitely don't want that."

My eyes sought out Carter as I entered the gym with the girls. He was already there with his team and their coach. Everyone turned to watch us as we passed them, and I just knew when Carter's eyes landed on me without even looking. They burned into me, bringing awareness to my whole body.

"Of course you're here. I'm not even surprised anymore," he said, and I turned to look at him.

"Don't make it sound like I'm here because of you. I'm a cheerleader, as you can see." I motioned at my navy cheerleading uniform.

His eyes took a slow dive over my body, and my breathing halted at the intensity in his gaze.

"Let me guess, you're a cheerleader because you love dancing. It has absolutely nothing to do with me." Sarcasm coated every word.

"As a matter of fact, yes, I love dancing," I replied seriously, conveying the truth with my eyes. "It's my biggest passion."

He must have recognized I was being honest, because his sneer fell and his lips parted in surprise. He crossed his arms over his chest, shifting his weight as he studied me, and I wished I could tell what he was thinking.

But people were already staring at us, and I didn't want to give them more to gossip about. I turned and went to my side of the gym. When I looked back over my shoulder at him, his gaze was still on me, and something flared in my chest. He quickly looked away from me, turning his back to me.

I expelled a long breath, catching Jacob's gaze.

"You okay?" he mouthed from where he stood with his teammates.

I nodded, giving him the thumbs up. Never been better.

Our coach arrived just then, and I willed myself to focus on our practice, but my attention kept drifting to Carter throughout the hourlong session. From the start, I noticed he was different.

Usually, he was the picture of confidence and determination during practice and games. He owned the court. But now, he mostly stood there shifting from one foot to the other, his gaze darting from one teammate to another and then to their coach as he gave them instructions. His hands never settled in one place.

One of the guys tossed Carter the ball, and I watched him bounce it between his legs flawlessly, then make a three-pointer. His skill and speed were still there, even if he didn't remember perfecting them.

Ten minutes after that, Carter cursed out loud and hurled the ball all the way to our side of the gym. The coach took him to task loud enough for us to hear him.

"That's not the way to do it, Reese. I told you if you need time—"

"I don't need time. I'm fine."

He didn't look fine, but then again, I'd be surprised if he actually admitted it.

"Zoe," my coach called out. I wrenched my gaze away from Carter. "Pay attention."

"Right. Sorry."

Jenna and Kim were observing me too keenly, and I decided I wasn't going to give them more material. Determined to keep my mind off Carter for the rest of the practice, I doubled down on the stunts Coach had us do.

Cheer practice turned out to be less exciting without Carter's loving gaze. Carter had used to love watching me perform. Our gazes would connect across the gym all the time, and he would often give me a thorough once-over, taking clothes off me just with his eyes. Once, he'd admitted that I could be too much of a distraction to him. So much so that his coach had to threaten to kick him off the team if he didn't fully focus.

His gaze had always made me feel so alive, so important. Like a flower opening up under the rays of the sun, I felt my happiest and most confident when I had it on me. Without it, I felt lonelier than ever, and the memories of our closeness—our connection—mercilessly taunted me as I drove home. The memories were too fresh, too powerful. What we'd had was a once-in-a-lifetime kind of love. Why had this happened to us?

The longing pulsed stronger in my chest, and I needed anything just to feel closer to him again, even if it was an illusion.

I dropped my backpack in my room and climbed up to the attic, my heart pounding harder as I got closer to it. A silly part of me expected Carter to be up there, to see him perched atop the window ledge, waiting for me. He would grin at me and follow me closely with his eyes as I approached him. Then he would pull me in his arms and press his mouth onto mine, drinking me in as though we hadn't kissed for a long time.

Fantasy turned into a memory, and I saw us sitting together on that ledge, with me leaning against him and his arms wrapped around my waist.

With my finger on the windowpane, I traced the shapes I saw in the distance. "I don't think I'll ever get used to it."

"Get used to what?" Carter asked.

"The view. I mean, look at it. It's mesmerizing how trees merge with the sky and it all blends in. We never had a view like this when I was growing up. All I ever saw through my windows were brick walls of the apartment blocks and dark alleys."

"This is a whole other world, for sure."

I laughed. "Yeah."

"How did you feel when you came here?"

I followed the lines of the clouds, trying to pick out some specific shapes. "It wasn't a fairy-tale princess-like moment, that's for sure. I didn't feel like I belonged, and I expected my new life to be over in just a matter of weeks. Mom has been in a lot of relationships, and I thought Dominic would be just one of many."

Carter's arms tightened around me. "And I didn't make it easy for you."

My lips twitched with a smile. "You didn't. God, at one point I even counted days until we were gone, just so I wouldn't have to see you again."

His lips trailed over the edge of my earlobe. "While I counted hours until I could see you again."

I turned to look at him. "Really?"

"I already told you I was attracted to you all that time. It turned out that even when I hated you the most, I kept looking for you. And whenever you entered the room . . ." His teeth dragged over his lip, and he shifted behind me. I could feel his hardness pressing into me, and a prick of desire formed low in my belly. "It was like I could finally breathe."

"I don't feel like I can breathe now when you're not by my side."

His hands started their journey down my shoulders, then my breasts, paying special attention to the two hard pebbles waiting for him . . . I arched into his touch. "I won't ever leave your side."

The thumping of a basketball blasted away my memory, and I blinked to focus my eyes on Carter shooting baskets on the basketball court below the window.

A sharp jolt of pain invaded my chest. I told myself to hold out hope, but I missed him so much. It felt as if I was missing a vital organ and couldn't function without it.

I couldn't move from my spot as I watched him, and that was when I noticed something was wrong. He made shot after shot, but he only looked more frustrated.

I went downstairs and stopped by the court, watching him hurl the ball at the wall. The sweat dripped off his face in rivulets. He was wearing a basketball jersey and shorts that clung to his body tightly enough to reveal the contours of his tapered waist and strong legs. His hair was a soaked mess. I loved it.

"You didn't lose your strength or skill, if that's what worries you."

He twisted around, startled. The sun glared onto his face, and he raised his hand to shield his eyes, staring accusingly at me. "How long have you been watching me?"

"Long enough to see you're not okay."

He fisted his hands. His steps were brisk as he went to fetch the ball, his muscles locked with tension. When he returned, he thumped the ball harder. It was painful to watch a haunted look settling in his eyes. Basketball had always been his outlet, a way for him to get rid of negative emotions, but this time, it seemed as if it only made things worse.

He took a quick look at me. His brows bunched together.

"What is it?" I asked.

The pounding of the ball turned even harder, if that was possible. He shot and scored. Then scored another shot.

Clenching his fists, he turned to face me. "I have no fucking clue what I'm supposed to do on the court. I feel as if I was grabbed up and dropped right in the middle of a foreign country. The rules are new, the people are different, and I'm supposed to act as if I have total control. Even Prescott and Jackson—I know them, but they've changed, and I don't know how to react sometimes."

"No one expects you to act as if you have total control."

"They do. All of you do. You all have these expectations of me, like we're all supposed to ignore the fact that I don't know what the fuck I'm supposed to be doing and continue like nothing has happened. I don't even know who I'm supposed to be! The guys at school, my friends, *you*—all of you keep talking about this guy that's not me."

My chest tightened for him, and I took a step toward him, wanting to console him. He noticed the movement and stiffened, forcing me to an abrupt stop. I hated seeing him like this. He was like a cornered animal, and I couldn't make a wrong step. I had to assuage his worries, not prioritize my own.

"I understand that everything is foreign to you, and I think that's normal in your circumstances. You should give yourself time. Figure things out day by day."

"I don't have time. My team expects me to bring us the state title. They expect me to lead our team like the previous year and prove we're unbeatable, but I don't even know our team, and I don't just mean how half of those guys are strangers to me. I mean our plays, tactics, strategies. Our strengths and weaknesses. I don't know who this basketball player I'm supposed to be is."

The ache in my heart deepened, and I would've done just about anything to take away his pain.

Throwing all caution to the wind, I closed the space between us and put my hand right across his heart. He took a sharp breath, his eyes dropping to my hand. I could feel his heartbeat quickening, and my fingers twitched with the urge to run them over his whole chest.

"You're going to figure it out. Just like the first time. You don't have two-years' worth of knowledge, granted, but it's in your blood. Basketball is in your blood, and you'll know what to do when the time comes. Trust your instincts."

He watched me raptly, his eyes shifting between both of mine over and over. My skin grew warm.

He stepped toward me, and I wasn't even sure if he was aware he'd done so. His heart was now beating with thundering intensity. He raised his hand as if to touch my face, but then he abruptly stopped. He dropped his hand, taking a large step away from me.

"*No.*"

"Carter?"

He glared at me. "This was all your plan. You're using my moment of weakness to try to manipulate me."

All the air left me. "You can't be serious."

"Don't think even for a second you'll get through to me. Your words mean nothing! You mean nothing. FUCK!" He hurled the ball across the court and headed inside the house.

My hands curled into tight fists. I didn't know whether I was feeling more hurt or furious. He wouldn't have the last word. Not now.

I went after him, catching him at the bottom of the stairs. "You seem to have overlooked one important thing, and that is, as my boyfriend, you shared with me all the details of your life, even those concerning our relationship when my mom and I first got here."

He stopped short and spun around to look at me.

"You've always been attracted to me. And you know that's true because you remember it, right? Even when you claimed you wanted me gone, you couldn't stop thinking about me. I invaded your thoughts every single day."

All the color left his face. He didn't blink. He looked as if he didn't even breathe.

I drew nearer to him. "So, I don't mean *nothing*. And I'm willing to bet you can't get me out of your head even now. But the difference is that you know you loved me at one point . . . and you're afraid the feelings are still there. That's why you're fighting me so hard. Fighting this"—I motioned with my fingers between us—"this pull between us that neither of us can fight off. But the more you try to fight it, the stronger it will be, and I think part of you knows that."

His chest was heaving. His hands were clenched into fists, his face just as tense. He was disarmed, thrown off balance, proving to me there was some truth to my words, and my chest ached so hard for him.

I was supposed to feel victorious.

But all I felt was sadness.

Finally, he said gutturally, "Fuck. You."

He rushed up the stairs and slammed the door to his room, also slamming another layer of sadness over my needy heart.

CHAPTER TEN

Two years earlier

THE FIRST FEW MONTHS AFTER WE MOVED INTO DOMINIC'S house had been tough for me. Carter had never warmed to me and Mom, and it seemed, with time, he was only becoming more bitter and ridden with anger. Dominic didn't know what to do with him, which led to endless, ugly arguments that created more scars and widened the rift between them.

In a way, I felt sorry for him. He wasn't even close to getting over his mom's death, and I knew seeing me and Mom every day was a constant reminder for him of what he'd lost. Dominic desperately wanted us all to be happy. Carter couldn't even begin to feel happy.

I went out of my way to avoid him, especially at school. Carter was like the king of Silver Raven Academy, and what the king wanted, the king got, and the king wanted me ignored. By the end of the first week, everyone saw me as an impostor and worthless, and no one wanted to make friends with me.

Not that I wanted to make friends with them. I didn't want to belong in their world. It didn't take me long to see they were all obsessed with status, power, and money, not necessarily in that order. If you didn't fit in, you were an outcast, and no one cared to see what was beneath the surface.

It didn't come as a surprise that the only friend I managed to make was a scholarship student, a girl who, like me, didn't belong. Summer was the only bright spot for me at Silver Raven Academy, reminding me that not all people were born douchebags. Or with a tendency to judge others. Or spurting insults whenever they pleased.

Like Carter.

Carter tried to antagonize me at every step. He had various insults at the ready for me, and when that wasn't enough, he brought out the big guns—humiliation. Today turned out to be the day for that.

I was taking a shower in the girls' locker room, applying the school-provided Coco Mademoiselle shower gel generously. The school splurged on consumables. The whole locker room was ultra-modern, with floor-to-ceiling mirrors lining a whole wall, hair dryers and wands, a dispenser with pads and expensive cosmetics, and beige leather benches. The built-in lights formed flowery patterns across the ceiling, completing the luxurious atmosphere.

Making the most of the toiletries, I took my time in the shower. Once I was done, I wrapped myself in a towel and stepped out of the shower stall. I reached for my clothes sticking out of my bag . . . only they weren't sticking out. They weren't there at all.

My heart accelerated. *That asshole.* I had no doubt this was Carter's doing. He must've arranged for someone to hide them somewhere. He had many blind followers who were ready to do his bidding at any time.

I wouldn't let him get away with this.

Armed with my fury, I marched into the boys' locker room to demand he give me my clothes back.

Hoots and whistles broke out around me, sending warmth to my cheeks. From the corner of my eye, I noticed almost all of the guys were either in their underwear, wrapped in towels, or in the process of stripping off their gym clothes. Making sure not to look at anyone, I made a beeline for Carter.

He turned to see what had gotten everyone's attention, and his eyes widened when he spotted me. Shocked? Good.

His gaze slid down my towel to my naked legs, and my gloating smile dwindled away, my body stiffening with awareness. I had the whole locker room watching me, but I was aware only of Carter.

Heat pooled in the pit of my stomach. It was hard not to notice how good he looked in his gym clothes. The material wrapped snuggly around his defined muscles.

Why did he have to be so hot?

Focus, Zoe.

Carter tore his gaze away from me, crossing his arms over his chest. "What are you doing here?"

"You know exactly what I'm doing here. You thought I wouldn't have the guts to get my clothes back? You're wrong."

Someone whistled. "Damn, dude. Your sister is hot."

Carter pierced him with a glare. "Shut the fuck up."

"Give them back," I demanded.

Carter smirked. It was a stark contrast to his cold eyes. "And what are you going to do to get them?"

"I'll stop myself from breaking your nose."

More hoots and whistles filled the room. I thought Carter would get angrier, but for a moment, there was wonder in his eyes.

He shifted closer to me. His scent hit me, and it was a challenge not to inhale the heady mix of his sweat and lingering traces of his cologne. My eyes went down his chest involuntarily, following each ridge of his muscles too intently.

Carter's smirk widened. "Show us your tits, and you'll get your clothes back."

My gaze flicked up as the guys roared with laughter, shame painting my face red. "You can't be serious."

"Come on, *sis*. Show them. It's not as if you're a stranger with showing off your goods. Girls like you and your dearest mommy think a little tits and ass is the way to get what you want."

Noise filled my ears, drowning out the laughter and hollers of the guys. It came from the fury building up from deep inside me—a fury born from a sense of injustice.

Just because my mom and I didn't belong in this world—just because my mom had to sacrifice a lot for us to survive—it didn't mean we were worth any less than them. We weren't *easy*. We had principles and pride too.

If anything, *he* was easy, with a different girl every damn week.

"Okay," I said.

The laughter ended abruptly. Carter's smirk vanished.

He titled his head. "Okay?"

"Okay. I'll do it. But only if everyone else leaves."

A muscle in his jaw jumped. He studied me for an extended moment, and then, without taking his gaze off me, he hollered, "Everyone, get the fuck out of here!"

The guys rushed in all directions to pick up their stuff, getting dressed in record time.

Once the locker room cleared and the door closed after the last guy, Carter tipped his chin at me in challenge. "So? What are you waiting for?"

I licked my lips. He followed the movement too closely. Now that we were alone, the room shrank to the two of us, and the air grew saturated with something I couldn't name.

I crossed the remaining distance between us with slow steps and stopped only a few inches away from him.

His nostrils flared around a sharp intake of breath.

Huh. Interesting. It seems my "bro" isn't as unaffected by me as he likes to pretend.

I brought myself up on my tiptoes to whisper in his ear. "Tell me, how many times have you imagined this? Seeing my tits. Be honest."

He let out a quick breath, his fists tightening by his sides. Another win.

"Never."

"Liar." My lips almost touched his ear, and he shuddered.

I almost laughed. This was too easy.

"I bet you think about them before you go to sleep." A low groan formed in his throat before he quickly suppressed it. My lips lingered over his ear, as if in promise of a touch. I could swear he was holding his breath.

I smirked. "But guess what? You're never going to see them." Just as I uttered the last word, I kneed him in the balls.

Crying out, he dropped to his knees and clutched his crotch. "Bitch!"

I yanked open his locker, and sure enough, my clothes were there. I grabbed them.

"The next time you try something like this, it will be your nose meeting my knee." I took small steps as I walked out of the locker room, feigning composure, but the moment the door closed behind me, I rushed off, my heart pounding in my chest.

My heart wasn't the only thing that had been pounding in that moment, and even long after that day, I sometimes allowed myself to imagine what it would've been like if I'd showed him my boobs . . . and he touched them.

The answer was clear.

I just wasn't so sure if I disliked the answer at all.

After that encounter in the locker room, it seemed as if we became more aware of each other, more conscious of our nearness. But that wasn't a good thing. It only poured fuel on our antagonism, leading to constant ugly moments.

One of those moments came when Adam Woodson, a guy two years older than us and one of the popular kids, started showing me attention at school. Carter did all he could to drive the guy away from me, first starting a rumor that I had an STD. I quickly rebuffed that, telling Adam I was a virgin, but Carter didn't stop there.

He showed up to mock me each time Adam stopped in the

hallway to talk to me. He always made sure to point out to Adam that I wasn't worth his time. When that wasn't enough and Adam asked me out on a date, Carter ruined my dress along with my hair and makeup by pouring syrup all over me fifteen minutes before Adam was to pick me up. I barely had time to go take a shower, blow dry my hair, and put on the first clothes I managed to grab from my closet, having to settle for not wearing makeup. I worried Adam would think I wasn't anything special all the way to the movie theater, but it turned out my natural look worked in my favor, because he told me then he preferred girls with no makeup.

We didn't hook up, but we agreed to go on another date. With that, I waltzed into our house around eleven, wearing a gigantic smile. Judging by the dark house, Mom and Dominic were probably asleep and Carter was still out with his friends. Even though it was past curfew, I didn't expect him for at least another hour or two.

With a pleased sigh, I entered my room . . . and almost screamed when I saw a figure sitting in my computer chair, the side of his face illuminated by the desk lamp.

I quickly pushed the door shut so Mom and Dominic wouldn't hear any commotion. They slept all the way in the other wing, but what if one of them decided to come see either of us? "What are you doing in my room?"

Carter didn't move. The dim light created devilish shadows across his body. The body that had been getting more muscular by the month. Too muscular to ignore.

How come he was two years younger than Adam but looking so much more mature and manly? At this rate, he'd be breathtaking when he got older.

"Did you have fun with Woodson? Did he pop your cherry?"

Warmth spread all over me. I took a step closer to him without thinking. "I thought I had it popped a long time ago. You said I had an STD, remember?"

His jaw twitched. I'd hit a nerve, but I couldn't pinpoint why. If I didn't know better, I'd say he was jealous.

"Is he a good kisser?"

"Why? You want him to give you a few pointers?""

He growled, and I felt a deep tug of satisfaction. I expected him to go off the rails any second now.

But he didn't. Instead, he brandished something he'd held beside him, as I'd just realized, the whole time. My blood froze. It was my diary.

"What are you doing? Give it back!"

I lunged at him, but he was quick to stand up and move around the chair, using it as a barrier between us.

"Ah, ah, ah. Not so fast." He opened the diary to the page his finger marked and started reading the entry out loud, all with a mocking, girly voice.

"Dear diary,

I'm finally going out with Adam. It's actually happening. How awesome is that? He's my first date. And if everything turns out alright, he'll be my first boyfriend.

A boyfriend. That sounds dreamy. I can't wait! But I'm so nervous. Like, we may be kissing. What if I embarrass myself? If I drool over him? Ugh.

That is, if Carter doesn't spoil it somehow. He must be planning something . . .

Ugh! I hate him!"

With each word, my cheeks burned hotter, and I wanted to fall through the ground.

"It's interesting that you should mention your 'brother' when it's an entry dedicated to your crush. Let's see what else you wrote about me."

He moved to turn the page, and I shrieked, moving fast.

"No!" I tried to grab the diary, but he was quicker, bringing it high above our heads and out of my reach. "Give it to me!"

I jumped to reach it, forcing him to take a backward step, then another . . . until we both crashed onto my bed, me ending up sprawled on top of him.

We both went still. In an instant, I noted the differences between our bodies. His chest and waist were all hard ridges, and his legs were strong and powerful. The contrast to my body brought a sweet ache between my legs.

Biting my lip, I reached for the diary above his head, but then he threw the diary to the floor, gripped my waist, and flipped us around, drawing a surprised gasp out of me.

His breaths heated my face. Every inch of me was conscious of his body on top of mine, and I couldn't drink him in enough.

He moved so that his knee was in between my legs, his hands trapping mine above my head against the mattress. The surprise in his eyes dwindled to lust as they swiped down my face, to my parted lips and my rising breasts straining against my shirt.

He groaned and shifted closer to me, drawing his knee higher, right against my most sensitive place. The ache there intensified. His lips had never seemed more tempting, more desirable.

His hand released my wrist to travel down across my arm, drawing fire to the surface of my skin. I didn't move an inch, breathing faster as his fingers moved past my shoulder, coming so tantalizingly close to my breast. My nipple puckered, as if inviting him to touch it. Since the bra I was wearing wasn't padded, it was all too visible to him, and I could see the moment he noticed it. His gaze turned feral, remaining on my nipple for several long, torturous seconds. I wanted to thrust my breasts up to his mouth. I *needed* to.

He licked his lips. "Tell me." His voice came out hoarse, deep. "Did you also react to him like this? Did you beg him to touch you?"

I jutted out my chin, giving him a sly look. "And why do you care?"

He froze. I could tell I'd flipped something in him, because the next moment, his eyes hardened. "I just want to prove you're easy, just like your mother."

My mouth went slack. How could I forget even for a second what a jerk he was?

"Not any easier than you. Tell me, how many times have you tested for STDs already?"

SHATTERED MEMORIES | 113

He snarled, pushing away from me. As suddenly as he was off me, the cold penetrated me, and I hated that I missed the feeling of our bodies pressed together.

"I hate you," he let out.

"I hate you too."

He gave me the finger and stormed off, and I slammed the door shut after him.

I sagged against the door, breathing more easily now that he was out of my room.

Too bad that I couldn't get him out of my mind as well.

CHAPTER ELEVEN

Present

T HE SOUNDS OF ARGUING COMING FROM DOMINIC'S OFFICE greeted me when I returned from school on Friday. The door was ajar, allowing me to overhear everything without having to resort to pressing myself as close as I could to the door.

"You can't be serious," Carter said. "There's no way I'd ever work for your company."

"We talked about this. You told me you were agreeing to—"

"I must've been out of my mind when I said that. Or on drugs."

"Carter, this is your future we're talking about, so be serious. We had a long conversation, and you agreed to join my firm eventually."

"I don't even know what I want! And now you're telling me I'm supposed to do something I've always been against?" He snorted. "You never gave up, did you? Even after two years, you're still pushing it."

Mom stopped by my side, her brows set low as we shared a long look of concern.

"You want to become an architect," Dominic said. "You mentioned a few colleges you wanted to apply to—"

"An architect. How fitting that I would choose the same profession as you."

"Are you saying I'm lying?"

"I'm saying you're full of shit."

There was the sound of a loud impact on a hard surface. Mom and I winced.

"Keep talking down to me and you're going to regret it, boy. I've been patient with you because of your condition, but my patience is reaching its limits."

I peered around the door and saw Carter's shoulders rising and falling quickly. It occurred to me just how much he must be feeling out of control in this moment. His confession on the basketball court had been playing constantly in my mind, reminding me how alone and confused he was.

"Even if I wanted to become an architect, I would've done it on my own terms, not yours."

"Maybe it's hard for you to believe, Carter, but it's the truth. And once you recover your memory, you'll see I'm not lying."

"It doesn't matter! Whether I recover my memory or not, I know what I *don't* want, and that's being close to you."

"Don't act like a brat. You're going to come work for my company, and that's final."

"No!" Something crashed, and Mom and I dashed inside. A flower-filled vase that had stood on one of Dominic's shelves lay broken near Carter's feet now.

Dominic rounded his desk to reach Carter, his face twisted with fury.

"Honey, don't," Mom said, rushing to Dominic's side. She placed her hand on his arm, rubbing it up and down to calm him, just like she'd done all the previous times when Dominic had lost it with Carter before they'd reconciled. "This is a lot for him to take in. You need to take it easy on him."

Carter's eyes narrowed to slits. "I don't need you to defend me, whore."

"Carter!" I shouted.

"I told you not to address Erika like that," Dominic barked out.

"Sure. Would you rather have me address her as 'mother'?"

"Get out," Dominic shouted, his face alarmingly red. "Get out now!"

If Carter's eyes had the ability to incinerate, Dominic would've been ash by now. "With pleasure." He passed by without even looking my way.

Swearing under my breath, I tore my gaze off Carter to look at Mom. She dropped into the armchair and released a deep sigh. She leaned her head against the headrest, closing her eyes, and I noted the dark shadows under them. The front door slammed, announcing Carter had just left. Mom flinched.

Dominic removed his glasses and rubbed his eyes. "I don't know what I'm going to do with him."

"We have to be patient," Mom said, massaging the back of her neck.

He gave her a half-smile. "Right. If he would at least try going to counseling. I tried to tell him it's for his own good, but he refuses to listen."

"He can't avoid it forever. In time, he'll see we don't have anything against him and we only want him happy. Then I'm sure he'll reconsider."

"Let's hope," Dominic muttered.

Hope. It seemed these days hope was all we had when it came to Carter.

If only that was enough.

The teachers had no mercy, already loading us down with homework. I didn't complain, because I preferred any distraction I could get. Along with dancing and working, schoolwork was the surest way for me to be productive instead of just moping around.

The situation at home remained tense. Carter spent most of

his time outside, going who-knows-where and doing who-knows-what, and whenever he came back, most often drunk, Dominic ripped him a new one. He demanded to know how Carter was spending his time, but he could never get anything out of Carter, and I couldn't do a single thing to help resolve the situation. I continued to write him notes, but other than them missing from where I'd left them by his door, I couldn't tell if he even read them because he never spoke to me about them. But I had a shred of hope since he wasn't straight up ignoring them.

I asked Mr. Dellucci, my boss and the owner of Bellezza, if I could work extra shifts so I'd spend less time at home, and it only took a few *no*s until I managed to convince him it wouldn't affect my grades and I wouldn't be exhausting myself. Mr. Dellucci acted like a grandpa to me, often claiming I was too young to overwork myself, but these days, even if it got too crowded and my tired feet would scream at me to get some rest, I preferred it to the emotional storm inside of me.

The work came with a major downside, though. Half of the Silver Raven students liked to come here, and since it was Friday, the place was crammed with my classmates. Their looks followed me the whole time.

When the news broke that I worked here, it was a hot topic for a while. No one would've said it to my face, but I heard it around school—they thought it was beneath any Silver Raven student to work and whoever did was a loser.

But they couldn't declare the girlfriend of one of their most popular students a loser, so they settled on giving me side-long glances and whispering among themselves when I wasn't looking. Now that Carter didn't have my back anymore, they were bolder in expressing their disapproval—they made jokes at my expense when I went to take their orders and laughed in my face. Furthermore, after my argument with Kim, she had started a rumor about me stalking Carter and threatening to off myself if he didn't get back with me. Some girls at school had already made sure to let me know I was sick, obsessed, and should go to therapy.

"Didn't you off yourself yet?" one girl asked me as I placed her drink on her table. "Because Carter isn't getting back together with you."

I imagined throwing the drink all over her. "I'll off *you* if you keep talking," I muttered to myself.

"What was that?" She gave me fake innocent eyes.

"I said, enjoy your drink." I turned to leave. "And pray I didn't spit in it." Her gasp brought a smile to my face, which widened when the door opened and Summer stepped in.

"Hey," she said, perching herself at the counter. "What's with the smile?"

"Our classmates are giving me a hard time because of that stupid rumor that I'm stalking Carter. So I just put one of them in her place."

She chuckled. "Way to go."

"Yeah, but that's not all. They're all looking at me like I'm a lowlife for working here, Sum. Their privileged asses have never earned a cent on their own, but they think they're so above me."

Summer gave them a glare. "Figures. They're the ones who should feel ashamed because they're nothing without their mommies and daddies."

"I know. The feel of holding my own money in my hands beats any humiliation they could come up with."

"I want that too. I can just imagine what it would be like if I became a professional makeup artist one day. That would be a dream come true."

A shadow crossed her face, and I knew what was on her mind. Her parents were against it. They didn't waste any chance to tell her that she was chasing an impossible dream; for them, Summer wasn't good for anything other than to serve Jackson's family one day, which had been their goal all along. As far as they were concerned, Summer wasn't going to college. They only saw it as a waste of time and money.

"Here's what I did last night," Summer said, showing me the screen of her phone. It displayed a TikTok video of her doing a new look. She'd started a TikTok account dedicated to makeup last year, and her account had quickly picked up followers. She'd already started to get requests, and she hoped that would be enough to open up a path for her into the industry.

I studied the explosion of purple around her hazel eyes, which gave her a sultry look.

"I wasn't sure purple was going to work, but it looks fantastic with that glitter in the inner corners."

I nodded. "Yes, it looks amazing. And look at those eyeliner wings. You've perfected it."

"All thanks to the countless hours of practicing on you." She winked at me.

"Don't forget me when you become famous."

She chuckled, her eyes turning dreamy, and I felt a little stab of envy. Despite her parents, she believed in her dream. She didn't seem to mind spending years of her life doing something that could turn out to be a failure. If she had a chance, I was sure she would grab it, and I wished I had her courage.

The door chimed, and I turned to see Carter come in, followed by Jackson, Prescott, and Prescott's bodyguard. My heart accelerated when they headed to a booth in my section. The girls turned to look at them, and a few of them started whispering, pointing at Prescott and pulling out their phones to take pictures of him. I was sure those pics would end up on tabloid websites in no time. His bodyguard stationed himself in a corner, his hawklike gaze scanning the room.

Taking a deep breath, I went over to their table. "Hey, guys."

They turned to look at me. Carter frowned, but then, as his gaze slid down my uniform, his face filled with confusion.

"You work here?"

"Yeah."

He rounded on Prescott. "Why didn't you tell me she works here?"

"Because you wouldn't have wanted to come, and this place has the best pasta in town."

Carter crossed his arms over his chest and pinned me with a glare. "What's your game?"

My brows rose high. "My game?"

"Why are you working here? You don't need money."

"Because, contrary to what you believe, I don't want to leech off anyone."

He gave me a long, assessing look, and it felt as though he was seeing me from a new angle, a look just like the one he'd had in the gym when he found out I loved dancing. Something like approval appeared in his gaze, and I felt my pulse ramping up at that, unsure if I was hallucinating. Abruptly, he dropped his eyes, reaching for the menu.

I cleared my throat. "Do you want me to tell you your favorite?"

He gritted his teeth, glaring up at me. "No." He barely looked through the menu before actually ordering his favorite—cheese ravioli with garlic bread and a Coke.

My heart gave a strong flutter. This was another thing that hadn't changed with his amnesia. I wanted to smile, but I kept a straight face.

I took all their orders and left, feeling Carter's gaze on me the whole time. Every part of me tingled, savoring his attention. Was it twisted of me to love his attention so much even if it was negative?

"I guess living with Carter is tough," Summer said once I delivered their drinks and got back to her.

"More like a nightmare."

"How do you feel about it?"

"Do you want the long version or the short one?"

"Give me all the deets."

I leaned my hip against the counter, sighing. I gave a quick glance around the room to see if anyone needed anything. "I don't know what I'm doing. Mom told me to show him how much I know about him and that I understand him, but it's so hard. Like there's a thick wall between us, and it's impossible to break it."

"If there's anyone who can do it, it's you."

"There's more. Carter's relationship with Dominic is getting worse by day, and it can't be helping his recovery."

Her lips turned down. "I saw on TikTok that Carter got super drunk at some party the other day. He stripped down to his underwear and jumped into the pool with one of his teammates—Dawson, I think—and two girls."

I grimaced. "I'm sure I don't want to hear the rest of it."

She looked away. "You're right. You don't."

My hands clenched. Jealousy roared deep within me, making me want to scream at the unfairness of it all. Maybe, if Carter had broken up with me because he'd stopped loving me on his own, it wouldn't have hurt as much. But because I felt this stupid hope that he still loved me beneath the layers of his amnesia, it only caused more pain. Doubts clawed at my mind, and I feared he was going to fall for someone else any day now. And then . . . then I didn't know how I would get over that.

Carter's eyes followed me closely when I returned to their table with a tray bearing their plates. It was unnerving. My hands shook as I placed the plates in front of them, and I internally patted myself on the back for not spilling or knocking anything over. My heart jostled in my chest when I returned Carter's gaze, and I felt as if I was drowning in the depths of his eyes.

I placed his plate last. "Here you go. Your favorite."

"My favorite?"

"Yep. You always ordered this when you came here to see me while I worked."

His brows arched up, and the way he kept looking at me had my chest tighten with longing. For a moment, it appeared as if he was processing this information, and I wondered if he realized how important it was.

He blinked, and his face closed off.

I moved to leave, but his hand darted out and grabbed my arm. My breath hitched as I looked down at him, catching him stare at his hand around my arm for an extended moment.

He snapped his gaze up to meet mine. "Stop writing me those notes."

I felt a flare of pain in my chest, but I smiled at him. "They're helpful, right? Maybe next time I can write down all the dishes that are your favorites these days."

His gaze flashed with anger, but I didn't stick around to witness it. I pulled my arm free of his hand and turned away, dropping my smile with a sigh.

I didn't make it far when I heard him say to Jackson and Prescott, "Nora and I are going to Dawson's party tonight. You coming?"

My stomach twisted sharply. They were going together to Dawson's party? As a couple, or what?

Resisting the urge to look over my shoulder at him, I made my way to Summer. I'd heard about that party, but I hadn't planned on going. It seemed my plans had changed.

"We're going to Dawson's party tonight," I said to Summer.

"We are?"

"Yep. Carter and Nora will be there, and I need to see what's going on between them."

"What would you do if they were together?"

What *could* I do? It wasn't as though I could order Carter not to date her. "I don't know, but I'll think about it when that time comes."

If that time came, I corrected myself silently.

Not that it was any consolation.

The Uber driver parked behind a long line of cars, and I felt as if I might start sweating any minute now. We were a little late arriving since I waited for Summer to come to do my makeup and then she spent an hour applying it, making sure my face looked stunning and flawless.

A song by Aurora was playing when we arrived, and I felt the urge to sway my hips; her music always did that to me. My eyes bounced from one figure to another, searching for Carter and Nora. I wanted to see them together, but I also dreaded it, so when I found them in the kitchen, separated from the rest of the people, it was as if someone had grabbed my guts and twisted them hard. Nora sat on the counter, and Carter stood too close beside her, wearing a smile as he listened to her talk. They looked as if there was no one else in the room but them.

I almost staggered as the image of them hooking up crystalized in my mind. Too suddenly for me to counter it, the fear that I'd lost him took hold of me. It was too potent, spreading too fast. *They can't get together. They just can't.*

"Do you think they've hooked up already?" I asked Summer.

"I don't think so. They're not touching or kissing."

"Even so, how can I break through his wall when she's around all the time?"

"There's still hope. If he liked her, they wouldn't be wasting time here just talking, don't you think?"

"I don't know what to think."

But I knew I needed to get them off my mind, or I'd drive myself mad.

Ripping my gaze away from them, I marched over to the kitchen island, which was loaded with all kinds of alcohol, Summer in tow. Her face darkened as she looked over my shoulder, and I looked in the same direction, spotting Jackson on the back porch, surrounded by a couple girls as he leaned against the railing. For a moment, under the dim porch lights with dark shadows edging him, he looked as if he were a king on his throne with a harem of his girls. They were all touching him in one way or another, and I thought back to a particular rumor circulating around our school of Jackson having orgies.

It was difficult to discount the rumor as the girl on his left kissed his neck, and the girl on his right shared a long, wet kiss with him. The girl in front of him played with the buckle of his belt, as if she wanted to take off his pants right there.

Summer was now making a point to look everywhere but in his direction. I guessed we both needed a distraction right now.

I grabbed two beers for us. We opened them and clinked them together. She tossed back the whole bottle.

"Sum—"

She raised her hand to stop me. "Don't. He's not important." It was a flat-out lie, but I kept my mouth shut. "My cousin will be happy to see you."

"Is he here too?"

"Yeah. I saw him post on his Instagram earlier. He's around somewhere."

I took several long swallows of my beer. Seeing Carter and Nora together must've made me desperate because I had half a mind to spend time with Jacob just to provoke Carter. But then I felt a stab of shame for considering using Jacob and guzzled the rest of my drink. It didn't take me long to reach for another beer. The alcohol created a warm buzz in my body, dulling the intensity of the pain residing deep in my chest. At some point during my third beer, Carter finally looked away from Nora and around the room, and when he spotted me, every part of me was set abuzz.

I smiled at him, saluting him with my drink.

His eyes went dark, and something stirred inside me. It was joy that I could affect him so easily. At least he wasn't indifferent to me, right?

I giggled and downed the beer in one swallow.

"Let's dance." I grabbed Summer by the hand and pulled her to the family room, where most of the people were dancing.

Another song by Aurora was currently playing (someone must be a fan of Aurora), and I started spinning and twisting, ignoring everything and everyone around me but the beat of the music that sent me higher and higher.

In only a few minutes, a thin sheen of sweat covered my skin. Heat coursed through me in waves as I raised my arms in the air and then ran them slowly down my body. The energy pulsed wildly around me. My hips circled with the rhythm of the song as I lowered myself down, then moved back up.

Carter appeared in my line of sight. His eyes were glued to me as he stopped by the doorway to watch me. Everywhere his gaze touched began to burn, amplified by the drinks in my system. The need to have him was overwhelming.

I wanted to dance for him. I *was* dancing for him.

I slid my hands from my neck down over my breasts and stomach, my hips moving from side to side sensually. Carter couldn't tear his gaze off me, and it was just like all those times I'd danced for him—his enraptured attention fed me and built desire deep within me.

I let my hands move down my sides, then my thighs, so, so slowly, licking my lips as his gaze followed the move. Even from here I could see his chest rising faster.

It could've been only seconds or minutes before the song was over. I finished my dance by blowing a kiss in his direction. Grinding his molars, he broke off our stare and turned toward Nora, who appeared by his side just now.

He disposed of the bottle he was holding, took her hand, and pulled her over near us to dance with her.

My heart contracted violently. I felt like I was going to vomit.

His hands landed on her hips, and he brought her close to him, so close they could be kissing if either of them moved any closer. Jealousy mixed with possessiveness rammed into me, robbing me of all breath.

This felt so wrong. Every inch of me screamed for me to go to break them apart. To put some sense into his head so he'd know he was mine and he shouldn't be with other girls. Not being able to do so set a heavy weight in my stomach, and I felt as if I was choking with the unfairness of it.

Summer placed her hand on my shoulder. "Are you okay?"

My fingers twisted the collar of my dress. "I need to be alone for a sec. I'm going out to get some air."

I went out as quickly as the crowds of people jammed throughout the house allowed me to. I passed a group of guys and girls huddled close together on the back veranda and stopped by the pool, taking in gulps of air.

The night was warm against my heated skin, and I started fanning myself with my hand. The torturous part of me created a fantasy of Carter pulling away from Nora and searching for me instead. The image was so vivid it took all the breath out of me.

"Zoe," someone called to me. I turned around to see Jacob approach me with quick steps. "Hey. Are you okay? You rushed out here like someone was chasing you."

"I'm okay. Sort of." I took a deep breath. "It's just too stuffy inside."

He cast me a boyish grin. "Yeah, that's why we've brought the party out here." He motioned at his group of friends. A few of them were girls, and they stared curiously at me. One of them was Tara. Her stare was harder than the rest of the girls'.

"Looks like you're having a good time," I said.

"It's even better now that you're here."

I smiled, but it was out of reflex rather than emotion. That seemed enough for him, though, because he followed me to the edge of the pool and sat down there with me.

I took off my sandals and dipped my legs in the cool water. It was just what I needed to quench the heat ravaging through me. Crickets sang their tune nearby. The clouds sheathed the moon and the stars. I wished the clouds could sheathe my pain as well.

"You look sad," Jacob told me.

"I must not be putting on a good enough mask, then."

"So, something *is* bothering you. Tell me. What's the problem?"

My feet slashed through the water, creating a distortion that captivated my gaze. "I don't think you really want to know."

"I want to know everything about you."

I met his gaze, and my heart bounced in my chest at how intense his eyes were. The moonlight and garden lights emphasized their depth—the depth that would've pulled me in had I been another girl, living another life. I looked away.

"It's Carter."

His fingers wrapped around my arm, making me look back at him. "Did he do something to you?"

"No. Uh, it's complicated. He—it seems as though he's going to hook up with another girl."

He released me, and although he said nothing, it felt like a barrier rose between us, making me already regret my words.

"It's probably just a fling. Knowing him, it's most likely something temporary."

Knowing him? Sure, Carter had gone through girls at a rapid pace back then, but hadn't our relationship shown Jacob that Carter wasn't just some player with no capacity to care or commit to someone?

I opened my mouth to defend Carter, but then I stopped myself. I didn't want to argue about Carter with Jacob.

"Still, it hurts seeing him with someone else."

"Something I completely understand," he muttered into his chin.

I rubbed my hand down my thigh, starting to feel a little uncomfortable. I didn't say anything.

Jacob turned so that he was facing me, bending one leg at the knee and tucking the other under him. "Say, do you think you'll ever be able to get over him? Start anew . . . with someone else?" His hand reached out and enveloped mine.

A movement to the side had me raise my eyes, and I saw Tara storming off into the house, her face shielded by her hair . . . passing right next to Carter.

Carter stood frozen like a statue on the veranda, his eyes two lasers as he stared between me and Jacob, and then at our connected hands. Nora came out behind him, giving him a confused glance before she took notice of what had gotten his attention. Her face fell.

For an extended moment, all Carter did was glare at me and

Jacob, and then, abruptly, he disappeared back into the house. Nora went after him.

I disentangled my hand from Jacob's. "I should head back inside."

The light in his eyes dulled. "Are you sure?"

"Yes."

"If it's because of something I said or did—"

"You didn't do anything. Don't worry about it."

I rose to my feet, but before I could move, his hand reached out to grab mine.

"If it's any consolation . . . I don't think you have to worry about him finding someone else. Because that right there?" He pointed at the spot where Carter had been moments ago. "He was totally jealous."

CHAPTER TWELVE

I DIDN'T GET MUCH SLEEP AFTER I GOT HOME FROM THE PARTY, SO I woke up earlier than usual and went to the home gym downstairs, planning to spend a few hours working out and dancing. It was my favorite way to start a Saturday. The home gym was the place where I could most be myself, leave all worries outside, and just feel.

Dancing had always been my refuge. Whenever life reminded me how hard it was, I turned to dancing, forgetting the loneliness I'd felt as a child without a father, the anger at the injustice of death and poverty, the burning desire to change my life circumstances. The burning desire to have my dad back.

I couldn't get my dad back. I couldn't erase the tragedy that had changed my whole life. I could only weave stories through motions, putting all the pieces of a dance together through choreography, and it was my outlet when I felt out of control.

I passed the state-of-the art exercise equipment that took over the right side of the gym and connected my phone to the sound system in the corner, putting on my playlist of songs by Aurora. After spending thirty minutes on the treadmill, then fifteen more lifting weights, I started dancing, letting the music guide me as

I did one of my choreographies, tracking all my movements in the mirrors taking up one entire wall. I enjoyed myself so much I completely lost track of time, my surroundings becoming just one fuzzy blur.

Sweat dripped into my eyes as the playlist ended and I finally stopped for a breather. My Lycra shorts and tank top were plastered to my skin. I became aware of my surroundings . . . and the figure in the mirror watching me from the doorway.

I sucked in a breath. "Carter."

His reply was silence. A taunting silence that stretched as he took in my soaked tank top and shorts that left my thick, toned thighs on full display.

His face transformed with tension as he stepped in. "Did you have fun last night? Getting cozy with Myers?"

My heart twinged. He'd always been adamant that he didn't want me, but what was this now? Why was he making me feel as if he didn't just hate me if that wasn't the case?

I wiped the sweat off my forehead with the back of my hand and faced him. "Just like you with Nora. What's going on between you two?"

His jaw settled into a hard line. He ignored my question. "You shouldn't be here. This is my gym."

"Things have changed, Carter. I'm also using it now."

"What for? Gearing up for pole dancing?"

I put my hand on my hip. "Is that supposed to be an insult or your fantasy?"

He bared his teeth. "If you think your body's something special, think again."

"Who are you trying to trick? I already told you I know you couldn't stop salivating over me back then. Not to mention when we were together. As a matter of fact, you often said, and I quote, 'You turn me on all the time. I can't focus on anything else when I'm around you.'"

His flaring nostrils were my only warning. He lunged at me, caging me against the pillar. His hands met the surface on either side of my head. His eyes were glittering jade pools of fury I couldn't look away from.

"I told you that Carter is gone. I don't give a shit about you."

"Then why did you mention Jacob? Plus, you looked pissed off when you saw me and Jacob last night. And don't tell me it's because you're 'furious I chose him out of all guys,' because that doesn't ring true."

"I couldn't care less what you think is true or not. As far as I'm concerned, you can go fuck the whole school, and I wouldn't even blink an eye."

Hurt pierced my chest like the sharpest dagger. He was always using hate to push me away. Always aiming for the deepest cut.

Suddenly, I wanted to throw him off. I wanted to shatter his control. To show him he wasn't so immune to me as he claimed.

I raised my hand and placed it on the side of his neck, right at his sensitive spot below his ear. His eyes widened.

"Tell me, Carter. If I do this, you won't be affected?" I stood on my tiptoes and kissed that spot.

His body turned taut like a tightly wound spring. I waited for him to shove away from me, but he stayed right where he was. I took that as the go-ahead to do it again.

My lips brushed against that spot, my tongue darting out to taste it. A strong shudder ran through him, and he tilted his head as if to allow me more space.

My heart soaring, I slid my mouth across the column of his neck, then up again to his ear. I'd already forgotten why I was doing this in the first place, losing myself in his scent, his closeness, the silkiness of his skin. It provoked my hunger for him, but I didn't move my hands to touch him for fear of breaking whatever this was between us, letting my mouth do all the talking.

My tongue flicked across the outer shell of his ear, causing more unmistakable shudders. And when I nibbled his earlobe, a low groan left his mouth, creating a throbbing ache between my thighs.

He took a step that had me completely sandwiched between him and the pillar and planted his hands on my hips, sending a ripple of pleasure through me. The evidence of his arousal pressed against me, and every nerve in my body went taut, making me dizzy with desire. I was brought back to a time when Carter and I were one, when our two hearts beat together as a whole. I needed to have more of him. Right now.

I placed my hands on his shoulders and sucked on a spot on his neck, just how he liked it. He hissed, his fingers digging into me. He slid his hand down to my ass and yanked me against him, bringing my center flush against his erection. His moan filled my ears.

"Do you see how good we feel together?" I rasped into his ear. "How we need one another? It's stronger than us."

I moved my lips back to his neck, but too late, I realized he'd gone still. Too still. He'd even stopped breathing.

I drew my face away to look at him and felt my stomach twisting. His eyes were icy hatred.

"Go ahead," he whispered roughly. "Keep proving me right. Keep proving what a slut you are."

My heart split open. My nails dug into my palms almost to the point of drawing blood. I felt like screaming with fury and pain, hating that he was always pushing me away in one way or another. Tears pricked my eyes, but I'd be damned if I let a single one out.

I stepped away from him and smiled sweetly. "No, Carter. I'm going to keep proving you wrong."

I pushed him aside, grabbed my phone, and left the gym without looking at him, doing my damnedest not to show him just how deeply his words cut me.

Mom had always told me I was a strong girl. Strong for living my life without a father, for never complaining about having so little, for growing up to be a good kid. She'd said that if there was anyone who would get back on their feet after a rough patch, it was me.

I'd never felt strong. Even less so now. Mom was so sure I'd be able to get Carter back, but with each passing day, we felt further and further away from each other.

The funny thing about longing was that it only grew stronger with distance, and mine was starting to suffocate me. It made everything hurt that much more. We'd strived to make as beautiful memories as we could, but the more beautiful they were, the more they wounded after they fractured. How much longer did I have to suffer through his insults? How much longer until enough was enough? Until I gave up on everything we'd had?

I was afraid of giving up.

Giving up would mean that our love, connection, and the memories we'd created together ended up meaning nothing. In a life full of disappointments, Carter had been a ray of sunlight warming my cold world and chasing away my loneliness. Time spent with him had felt special, momentous. He'd left his permanent mark on me. I couldn't imagine life without him.

To rub salt into the wound, I had to keep seeing him every day, and each time I saw him, loss drove the stake of pain deeper into me, and I couldn't escape it, even at school.

Cheer tryouts were supposed to be my refuge, but when I entered the gym and saw Nora stretching out on the sidelines, all my excitement fizzled out.

There was my answer. She was going to try out for the team.

As though sensing my attention on her, she looked over at me. Her face twisted uncomfortably for a second before she smiled at me and waved. I guessed she must've found out about my relationship with Carter by now. I didn't wave back.

I moved toward where Denise, Trisha, and Amalie stood talking, but I didn't make it five steps when Nora intercepted me.

"I'd like to talk to you for a sec," she said.

My stomach stirred uncomfortably. "Sure."

"I hope things won't be awkward between us since . . . you know."

I wasn't going to make it easy for her. "Know what?"

She frowned. "Since you and Carter broke up, and I'm interested in Carter."

Is he interested in you?

After the party, Kim had started a rumor that they were going out, but when I texted Prescott about it, he told me it wasn't true. For how long, though?

"You said it yourself, we broke up. He's free to do whatever he wants."

She cocked her head. "You really think that?"

I wanted to say no, but what difference would it make?

My stomach twisted sharply, and it was a challenge not to show the pain on my face. "Yes."

"That's cool, then. Phew." She imitated wiping sweat off her forehead. "I'm relieved to hear that. I wouldn't want to step into someone else's territory."

Yet, you were on to him from the outset. "You're not." *Lie.*

"Okay, then. Good to know. Nice talking to you."

I didn't say anything, grimacing the moment she turned her back to me. I went over our conversation in my mind, trying to spot any sign of bitchery on her part, but I came up short.

If only she was a bitch. But no, she had to be Miss Perfect.

Perfect for Carter.

I hated that.

I wanted to hate her dancing and stunts too, but it was just another thing that went in her favor. The first recruits were good, but Nora outdid them all. Her expressions and cheers had energy behind them. I performed a routine, and she copied it flawlessly. Her skill showed in every way, and I could feel my heart shriveling in my chest. Even the coach looked at her as though she was sure she would be good for our team, and I just knew Nora was in.

Was there anything this girl was bad at?

Her friend was sitting on the bleachers, waiting for her, and when Nora finished, I heard her say, "You're going to make it for sure. And then you can cheer for Carter at all his games!"

Nora glanced at me as she responded with a satisfied laugh, and my mood sank even lower.

Carter and I were getting further and further away from one another, while they were getting closer and closer.

I felt as though I was going to be sick.

CHAPTER THIRTEEN

THE REST OF THE TRYOUTS DID NOTHING TO IMPROVE MY MOOD, so I decided to stop by my favorite coffee shop on my way home from school. I was sure coffee would perk me up.

I went inside and ordered a double mocha. A few minutes later, I headed to my car with my mocha, ready to lose myself in its delicious taste, but the nearby throbbing bass of music stopped me. I turned to see a dance studio around the corner, its purple-black logo decorating the floor-to-ceiling windows. It was the one Mom had mentioned to me.

My feet took me toward the window before I was aware of moving.

The sun clashing against the glass made it difficult to discern what was going on inside, and I had to take off my shades to be able to see better. There was a dance group in the middle of choreography for the song currently playing.

My blood rushed through my veins. I followed them closely, my brain already picking up on the moves and storing them for later. It was the kind of song that made it almost impossible not to move your hips and arms, and I almost did just that. I couldn't

SHATTERED MEMORIES | 137

prevent my head from bobbing, though. Something deep inside me urged me to go inside, to join them. But I didn't move an inch.

As I watched the choreographer instruct the front row dancers on a spin-down sweep, an image crystalized in front of my eyes. It was of me in there with them, living through the music and letting it flow freely through me. Letting it lead me through life.

"My sweet daughter is going to be the best dancer in the world."

My fingers tightened around my cup of mocha, threatening to spill it. I tried to block the familiar pain. It didn't matter how dancing made me feel. It didn't matter that I would love to do nothing more than dance for the rest of my life. I was *not* giving up on my plan of securing a stable job.

Tearing my gaze away, I turned to head back to my car, only to almost bump into a tall, muscular body. I raised my eyes and internally cursed when I saw it was Brandon Mead, the captain of East Creek High's basketball team. The last time I'd seen him was when we won the first round of the playoffs last season. He looked even more vicious now, with a low buzz cut, tattoo of a snake coiling up his neck, and black leather clothes that had seen better days.

His lips crooked in a smile. "Hey, Pom-Pom. What a pleasant surprise."

What a liar. From the moment he'd first seen me, he'd made it his mission to antagonize me. I'd been his target because I was Carter's girlfriend, and Brandon really, really hated Carter. I didn't know why, but I guessed it was because Carter was everything every guy wanted to be—smart, handsome, rich, and popular. Brandon was none of those. Plus, he wasn't nearly as good at basketball as Carter.

"What are you doing here, Brandon?"

He laughed, pulling out a cigarette and a Zippo lighter. "Always so defensive with me. I'm just passing by. You?"

"None of your business." I tried to leave, but he caught my arm, stopping me. I glared at him. "What do you think you're doing?"

"Come on, Pom-Pom. Why can't you be nicer to me?"

I yanked my arm out of his grasp. "Do you really have to ask? You and I are not friends."

He put the cigarette in his mouth and lit it, flicking his Zippo shut with a loud click. "Didn't anyone ever tell you you're not sexy when you're bitchy?"

"Goodbye, Brandon." I made my way around him.

"Tell me, is it true that Carter ended up with amnesia after saving some girl from a fire?"

I stopped, digging my fingers into my palm and imagining it was his neck I was digging them into. "None of your business," I said again.

He flipped his Zippo open and closed a few times. The clicks were getting irritating. He expelled a long stream of smoke. "That's so noble of him. Risking his ass for some girl. Are you jealous?"

I gave him an incredulous look. "Are you serious?"

His raspy laugh grated on my nerves. "Come on. I know I'd be jealous. I even heard he broke up with you."

"Fuck off, Brandon."

His lips remained fixed in a smile. "Ouch, I touched a sensitive subject. So, it's true. He broke up with you. Not that it's any shame, because the guy's a real dick. You can do so much better."

"The pot calling the kettle black."

He laughed. "That's where you're wrong, Pom-Pom. He's got nothing on me. Want me to show you?" He reached out and skidded his fingers down my arm.

I'd had enough of him. I shoved his hand away and continued walking.

"Tell Carter that, amnesia or no amnesia, we're not done," he shouted after me, no trace of amusement in his voice now—only malice. "He'll get what's coming for him."

I didn't slow my steps, refusing to even acknowledge his threat despite the shiver that raced down my spine.

"We'll see each other again. Stay out of trouble!" His laughter followed me all the way around the corner, and I released a long breath once I was out of his sight.

I didn't know what his deal was now, but I wasn't going to give it another thought. I had a lot on my mind already without him and his ridiculous obsession with Carter.

I entered the house and went up to my room to change my clothes, then made my way to the kitchen. I expected to see Mom and Dominic there, but there was only Carter, looking through the fridge.

He didn't even glance at me as I set to making a smoothie. Each time we passed each other, I held my breath, and my core pulsed in response to his nearness. The images of us in the gym unfolded in front of my eyes, despite the disastrous ending to it.

I coughed, forcing the images away. My face heated as I sneaked a peek at him.

He was already looking at me, and a knot formed in my stomach at the anger I found on his face.

"You must be pretty satisfied with yourself," he said.

I set the milk on the counter. "Why?"

"Because you manipulated me into giving in to you in the gym."

My jaw dropped. *"Manipulated you?"*

"That's your specialty. It's how you got me to start dating you in the first place."

My hands curled. "Oh really? Did Prescott and Jackson even tell you how you and I got together?"

He straightened up, his expression briefly giving way to uncertainty. "No."

"But you know everything about it, right? You know everything about our relationship and what we were like together."

"What are you getting at?"

He was always jumping to conclusions and refusing to see reality. I took my phone out of my pocket and opened the video gallery. "Here. See just how much I needed to manipulate you to be with me." I slid the phone over the counter.

He held my gaze for a long second before he reached for my phone, sitting at the counter, and played the last video, which I'd taken about four months before. Carter and I had been hiking in the woods on the outskirts of Pine Hills. He used to tease me with bugs, knowing they disgusted me. He'd always bring them to my face and laugh when I scrambled away, and I'd captured one of those moments.

"*Baby, you know I hate bugs,*" my voice rang out, followed by a giggle. "*Stop! Don't bring it any closer! Yuck!*"

Carter laughed in the video. "*Say hello to Bugsy.*"

I'd shrieked. "*Get that away from me.*" I'd darted backward, but he'd followed me closely.

"*Come on, it won't eat you . . . much.*" He'd made a chomping motion with his mouth, chasing me around.

I felt a crushing weight in my chest, and I had to move, unable to stay in one place. Carter stared transfixed at the screen, but his face told me nothing.

"*Stop! Don't come any closer!*"

More laughter had poured out of him. "*Come kiss Bugsy.*"

I'd tried to run away from him, but he'd been way faster than me, managing to bring the bug within inches of me. But then he'd dropped the bug and grabbed my arm, spinning me around and into his embrace.

"*I take that back. I want you to kiss only me.*" He'd grabbed the back of my head and pulled me in for a kiss, the camera capturing it all.

I'd chuckled between our kisses. "*Carter Reese, are you jealous of a bug?*"

"*Shut up.*" Grinning, he'd pinned my lips to his.

The video ended with us on the ground, his lips making a trail down my neck and his hand reaching for the hem of my shirt to raise it. Then there was just silence in the kitchen.

"That place in the video is your favorite place to hike. But you know that, because it was your mom's favorite place to hike."

His eyes clashed with mine. "How do you know that?"

"You told me. You told me a lot of things about you and . . . and your mom."

His gaze trapped me for several seconds, making it difficult for me to breathe. Then his eyes dropped to my phone.

"We were happy," he said quietly, almost as if confessing it to himself.

"Yes," was all I could say.

"Did we argue a lot?"

I smiled bitterly. "If you're digging for some dirt in our relationship, I'm afraid I'll have to disappoint you. We rarely fought. And those times we did, it always ended with sex."

He shifted in his chair, and his eyes got a shade darker. "Was everything with you about sex? For all I know, I could've just used you for fucking."

Part of me wanted to tell him off because he was always treating me like shit, but I didn't want to get in yet another fight with him.

"Sure, tell yourself that. Or go through more videos in my gallery. See for yourself if sex was all there was to our relationship."

He took me up on that, opening another video. It was of me behind the wheel of Carter's Maserati while Carter filmed me from the passenger seat. I was rushing down a highway, the driver's window open all the way. The wind sent my hair flying all around, which in turn caused me to laugh non-stop. I looked wild and carefree. I loved speed and driving on highways, and when I drove fast, it made me feel invincible. It dulled all my insecurities and fears. Carter had let me drive his car on the highway all the time, saying I never looked sexier than when I was behind the wheel of his car.

"This feeling is the best," I'd said.

He'd chuckled. *"You're addicted to it, admit it."*

"Of course I am. It's like anything is possible when you're moving at high speed. Like you could fly."

"I know. You don't feel chained."

"Exactly. The rest of the world doesn't matter. Just you, your car, and this never-ending road."

I closed my eyes now, almost smiling at the memory.

"*That's how I feel with you,*" Carter had said.

I remember looking at him practically with hearts in my eyes. "*Really?*"

"*Yes. When I'm with you, there's no pain, or loneliness, or the feeling that I'm not good enough. You make all that go away.*"

Carter's brows went low at this, and I held my breath as I observed him. I expected him to stop the video, but his stare was fixed upon it.

"*You're never alone, Carter. You'll always have me,*" I said in the video.

"*I know. And I have proof of it.*" He'd motioned to my tattoo and grabbed my wrist, leaving a quick kiss on his special spot that had left me breathless.

Carter's fingers flexed around the phone as the video ended.

My chest tightened. I went over to the window and watched the birds create spellbinding circles across the sky. Almost as spellbinding as the feeling of love in my chest that rapidly gained intensity. Carter played another video, then another, until the longing within me was too much to take.

It had been a mistake to send him down memory lane. It meant so much to me. It could mean as little as nothing to him.

I marched over to him and grabbed the phone from his hand, finally silencing it. "That's enough."

His hand stayed where it was on the table, his fingers curled around the empty space my phone had occupied. His face remained blank, and his eyes were set on a spot in the distance, glazed over. My heart pumped harder.

I sat at the counter. "What are you thinking?"

He snapped his gaze up to mine. "What do you think I'm thinking? Do you think this'll trigger something in me? Did you hope that once I saw us all happy and in love, I'd be that guy again?"

I looked away, biting my lip. Damn him.

"Well, here's a newsflash for you—I only feel more like an intruder."

I frowned. "An intruder?"

"I see that guy, and it's like it's someone else's life. I didn't live that life. Someone else did. And you keep clinging to that guy, but at this rate, he's not coming back."

"That's not true. There's a big chance you'll recover your memory and—"

"And what if I don't?" he shouted, and I saw it for the first time—fear.

He's afraid he won't ever regain his memories.

"Even if that turns out to be the case, you'll rediscover yourself. You'll find sense."

"How?" The word was uttered gutturally, hopelessly, and it hurt me that I could do nothing to bridge the gap between us. That I couldn't touch him, hold him, *love* him.

"Trust in yourself."

His gaze connected with mine and didn't let go, and it was wreaking havoc on my heart. With each second that rolled by, I felt weaker for him, more desperate because of the rift between us.

"Your notes, this. Why are you always helping me?"

Because I love you. "You know why."

"Even after everything I've said to you."

I remained quiet.

He continued staring at me, and the tempo of my heart increased. I wished he could say anything to change our relationship. To give me a chance.

Before either of us could break the silence, Dominic entered the kitchen. "Good, you two are here. Can you come? We'd like to talk with you."

Carter and I looked at each other. What was going on?

We followed Dominic into the living room. Mom was seated on the sofa, and Dominic took a seat next to her.

Carter leaned with one shoulder against the wall and crossed his arms over his chest.

"Please, have a seat," Dominic told me. "You too, Carter."

"I'll stand."

Dominic sighed, but he didn't say anything. I sat down in the armchair.

"Is everything okay?" I asked Mom.

She smiled at me. "Yes."

"What's this about?" Carter asked.

Mom's smile wobbled on her lips, and Dominic took her hand in his. He gave her a soothing look before he turned to address us. "I proposed to Erika last night, and she said yes."

I gasped. My eyes snapped to her hand, and there it was—a diamond ring that glimmered brilliantly in the daylight.

"That's wonderful!" I burst out laughing, my heart swelling with happiness.

Mom laughed with me, reaching out to cover their joined fingers with her bejeweled hand. They looked so perfect together, so happy, and I felt immense relief. After so many years, after losing my dad and working herself to the bone to provide us with food and a roof over our heads, Mom was finally getting her happily ever after.

"You've got to be joking," Carter let out.

I looked at him, and the smile I'd had from the moment Dominic dropped the news disappeared.

His face was screwed up with fury. I didn't think he was even breathing. There was a look of betrayal in his eyes, like his whole world had just spun off its axis.

"You two disgust me."

Dominic stood up. "Carter—"

"How does it feel to build happiness on someone else's unhappiness?"

Mom face crumpled.

"This was a long time coming, son. Erika and I love each other and want what's best for this family. I hope you'll learn to accept that one day."

"What's best for this family? You mean, what's best for you?"

"Son—"

"Screw you." Carter darted out of the room, ignoring Dominic's calls to stop.

Mom leapt up and rushed after him. "Carter, please wait." She caught his shoulder.

He yanked his shoulder out of her reach. "Don't put your hands on me."

"I really wish you'd understand. I love your dad more than I ever thought was possible to love a man. And from the moment I set foot here, I've loved you as a son. I want you to be happy. I can't be happy if you're not happy."

Carter's face turned to granite. "Don't you fucking dare mention me and 'son' in the same sentence. I'm not your fucking son."

I got up, rushing to them.

Dominic moved over to step between them. "Don't talk to her like that."

Carter glared at him. "Try to stop me."

"Carter," Dominic growled in warning.

Mom gave Carter a pleading look, tears collecting in her eyes. "Please, try to understand. I know now that Dominic and I made a mistake. We started our relationship too soon after your mom's death, and if I could go back in time, I'd change that. But we can't change our past. All we can do is do better."

"Spare me your philosophical bullshit. I will never accept you, you hear me? Never."

Mom brushed away the tear that slipped down her face, her hand trembling. "You and I patched up our relationship before your accident, and you accepted me. We can do it again. I can show you that there's no reason to mistrust me and that all I want is what's best for you."

"What's best for me is to see you gone, whore."

"That's enough out of you!" Dominic's hand landed against Carter's cheek in a hard slap.

Mom and I both stared in shock at them. Pain sliced through my heart as Carter's eyes filled with anguish.

"Keep proving to me what a bastard you are," Carter said.

Dominic's face had gone red with fury. "I've been patient with you, but I told you not to talk to her like that."

Carter balled his hand. "I'll talk to her however the fuck I want!"

"I won't allow you! So, you better learn to treat her right, or else."

"Or else what? I don't give a shit what you want. I'll never accept her as your wife, and if I have to, I'll make sure to show her every single day she doesn't have the right to be here—"

"She has every right!"

"She has no right! She's a fucking intruder—"

"She's pregnant!" Dominic boomed.

I caught my breath. What?

Stunned silence fell between us as I gaped at Mom. Carter stumbled a step back, his face a picture of disbelief.

"You're pregnant?" I asked Mom.

She nodded, her hands going to her stomach to cradle it. Joy swelled in my chest. I was going to have a sibling!

Carter's feet shifted back another step. "That can't be true."

"It's true. And as I said, you'd better learn to treat her right, because she's not going anywhere."

More anguish shaded Carter's eyes, and he looked between each of us. His gaze stopped on me. There were so many emotions on his face, and each created a tear in my heart.

His jaw clenching, he ripped his gaze away from me and left.

Something split open in my chest. How did such a beautiful moment turn out to be so ugly? I so wished he would see this differently, that he would realize how unreasonable he was being and we could be so happy if only he demolished the wall between us.

Why did he have to lose his memories? Just . . . why?

"Are you okay?" Dominic asked Mom.

She nodded, tears finding their way down her cheeks.

"Don't cry, darling. This was supposed to be a happy moment." He pulled her into his embrace.

"It's okay. It will pass."

"Dominic's right." I put a hand on her shoulder. "We should celebrate, not cry."

"Oh, honey." Mom released Dominic so she could hug me.

I wound my arms around her tightly. "I can't believe you're pregnant. I'm going to have a brother or a sister." I laughed. "We definitely should celebrate."

"We will."

"Do you know the sex of the baby?"

Dominic chuckled. "We don't know yet. It's still too early to determine."

I placed my hand on Mom's belly, feeling the small swelling that indicated her baby bump. How had I missed this? She'd been wearing billowy clothes, and now I knew why. "It doesn't matter, as long as the baby's healthy. But why didn't you tell me anything, Mom?"

"I wanted to, but then Carter's accident happened, and we agreed we would wait to reveal it until things got better with him."

"But I got a little impatient with the proposal, so here we are," Dominic added.

The engine of Carter's Maserati roared in the driveway, and my stomach jumped. What the hell was he doing?

I looked between Mom and Dominic in alarm. "Carter shouldn't be driving! What if he causes an accident?" I ripped open the front door in time to see his car tear out of the estate, his taillights quickly becoming two distant spots. Where was he going?

Dominic cursed into his chin. He took off his glasses and pressed his fingers to the spot between his brows. "This is a ca-tastrophe." He looked at Mom. "Do you see that all our patience is useless? Things are only getting worse."

"I know, but he's your son. We can't give up on him."

Something passed between them, and I didn't like what I saw.

"What are you talking about?" I asked.

Dominic replaced his glasses. "I'm thinking of some options for Carter in case this continues."

"What options?"

"Like telling him to move out."

My stomach dropped. "No."

Mom shook her head. "We won't tell Carter to move out, sweetie."

Dominic's expression didn't inspire confidence, and my stomach turned over. I didn't even want to imagine how Carter would feel if he ever heard Dominic had considered asking him to move out. It would be devastating for him.

I didn't like this. I didn't like this at all, and worst of all was I was completely helpless to do anything about it. There had been too much bad blood between us already. Now this? How could we get past this?

"This is his home, Dominic. He shouldn't be forced to leave it because of us."

"And I agree," Mom was quick to say, putting a hand on my shoulder. She looked at Dominic. "We talked about this, and I already said I don't want that, darling."

Dominic released a long sigh. "I know, honey. I don't want to do anything that will make you unhappy, but we also have to think about our child. You're pregnant. You can't be exposed to stress during this time, and I won't allow Carter to put your health or our child's health at risk."

He was right, but suddenly, the picture became clear to me. It was the same picture I'd tried to deny since the beginning, and that was that Carter always came second in Dominic's life. Now that they were having a child? Carter would be even less of a priority for him.

A new kind of fear took root deep inside me.

If one day Dominic was forced to choose between Mom and their child or Carter . . .

Carter would lose, and then . . . then I had no idea how we would ever glue our family back.

CHAPTER FOURTEEN

Over a year and a half earlier

AFTER THAT EPISODE IN MY ROOM WITH MY DIARY, A CHANGE took place between me and Carter. It wasn't as though our relationship had improved, no. But I was definitely more aware of him and interested in his whereabouts. Or in what he was doing with the line of girls waiting for him to throw them even a crumb of his attention. Or in what he really thought about me.

He acted differently too. He was constantly looking for me at school, and I caught him turning to look at me in class too many times to count. That, and he was always asking me about my love life. Not that I had any life love, because after that night with Carter on my bed, boys just didn't have the same appeal anymore. Adam Woodson had taken me out on another date and tried to kiss me, but I'd stopped him before he could and told him I wasn't interested in him. A few more boys asked me out, but I turned down each of them. I totally blamed Carter for that. More precisely—the memory of his body against mine.

As for Carter, he'd grown even more handsome over the course of last few months, and the girls just couldn't stop talking about him. Some of them (those who weren't avoiding me like I was a leper) kept asking me for his phone number or if he was seeing anyone. And each time, I repeated the same lines: "Trust me, you don't want to be with him. I mean, the guy tested positive for STDs twice already!" It worked like a charm every time. Though, his reputation at school remained intact, much to my chagrin.

Carter was playing into his role of a popular, rich guy at school. There, he was always in charge, always in control. His life was an adventurous, carefree roller coaster, spent driving fast cars—even though he was too young to even have a license—and partying with countless girls whose names didn't even matter to him. His social media only enforced that image. Whatever Carter did set off a trend, and no one could bring him down.

At home, it was a different story. He'd been hiding his true self for so long, but now that I'd started to pay real attention to him, I was beginning to see a chink in his armor.

He fueled himself with hate, using it as armor against me and my mom, but inside, he was crippled with pain. And he was lonely. He needed someone to care, and that wasn't his dad, as tragic as it was.

I didn't know how to explain Dominic's lack of interest in his own son. Furthermore, I didn't like how he always used physical violence to deal with Carter's temper, just like the day when we arrived at their house. Even almost a year later, Carter couldn't escape the grip of his grief, and Dominic didn't make it any easier for him.

Carter often had screaming nightmares in which he was calling for his mom. The first time I heard him scream, I rushed into his room all panicked and tried to wake him up, assuring him he was okay. Instead of thanking me, he kicked me out of his room, using a palette of colorful insults.

After he got into one fight too many on school premises, Dominic sent him to a counselor, but Carter hadn't been making much progress there. I tried not to care but seeing a vulnerable side to him only made me more susceptible to the feeling growing in my chest day by day.

So, when I headed outside to the back porch and caught him crying on the porch stairs, it hit me with the force of a hurricane. I wanted to leave him to it, but my feet stubbornly took me to him.

I peered at his face. Something in my chest ached at the sight of his red eyes and tears streaking his cheeks.

"Are you okay?" I asked him, and he jerked in surprise.

"The fuck are you doing sneaking up on me?" He turned his head away from me, but I managed to catch a glimpse of his reddening face before he hid it. He wiped at it with his hands in two brisk moves.

"You're crying."

"Go away!"

There was a framed photo in his lap. It was of him and his mom, taken, it seemed, a few years before. Carter had had longer hair then, and there was a joyful look in his eyes that was missing now.

I dropped down on the step next to him. I didn't bother putting any distance between us, so I was all too aware of how near he was to me. This was the first time we'd been this close since that night in my room. The memory heated my skin.

He scowled at me. "What do you think you're doing?"

"Do you miss her?"

"Are you serious?"

I met his glare head-on. "Very serious."

"What are you now? My therapist?"

"I'm just trying to help."

He snorted. "I don't need *your* help."

"But you need help. I mean, look at you. Hiding out here crying."

His face darkened with rage. "I think you'll want to consider carefully your next words, trash. Otherwise, I'll make you regret it."

"Do you think that throwing insults at me will make you a tougher guy? Or admitting that you have issues like the rest of us will make you any softer? It's okay to cry, Carter. It's human to cry."

"So, what? You expect me to open up and shit? You're nothing to me."

I ground my teeth together. "Sure. Clam up. Because it works for you oh so well." I rolled my eyes.

I pretended my reaching out to him wasn't a big deal, but my heart was hammering against my chest, and there was a heavy weight in my stomach at seeing him in pain. I wished I could help him; that was a first.

"It's not like you can help me," he said into his chin.

"Sometimes, even listening helps, Carter."

His fingers gripped the photo in his lap. I expected him to leave any moment now. But he didn't.

The silence stretched, and I wondered if I should just stand up and leave him alone.

"It's her birthday today," he suddenly said. "She would've been thirty-seven."

A deep ache formed in my chest, followed by something else I didn't want to acknowledge. I observed the birds making spirals in the sky. I felt for his mom. I really did. She died so young, just like my dad.

He wouldn't meet my eyes, and I said, "I'm sorry. She didn't deserve that."

"Yeah." He ran his hand down his face, taking in a long breath. "My dad was all she ever knew, and he didn't even care. He acts like her death was just a failed business transaction—unfortunate, but it's business as usual. He hasn't shed a single tear. While she . . . she shed countless tears over the years. All for him."

"They weren't happy together."

"They weren't. She was madly in love with him, but it didn't matter. And it's fucking ironic how she did everything she could to make *him* happy. A doting wife. Never complaining. Accommodating to *his* needs." His lips formed a sneer. "She even used to wait for him when he wouldn't come home because he was supposedly swamped with work. Something else always took priority." He fisted his hand. His knuckles whitened.

"I guess she was lonely."

"She was. She was lonely and miserable, and she started spending days closed in her room. He didn't even care to pull her out of it. And no matter what I did to try to help her snap out of it, it didn't work. She didn't even see me. She was all about *him*."

His eyes weren't red anymore, but they carried pain originating from deep inside him, and I felt warmth growing inside me because he was opening up to me. Because he was letting me see his pain.

My hand twitched with the urge to cover his. But I kept it on my thigh.

"Her dying did my dad a favor."

My mouth fell open. "Don't say that."

"But it's true. The further proof of it was when he brought you and your mom to our house just weeks after her death. What kid would get over that easily?"

I averted my gaze. I didn't know what to say, because he was right. I knew if I were in his place, I wouldn't be okay with it either. Perhaps that was why I understood his hostility toward us. I couldn't really blame him for seeing us as intruders.

"I wish Dominic appreciated her," I said. "I wish they were happy."

He threw me an accusing gaze. "But then you and your mother wouldn't be here. You wouldn't be rolling in the money."

I glowered at him. "We aren't 'rolling in the money,' Carter. I get why you hate us, but we're not bad people. And I don't care whether Dominic's rich or not."

"Oh, yeah, you said that when you got here too. You said you expected you'd be gone in no time, but look at you. Still here. Still using all the privileges."

"If you think my mom is so obsessed with your dad's money, why do you think she doesn't want to marry him, huh?"

It was no secret that Dominic had wanted to marry Mom from the start. However, she refused to get married to him out of respect toward Carter. She thought it would be too much for Carter if, on top of everything, she and Dominic got married.

"She's just playing hard to get so she'd keep Dad wrapped around her finger."

This asshole. He could find any excuse to hate her even if the facts proved something different.

I shook my head. "Whatever, Carter. I tried to have a normal conversation with you, but I see that's impossible." I jumped to my feet.

He grabbed my hand, preventing me from leaving. "Hold up."

My heart lurched to my throat, my skin tingling where he held me. I looked down my arm at him. "What?"

His gaze skated over my face, bringing heat all over my skin. It became hard to breathe.

"I keep thinking about it."

"About what?"

"About what happened in your room."

I felt myself growing hot. There was no more pain in his eyes, only desire—a desire that matched mine. It was hard to ignore how kissable his lips looked, or how smooth and flawless his skin was. Or how strong his hand felt around mine. How I imagined it all over me.

"Nothing happened in my room."

He stood up. Since he was standing one stair beneath me, his eyes were now almost level with mine. His warm breath caressed my lips. I drew in a quick breath through my mouth.

"Really? So, you want to tell me you weren't thinking about me on top of you? You weren't imagining what would've happened if I hadn't left?" He moved his lips to my ear and whispered, "I bet that if I read your diary now, your fantasies about me would be filling every single page."

Damn him, how did he guess that?

I closed my eyes, unable to stop the shudder coursing through my body. Him whispering in my ear turned me on, big time. Moreover, he kept his lips at my ear, as if taunting me with the possibility of a touch.

My nails dug into my palms. I was tempted. So tempted to

move just a little, enough to have his lips connect with my skin. I was tempted to dig my fingers into his shoulders and see if they were as strong as they looked. But he was my enemy. It didn't matter that he'd been so honest with me for the first time ever. He was a snake. I didn't trust him not to bite me when I least expected it.

Reining in all my self-control, I took a step away from him and gave him a smug smile. "Not really, but thanks for revealing to me *your* fantasies. A little pathetic, if you ask me, but you do you." I winked at him, and before he could flip his lid, I went into the house.

Now I could add another fantasy to my previous ones, and it was the one I'd never admit out loud—him having his way with me on those porch stairs.

CHAPTER FIFTEEN

I TOSSED AND TURNED IN MY BED, UNABLE TO SLEEP. IT WAS PAST midnight, but Carter still hadn't come home. Dominic had called him a dozen times, but he never answered his calls. I'd texted Prescott and Jackson to check if he was with them, but they hadn't seen him or heard from him at all. What if he'd really ended up hurt somewhere?

The night of Carter's accident returned to haunt me, and I grabbed my phone for the umpteenth time with the intention of calling him to confirm he was okay. Just before I pressed the *call* button, one of the deck chairs by the pool scraped against the pavement.

I kicked my sheets away and rushed out onto the balcony, my heartbeat accelerating. Carter dropped into the deck chair.

I didn't waste a second and sprinted downstairs.

Relief that he was okay mixed with anger, and I darted out of the house ready to tear him a new one. I only got angrier when I saw he was totally drunk, splayed across that deck chair carelessly.

"What were you thinking? You had me so worried!" I lowered myself into the deck chair next to his. "Where have you been?"

"Does it matter?" he slurred.

"I thought something had happened to you."

He had his arm covering his eyes. He only smiled. "Wouldn't that be convenient? If I was gone?"

My insides froze. "Don't say that."

"I think it would be very convenient. Just like my mom. Then he'd have a clear path."

Oh God. My hand twitched with the need to touch him, and I almost did, raising my hand toward him, but I forced it back down.

"Stop talking bullshit. That's not true."

He finally removed his arm from his eyes and grinned at me, only his smile didn't touch his eyes. His eyes were dark, desolate, and my heart wanted to bleed out. "He doesn't give a shit about me, don't you see? He's got a new life now. A new family."

"You're his family, Carter."

"Then why isn't he here now? Isn't he supposed to be worried about me?"

"Is that what this is about? You drove away to get his attention?"

He sneered. "Don't be stupid. I drove away because I needed to get the fuck away from here." He closed his eyes and tilted his head back, a pained expression settling onto his features. "This place doesn't feel like home anymore," he whispered so quietly I barely heard it.

This time I couldn't stop myself from touching him. I leaned over and placed my hand over his.

His eyes snapped to look at me, and I immediately said, "I'm just trying to comfort you, Carter. Nothing else."

"What makes you think I need your comfort?" But he didn't move his hand away, closing his eyes again.

Something swelled in my chest that he was allowing me to hold him. It took everything in me not to do more.

"I wish you'd see you have a family here. This is your home, no matter the circumstances."

He shook his head, his eyes remaining closed. "Then why does it hurt so much?"

"You've suffered a serious injury, which also affects your mental state. Everything's a mess in your head. Maybe once you recover, things will be better. No, they *will* be better."

"I doubt it. Because he'll never stop prioritizing *her* over his own son."

I bit my lip, hurting for him. I wished I could tell him Dominic cared about him the most, but how could I, when I wasn't sure about it myself?

"He will always be your dad, Carter. Nothing will change that. Don't you see how worried he is for you? Don't you see that he wants you two to have a good relationship?"

"We can't have a good relationship," he let out, pain suffusing each word.

"Why not?"

"Because that would be pissing on all the pain my mom went through because of him."

I felt a twinge in my chest. He was all rough edges of pain and anger, and I worried that would only poison his mind more until there was nothing good left.

I brushed my thumb over his knuckle, and he opened his eyes to watch the move. My pulse picked up. "You think your mom would want you to hate your dad for the rest of your life?"

His eyes followed my thumb closely. I wanted to lean even closer to him, basking in the feel of his smooth skin under mine. "I don't know how not to hate him. Especially now with a baby on the way."

"The baby doesn't have to change anything."

"The baby will change everything. Things are already changing. He's marrying your mom. We're going to be a family for real."

"Is that so bad?"

His eyes met mine. They were so dark, they seemed black in this light. "I never saw you as my sister. I never will."

That statement wasn't charged with hate. It was charged with something else, something that had been coursing through my veins ever since the first time I realized I wanted him. Right now, he felt different, unlike the hateful Carter he'd been since his accident, but he was also drunk.

He grabbed my hand and turned it over to reveal my tattoo. His gaze shifted to his own. "What did you do to make me get this tattoo?"

His fingers created a burning imprint on my skin. His thumb rested on the inside of my wrist and my pulse, which now pounded fast, revealing how much he affected me.

"Actually, it was your idea." My heart gave a flip in my chest when his eyes reconnected with mine. "You said it would be a perfect anniversary gift. It was our declaration of forever."

His eyes glimmered. I couldn't breathe as his fingers tightened around my wrist, and his thumb moved up and down across my vein. His tongue came out to wet his lower lip, and almost imperceptibly, he drew me closer to him. I wished I knew what he was thinking. If, deep down, despite all the hate and misconceptions, he could still feel our connection.

"It sounds like I was a fool, then."

"No, Carter. You were the guy I fell for—always showing me life was more than just one dark shade."

His eyes widened. "How do you always do that?"

"Do what?"

"Make me lap up everything you say."

Butterflies exploded in my belly. He pulled me even closer, and my scent must've wafted over to him, because he tilted his head toward my neck and took a long inhale. He emitted a sound from the back of his throat, sending heat through every part of me.

"What's this scent?"

"Cherry and rose. Your favorite perfume."

He raised his gaze up to look at me. "My favorite perfume?"

"Yeah. You always wanted me to wear it."

His pupils dilated. He closed his eyes, and, his brows knitting, he took another inhale of it, as if he couldn't resist it, his nose skimming across my skin. I bit back a moan, starting to pant.

"Carter," Dominic called, and I spun my head around to see him step out of the house.

Carter released me immediately, turning away from me. Damn it.

"We've been worried sick about you. Where have you been?"

"Like you care."

"Of course I care. You shouldn't have been driving. You could've gotten yourself killed."

Carter pushed himself off the deck chair. He wobbled as he stood up to his full height. "I'm sure that would've been devastating for you."

"Stop with that nonsense."

"More like the truth. You don't give a damn about me. So, go back to your future wife and kid."

He moved to leave, but Dominic stopped him, grabbing his arm. "Carter, this behavior has to stop. I can't change the past. I can't fix my mistakes, but I can sure try to do better, especially now that we're having a baby. This family is not whole without you. I hope you can see that and give me a chance to prove I care about you."

Carter shoved Dominic's hand off him. "What I see is that you're doing just fine without me. So, stop pretending and leave me the fuck alone." He pushed Dominic aside with his shoulder as he passed him by.

Dominic's shoulders sagged as he watched Carter leave. He looked like he'd aged overnight, and there wasn't even a hint of the powerful man he was.

"I'm sorry," I mouthed to him.

He offered me a half-smile. "It's been a long day, huh?"

More like a long month.

"You should go to bed. It's late."

"Yeah."

I followed him inside the house, but I knew there was no way I'd fall asleep easily after this, after Carter had touched me and the things he'd said. Dancing myself into exhaustion was always the solution when I couldn't sleep, so, not bothering to change my clothes, I headed to the gym instead.

CHAPTER SIXTEEN

S INCE DOMINIC AND MOM WANTED TO GET MARRIED SOON, MOM hadn't wasted any time scheduling a meeting with a wedding planner. They wanted a small wedding with only twenty people, and after some consideration, they had decided to get married on November tenth, three days before Carter's eighteenth birthday. Mom had her hands full with the organization and her job, refusing to listen to Dominic or me and take a few days off. In addition, they had chosen a room for the nursery, and she'd taken it upon herself to decorate and furnish it.

Time rolled by, and before long, the Friday of the first basketball game was upon us. My squad and I pulled our weight with a routine that was more complex than usual with some serious acrobatics, because the game was a big deal. It was one of the few exhibition games before the season started in about a month, but we had a superstition here at Silver Raven Academy—the outcome of the first match would be the outcome of the season. Whenever we won first matches, we were the champions. So, my squad had to be 100 percent ready.

Cheer practices hadn't been the same since Nora had made the team. She was always nice to me, but there was an undercurrent of tension between us, and we never talked to each other unless necessary. She was a fast learner, and she got along with everyone, especially with Jenna and Kim, who were too eager to take her under their wings like the harpies they were. They would often stand on the sidelines to talk with her, and I was sure they were brainwashing her with the latest gossip when they weren't trying to make her fess up to whether she'd gotten together with Carter yet or not.

The basketball team had also stepped up their practices, and their excitement was palpable in the air. They were ready to crush our opponents, so in sync, and it had been fascinating to watch them practice. The only weak link there was Carter.

He'd lost his temper a few times in the week leading up to the game, and it didn't help that he and Jacob didn't get along. Carter had often complained about Jacob's assists, and whatever Jacob did, it wasn't good enough for Carter. Their antagonism created tension in Carter's team, and since they couldn't afford strife at this time, everyone was full of jitters come Friday.

We'd won against Northwest Valley High five times, but it was rumored their team was strong this year courtesy of a few transfers, so anything could happen.

The bleachers were packed with students and parents when my squad entered, and all eyes went to us. We had blue uniforms and matching pom-poms we were shaking in greeting as we chanted, "Ravens for the win! Ravens for the win!" The crowd grew louder in response.

"You go, girls," one guy shouted, and I smiled.

I swear sometimes it was like some of them were here just to watch *us* perform.

Our team entered the gym, and my eyes latched onto Carter in his black uniform. He'd always looked sexy on the court, always dominating his games with his determination and a kind of ruthlessness, and it was a challenge for me to keep my eyes off him. Not that I had to now that the game was starting and I could feast my eyes on him as much as I wanted.

The game was tense from the start, and everyone's attention

was on Carter. I hadn't been sure if the coach would allow him to remain as captain, but he must've thought Carter would be able to handle it. And he did handle it, despite all the odds. He stayed on top of his game and led his team effectively, leaving no doubt that he was in his element. Jacob also did well, passing the ball to Carter each time he found him open and vice versa, the hostility between them temporarily forgotten.

Unfortunately, Northwest Valley High played well too, and the score was mostly tied during the first two quarters. The crowd exploded into shouts of joy when our team took the lead at the end of the second quarter.

"Go, Ravens, go! Go, Ravens, go!" we chanted from the sidelines, excitement pumping through our veins. "Win, Ravens, Win!"

Energized by adrenaline, I led the squad through our choreography during halftime. Our moves were synchronized down to the very last second, and I felt high on anticipation and attention, losing myself in the blur of colors and sounds.

As the game progressed, our team led by ten, then fifteen, then twenty points, and we all joined in booming cheers. Carter definitely played better now, and I wondered if the cheers were feeding him. If he was finally enjoying himself on the court. My heart pumped wildly each time he scored or got pushed by an opponent and the referee signaled a foul. The opposing team targeted him the most, but luckily, Jacob made up for it.

In the end, we beat Northwest Valley High by twenty-three points. Everyone went into a frenzy, and the whole team rushed toward Carter, swarming him. I jumped, cheering with others at the top of my lungs.

Trisha turned toward Amalie, Denise, and me. "We did it!"

I hooted with laughter. "Yes!"

Carter stepped away from the teammates surrounding him. He was still smiling when his gaze roamed over the sidelines until it found mine, and my heart gave a kick against my chest. For a brief moment, I could pretend that smile was all for me, and my chest heaved with love.

But then Nora raced over to him and jumped into his arms. With a sickening twist of my stomach, I watched her wrap her legs around his waist and bury her head into his neck. My face froze in a grimace.

Before I could unglue my gaze from them and turn to leave, someone tipped my head to the side and a pair of lips claimed mine. With a start, I registered Jacob's face. His hands splayed over the sides of my head to hold me in place.

Only faintly, I heard mixed gasps and giggles from my squad. The smell of Jacob's sweat mixed with soap permeated my nostrils as the moisture from his face transferred to mine. Just then, I felt his tongue searching for access to my mouth, and I shoved him away.

"What the hell are you doing?"

His brows knitted together as he regained his balance, the desire on his face petering out when he saw I wasn't in the least happy about the kiss. Over his shoulder, I found his friend Tara standing a few feet away from us. Her clenched fists and furious eyes were the last thing I saw before she darted away.

"I'm sorry. I thought—it was just spur of the moment . . ."

"Spur of the moment? You had no right!" I looked at Carter. He was watching me and Jacob, wearing such an expression of rage it almost had me swaying.

"Just leave me alone." Spinning on my heel, I made a quick exit.

"Zoe, please wait!" Jacob called after me, but I ignored him.

Summer intercepted me before I entered the locker room.

"I saw what my cousin did. I can't believe him! Are you okay?"

"He crossed the line, Sum. And to make it worse, Carter saw it too. Did you see how he looked at me?"

"At least that's a good sign, right? It means he cares."

I yanked my hair out of my ponytail and ran my hand through it. "I don't even know! He's always so cold, but then he reacts like that when he sees me with Jacob. I don't understand him at all.

And then there's Nora. Have you seen her climbing all over him? It's nauseating."

"I know. He's such a jerk for stringing you along like this."

I sighed, supporting myself against the wall. A few girls from my squad passed, and we smiled at each other.

"I'm pathetic," I breathed out.

"You're in love."

"No, I'm pathetic. I'm running around in circles waiting for him to show me even a flicker of attention."

"You're hopeful."

I shook my head. I was sickened by the emotional roller coaster Carter had me on. I was disappointed in myself because I was allowing him to pull me in, then push me away, while I was trying to get through to him but only getting nowhere. I was fighting so hard not to let our love and memories go to waste, but at this point, there seemed to be no end to his hate.

"Anyway, everyone's talking about the afterparty. Are you going?"

"No, sorry. I'm not in the mood. I think I'll be going to bed early."

"Then I won't go either. More time for me to play with some new eye shadows I bought."

She left, and I headed for the shower, yearning for the hot water to clear my mind and wash away all the poison coursing through my veins.

Mom and Dominic had gone to bed early, so downstairs was cloaked in darkness when I got out of bed to get some snacks. I hadn't been able to sleep, tossing and turning in bed as I imagined Carter and Nora together at that party, and I'd finally given up after an hour. Not even reading the latest novel from J.R. Ward helped me keep my mind off them. I'd kept rereading the same paragraph.

As I stepped into the kitchen, my eyes caught on a figure sitting at the counter, and I stopped mid-step, pressing my hand over my mouth to suppress a scream. It took me a few heartbeats to recognize it was Carter.

I gulped a breath, rubbing my arms against a chill. "Carter. What are you doing here sitting in the dark?"

He raised his head to look at me, and even in the darkness, I could see him take in all of me, his gaze lingering on my breasts and belly button. My insides stirred. His hair was disheveled, like his fingers had threaded through it repeatedly. Or Nora's fingers.

"What does it look like?" he slurred.

I frowned. *Okay.* I quickly turned on the under-cabinet lights and grabbed a bowl from the cabinet. I could feel his gaze follow me the whole time.

"You said you were going to keep proving me wrong. Was that what you were doing earlier?"

"What are you talking about?"

"You know exactly what I'm talking about."

Was he serious? I stepped into the pantry and pressed the light switch, locating my snacks. "You're talking nonsense."

His chair made a scrapping sound against the floor as he stood up. "Nonsense? You kissed, right? I saw. The whole fucking world saw."

I inhaled sharply, turning to look at him. "Funny you mention that since you and Nora couldn't take your hands off each other. Did you two have fun at the party? Did you sleep together?"

Fury cut through his eyes. He eliminated the remaining space between us, and my pulse quickened. He was so close to me now, and my stomach fluttered when he framed my chin with his fingers, making me look at him. I yanked my chin out of his grip, but he repeated the motion. It was hard for me to breathe, desire awakening deep in me.

"You're doing it on purpose. Fucking around with Myers to hurt me."

"You couldn't be more wrong."

"I don't believe you."

"But it's true."

I tried to step away from him, but he kicked the door closed and caged me against it, causing my heart to thunder against my rib cage. The pantry was barely big enough for both of us, which made me all the more aware of his proximity. His scent mixed with his cologne overwhelmed me, and I could feel my nipples hardening underneath my sleeping top as our chests brushed against one another. His gaze went down my body, cataloging everything.

He emitted a low growl. "Those shorts and top look so tiny, it's as if they're non-existent. I can see everything."

An ache throbbed between my legs. "What do you want, Carter?" My voice sounded raspy even to my own ears.

"For you to stop messing with my head."

"I'm not doing that."

"Yes, you are. Always."

My stomach quivered. "Did you sleep with Nora?"

"I can't even touch her," he snarled.

I couldn't get enough air into my lungs. "Why?"

"Because your fucking face is the only thing I see."

My breath fluttered. "That can't be true."

"Oh yeah? Then why do you think this is?" He grabbed my hand and pressed it against his hardened length.

"You don't like me."

"So? This means nothing."

Fury and pain gripped my chest. He so wasn't fair. "Then leave me alone."

"Why should I? You keep throwing yourself at me. Maybe I was going about this the wrong way this whole time. Maybe I should take you up on that, so I could finally prove you're just like your dearest mommy."

My hands started shaking, and I felt the urge to strike him hard. "Go to hell, Carter." I shoved him away, but he stepped back into my space.

Before I could even say anything, his lips landed on mine. It was like a strike of lighting, causing my whole world to spin out of control. I raised my hand to push him away, but then his tongue invaded my mouth and connected with mine, and I was swarmed by pleasure. Everything in me went haywire, responding to him with alarming need—a need that had boiled deep within me all this time, waiting to be unleashed. And when his arms wrapped around my waist and molded me against his hard body, all my restraint vanished, already forgotten.

Kissing him was like coming back home. I was finally kissing him after so long, and it was like he was nourishing me after weeks of starvation. It was electrifying, addictive, and more arousing than ever before. I'd never starved for his kiss more, for the silkiness of his tongue on mine, and I wanted him to possess me. To have all of me. I moaned as his hands slid inside my shorts and kneaded my ass, pressing me flush against his hard-on.

This was what I'd missed all this time. This familiar urgency and raw need. These kisses and hands that promised pure pleasure.

His hands slid up my hips and waist to my shoulders. He brought my arms up and pinned them above my head against the door. Holding my wrists together with one hand, he raised my top with his other hand, revealing my breasts to him.

He took a quick breath. His eyes glinted like emeralds in the night as he studied them, and I could feel myself throbbing harder.

He cupped a breast and ran his thumb over the beaded tip awaiting him, sparking pleasure deep within me. I moaned. He groaned at this, and he gave my nipple another flick of his thumb before he lowered his mouth to my neck and left a line of hot, wet kisses all the way to my breast. My back arched when his lips wrapped around my nipple and sucked on it.

"Carter," I breathed out. I squirmed against him as he tortured me with his tongue and teeth, making me ache for him. He moved to the other nipple and swiped his tongue over it. "*Yes.*"

He released another groan. His hand went under the waistband of my shorts and cupped my heat over my panties. I bucked against him, moaning his name loud.

"Fuck," he hissed, tightening his grip on my wrists above my head.

His finger pressed against my throbbing nub, and my hips shot forward. This was so familiar. He was touching me just like he had the first time, and that fact had me even more aroused. It was calling for everything in me to surrender.

I looked down to his hand, and the sight of him touching me, holding me completely to his mercy, almost pushed me over the edge. As though sensing I was close, he shoved my panties aside and pressed his fingers directly against my sensitive flesh.

My legs almost gave out on me. I was drowning in pleasure, and I gyrated my hips in rhythm with his fingers, so close to bursting, so goddamn close.

But then I looked into his unfocused eyes, smelling the whiskey on his breath, and the recent memories rushed back to me, reminding me why I shouldn't allow him this.

He was drunk and . . . he didn't want to be with me.

I didn't want to soar high only to crash down hard.

"Carter, don't."

He stopped and met my eyes.

"You're going to regret this, and I don't want you to hurt me more than you already have."

He needed a second to process my words. Abruptly, he pulled away, leaving me panting against the door. Too quickly, the desire in his eyes was gone.

He gave me a derisive once-over, making me aware of how disheveled I must look. "There's nothing to regret because, as I told you, this means nothing."

I pressed my lips together to stifle a cry.

"But thank you. You seem like a bad fuck, so you saved me from wasting my time." With that, he opened the door and walked out.

And as I watched him leave, I felt it—*enough is enough.*

I couldn't keep going around in circles. I couldn't keep letting him walk all over me again and again. I couldn't keep hoping against hope when I always ended up hurt. I'd kept banging my head against the wall like the lovesick fool that I was, hoping for his love—for a morsel of his attention—trying to make him see me, need me, *love me*, simply refusing to give up on him no matter what insult he threw my way.

Maybe he was attracted to me, but it didn't mean a damn thing when he didn't want it. When he didn't want to love me.

I'd been fighting it all this time, but I had to admit it—I'd lost him. And the worst part of it was that even if he got his memory back, there was a possibility it wouldn't change a single thing.

"Carter."

He stopped and looked over his shoulder at me.

"I'm done."

His eyes went wide. "What?"

I swallowed past the obstruction in my throat, past the heavy feeling claiming my chest and threatening to paint my world dark. I was going to break down into pieces once I was alone.

"I'm done chasing after you. Whatever I do or say, it doesn't matter. You just keep hurting me." I closed the space between us, the pounding of my heart ringing hollow in my ears. "I finally realize there's no chance for us to be together anymore. You won't ever love me again. So, you can be sure I won't bother you from now on."

He paled, not a single muscle on his face moving.

I didn't wait for him to say something. My legs and heart heavy, I left the kitchen, ignoring my heart that begged me to stop as I moved right past him.

CHAPTER SEVENTEEN

I WOKE UP TO SEVERAL MESSAGES FROM JACOB IN WHICH HE APOL-
ogized for kissing me and asked me to forgive him. Refusing
to deal with him today, I dressed and went with Mom to look
for her wedding dress, leaving the house at the first opportunity. I
needed any distraction I could get so I wouldn't break down into
a thousand pieces.

Mom would be five months along at the wedding, and her
dress would have to accommodate the bump. So far none of the
dresses had attracted her attention, though they were all stunning
and embroidered in fine detail. Dominic had insisted on only the
best for her, so each dress was worth at least a few thousand dollars.

"We'll find something," I told her after we left the final bridal
shop for the day.

"I've spent my whole life thinking I'll never get to wear the
perfect wedding dress, and now that I've got the chance, nothing
seems right."

"What was your wedding dress like when you married Dad?"

"Simple. More of a summer dress than a wedding dress. But
that was the only dress we could afford."

"Now you can compensate for that."

"The price of the dress doesn't matter. Only that you're happy with the person you're marrying." She examined my face. "You've been looking down the whole morning. Is something the matter?"

I avoided her gaze, my heart twisting painfully in my chest. "Don't worry about me. I'm fine."

"You're not fine, honey. Tell me."

I gnawed at my lip to divert my attention from the emotional pain, looking out in the distance. "I'm done chasing after Carter. He keeps pushing me away no matter what I do, and I can't take it anymore. I told him so last night, and I know it's a good decision but . . . but I love him." I bit into my lip harder. This outing was supposed to be my distraction.

Mom ran her hand through my hair, tucking a lock behind my ear. "I understand how hard that decision must be for you. But given the circumstances, it really is a good decision."

"But you told me to try to be patient with him."

She palmed my cheek. "Not at the cost of your happiness, honey. Your happiness always comes first."

"I don't feel happy right now."

"I know. But I'm sure in time it will get easier for you, and you'll find someone else. And before you know it, Carter will be just a distant memory."

A distant memory. After all that love, effort, and countless moments spent connecting with each other.

"Don't be sad, honey. Everything will be okay. Come on, let's get something to eat."

Mom took me to a five-star restaurant owned by one of Dominic's friends. The moment we stepped inside, we were welcomed with Hollywood smiles and royal treatment. Something I'd never get used to.

The server had us seated at the best table near the ceiling-high windows, with a view of the town's square. We were brought wine, which Mom declined but was happy to allow me to drink.

I raised my brow at her.

She giggled. "Just this one time, to celebrate. We never got the chance to make a toast to this baby, just you and I."

I smiled. "If you say so." I didn't feel like celebrating, but this outing was all about Mom, so celebrate I would. I clinked my glass against her glass of orange juice and took a sip. The wine had a refined taste that lingered in my throat long after I swallowed it, and I sipped more as I studied our glamourous surroundings and the patrons. "Classy."

"Just like everything else in Dominic's world."

"It's also your world now."

"Right. Is it bad to say I already feel as if it's where I belong?"

"Not at all. You deserve this. And much more."

She took a swallow of her juice, her face contorted with guilt. "Do I? Carter doesn't think so. When Dominic proposed to me, he assured me everything would be okay, but I don't know. I feel like we're doing Carter wrong. I told Dominic maybe we should postpone the wedding, but he wants us married before the baby's born."

My teeth gnawed at my lip. She'd always put Carter's interests first, but this time, she should put herself and the baby first. "You're not doing him wrong. This is your happiness with Dominic we're talking about. Carter should stop being so selfish and start thinking about others. Either way, that is your day. It should be perfect, so don't let him spoil it for you."

She gnawed at her lip, caressing her stomach distractedly. "You're right."

"I know I am."

"I just want us to be a family."

"There's still time until the wedding. You never know. Maybe he'll change his opinion. Or maybe his memories will come back." My stomach churned with fear. Seeing the way things were, I wasn't so sure he'd ever regain his memories, and it was something that had gnawed at me from the corners of my mind all this time. "You're still working."

"Because there's a lot of work to do. We have some important clients, and I can't afford to leave Dominic all on his own."

"He's not all on his own. He has a ton of assistants. Besides, you still have dark circles under your eyes. Are you sleeping well?"

"I am, but I've been feeling more tired than usual these last few weeks. But that's pregnancy for you."

"I know, Mom, but try to take it easy. You sacrificed your happiness long enough."

"Oh sweetie. I haven't sacrificed anything."

"Yes, you did."

I'd never forget everything she'd done for me. She'd been fighting her whole life. Even before Dad died, she'd had to deal with poverty as a trailer park kid. Her dad was an alcoholic and gambler, and her mom barely scraped together a living as a waitress. When Mom left in search of a better life, she'd only had a hundred dollars in her pocket. And she'd found a better life—with Dad. But the fairytale didn't last long, ending the moment Dad died of a heart attack.

I had mostly vague memories of Dad, but my memories of Mom of that time were perfectly clear—she'd always smiled for me, never complained, and made sure to never let me see a single tear or to show fear in front of me. Even when she was struck with grief and without anyone to rely upon. She'd tried her best to spare me from knowing just how bad it was, and she never gave up. So now, finally—*finally*—she deserved to be selfish and think about her own happiness.

"You never told me how hard it was for you to raise me without Dad."

"That's because everything was worth it just to see you happy."

"But you weren't happy."

She gave me a soft smile. "That doesn't matter, honey. I'm happy now." She gave me a long look. "Do you see now that we have a permanent place in Dominic's life?"

I nodded, unsure why she was asking me this.

"Dominic will officially become your stepdad. He'll always have your back. So, you don't have to work so hard."

"Mom . . ."

She sighed. "You always try to rely only on yourself."

I looked away.

"We won't end up on the streets."

"I know."

"Then why don't you take it easy and stop thinking about negative outcomes?"

My lips parted. She was right—Dominic was officially becoming our family and we were staying for good. Our life at the Reeses' house wasn't just a pit stop before life threw us another curve. Their love was for life.

Throughout all my pessimism, there'd always been a part of me that hoped Mom and I would get a reprieve. I hadn't gone so far as to hope we could have lives out of Hollywood movies, but I'd hoped we wouldn't always have to count our every cent or worry about price increases.

This was finally our reprieve.

"So, how about quitting your job? Dominic is more than happy to help you with college."

"I don't feel right about that."

"Why? Look at him as your dad. No, he *will* be your dad from now on."

"That's the thing. I can't see him as my dad," I muttered, unable to look her in the eyes, finally admitting my true feelings.

I could hear her quick intake of breath, and when I saw the hurt expression on her face, I wished I hadn't said that.

"There's nothing wrong with Dominic, don't get me wrong. It's just that . . ."

"It's just that you haven't gotten over your father's death."

The words rang sharply between us, filling my lungs with something heavy and painful. It was ironic that I would miss him now more than ever after finally giving up on Carter.

Mom and I never talked about Dad, and I'd never asked her about him. It wasn't because I hadn't been curious. It was because I knew his death had left permanent scars on her too, and I didn't want to make it harder for her by talking about him. But that meant

I hadn't been able to vocalize my own feelings—the pain that had constantly followed me since his death. The loneliness. The loss. I'd kept my grief locked deep inside me and never let it out. Never revealing to her that I'd never gotten over his death. That no partner of hers would be able to fill his shoes.

That his passing was what had me so distrustful of life and others.

Moisture collected in Mom's eyes, and she reached across the table to cover my hand. "I'm so sorry," she whispered.

"About what?"

"We've never talked about your dad." Her fingers squeezed tightly around my hand. "We never talked about how his death affected you."

I dropped my gaze. "It's okay."

"No, it's not okay. You talk about my sacrifices, but you had to sacrifice a lot too. You always tried to make things easier for me, even at the cost of your happiness."

"And I don't regret it."

"But it's been hard for you too. All the more so because you kept it all inside." Her eyes glittered with sadness. "Do you miss him?"

I studied her engagement ring, briefly blinded by its glint under the bright restaurant lighting. "I try not to think about that."

"But do you?"

I nodded, sucking in my lip between my teeth. I had only two clear memories of him. One was the happiest memory of my life and the other was my most painful, and both controlled my choices in life. But I couldn't admit that to her.

"I should've broached this subject sooner. *Years* sooner." She shook her head with regret, but I didn't want her to feel regret or beat herself up. We were here on a happy occasion, not to dwell on the past.

"I don't blame you, Mom. So, don't worry about it."

"I know you don't, but that doesn't make it okay. If you need to talk about him, sweetie, we can. Anytime. Anything you want to know."

I took a gulp of my wine and lowered the glass with a clank. I watched the liquid swish around inside the glass. "What . . . what was he like?"

She took a handkerchief out of her purse and dabbed at the corner of her eye, her lips curving into a smile. "He was kind. We met when we both volunteered for a non-profit dealing with victims of domestic abuse, and from the get-go, it fascinated me how compassionate he was. It didn't take me long to fall for him."

"And how about him? Did he fall for you right away?"

She giggled. "You bet. He asked me out the same day we met." Her eyes glazed with happy memories. "Oh, we had a wonderful dinner. We realized we had so much in common, and I just knew."

"You knew what?"

"That he was the man of my dreams."

I chuckled. "How about you? Do you ever miss Dad?"

"I do. But now I have Dominic. He makes everything easier."

A smile tugged at the corners of my lips. "I'm so happy for you. I'm sure you'll have nothing to worry about from now on."

"Same to you, missy. Think about what I said. Quit your job and chase after your dreams."

The waiter showed up with our food, and I was glad he'd decided to come just then because he saved me from having to reply.

I didn't want to make her false promises. Maybe Mom and I weren't going anywhere, but there was nothing wrong with relying on myself.

Especially when I didn't know how to conquer the fear of letting go . . . and getting my heart irreparably broken.

Beyond what it had already been, anyway.

CHAPTER EIGHTEEN

I PARKED MY AUDI IN MY ASSIGNED SPOT AND OPENED MY UMBRELLA as I got out of my car. It was raining heavily today, and the wind was sending my hair in all directions, turning it into a mess—just like how I felt inside. And if there was anything that could make my mood turn from bad to worse, it was gloomy and cold weather. I should've stayed in bed.

I rushed into the school lobby, cursing myself for not having the forethought to tie back my hair. All the more so when a quick glance told me all the other girls had their hair styled to perfection.

So, they weren't just immune to poverty. They were immune to bad weather as well.

Some girls turned to stare at me, and I started to flatten my hair with my hands. But then I picked up on their whispers, and I started wishing it was because of something as trivial as the state my hair.

Jacob's kiss was a hot topic trending on social media. The video of me pushing him away after that kiss made the rounds on TikTok, but that didn't stop a rumor that we were together from going around. There was even a rumor that Jacob had cheated on me, but I was so desperate for him that I got over it just to stay with him. Judging by the cunning look Kim gave me when I saw her and Jenna on my way to lunch, it was all her doing.

Summer joined me near the cafeteria. "Hey."

"Hey, yourself."

She gave me an appraising look. "You don't look good. Did you sleep last night?"

"Barely."

"Did something happen?"

"You could say that." I recounted my decision to give up on Carter. "I won't be keeping my hopes up any longer."

Her lips turned down. "I'm so sorry, Zoe. I was really hoping you'd be able to get him back."

"Yeah, well, life sucks."

Amalie jumped in front of me. "What's up? What's with the sad face?"

Trisha and Denise stopped beside me. "The dark circles under your eyes are visible from space," Trisha said.

"Just what I needed to hear."

She gave me a concerned look. "Is everything alright?"

"Not really. I officially gave up on Carter."

"Oh."

Amalie's lower lip stuck out. "That's so not fair!"

"Why did you give up? Did something happen?" Trisha asked.

"It's just that I can't take his attitude anymore. I've been trying so hard to keep him without realizing there's nothing to keep because I've already lost him. So, I won't be keeping my hopes up anymore."

Denise placed her hand on my shoulder. "Hang in there, okay?"

Amalie bobbed her head. "Yeah. And you'll find another guy in no time!"

She looked so childishly sure about it I had to laugh.

Trisha wound her arm around Amalie. "There's always Jacob."

My smile fell. "Let's not go there."

"Speaking of Jacob," Summer said, motioning with her head at something behind me.

I turned to see Jacob coming up to me, his expression pinched.

He ran his hand up and down his neck as he stopped in front of me. "Hi. Can we talk for a minute?"

A few passersby tossed us curious gazes.

"Okay."

I gestured for my friends to enter the cafeteria without me and followed Jacob to a nearby corner where we'd have some privacy.

"What did you want to talk about?"

He dropped his gaze and pushed his hands into his pockets. "You didn't reply to my texts. I know I messed up. I'm really sorry for that."

I folded my arms over my chest. "I don't know, Jacob. You went way over the line."

"I know. I'm an idiot. I like you, Zoe. I've liked you all this time, and I just—" His voice trailed off. He shook his head, the locks of his hair brushing against his cheeks. "When we won and I saw you right there . . . you were so beautiful in that cheer uniform. I had to kiss you." My brows dipped low, and he was quick to add, "I know that was wrong."

"So wrong."

His throat worked. "I know there's no excuse for what I did."

I glanced to the side. I didn't know what to tell him. Despite knowing he liked me, I'd always thought we could still be friends. I wasn't so sure about that now.

He shifted his weight. "Look, I want to make things right. Please let me make things right."

"How do you mean to do that?"

"I'll take you out this Friday. And you get to pick your favorite place."

I chewed on the inside of my cheek. "I don't know, Jacob. I don't want you to get the wrong impression."

He raised his hands in the air. "Don't worry about it. We'll go just as friends. What do you say?"

I released a deep breath. "Fine. I'll text you the place."

"Yes!" He fist-pumped the air, and I had to smile.

We moved to go to the cafeteria, when I heard voices close by. I looked over my shoulder. Nora was standing with some guy at the end of the hallway, and judging by her body language, the conversation wasn't friendly.

Jacob was holding the cafeteria door open for me. "Are you coming?"

"I'll be there in a sec. You go inside."

"Okay. Catch you later."

I nodded, then moved close enough to be able to overhear Nora's conversation. It was only after I stepped behind a corner and peered around the wall to look at them that I recognized the guy. It was Brandon.

What was he doing here? And more importantly, why was he talking with Nora?

Nora's hands were balled at her sides. "Why did you come here?"

He wore a sly smile on his face. "I told you. I had to see you once I found out you transferred here. You blocked me on social media, and you don't reply to my texts."

"I told you many times I want nothing to do with you."

He shifted closer to her, and she went rigid. "And I told you, we're not done."

Brandon and Nora had been together?

She spun toward me, and I ducked behind the wall so she wouldn't see me.

"If you don't leave me alone, I'll report you, and I mean it this time."

Her heels clicked against the floor as she headed toward the lunchroom. I held my breath when she passed right by me, hoping she wouldn't see me. She didn't. She didn't even look over her shoulder before she yanked open the cafeteria door and disappeared inside.

I peeked around the wall to see if Brandon was gone so I

could leave, and I almost connected with a solid wall of muscle. I yanked my head up, meeting Brandon's amused gaze.

"Didn't anyone ever tell you that you shouldn't eavesdrop?"

I took a step away from him. "How did you see me?"

He released a chuckle. "You didn't think I'd notice you? Come on, Pom-Pom. You're surely smarter than that . . . oh wait. You're not."

"What do you want from Nora?"

"I fail to see how that's any of your business."

"It looked as if you were harassing her. I can't just pretend it's nothing."

"You worry about yourself, 'kay?"

"You have no business here, so leave."

His smile fell. So fast that I wasn't even aware he'd moved, he got in my face and cornered me against the wall. "You don't get to order me around, bitch. I'll let it slide this time, but the next time you talk back to me, you'll be sorry." His brown eyes were shaded with blazing fury. Something told me not to mess around with this guy, because he meant his threats.

Like nothing had happened, he pushed away from me and cast me a big smile. "See you around, Pom-Pom." He flicked a strand of my hair off my shoulder and walked away like he owned the school.

Only after he was gone, I could release the breath I'd been holding.

What was this guy up to? And what did he want from Nora?

After winning the first exhibition game, the basketball team was upbeat about the start of the upcoming season, and even Carter looked as though he was enjoying being on the court for a change. He was starting to control himself better during practices, and he didn't lose his temper as often as before. He and Jacob managed to tolerate each other long enough to make the most out of their plays.

As for my squad, the coach wanted us to change some parts of our routine, and we spent the whole practice improving our switch ups in level two pyramid. Nora and Trisha were on top, assisting me with a flipping stunt, but it was far from perfect since Nora's mind wasn't in it.

After the fourth flip that had Nora almost pull my arm out of its joint, I dropped on the ground and directed a glare at her. "Focus, Nora."

"Yeah, sure," she replied without even looking at me.

I stepped closer to her until our feet were almost touching. "I mean it, Nora. This isn't just about the routine or wasting everyone's time. This is also about our safety. We don't want anyone to end up injured."

There was something frantic in her eyes, but it was gone before she raised her gaze to look at me. "I'll do better."

She fidgeted with her hands as she moved back to her position, and I thought about the way she looked when I caught her with Brandon. She was genuinely scared, and after how he'd cornered me, I wondered if he was physically abusive toward her. There had to be a good reason why she was trying to avoid him so much.

This time, we managed to do the stunt right, but the coach didn't let us go until she was completely satisfied. As a result, my muscles were sore, and I craved a long shower to relieve the pain.

I did just that, and the locker room had emptied by the time I was done. My muscles still ached, but nevertheless, I planned to hit the gym as soon as I got home from work.

Hanging my backpack over my shoulder, I made my way to the parking lot. As I neared my car, I heard familiar voices. I looked to my right and saw Carter and Nora deep in conversation.

They were leaning side by side against her car, their backs to me. Nora was smoking.

She had the nerve to smoke on school property. Huh.

From this distance, I couldn't tell what they were talking about. I clutched the strap of my backpack in indecision. I should go home. Their conversation wasn't any of my business.

I resumed walking toward my car, but I didn't take more than five steps before I gave up and ducked behind the nearest car. From there, I moved alongside cars until I reached the car parked diagonally to hers. I peered around the car, making sure they didn't spot me.

"You always smoke when you feel stressed. Did something happen?" Carter asked her.

She was quick to offer him a smile, expelling smoke through her nose. "Pop quizzes. They can suck your soul out." *Pop quizzes. Right.* "But what about you?"

"What do you mean?"

"You've been more distracted than usual this week. What's got you thinking? Basketball?"

"No."

"Then, what? You know you can tell me anything." Her voice was sugary and compassionate. I hated it.

"It's a long story."

There was hurt on her face because he clearly didn't want to talk to her about whatever was troubling him.

"Does it have anything to do with Zoe?"

His jaw clenched, and his eyes set on a spot in the distance.

My treacherous heart gave a jump. It would be so easy to delude myself into thinking he was down because of what I'd said about giving up on him.

"I see," Nora said under her breath.

"Sorry." He ran his hand down his face. "Everything's a mess at my house, and it's just that . . . everything's so fucking confusing."

She took a drag of her cigarette. "Is everything okay with your dad?"

"Not really. He's getting married to Zoe's mom."

She gaped at him. "Really?"

"Yeah. She's pregnant."

"Oh. Congratulations, I guess?"

"You guessed wrong."

"You didn't tell me much, but I've deduced that you don't get along with her."

"I don't."

"But why? Is she a bad person?"

No, my mom is not a bad person, I wanted to shout. I waited with bated breath for what he was going to say.

"I don't know," he said quietly, and the organ in my chest constricted. "On the surface, she's all nice and friendly." *On the surface?* "But what kind of woman would have an affair with a married man? What kind of woman would jump at the first chance to move in with the man right after his wife died? A wife that loved him so much and fought for their marriage until the end?"

"Ouch. I'm sorry about that. That's . . . messed up."

"And now they're acting as if they didn't do anything wrong, as if they haven't built up their relationship on lies and other people's misery."

I curled my hands into fists, starting to shake. I wanted to go over there and shout at him not to badmouth my mom and Dominic, but I didn't want to reveal myself to him.

"Dad doesn't care how I feel. He just cares about his 'perfect' fiancée and her snowflake of a daughter."

Fury slammed into me, stealing my breath away. *Snowflake of a daughter?*

Nora cocked her head, studying him closely. She quickly looked away and took another drag. "She really gets on your nerves that much? Zoe?"

He raised his eyes to look at her. "What do you mean?"

"I thought that since you two were together . . . that you'd have some lingering feelings for her."

"I have amnesia. I don't remember being with her."

"But you surely feel something when you're next to her."

My pulse beat in my throat. My mouth was now dry because I was breathing through it, taking lungsful of air.

"Yes. Disgust."

I clamped my lips together. Why was I still listening to them?

Why was I listening at all? I willed my feet to take me away from this torture, but just as I started moving, she asked, "Are you sure that's all?"

He didn't reply for so long that I began to wonder if he meant to at all. His gaze was on his shoes, confusion playing across his features.

"There's something," he finally said.

My heart gave a flutter.

"What?" she asked almost breathlessly.

"A sense of familiarity. Her scent . . . her touch . . . it feels like . . ."

"It feels like what?"

I held my breath.

"Like everything's how it's supposed to be."

Pain spread through me, and I couldn't fill my lungs with enough air. I wanted to cry, cursing life and everything that had brought us to where we were today.

"Do you want to be with her?"

I waited for him to say "no," but he remained quiet.

I pressed my hand against my mouth. Why wasn't he saying anything? He should be saying "no." He should clearly be stating that after everything he'd put me through.

Nora studied her cigarette. Pain blending with jealousy flashed over her face.

"You know what I think?" she asked.

"Hmm?"

"I think you're getting closer to her, and you don't even know it."

"I don't want that," he clipped out.

"But you obviously can't fight it."

He didn't say anything to that either.

"You never told me about that tattoo on your wrist."

"There's nothing to tell."

"It has to do with her, right? She has the other half of it."

His gaze went to the tattoo. His hand curled. "Yes. But that's in the past. The tattoo doesn't have any meaning for me now."

A wave of pain hit me right in the chest because what else had I expected? But then Nora asked, "Then why are you always staring at it?"

My eyes widened. Say what?

Carter pushed himself off the car and gave her an annoyed look. "You must've imagined it. Look, I really don't want to talk about Zoe, so let's just drop it, okay?"

Her gaze lowered with hurt, but she recovered quickly.

She finished her cigarette. "We can leave now. Going straight home?"

He nodded, and they got into her car.

I took that as my cue to leave as well.

By the time I reached my car, Nora had driven out of the parking lot, and I took my time starting the engine, allowing the long-suppressed tears to come out. If only my love for him would cease. If only it wasn't making me so weak for him. If only he didn't put another memory into the box of my beautiful memories of him—the memory of his hot kisses and touches in the pantry that consumed me despite all our previous antagonism.

So many questions plagued my mind, each revolving around what Carter felt toward me. Why did he have to be so complex? Why, just when I was determined to forget about him, he had to go and say those things?

"Fuck you, Carter. Fuck. You."

I started the engine only after my last tear dried, and by then, the parking lot had been completely empty for quite some time.

CHAPTER NINETEEN

"I S IT TRUE? YOUR MOM AND CARTER'S DAD ARE GETTING MAR-
ried?"

"So, Carter is officially becoming your stepbrother now, huh?"
"I heard your mom's prego. Congrats!"
"Lusting after your stepbrother??? Yuck."
"You should delete all the photos and videos with Carter from your social
media. You two are history."

I grimaced at my DMs, my hand clutching the phone shaking.
Social media was flooded with posts about my mom and Dominic,
and I suspected it all had to do with Nora finding out about it. It
wasn't difficult to deduce that she hadn't wasted any time letting
Kim know about the latest events, since new rumors were already
circulating.

"Isn't it weird to be in love with your stepbrother? It would be too weird
for me."

My heart twisted in my chest. That did it. With punching fingers, I logged out of all my social media, deciding to stay off it
until the jackals pounced on someone else.

I didn't need people's judgement. I'd already gotten my fair
share of it back in the day when Carter and I first got together.

They had all been too ready to pour scorn on me until Carter threatened to make them regret it if they didn't stop.

As if they hadn't given me a hard time already since the breakup. When would all this stop?

A night out with Jacob was exactly what I needed to forget about drama, if only for a few hours, so come Friday, I rushed out of the house with more enthusiasm than I'd counted on.

We went to the amusement park on the outskirts of Pine Hills. It was the largest amusement park in the state, and it attracted people from all around. When we arrived, Jacob had a hard time finding a parking spot, squeezing his Honda between an old pickup truck and a sleek Mercedes.

My hair usually refused to stay curled for long periods of time, but tonight was my lucky night, because my curls held out, and they framed my face enticingly. My chocolate eyes popped with eyeliner and dark shadow, creating a stark contrast to my cherry red lips, thanks to Summer's last-minute advice. I'd dressed in a navy dress that hugged my waist tightly but flared out at my hips and had built-in cups that pushed up my overflowing breasts. It was fancy but casual enough for the occasion. I'd noticed Jacob had a hard time focusing on driving, his eyes shifting every few seconds between my boobs and legs.

He looked good himself, with his blue-and-white hoodie, ripped jeans, and disheveled hair that reached the collar of his hoodie. Many girls would want to run their fingers through it, and I recalled his best friend, Tara.

"Where do you want to go first?" he asked me, barely managing to keep his gaze above my breasts.

"Anywhere is fine."

He took me on a roller coaster. It turned out we both loved adrenaline and roller coasters, so we had a great time, laughing and screaming at each high drop. My heart pumped at about a hundred miles a minute when we got off, and I couldn't stop laughing.

"Okay, so how's that for adrenaline?"

I chuckled. "I think I'll have to recover before we ride something else."

"Why don't I buy you some ice cream? It's good for recovery." He winked at me.

"Just what I need. Lead the way."

A few guys moving in our direction checked me out, and I sensed Jacob move so that he was closer to me. It made me aware of his hand dangling too close to mine, and I placed my hand on my purse just so he wouldn't get the wrong impression and try to hold it. I'd reiterated that this wasn't a "date" date when he came to pick me up, but he kept giving me these glances that were full of meaning.

"I've been meaning to ask you," I started. "What's the deal with you and Tara?"

He arched his brow. "The deal?"

"Yeah. You're best friends, right?"

He laughed, his eyes crinkling. "Yes. We've been best friends since kindergarten."

"And there was never anything between the two of you?"

He gave me a confused glance. "Me and Tara? No way. Never."

"Why not?"

"Because she's like a sister to me. I never saw her that way."

Ouch. So, Tara's crush on her best friend was one-sided.

I wondered why. If I could use one word to describe Tara, it was *spitfire*. She was short and slender, with tomboyish looks. Her uniform was never in place; either her shirt was untucked, or her skirt was tilted, or she wore biker boots, all with fishnet tights. Even her hair rebelled against the "norm," with streaks of green permeating her shoulder-length black hair. She was definitely unforgettable, someone you couldn't ignore in the room.

I guessed she wasn't his type. That had to be it.

"She seems like a nice girl."

He barked out a laugh. "Yeah, she is. Not many people would say so, though, since she's so loud and opinionated. She's always getting in trouble for not being able to hold her tongue."

192 | VERA HOLLINS

"I guess that's where you jump in. To rescue her."

He grinned. "It's no joke. Sometimes I really feel like her big brother. I'm always pulling her out of trouble."

Big brother. Double ouch.

We stopped at the ice cream truck, and I chose chocolate ice cream. I took the cone from the vendor with a smile and turned around as Jacob gave his order. My smile dropped along with my heart when I spotted Carter and Nora coming our way together.

Carter was dressed in black jeans and a black hoodie, his hair slicked back with a few strands hanging over his forehead. The dim light pouring from the lamp posts enhanced his features, accentuating his long cheekbones and sharp jaw. He was so beautiful it hurt to look at him.

Nora was wearing high-waisted jeans and a tight tee tucked into them. The outfit accentuated her curves, and as they passed a group of guys, all of them gave her ass a lingering stare. A DSLR camera hung from around her neck, uncapped and ready to shoot photos.

Carter and Nora definitely complemented each other; they looked like the perfect couple.

Suddenly, I had no desire to eat my ice cream.

As if sensing my gaze, Carter looked in my direction, and his whole face changed. My fingers flexed around the ice cream cone as his gaze slid over my body like velvet, exploring every inch of me. My heart sped up, and I hated the current of desire that so easily gushed through my veins.

Jacob turned with his ice cream in hand, and it was then that Carter noticed him. His face darkened, his hand curling into a fist by his side.

They had to pass us to join the ice cream queue, and my body shuddered with awareness when Carter moved right by me and stopped at the end of the queue. He turned to glare at us. Nora clasped the strap of her camera, looking between Carter and me.

"So, the rumor is true. You two are going out," he said.

My teeth clenched together. I couldn't believe this guy.

"And so what if we are? It has nothing to do with you."

The veins bulged out in his neck as he took a step closer to me. "Up until now, you've clung to me like a bad rash, and now you're with him. You really are desperate for cock."

I blanched, my pulse leaping. I hated him for not just humiliating me but also for doing it on purpose in front of Jacob and Nora.

Jacob took a threatening step toward him. "Don't speak to her like that."

Carter squared up, his eyes flashing with rage. "What the fuck did you just say?"

I brought up my hand in front of Jacob's chest to stop him from getting any closer, never taking my eyes off Carter. "Didn't you say that as far as you're concerned, I can go fuck the whole school? So, I don't see the issue."

Carter balled his hands into shaking fists, for once unable to come up with any retort.

I linked my arm with Jacob's, and Carter's gaze dropped to our entwined limbs. "Let's go, Jacob." I steered him away.

"What the hell is his problem?" Jacob asked a minute later.

"Beats me. I think, at this point, he simply enjoys antagonizing me."

"That or he's jealous."

My stomach took a dive. No, he didn't get to be jealous after he'd rejected me so many times.

The mood had changed. Jacob remained silent as we walked around, and neither he nor I touched our ice creams. But I refused to let Carter spoil this evening for me. A nearby fun house grabbed my attention. It had a clown face as an entrance.

"Say, what do you think about the fun house?"

"Sure." He smiled at me, but it didn't reach his eyes.

Only after we ate our ice creams and went to grab the tickets, I remembered the fun house might not be such a good idea because of the dark, but then again, I'd be with Jacob. I'd ask him to stay close to me if it got to be too much.

We were just about to pass through the clown's grinning mouth when Carter and Nora showed up right behind us. Carter didn't take his gaze off me, daring me to say something.

Was he following us, or what?

"Are you fucking kidding me?" Jacob muttered.

"Just ignore them," I told him.

That was easier said than done since besides the four of us, there was only one other couple at the entrance. As Jacob and I ventured further inside, Carter and Nora were right at our heels. It was impossible to speak without them overhearing.

I grew overly conscious of Carter. The hair on my neck rose, and my heart pumped harder, and it had nothing to do with the darkened rooms and creepy sounds. I could feel his gaze on me, almost engulfing me in its intensity. Each time I bumped into Jacob accidentally, I could practically sense the force of his gaze getting just that much stronger.

Jacob didn't look any more comfortable than me. "If you want, we can go somewhere else," he told me in a low voice.

"No way. We won't give him that pleasure."

The house had too many corridors, and some of them were too narrow, barely allowing one person to pass. The lighting was growing dimmer, until at one point, it all went off. I made it a point to stick close to Jacob, but then the floor underneath me literally moved, spinning me around, and I completely lost my orientation. I reached out for Jacob, or where I thought he was, but he wasn't there.

"Jacob?" I stretched out my hands to try to feel something. "Jacob, where are you?"

"He can't hear you," I heard Carter's voice right next to me.

Goosebumps erupted all over my skin, and I clamped my teeth down on my lip. "Carter?"

With a low buzz, the lights came on, and I met Carter's impassive gaze. Jacob and Nora were nowhere to be found. We were all alone in a long, poorly lit hallway.

My hand went to the wall beside us, and only now I noticed the concealed hinges in it. It was a rotating wall, standing in the middle of a circle that also rotated along with it. Carter and I must've been standing within the circle, since only the two of us were transferred to the other side.

I pushed against the wall, trying to see if it could be moved, but of course it couldn't.

"Just great. Now what?" I asked.

"Now we try to find a way out. And it's certainly not that *wall*." He motioned with his head at the wall with a snort, as if mocking me for even thinking we could get back that easily.

This was getting better and better. Jacob and I were separated, and I was stuck with Carter.

To make things worse, because of my fear of the dark, my first instinct was to snuggle up to him. I tried to block the memories of doing just that in the past. I ran my hands up my arms, hugging myself as I fell into step with him. The shadows twisted and twirled, urging me to move closer to him.

"Boo!" A guy in a creepy clown costume jumped at us from behind the wall. He sent me stumbling backwards a few steps, a scream lodged in my throat.

I pressed my hand against my chest. "Jesus!"

The guy guffawed, his disturbing, wide smile stopping just short of slamming into my face when he bent toward me. "Want us to get mad together, little girl?"

I shuddered. He was good; he was giving me the creeps. "How about not?"

"Awee, the little girl is scared. Are you sure you don't want me to fix you?"

Carter stepped between us, glaring at him. "Step away from her if you don't want *me* to fix *you*." I raised my brows, dumbfounded. He directed his glare at me over his shoulder. "You better follow me if you want to get out of here."

I stepped around the guy, keeping my eyes on him until we were around the corner. His laughter trailed after us.

This was a prelude to more creepy clowns showing up, each of them trying to corner us in. Their laughter almost drowned out the circus music playing from the speakers. I released a relieved sigh when we made it out of their sight, but then the corridors narrowed, and the increasing darkness gave rise to thicker shadows.

I hugged myself again, whimpering when I looked to my side and saw nothing but pitch dark.

Carter stopped and turned to look at me. His gaze skimmed down my body, pausing briefly on my legs.

"What do you have to be so afraid of?"

"I don't like the dark."

He rolled his eyes. "That's ridiculous."

"That's not what you said when I confessed that to you the first time."

His face turned serious. He held my gaze, and it felt like his presence was shrinking the space.

My breaths turned shallower. I could pretend it was from fear, but I knew better.

He wet his lips. "What did I say?"

I looked away.

"Tell me."

"You told me you were always going to be there to protect me. And then you kissed me. It was our first kiss."

The space between us seemed to shrink even further. His eyes inched down my body, slowly, so slowly, setting my every nerve on fire.

"Did you wear that dress for Jacob?"

I averted my gaze.

He took a step closer to me. "Or for all the guys out there who were looking at you tonight?"

My eyes met his. "How do you know they were looking?"

He took another step. "Because I was watching for it."

My heart started hammering against my rib cage.

"They all wanted you." His gaze didn't let up. "Jacob wants you."

"I could say the same about Nora and you."

He angled his head, his gaze narrowing at me. "Are you doing this because of her? You're going out with Jacob because I'm hanging out with her?" He almost completely closed the distance between us. "Or to make me pay attention to you?"

I had to will myself to keep breathing. "I told you I'm done, Carter. You can do with Nora whatever you want."

To my surprise, his features twisted with anger, and his gaze dropped to my mouth.

My heart began pounding at a punishing tempo. I couldn't tell what was happening with him. He was supposed to be happy that I wasn't after him anymore. He shouldn't give a damn about me and who I was with. Instead, he was bothered that I spent time with Jacob. Then there was what he'd said to Nora in the parking lot. It only made it harder for me to predict his next move.

He took the last step separating us, and all my senses heightened. "Are you sure you're done? Because you don't look done to me right now."

I clenched my teeth and fists. "I'm here with Jacob, aren't I?"

His gaze turned into a glare. "You move on real quick, huh?"

"And what do you want, Carter? You want me to desperately chase after you? To face your rejection over and over again? I have more self-esteem than that."

He sneered. "You sure about that?"

I dug my nails into my palms. Over and over, he was hurting me, and I hated him for that. I hated how easily he could use his words as weapons and hurt me from deep within.

"At least I don't act like a jealous prick."

"What?"

"What are you even doing here? What, you suddenly love fun houses?"

He averted his eyes. "That's none of your business."

"You sure about that?" I mimicked him.

"Drop it, Zoe."

"You *hate* fun houses, Carter. You were five when your mom took you to one and you lost her inside. You were stuck for an hour until someone found you crouching in a dark corner. You never stepped foot in one again."

His cheekbones sharpened with anger. "That's enough!"

"You can pretend you're here for a thrill all you want, but I know that's not true. It has something to do with me."

He grabbed me by my upper arms. "I said, *enough!*"

"No! I've had enough! Of *you!* Of your bullshit! Of you always hurting me and insulting me and treating me like—"

Something crashed loudly right next to us, making me scream. The lights flickered on and off, then went permanently off, and I jolted violently.

Carter's arms wrapped around me, the way they had so many times before, and I went still from head to toe. I couldn't see anything, my eyes darting around in total blackness.

My breathing accelerated. I blinked rapidly, as if that would allow me to see something, but of course it made no difference.

"I can't see anything. It's too dark." My voice quivered.

His arms tightened around me. I could feel myself trembling, or was that him? "Nothing's going to happen to you. You're safe." His voice was soft, sounding exactly how I remembered it when he'd comforted me before.

I buried my head into his shoulder without thinking. "I hate the dark. I hate it, hate it, hate it."

His hands went to the small of my back, pulling me even closer to him. His warm breath caressed the side of my face, stirring something deep inside me. I kept expecting him to push me away, but he didn't. No, he held me as though he had no intention of releasing me anytime soon.

I closed my eyes, allowing myself to soak in the feeling of his hands on me. Of the wall of solid muscle pressed against me. Of his scent that drove me crazy. His body was a taunting promise of pleasure but also security, and I wanted to stay in his embrace forever. When he was holding me like this, I struggled to remember all his hate and my heartache.

The dim lights flicked back on. I tilted my head upward to

look at him up close. His lips were a breath away. His green eyes were molten lava. The lines of his face were satiny, calling for me to touch them.

His hands went to my hips and dug in. I gripped the back of his shirt.

"Better now?"

I nodded. "Thank you."

He still didn't release me, looking down at my mouth. My lips parted.

"How did our first kiss happen?" he asked quietly.

"It's a long story."

"Did you look at me before our first kiss the same way you're looking at me now?"

My heart skipped a beat. His hands moved from my hips to my ass inch by inch, until his fingers were almost splayed all over it.

I closed my eyes against the surge of desire that almost knocked all the air out of me. I was so weak for him. He was like a drug, and it would be so easy to just lean in and press my lips to his. It made everything hurt all the more.

"I let you go, Carter. So what do you think you're doing now?"

He stiffened. Before he could say anything, Nora called out, "Carter? Carter, are you there?"

"Zoe?" Jacob's voice followed. "Zoe, we're here." Carter released me right before they showed up around the corner.

I dropped my gaze, unable to look Jacob in the eye. I was certain that my face was flaming red, and for once, I was glad of the poor lighting.

"There you are," Nora said. "We've been looking everywhere for you."

"Let's go," I muttered to Jacob as I stepped over to him.

He frowned. "Is everything okay?" He whipped his glare to Carter. "Did he do anything to you?"

"No, everything's fine. It's just that I think I've had enough of this place." I moved to leave.

"Carter, are we going?" Nora asked him, and I looked at him over my shoulder when he didn't answer her.

He watched me and Jacob leave, not moving a muscle, and I only let out the breath I was holding once we were out of his sight.

Jacob and I didn't talk much after that, and that was fine by me. The memories of me and Carter in that fun house did the talking, compensating for the silence more than enough.

CHAPTER TWENTY

One and a half years earlier

T HE SCHOOL WAS TAKING US ON A SKI TRIP, AND FOR DAYS IT was all I could think about. I'd never been anywhere on a trip. I'd never even left the state. So, when I heard we were going to a luxurious ski resort for a week, I immediately googled ski wear and other things I'd need, never mind that I had no clue how to ski.

Since it was my first school trip, I couldn't wait for the bus ride with my classmates, but I hadn't counted on Carter sitting behind me and Summer with Jackson. The whole time, I was super aware of him, an undercurrent of attraction pulsing between us each time I turned to talk to someone behind me and I caught him looking at me.

That didn't mean we found ways to spend more time together; on the contrary, we refused to spend time alone with each other and always found excuses to go our separate ways. If I saw him going into the coffee shop in the lobby of our hotel, I decided I could drink coffee another time. If he saw me and Summer in the line for the cable car, he turned around and took Jackson and Prescott elsewhere. And if we happened to be walking toward one another in the hallways, we pretended we weren't even aware of one another.

But we could only avoid each other for so long.

The second day of our trip, I met Summer's cousin Jacob Myers. He gave me hints that he liked me right from the start. Since he was an advanced skier, he was particularly interested in helping me learn to ski. I lost count of how many times I fell, but it was fun, and Jacob was super cool about it.

Unlike when other guys had hit on me, I liked Jacob's attention. There was something about him that set him apart from the others. Maybe it was his sharp intellect, or an attentiveness that made you feel as though he cared about everything you said. Then there was his charm; the guy was super handsome, and he knew it.

It didn't take long for me to decide I could date Jacob if he asked me out.

It didn't take long for Carter to decide that was a terrible idea.

Once Carter realized I was spending all my time with Jacob, he put him down any chance he got and even "accidentally" shoved him when he passed him going down the ski slope.

That was the reason for our newest argument as our group made its way to the terrain park on the outskirts of the resort. I'd grabbed Carter's hand and pulled him behind and away from Prescott and Jackson, demanding he walk with me so he could explain why he'd shoved Jacob. We lagged behind the others as we all followed the path through woods buried under heaps of snow. Tree branches curved over us like skeletal fingers.

"What the hell is your problem?" I asked him, almost stumbling when I stepped into a too-deep patch of snow. "Jacob could've broken his leg or something."

Carter didn't even deign to look at me. "But he didn't."

"You have some serious issues, dude. He didn't deserve that. He's amazing, and I like hanging out with him."

"He just wants to fuck you."

The wind picked up, and even though my jacket did a good job of protecting me from cold, I was starting to get colder. I wrapped my arms around my waist.

"So? Since when do you act like a concerned brother? It's my business what I do with guys."

"So, you want him to use you."

"Has it maybe occurred to you that *I* am using *him*? Maybe I'm tired of waiting for the right guy to have sex with."

He stopped and glared at me. I stopped too. "Really? So you're going to give it up to the first guy who shows you any interest?"

I put my hands on my hips. "Why? Want the spot for yourself?"

His eyes smoldered, making my blood and insides heat.

I glanced away, only then noticing that I could no longer see our group in the distance. The snow had started falling again, and the sky had darkened. The weather forecast said today would be a clear day, but it didn't take a genius to see there was a storm coming. More snow accumulated on the path, and it had become difficult to see where we were supposed to be going.

"We should find the group. We're going to get lost at this rate," I said and headed in the direction our group had gone.

The snow and fog that had descended made it difficult to see anything in the distance. We started calling for the others, but there was no way anyone could hear us with the wind howling. Everywhere I looked, the trees looked the same. There was no telling from which way we'd come. We tried going back, only to realize we were walking deeper into the woods.

I stopped and reached for my phone. "I'm going to call Summer. She'll let the teachers know we're lost." I unlocked my phone and cursed.

"What?" Carter asked.

"There's no signal."

"What? No way." He took out his own phone. "Shit!"

"Guess that means you don't have signal either."

He gnawed on his lip, sweeping the area with his gaze. "We'll have to find the right way. There's no other choice. Come on. We have to go back."

"Go back? Go back where? We don't even know where *back* is!" I grabbed my head with both hands. My feet were already so cold I couldn't feel them, and my body quaked with shivers. This was bad. "No, no, no. This is not happening."

He turned and grasped my shoulders, making me look at him. "Zoe, now's not the time to lose it. We have to keep moving. Follow me."

He caught my hand and pulled me after him, and I made sure to keep up. I was already tired, and my muscles were protesting the strain. He trudged through the snow without a single complaint, never slowing down. He showed no emotion—no fear or anxiety—but he couldn't have been any more prepared for this than I was. He walked ahead of me, blocking the worst of the wind with his broad shoulders, his black ski jacket the only thing I could see as I huddled behind him. Strangely, I felt safe with him, and somehow, I knew we would be okay because he was here.

"What do you think, how long will it take them to figure out we're missing?" I asked.

"I don't think it'll take them long."

The trees surrounding us seemed never-ending. There was more snow here, and the fog prevented us from seeing more than a few feet ahead of us. It grew steadily colder, and I couldn't think about anything except that I needed to get warm. My hands were numb in my gloves, and my nose was burning from cold.

"Do you even know where you're going? It feels like we're only getting further off course."

"If you think you can do better, lead the way."

I checked my phone again, but there was still no signal. I shouted for help. Then shouted again. After the tenth time, my throat gave out on me.

"Save your strength," Carter told me. I shuddered, and his fingers wrapped more firmly around mine. "Are you cold?"

"*Am I cold?* I'm freezing to death here!"

"We need to find shelter."

My pulse accelerated with panic as the realization finally hit. We wouldn't be able to get back to the hotel. Not today.

"And how do you think we'll do that? I don't see anywhere to hide from this weather."

He didn't reply. He just kept going forward.

I didn't know how long we'd been walking. It could've been minutes or hours before we stumbled upon a cabin sitting amid the sea of snow. At first, I was sure it was a mirage, a product of my desperate mind, because it was literally in the middle of nowhere, but when I blinked, it was still there.

"I can't believe this." I started to laugh. "We can take shelter there." I released Carter's hand and rushed forward, the sudden burst of adrenaline giving me strength to increase my pace after so much walking and trying to stay warm. "You think there's someone inside?"

"Doubtful." Carter looked as exhausted as I felt. His eyes and mouth appeared strained. "It doesn't seem like there's anyone in there."

We stepped onto the wraparound porch. Carter tried the door, but it was locked.

"We have to break in. Get out of the way," he told me, and after I moved, he kicked the door.

The door gave in on his second kick, and we rushed in. It was cold inside—clearly no one had been here recently—but it was an improvement compared to the howling wind and cold snow outside.

The cabin was simply furnished, with a couch and a coffee table holding court in the living room, looking over the fireplace in the corner. There was an adjoining kitchen, and next to that a hallway that probably led to the bathroom and bedroom.

"We need to get warm. You go find some blankets, and I'll look if there's firewood outside," Carter said.

I nodded, removed my backpack, and set about doing as he'd said. I found the bedroom at the end of the hallway, and inside the

206 | VERA HOLLINS

room was a cabinet with blankets, sheets, comforters, and pillows. I selected the two thickest blankets.

I stopped in the kitchen on my way back to the living room and found canned food in the cabinets. The refrigerator was without power, but it contained unopened bottles of water and soda. I checked the expiration dates and was relieved to find they were still good for a few more months. There was only one big bottle of water and a couple candy bars in my backpack, and I didn't know how long we would be staying here. We needed any food and water we could get.

I pulled out my phone and saw there was still no service. There was no landline here either, I discovered after a quick search.

Carter had yet to return, so I used the opportunity to go to the bathroom and empty my bladder. Just as I made my way once more to the living room, Carter pushed through the door, carrying several logs.

"There's firewood behind the house. It's covered by a tarp, so it's usable." He dropped the logs by the fireplace and gave me a long look. I was standing with my arms wrapped around myself, shivering uncontrollably. His brows drew together. "I'm going to start a fire, so you'll be warm soon."

I felt like melting on the inside. He cared about me.

I sat down on the couch and watched him work, fascinated by the purposeful way he stacked the wood. "How do you know what to do?"

"Boy Scouts."

Right. Why wasn't I surprised that Carter, who was always on top of every situation, was on top of this as well? And not once did he lose his cool.

"I checked the kitchen while you were outside. There's canned food in the cabinets and water in the fridge. I think the power's turned off, though."

"There must be a breaker box somewhere."

"I'll go look for it."

I found it at the end of the hallway by the bedroom door.

Once the fire was burning, Carter tried to get the electricity on, but it wasn't working.

"We'll have to do without it."

I went to check if there were at least any candles, but there were none.

"At least th-th-there's fire." My teeth chattered.

His lips pursed together. "Let's get you warm." He took my hand and led me to the couch, which he'd dragged closer to the fireplace. We sat down together and wrapped ourselves in the blankets. I tucked my legs under me and tightened the blanket around me, digging my fingers into the material.

He looked down at me. "Better?"

I smiled. "N-N-Not really."

"Come here." He turned so that he was perched against the back and armrest, one leg bent on the couch and the other anchored on the floor, and opened his blanket in invitation. I sat in between his legs with my back to him, knees drawn up tight to my chest, and he wrapped his arms and blanket around me, pulling me against him. His leg pressed closer to me, caging me in. It was too cold, and we were lost who knew where, but right now, all I could think about was how strong his body was behind mine. The allure of it. How these past few months were all spent with me fighting not to think about him and his delectable body but failing miserably at it.

"Are you worried?" he asked me.

"It would be a lie if I said no. How long will we have to stay here? Will we ever get back?"

"Don't think that way. The storm will pass sooner or later. Then we can try to find our way back."

"What if it lasts for days? What if we only get more lost?"

His hand found my knee through the blanket. He squeezed it. "Take it easy. We'll be okay."

His body heat and the warmth from the fireplace were starting to work miracles, and I wasn't trembling anymore. I snuggled even closer to him.

"How can you be so calm?"

"Because panicking will get us nowhere."

"I never would've imagined I'd get lost in the woods. I mean, this trip was supposed to be memorable, but not like this. I've never been anywhere other than my hometown and Pine Hills, which is why I was so happy to come on this trip, but of course, this had to happen."

"Why haven't you ever been anywhere?"

"I think you can guess." I tossed him an ironic smile over my shoulder. "No money."

He didn't say anything to that.

The fire crackled in the fireplace, flames dancing in captivating twirls. For a while, I was able to forget why we were there. I could pretend this was just me and Carter sharing a quiet moment together somewhere.

"Where would you like to go if you could anywhere?" he asked me.

"The real question is, where wouldn't I go? I've always wanted to go on a trip around the world. See as many countries as possible."

"Okay, what country comes to mind first?"

"Australia. I want to see kangaroos and koalas."

His chest vibrated with laughter.

I arched my brow at him. "What's so funny?"

He was all smiles. "Nothing. That's just cute." I was too busy staring at his gorgeous smile to register what he'd said at first, but when I did, I blushed and turned back around.

I didn't know what there was to blush about nor why Carter could fluster me so easily, but it was what it was. I stared straight ahead, pretending my heart wasn't galloping in my chest and I wasn't overly aware of every inch of his body pressed against mine.

The time flew by with Carter by my side, and before I knew it, darkness was falling, swallowing our surroundings within an hour. Everywhere I looked, there was darkness, its edges softened by the firelight. The wind wailed and rattled the windows. A strong shudder passed through me, but this time it was from pure fear instead of the cold.

"What's wrong?" His softened voice was directly in my ear, raising goosebumps on my skin.

"I hate this."

"Hate what?"

"The darkness. I don't like the dark."

His arms wound more closely around me, and his scent washed over me. His lips were now almost touching my ear.

I closed my eyes, biting my lower lip.

"Don't worry. I'll protect you. I'm always going to be there to protect you," he whispered.

Heat surged through me, past all the cold, fear, and uncertainty, and I thought my heart might implode in my chest. Had he really just said that?

I turned my head to look at him and released a shuddering breath when I found fierce tenderness in his eyes. His gaze dropped on my lips . . .

I held my breath.

He let out a low groan. "Don't look at me like that."

"Like what?"

"Like you want me to devour you."

"Do *you* want to devour me?"

His eyes darkened so much they were the color of evergreens at midnight. "Always."

"Then why do you always treat me so badly?"

"Because I'm fighting how I feel for you, baby. I'm already too addicted to you." His eyes shifted between my eyes and mouth.

"Show it."

"*Fuck.* You're playing with fire," he said in a rough voice.

We'd been playing with fire for weeks, circling around each other. As much as I wanted to pretend I didn't find him attractive, as much as I wanted to ignore the pull he had on me, it made no difference. He was always on my mind, and I wanted to know what it was like to be kissed by him. To be his.

So, I gave in. "So what?"

The raw lust in his eyes was my only warning. He grabbed my chin and pressed his lips down on mine, taking in my quick exhale of breath.

Our lips molded together like it was the most natural thing in the world. In an instant, he turned me around, and I kneeled as I clutched his head with my hands, the blanket pooling around me. Our lips brushed against each other over and over again, our breaths frantic. We were puppets of this need that had built up in us over time, demanding to be satiated.

He pushed his tongue deep into my mouth, and it was heaven. He kissed as though he wanted to possess every inch of me, as if he was drunk on my taste and couldn't stop. Without breaking our kiss, he took off my jacket, then his, and then his hands turned restless, roaming over my arms, my shoulders, my back. I yanked at his hair when his hands went down my back and grabbed my ass, hauling me flush against him. I felt myself growing wet.

He growled and drew away. We were both gulping for air.

"You feel so good. I've wanted this for so long."

"And why is that?" I needed him to say it, to admit exactly how he felt toward me. No more lies or denials.

"Because I want you so badly."

"Just *want* me?"

His eyes probed mine, searching long and deep. "No, not just want. *Need.* I need to feel you. Need to have you by my side."

"Does that mean you don't hate me?"

"Do you hate *me?*"

"Not really."

"There's your answer."

Warmth brought me to life, and I moved my mouth back to his. His hands immediately latched onto my hips, and I lost myself in the feel of them. This time, they were even bolder, coming up to my breasts. He cradled them in his hands and pressed his lips to my neck. His tongue darted out, sending a bolt of pleasure all the way down to my center. His fingers brushed over my nipples, then pinched them, elongating them into hard peaks that begged for more.

And he gave them more. He raised my shirt, yanked my lace bra down, freeing my breasts, and took first one, then the other into his mouth.

"Carter." I arched my back, beginning to pant.

Everything within me burned. I'd never felt this way. Never.

His tongue circled my nipple, then rewarded it with a slow lick, while his fingers played with the other. I rocked my hips, needing him to fill that empty space inside me. I'd never wanted anyone before the way I wanted Carter. I'd never wanted to sleep with anyone but Carter.

"You have no idea how often I've imagined doing this to you. Too often," he said.

"I imagined it too."

He grunted and dug his fingers into my ass as he sat on his haunches, positioning me across his lap. He mashed his erection against me.

He groaned. "Tell me this feels as good to you as it feels to me."

I closed my eyes, biting my lip. "It feels amazing."

He tightened his grip on my ass and started grinding me against him. It felt as if there were no clothes separating us, and the friction quickly built pleasure inside me. His lips moved over my jaw, leaving frantic little kisses that sent fire through my veins. I tilted my head to allow his mouth access to my neck and moaned when he sucked the spot that was the most sensitive, right at the juncture of my neck and shoulder. The mix of sensations was almost too much.

He ground harder against me, moving faster and faster. My mind went totally blank as my body surrendered to ecstasy, and then . . . then I combusted into flames, crying out his name with a need stronger than anything. This was his own undoing, and he unzipped his jeans in one motion, yanked a spare shirt out of his backpack he'd dropped by the couch, and finished into it.

He tucked himself in. I thought now that the moment was over, he would pull away from me, but he drew me to him and laid us down, spooning me. His arms wrapped around my waist.

For a minute, I could only revel in what we'd just done and how good it had felt. How good it felt to feel his body like this next to mine. We fit so well together.

What was going on between us?

"Carter, contrary to what you've been claiming, I'm not the kind of girl to do this with just anyone."

"I know."

The certainty in his answer had me silent for several moments.

"Then what does this mean for us? Where do we stand?"

I could feel his gaze on me, and I shifted to look at him. A soft smile played on his lips.

"It means we're together. No more masks. No more running away."

"Just like that?"

He grinned this time. "Just like that."

And *just like that*, everything felt right. As if we were right where we were supposed to be. Like we'd finally found each other after a lifetime of darkness.

We were found the next morning. The rest of the trip passed in a blur of people fussing over us, long talks with the rescue team and police, and phone calls with our parents. We didn't have a minute when we weren't surrounded by other people, answering their endless questions.

But none of that mattered because we were now together.

And it felt as though it was just the beginning of the love story of our lives.

CHAPTER TWENTY-ONE

Present

THERE WERE ONLY THREE WEEKS LEFT UNTIL THE START OF the basketball season, and the whole school was pumped-up for it. We'd quickly reinforced our reputation from last year, having won both exhibition games this week, and the atmosphere on the team had improved greatly. Their teamwork was up to scratch, and they were confident they'd be going to the finals.

Everyone wanted a piece of Carter, and I kept seeing posts on social media about Carter hanging out with different people at various places, partying like there was no tomorrow. After that night in the fun house, Carter made it a point to be as far away from me as possible, and at home, he pretended I didn't exist.

In a way, his ignoring me made it easier for me to keep my distance from him, but my feelings were a different story. My heart still beat for him, and at night, I fell asleep to the memories of his heated kisses. He plagued my dreams, in which he was the old Carter, and I hated the moment when I had to wake up and embrace the harsh reality.

It didn't help that not only did I have to see him at home and school, but we also for the most part had practices at the same time. Today was the worst, because he and Nora spent all our breaks on the bleachers, watching videos together on his phone and laughing, and it took everything within me not to stare at them like some pathetic fool.

The cheer squad finished practice a few minutes after the basketball team, and we all headed out to the parking lot together. The guys were joking and flirting with us, and even promised they would win the next game for us. All conversations halted as two pickup trucks rolled up in front of us and a group of guys from East Creek High piled out of the beds of the trucks, with Brandon as the clear ringleader.

The whole basketball team stopped, some of them crossing their arms over their chest and assuming a wide stance.

Carter looked between the guys on his team with furrowed brows, then at Brandon and his guys, and it dawned on me that he didn't know who they were. Carter and Brandon had only met last year, when we played an away game against East Creek High. They had taken an instant dislike to each other.

I glanced at Nora. She'd paled, her gaze darting between Carter and Brandon. Kim pulled out her phone and began filming.

"Reese!" Brandon wore his signature creepy smile. "I hear you're making waves."

Carter flexed his jaw, folding his arms over his chest.

"What's with that face? Is that any way to greet your old buddy?"

Carter frowned, as if not sure whether Brandon was really his old friend. He looked at Dawson, and Dawson shook his head, telling him something I couldn't hear from where I stood. Carter's face darkened.

Brandon laughed before Carter could say anything. "Ah, right. You don't remember me. How rude of me." He *tsk*ed and flicked an invisible speck from his shoulder.

Carter's whole body tensed as he stepped forward. "What do you want?"

"Just checking out our competition. You were lucky last year, but you won't be so lucky this time."

"Only if you finally learned how to play ball," Strider said, a taunting smirk accompanying his statement. "Your team was pathetic last year."

Brandon's fake smile dropped. He moved in on Strider, but Carter blocked him, getting into his face. "Where do you think you're going?"

Nora rushed to them. "Enough!"

Brandon jerked his head toward her, and his eyes widened. They sharpened with fury as she stepped between them with wide arms to shield Carter.

"Leave Carter alone."

Brandon was still for a long moment. He didn't even seem to breathe. The air was tight with tension, so tight I was afraid even the slightest move from any of them would result in a brutal fight.

I could see the moment everything clicked in Brandon's head—when he became aware there was something between Nora and Carter. The air around him thickened with danger.

He bent down to get in her face. "You're with *him* now?" he hissed.

Carter pushed Nora behind him and kept her there with his arm in front of her. "Talk to her like that again, and you'll leave here on a stretcher."

I knew I shouldn't be jealous of him defending Nora (anyone decent would protect a girl in danger), but I couldn't help it. My jealousy festered when she looked at him with eyes full of gratitude, as if he were her knight in shining armor.

Brandon raised his gaze to the sky and ran his hand through his hair, spinning away on his heel. He looked unhinged. He paced a couple steps back and forth before he saw me, and his expression changed at once. A calculated smile twisted his lips.

"And look who we have here. Your bitch." He addressed Carter, but he never took his eyes off me as he crossed to where I stood. He raked his eyes over my body, and I felt like shivering with disgust. I didn't know what Nora had seen in this guy, because each time I looked at him I only felt revulsion.

He stopped a step too close to me, and I had to fight the urge to take at least ten steps back. "Who needs those two, right? Why don't you come with me? You'll have the time of your life with me."

"If getting the creeps is your definition of the time of my life, I'll pass."

He bared his teeth, and before I knew what was happening, he shoved me to the ground. As I fell, I scraped my knees against the rough pavement, and I cried out at the sharp pain.

"Zoe," Jacob bellowed.

Brandon bent and grabbed the collar of my uniform, holding his cupped hand to his ear. "What did you just say, bitch?"

Jacob bolted toward us, but Carter was faster. He pounced on Brandon, slamming his fist right into his face. The force of the punch had Brandon crashing to the ground.

"Don't touch her, you son of a bitch!" Carter shouted, his eyes two pits of unrestrained rage. Brandon didn't have time to recover before Carter started kicking him in the ribs, then his stomach, a feral expression on his face, and I could only stare at him in shock.

He looked as though he was going to kill Brandon, kicking him over and over again until Brandon stopped moving on the ground. Wheezing, Brandon struggled up onto all fours and began to crawl away from Carter, and I might've laughed at how pathetic he looked if only I wasn't so surprised by Carter's behavior.

Brandon's friends stepped forward, but Jacob and the other guys from our team joined Carter, outnumbering Brandon and his buddies. Realizing they didn't stand a chance, they started to withdraw.

"Get the fuck off our turf. And if you come here again, we'll kick all your asses," Strider snarled at them.

Carter hovered over Brandon, his chest heaving with quick gulps of breath. He pinned him with a glare. "If you touch Zoe again—no, if you even *breathe* in her direction—I'm going to make you regret you were ever born."

My heart lurched in my chest. I was beyond stunned now.

Brandon stumbled when he tried to get up. He managed to get to his feet on his second try. He spat blood on the ground and wiped at his mouth with the back of his hand.

"This is not over, Reese," he hissed as he backed away.

Carter never took his eyes off Brandon, even as his teammates helped him into the back of one of the trucks before they blazed out of the parking lot.

"Let's get you up," Trisha told me. Along with Amalie, they helped me to my feet. I winced and my knees protested, blood oozing from my scrapes.

"Oh gosh, you're injured," Denise said.

"Just a few scrapes. It's not a big deal."

"Are you sure?" Jacob asked, already by my side.

"Yes. It looks serious, but it's nothing."

Carter finally looked in my direction. His attention shifted to my knees, and a dark look crossed his face. He made a step toward me but then stopped as his gaze flicked to Jacob. His hands fisted. A muscle working in his jaw, he turned around to leave.

"Wait." I made my way to him. Kim was of course filming everything with her phone, so I lowered my voice so only Carter would hear me. "Why did you do that? Why did you protect me?"

His gaze moved between my eyes. "Because I can't let anyone touch you."

What?

He pivoted and went to Nora, and together, they got into her car. Only then, my heart restarted in my chest, having stuttered to a stop at his parting words.

Jenna and Kim looked ecstatic, and I wished I could wipe the smiles off their faces.

"That was pathetic," Kim said to Jenna, *still* filming. Bitch. Not for the first time, I wanted to grab her phone and smash it against the ground so she couldn't film others' private moments anymore.

Jacob placed his hand on my shoulder. "Do you want me to take you to the nurse?"

"No, thanks."

"Can you walk?"

"Yes. Thank you, Jacob."

Nora started her car, and I watched as she and Carter left the parking lot.

"You know, if what just happened with that guy is any indication, Carter obviously still feels something for you," Denise said, noticing me looking after them.

I looked away without saying anything, my chest aching. Even if he did feel something, what was the point? Whatever he felt, it didn't matter when he was always fighting me. Just like two years ago.

It seemed Carter's natural response was to fight me.

I didn't want to analyze what that actually meant. I was sure I wouldn't like the answer.

❁

I winced as I sat down on my bed to bandage my knees. The wounds weren't serious, but it was going to be hard to dance with them. I'd have to avoid dancing for at least a couple days if I wanted them to heal, and I didn't know if I'd be able to do that. These days, dancing was like a drug to me—a much-needed fix to escape my heartbreak. Not to mention that I had to be in good shape for the start of the basketball season.

I was about to apply the last bandage when Carter entered my room unannounced.

"Haven't you ever heard of knocking?"

He came to a halt mid-step when he saw what I was doing. An emotion I couldn't read passed briefly across his face. "Does it hurt?"

"Way less than being treated like shit by you. What are you doing here?"

"I wanted to check on you."

I raised my brows. "What? Don't tell me that you care I was hurt." He looked away, pushing his fisted hands into his pockets. That, along with my frustration at his behavior in the fun house, caused anger to bubble up inside me. "You're unbelievable, Carter. You treat me like shit, then you're nice, then you push me away again, and now you act like you care. You're giving me whiplash."

"You think I'm not giving myself whiplash too?" he snapped.

Jerking my head back, I opened and then closed my mouth.

His gaze drifted over my belongings scattered around the room—the shirt hanging off my chair, the figurines decorating my desk and nightstands, my romance books overflowing from my bookshelves, my dancing portraits and the photos of us on the shelves. His brows scrunched together. My cheeks heated; I didn't want him to use the fact that I still kept our photos as an argument that I was pathetic and hung up on him.

He looked down the length of his nose at me. "Why isn't Jacob here being your nurse?"

My brows arched. "Because he has no business doing so."

"So, you're not together?"

I forced a laugh out, shaking my head. "I know you enjoy jumping to conclusions, but, no, we're not together."

I didn't know what to make of his expression. Was it relief? Surprise? Satisfaction? It only made me more confused and, in turn, angrier.

He combed his fingers through his hair, shifting his weight.

"Jackson and Prescott brought me up to speed about that Mead guy. Has he ever hurt you?"

"You mean other than acting like a jerk like today?"

He nodded.

"Yes. He always used every opportunity to provoke you by messing with me."

"Did I teach him a lesson?"

My lips curled into a brief smile. "Every time. But now we're coming to the million-dollar question—why do you care?"

He looked away. "Because I don't want to hear I've been a wuss these last two years."

"Yeah, right." I stood up and flinched at the sharp pain in my knees.

"Easy." He rushed over to me, grabbing my elbows to help me balance. He made me sit back down.

My heart stuttered when he sank to his knees in front of me. He put his hands on my thighs, his eyes zeroing in on the unbandaged scrape.

"Let me do it."

It felt as if the world stopped as he took the bandage and put it tenderly on the scrape.

I swallowed thickly. I forgot to breathe when he didn't remove his fingers from my skin, leaving them on my knee. Seconds rolled by without either of us moving, and I struggled to take enough air into my lungs. He raised his gaze to look at me, his pupils almost eating up the green of his eyes.

"When I saw Brandon push you earlier, I . . ."

My mouth went dry. "You what?"

"I never wanted to hurt anyone so much in my life." He pressed his fingers into my skin, and I bit the inside of my cheek as my core throbbed in response. My skin was burning under his hand. I wanted that hand to go up, under my skirt, until it reached my most sensitive spot.

As if reading my mind, he moved his hand up a few inches, and I almost let a moan out.

Shit. How could I move on from him when he was always giving me mixed signals? When it was so easy for him to make me want him badly?

I forced the words out. "A strange reaction, considering you don't like me."

He blinked twice. His face hardened, and he removed his hand from my thigh. I mourned the loss of his touch, the lack of it leaving a chill on my skin that went all the way to my center. "Why do you have to be so bitchy?"

I recoiled and raised my brows at him. "Are you really asking me that?"

"Whatever." He straightened up and turned to leave.

But before he left, he looked at me over his shoulder, his hand on the handle. "Make sure to stay away from Mead." Without waiting for my reply, he stepped out and shut the door.

CHAPTER TWENTY-TWO

S INCE I COULDN'T DANCE, I PICKED UP EXTRA SHIFTS AT WORK, drowning my frenzied thoughts in the sea of orders, chatting with customers, and cleaning. It was my way of forgetting the chaos that was Carter and his hot-and-cold behavior. Not that I could forget the look on his face as he revealed how he'd felt when he saw Brandon push me. Or when he touched me so intimately.

Work was supposed to exhaust me, but I got off my shift with extra energy that left me craving an hour of physical activity. I'd just stepped out of Bellezza, planning to head home and hit the gym, when my gaze landed on Brandon, leaning against the tree across the road.

A cigarette hung from his mouth, its smoke twirling upward. A nasty bruise had formed where Carter had punched him, and it added to his menacing look. He didn't take his eyes off me.

What the hell was he doing here?

After that scene in the parking lot, it didn't take long for Kim and Jenna to dig up Nora's past. The details of her relationship with Brandon came to light, shifting the spotlight from me to Nora for a change.

Nora had gone to East Creek High too. She'd been dating Brandon for a year when things started spiraling between them, until finally their relationship came to an ugly end. He'd turned out to be easily angered and violent, and, yes, he'd raised his hand to Nora several times, until she decided to leave him. At that time, she got the scholarship at Silver Raven Academy, which was a way for her to put distance between them. This explained their encounter in the hallway.

Brandon obviously had a lot of issues, and I wasn't sure he had any boundaries. A shiver coursed through me the moment I turned my back on him as I made my way to my car. I increased my pace just in case, expecting him to come after me, but when I unlocked my car and looked over my shoulder, I saw he hadn't moved away from the tree. He hadn't moved his gaze away from me either.

Slamming my car door and stepping on the gas, I tore out of the parking lot. A look in the rearview mirror confirmed he was still watching me, all the way until I turned the corner.

Maybe he was just waiting to meet someone. Yes, maybe it was a coincidence that he was there.

I didn't want to consider any other alternative.

"So, you don't want a wedding rehearsal or a rehearsal dinner?" the wedding planner, Mrs. Gibson, asked, straightening her glasses on her nose. She wore a black suit and a bun, not a single strand of hair or piece of clothing out of place.

She'd been in our living room for over an hour, discussing everything from the arrangement of flowers to the wedding cake. She had an assistant with her, who was diligently taking notes, her fingers flying over her tablet as she tried to put all the details down.

I'd been sitting on the windowsill listening to them the whole time as a way of distracting myself from the fact that Carter was currently in the backyard chilling with Nora. Their laughter filtered inside every once in a while, and I had to take deep breaths so that the pain in my chest would ease up.

"No, since it's a small wedding, we want things to be simple," Dominic said.

Mrs. Gibson's assistant took a note.

"And have you finally decided on the venue?" Mrs. Gibson looked between Mom and Dominic over the rims of her leopard boho glasses, her face expressionless, but the tone of her voice said plenty. Since they had been undecided on the location, Mrs. Gibson had sent them a list of popular venues in town, and while they had narrowed down their options, they still hadn't made their choice. Mrs. Gibson clearly wasn't happy about it.

"We've talked about a few," Dominic answered.

"Mr. Reese, I'm afraid we have to decide on the venue right now. I've put in some calls, and they're waiting for you, but they can't hold a spot for much longer."

"There's one place," Mom said meekly. She wrung her hands together.

Her head was tilted down, and at that angle, the outdoor light shone directly across her cheekbones, exposing the pale color of her skin and deep under-eye circles. I'd thought she'd muster more enthusiasm as we got closer to the wedding, but it looked as though the opposite was happening. She was supposed to be the happiest bride there was.

Dominic took one of her hands into his own. "Yes, darling, anything you want."

"The hilltop hotel, where you took me on our first date. With its breathtaking view of Pine Hills."

Dominic's face lighted up with a big smile. "That's an amazing idea—"

"No fucking way."

We all whipped our heads toward the voice, and my heart

lurched. Carter was gripping the doorjamb, his face twisted into an expression of pure rage.

"You're not going to get married there."

Dominic's forehead creased in a deep frown. "Carter, stay out of this."

"I didn't say a word as I watched you go about this wedding as if it's the most important fucking thing in the world. But I refuse to let your slut steal another thing from my mom."

"Carter!" Dominic erupted, rushing to his feet.

Mrs. Gibson's gaze bounced around the room. Mom looked as though she wanted to disappear into thin air.

Dominic marched over to Carter. "Apologize right now!"

"I will not apologize! That place was special for my mom." He snarled at Mom, "It's where she fell for Dad, and you knew that. And now you're going to take that away too. What, her husband and house weren't enough? You want her special places too?"

Mom whimpered, pressing one shaking hand against her stomach and the other against her mouth. "It's not like that."

I stood up, anger blazing its way through me. Mom was already feeling guilty enough, walking on eggshells around him. On top of that, she was pregnant.

"Stop talking to her like that! She's fucking pregnant! You better stop saying things that would upset her, or I swear to God, I'll—"

Carter shifted his sneer to me. "You'll what? You can't do shit to me."

Dominic raised his hand and slapped Carter with a force that had him slumping against the wall.

We all gasped. Mrs. Gibson's eyes had gone wide.

Mom hoisted herself up. "Dominic, no," she whispered.

Carter glared at Dominic with a sickening amount of hatred as he pulled himself up, breathing loudly through his nose. "That was the last time you'll ever raise your hand to me." He lunged at Dominic, using his hands to shove him to the ground.

"Carter!" Mom and I both shouted. We rushed to their sides as Carter moved to sit on top of Dominic, his fist at the ready.

"Stop!" I wound my arms around his neck from behind and pulled.

"Don't do this, Carter," Mom pleaded, crouching next to Dominic. She shielded him with her arm.

"Get the hell away from him!" I yanked Carter harder, and I almost collapsed when he stopped resisting suddenly, letting me pull him back.

Dominic was breathing heavily, observing Carter with wide eyes. There was shock and disappointment in them, and it stung seeing Dominic look at his son that way. The line had been crossed, and I was afraid this could never be forgiven.

Mom helped Dominic get to his feet, and he gave her hand a tight squeeze before he faced Carter. There was a look on his face that was so similar to Carter's whenever he pulled his barrier up, and now I knew who Carter had gotten that look from.

"You'd hit your own father?" Dominic asked him incredulously.

Carter climbed to his feet, wrenching himself out of my reach. "Are you still my father? Or did you stop being that the day you turned your back on me and Mom? When you brought this woman with no shame or conscience into our lives?"

Mom's face lost all color, and she pressed her hand against her chest, her expression stricken.

"Carter, please, don't say that—" she murmured.

And then she dropped unconscious to the ground.

The drive to the hospital was a sickening blur. It was a blend of panic, bouts of fear, and confusion as Dominic and I stared at Mom's unconscious body on the stretcher. Countless scenarios played out in my mind, the most dominant being that there was something wrong with the baby. Mom hadn't looked good lately, but now, with what had happened with Carter . . . I was so afraid for her and the baby. What if she miscarried? What if her life was in danger as well?

Dad's face filled my vision, and I closed my eyes, fighting against the fear that I was going to lose Mom too. No, if that happened, I . . . I wouldn't be able to bear it.

Tears pricked my eyes, and before I could suppress them, one slid down my cheek.

I pressed my hand against my mouth. "This is all our fault. We didn't take good enough care of her."

"No, it's all my fault." Dominic's hands balled on his lap. He didn't take his eyes off Mom. "I shouldn't have allowed things to go this far with Carter. I was supposed to take better care of her. I was supposed to protect her. And if something happens to the baby—"

I covered his hand with mine, swallowing past the lump of fear in my throat. "It won't. She has to be okay. She has to."

He didn't say anything, and that only increased the fear pumping through my veins. He looked lost in his own world, his eyes red-rimmed and filled with concern and anxiety, as we arrived at the hospital and then waited for the doctor to come out of Mom's room.

I supported myself against a wall, staring at the poster across from us that described the importance of ultrasounds and regular preventive checkups. I was angry at myself for being too obsessed with Carter and getting back with him to think about Mom and the baby. I should've made sure she worked less and focused on herself and her well-being. I should've done something more, something other than pining stupidly for Carter.

My chest tightened with rage when I thought about his words, the look in his eyes as he spurted all those insults. To see the guy I loved so much be so cruel, so relentless in his hate . . . it was so painful.

If anything happens to Mom or the baby, I'll never forgive him.

The doctor came out of Mom's room shortly after, and we both rushed toward him.

"How is she?" Dominic asked before I could.

"And the baby?" I added.

"She's awake and well. The baby is fine."

Immense relief shot through me, and I felt as though my legs would go out from under me. *They're okay.*

"What caused her to pass out?" Dominic asked.

"We're going to run more tests, but based on our initial examination, she collapsed because she's anemic."

"Anemic?" Dominic asked.

"Yes. Has she complained of exhaustion or weakness recently?"

"She mentioned she tired easily, but we chalked it up to the pregnancy," Dominic said.

"She's looked tired lately," I said. "I told her not to work that much, but she didn't listen."

Dominic rubbed the spot between his brows. "I knew it was too much for her."

The doctor nodded. "Yes, she needs to slow down. Has she been anemic before?"

"Not that I'm aware of." Dominic raised his brows at me. "Zoe?"

"No. She never had anemia before."

"Iron-deficiency is not unusual during pregnancy. Now that she's carrying a child, both she and the baby need more iron, so you'll need to make sure she gets enough from now on. Otherwise, you're risking premature birth or low birth weight."

Dominic nodded, relief written all over his face. "We'll do that."

"I'll keep her under observation overnight, until all the test results come back."

"Can we see her?" I asked.

The doctor nodded. "Yes, of course. You can go inside now."

I hurried into the single-unit room. Dominic had specified when we arrived that Mom was supposed to receive the best care, and the hospital had obviously complied. The room was nothing like a regular hospital room. It was sparkling clean, bright with floor-to-ceiling windows, and adorned with plants occupying all the corners. A flatscreen TV and high-tech machines surrounded her sturdy hospital bed. There was no sickening smell of antiseptic in the air, only an air freshener.

Guilt squeezed my heart when I saw her in the hospital bed. She was even paler now, and the blue-dotted white hospital robe she wore swallowed her thin frame. I cursed myself for being so negligent.

"I'm okay," was the first thing she said, smiling at me.

I smiled back at her. "I know. I think you'll be ready to climb the Himalayas any day now."

She laughed, then opened her arms to hug Dominic as he leaned over to kiss her. The intensity of their kiss showed exactly how much he'd been worried for her.

He pulled away, and she reached for me. I rushed into her open arms, wanting to bury my head into her neck the way I'd done as a kid.

"I'm sorry, Mom. I'm so sorry."

"What do you have to be sorry for?"

I hugged her tighter, fresh tears pouring down my face. "We were supposed to take better care of you. I should've seen there was something wrong."

She put her hands on my face and made me look at her. "Honey, that's not your fault at all. It's all mine. Both of you told me to slow down, but I didn't."

I shook my head. "No, don't say that."

"It's alright, honey. It really is." She wiped the tears off my face one by one with her thumbs, and my heart constricted. I couldn't lose her. I was going to make sure she was healthy 100 percent from now on.

Dominic reached for her hand, taking a seat by her side. "How are you feeling now?"

"Definitely better after the IV." She motioned at the cannula plastered to her elbow crease. My chest throbbed, because I hated looking at cannulas and also because Mom was afraid of needles.

"Doctor Patal will keep you overnight," Dominic said. "But once we get home, we'll make sure you get enough rest. You don't have to come to work until you get better."

Mom's face screwed up. "I'm sorry, darling. I was supposed to take better care of myself."

"No, don't say that." He brought his lips to her hand. "It's not your fault."

"It is. I shouldn't have been so irresponsible."

"It doesn't matter now. From now on, we're going to do better."

She nodded, biting her lip. "We have to." Her eyes started to close.

"You need some rest. We'll leave you to it, okay?"

"Okay."

"I'm going to grab some coffee and then I'll be right back."

Her lips twitched with a smile, her eyes remaining closed. "I'll be here."

Dominic and I quietly walked out, and he closed the door behind us. I was about to take a seat in a chair across from her room, but Dominic put a hand on my shoulder.

"You should go home. I'll stay with Erika."

"No, I want to stay with her too."

"You have schoolwork to do. There's no need for you to stay here the whole day."

"But—"

"No *buts*. As you can see, it isn't anything serious, so don't worry. I'm going to come home later to grab her an overnight bag. You can pack it for her, okay?"

I couldn't argue with that. "Okay. I'll do that."

I moved to leave, but then I turned to look at him. "We can't allow this to happen again. I'm afraid that if she's exposed to more stress, the next time . . . the next time, she—"

"Shh." He reached for me and hugged me. I leaned my head against his shoulder, gripping the back of his jacket. "It's going to be okay."

"How? You've seen Carter. He won't stop."

His whole posture stiffened for a second, and I was afraid of what he was going to say next.

But all he said was, "You better go home now. And don't worry about a thing."

As if it were that easy.

CHAPTER TWENTY-THREE

DARK CLOUDS CONVERGED ACROSS THE SKY AS I HEADED home, and it matched my headspace. I couldn't stop thinking about the sound of ambulance sirens and the image of Mom's unconscious form.

As I'd rushed across the room toward her, willing her to move, to open her eyes as though nothing had happened, I had the feeling of déjà-vu. It was exactly like when Dad died, when he had a heart attack and crashed to the ground right in our living room. Mom had been frantic, trying to rouse him, but he never woke again. That quickly.

I was terrified of it happening again. She was the only parent I had left.

I was so deep in thought, the Uber driver had to tell me twice we'd arrived at the house. I dragged myself out of the car and made the short walk to the front door. The first splatters of rain fell on my head and shoulders. Nora's purple Audi was still in the driveway, and the anger I'd felt at Carter earlier returned with full force.

As I approached the front door, it opened, and Carter and Nora stepped outside. They were smiling at each other.

My lungs expanded around a quick intake of air. He could smile after what had just happened?

And *that*, combined with Mom's blackout, made me lose it.

His smile dropped when he spotted me. I marched past them and inside the house, not giving them a single look.

"Zoe," he called after me. "Zoe, hold on."

I paid him no attention. I'd reached the second-floor landing when I heard Nora's car pulling out of our driveway and leaving. Tears flooded my eyes and spilled out as I continued up to the attic. Opening the door, I yanked off my jacket and dropped it to the floor.

I hadn't heard Carter following me, so when footsteps shuffled behind me, I twisted around to look at him with my heart in my throat.

"What are you doing here? Get out!"

He wasn't looking at me. His gaze shifted around the attic, his eyes widening with surprise. He observed every piece of memorabilia that was ours—our photos together taped on the angled ceiling, the TV and the movies piled around it, his basketball jersey still hanging off the beanbag hammock. His architectural book faceup on the carpet. His whiteboard.

"Didn't you hear me? I need to be alone. Go away."

His eyes were brimming with an emotion I couldn't read when they shifted to me. "I won't leave you alone when you're not okay."

Anger accumulated in my chest until it bubbled over. "You don't give a shit about me, Carter, so don't pretend you do! I don't want you here, so get out."

"How are your mom and the baby?"

"You don't give a shit about them either! Now, leave!"

"I won't fucking leave until you tell me they're okay!"

"They're fine! She's anemic, that's all. Though I doubt you're happy about it because you'd like nothing more than to see her gone."

"That's fucking bullshit."

"Is it? 'The intruder' would be getting what's coming to her. You'd finally get your justice."

He got in my face. "I said, that's bullshit. No, I can't stand her, and I'd rather never see her again, but I'm not a monster. I don't want her or her baby to die."

"Then why don't you pay attention to what you fucking say? She could've lost her baby because of you!"

He winced; his nostrils widened around a frantic, loud intake of breath and he looked away. There was anger on his face, but also confusion and sadness—sadness so deep it slashed into my already battered heart. "I . . . I didn't intend for that to happen."

"Oh, yeah? Well, *think*, Carter. Your actions have consequences! She's in a fragile condition, and if you keep treating her the way you did today . . ." I squeezed my eyes shut. I shook my head. "Do us both a favor and leave me alone already!"

"I'm not going to leave you alone right now, so stop asking." He motioned with his head around us. "What's all of this?"

I dug my nails into my palms to the point of hurting myself. "Just leave, Carter. *Please.*"

He took another step in. "What's all of this?" he repeated in a harder tone.

"It doesn't matter."

"What. Is. All. Of. This?"

"Us!" I screamed, having had enough of him. "This place is us! The place where we used to spend most of our time. We used to talk to each other for hours here, discussing our dreams, desires, memories. Everything and nothing. That whiteboard over there"—I pointed at it—"you used to plan your buildings for contests on it. You wanted to focus on affordable housing so low-income families would be able to get quality housing without having to pay for it through their teeth! We used to watch movies there"—I pointed in the direction of the TV—"and we often argued whether we would watch dance movies or horror movies, your favorite. And there . . ." My finger pointed at the carpet in the center. "You took my virginity there."

I hadn't realized that, while I was talking, he'd been advancing on me until I was almost pressed against the wall. His eyes burned with raw intensity, looking at me the same way they had looked at me before his amnesia. With desire that had no limits—desire that matched my own. They were burning ever so intensely, and it became difficult for me to breathe.

"And this wall?" he asked in a hoarse voice, motioning at the wall behind me as he caged me against it. "Did we do anything against this wall?"

My heart was a thundering mess. I swallowed hard and shook my head.

"Then how about we fix that now?"

His lips crashed onto mine, cutting off any response I might've made. His hands were all over me, moving with a need that was so like the old Carter, but also not. It was thrilling—the heady mixture of the familiar and the new, which was his potent urgency, his uncontrollable desire.

But this shouldn't be happening.

I slammed my hands against his shoulders, trying to push him away. "Don't do this."

"Why not? You want it."

My heart wanted to jump out of my chest. "I don't want it."

"Then why did you kiss me back just now?"

As if to prove it, he returned his lips to mine and opened my mouth to his. The moment his tongue connected with mine, I knew I was lost and wouldn't be able to resist him.

I grasped his shoulders and dug my nails into them as hard as I could, punishing him for making me this weak. He dragged his lips to the side and nibbled along my jawline.

"You want this as much as I do," he rasped out, taunting me. Bastard.

"I hate you."

"You don't hate me."

"You hate me."

His eyes grew intense as he pulled away to look me directly in the eyes. "I don't hate you."

He brought my arm up beside my head, so that our tattoos met perfectly. His gaze lingered on them before he did something that caused all the breath to surge out of my lungs—he pressed an open-mouthed kiss to my tattoo, right on his special spot.

Just like before. He was doing the same thing . . . there was another piece of my Carter in him.

My heart filled with a surge of love that threatened to engulf me. Even now it beat for him. Even now it took strength from the love I felt for him.

He locked my arms around his neck, urging me closer to him. I was aware of each inch of his body pressing against mine, of his hard muscles and tight planes. It felt so good having him against my softness. I yanked his hair, partly with need, partly to punish him more.

In response, he seized my bottom lip with his teeth and grabbed my butt, yanking my lower body against his. I moaned.

"We shouldn't do this."

His hands kneaded my ass. "Then stop me."

This was my chance to end this insanity. I should end it right now. But I'd been away from him for too long. This felt like bursting through the surface to gulp a breath of air after minutes of drowning in the water. And after the emotional turmoil of this day, I couldn't handle him not holding me.

"No." I breathed him in. "Make me forget." I pressed a hard kiss to his lips. "Make me forget why this is wrong."

"Anything you want, baby."

He slid his mouth to my throat and licked all over my throbbing artery. I released a loud moan. His hands went to the hem of my shirt and took it off in one jerky move, leaving me in my bra. He drew away to look at my breasts, and the look of desire in his eyes made my center pulse hotly. He buried his head between them like he was starving for them, mashing them together with his hands. He groaned, and I felt myself pulsing harder.

He pulled one cup down and brushed his thumb over my nipple. I arched my back, grabbing his sleeve. *Yes.*

This. This was what I'd needed all along. I'd missed his touch so much. I'd missed this rush of pleasure deep inside me. I'd missed the way he watched me unravel in front of him. Only this time, it was more intense, because he was looking at me as though we were being intimate for the first time, thrill and anticipation converging with desire in his gaze.

He unclasped my bra and tossed it to the ground, wrapping his lips around my nipple. I almost shattered with pleasure. His hand slid to the zipper of my jeans and unzipped it with an urgency that had me pushing myself against his hand. He shoved it inside my panties and palmed me.

"Carter," I moaned. His fingers moved right over the spot that throbbed for him. "That's . . ."

"Tell me. That's what?"

"That's so good."

"Yeah? Let's make it better."

He dropped to his knees. I watched him with wide eyes as he yanked my jeans down along with my panties.

He smirked, looking up at me with dark, hooded eyes. "You're wet."

With that, his mouth covered me, and it was all I could do not to collapse. I grabbed his head, and he hooked my leg over his shoulder, exposing me fully to him. He growled, sending vibrations deep into me along with his tongue.

He brought his thumb to my swollen nub and started stroking it in tiny circles. Pleasure robbed me of all coherent thought and built quickly, until it overloaded my senses. I couldn't stop moving my hips against him. Before I knew it, I soared, moaning loudly and convulsing as the waves of my orgasm hit me.

He didn't wait for me to recover. He got to his feet and pulled his sweatpants and underwear down, revealing his long length.

"Condoms are there." I pointed at the drawer in the corner.

He retrieved a condom and sheathed himself in just a few

seconds, keeping his eyes on mine the whole time. I kicked my jeans and panties aside. He picked me up, coaxing my legs to wrap around his strong torso. This was our favorite position, and I almost smiled because it was how he wanted us to do this now.

I was so ready for him, and he slid inside of me in one quick, slick move. Pleasure burst through my center, tearing a moan from my mouth. He was finally filling the void inside me that had always needed him. He was finally making me complete.

"Zoe," he moaned, his eyes widening, never looking away from me. He was devouring me with his gaze, looking at me as if he was seeing all of me—like he could feel just how special this was. Like he could feel our connection.

"This is . . . fuck. It feels so good." He pulled out until only his tip remained inside of me, then rammed back into me.

"Carter!" I screamed, digging my nails into his shoulders.

"So fucking good."

He tilted me so he could go even deeper, and I could feel him everywhere. He drew out and thrust back in, eliciting another scream from me. He groaned. His thrusts became harder, setting my nerves afire with pleasure. It had never felt so good before. I didn't know whether it was desperation, or it was because this felt like it was our first time, but I knew this differed from all our previous times.

Our lips clashed together, and we tasted each other with urgent need that left us wanting more. We moaned into each other's mouths, our bodies meeting in a frenzy as his hands guided me on him faster and faster.

"Carter! Yes, just like that . . . Carter, I missed you. I missed you so much."

At this, he pumped into me even harder, and it was all I needed to come again. I called his name as the pleasure blinded me, which only spurred him on. He didn't stop, going faster, prolonging my pleasure until nothing else existed, until he, too, went over the edge, emptying himself deep inside me.

More love surged through me and guided my arms to tighten

around him. I left a kiss on his cheek, feeling more sated and calmer than ever.

Shuddering, he pressed me closer to him. He didn't let go of me, instead just breathing me in, and I laid my forehead against his. I closed my eyes.

As our breathing slowed, reality returned piece by piece, and that sated feeling started seeping out of me. I knew that whatever had just happened between us was over. Haunting memories and pain returned full force as I opened my eyes.

I felt sick.

How had it come to this? All our smiles and perfect moments? How had we reached this disharmony?

He drew himself out of me and lowered me down.

I reached for my panties and jeans, rushing to get them on. "I think you should leave."

He raised his eyes to look at me as he pulled his underwear and sweatpants back up, his forehead creasing. "Do you regret this?"

"What do you think, Carter?"

He just stared at me, and I saw various emotions warring for dominance on his face. Pain, anger, confusion. With each passing second, I felt more off balance, and I couldn't take him looking at me any longer.

So, instead, I picked up the last of my things and left.

CHAPTER TWENTY-FOUR

FTER THAT, I MADE SURE TO AVOID HIM. I SPENT THE ENTIRE evening in my room, more than aware that he was also in his room, and I held my breath each time I went downstairs to the kitchen, expecting him to show up.

In the morning I opted for a run around the estate instead of the gym because he was working out in there. Running and the music in my earbuds proved to be a feeble diversion because my mind refused to give up on the images of our entangled bodies or the sensation of him inside me. Or the pleasure that provided me with the much-needed abandon. Or him saying he didn't hate me.

Even my dreams contained him. I'd dreamed of us in that cabin when we got lost, but this time, we went all the way, with me chanting his name as he finally entered me—as he finally showed me what it felt like to be *one* with someone, no boundaries or insecurities between us. In the dream, I remembered exactly how it had felt knowing he was my forever. It had felt so real that I woke up with tears on my pillow, and even after I exhausted myself with running, I couldn't quell the urge to cry.

What made things worse was knowing that the sex hadn't meant anything more to him than a means of physical release.

Of getting rid of the pent-up angst accumulating between us all this time. But for me, it had meant everything, and what hurt the most was knowing it amounted to nothing in the end. It had only added another scar on top of ones he'd already made, and I hated myself for allowing him to make that cut. And if I didn't already have enough reasons to regret it—I felt like I'd betrayed Mom by giving in to him.

The sound of Dominic's car in our driveway broke through my dark thoughts. They were here.

I bolted outside and into Mom's hug. "Mom!"

Her lips widened into a smile as she wrapped her arms around me. She placed a kiss on my forehead. "Sweetie."

"How are you feeling? Are you tired?"

"You asked me that already when you called this morning. I'm fine. It felt like I went to a spa instead the hospital with the kind of treatment I received."

She did look better, with no under-eye bags for a change. Her cheeks had color, and her eyes were glowing.

Dominic grinned, putting Mom's arm around his. "Wait until you see what Mrs. Hopper made for you."

I giggled. "Yeah, she couldn't decide between two dishes, so she made four."

Mom shook her head with a smile. "Should I be worried about gaining too much weight?"

I rubbed her stomach. "We need to make sure my lil' sis or bro gets enough food. They're going to be one healthy, big baby by the time they're born."

Mom chuckled. "That doesn't mean I should become a walrus."

I laughed but trailed off when I caught Carter watching us through the living room window. His face was blank, so I couldn't tell what he was thinking.

Warmth spread through my chest and face. I couldn't stop my brain from taking me back to what had happened in the attic. I hoped I didn't look as red as I felt.

Abruptly, he turned and moved out of sight.

My insides knotted as we entered the house. I looked to the living room, waiting for Carter to appear, but he never did, and I didn't know whether I felt relieved or disappointed, because for some reason, I'd hoped he'd at least come to apologize to Mom.

"Wait until you see the big surprise," Dominic told Mom, sharing a smile with me as we climbed upstairs. We were both excited to see Mom's reaction when she saw their bedroom.

Dominic had bought a thousand roses for her, and they now occupied all the available surfaces around their bedroom. I'd blown up balloons with a "Get well" message and tied them to the chairs, nightstands, and her vanity table. A basket of fruits sat on the end table.

Mom's face lit with happiness as she stepped in, and she released Dominic.

"You didn't have to," she told him.

"That's nothing. You deserve so much more."

"He's right, Mom. Only the royal treatment for you from now on."

She went to the bouquet on the nightstand and bent to smell them.

"Roses. My favorite."

"And here's another favorite for you." I pulled a bag from behind the armchair and handed it to her.

She looked inside and found the latest book by one of her favorite authors, a gift I'd purchased earlier. Her lips parted, then curved into a shining smile. "Oh, honey. You didn't have to," she repeated as she studied the cover. She put the book back into the bag and pulled me into her warm embrace. I inhaled her motherly, cinnamon scent and instantly felt reassured.

"Now that you're going to rest more, you'll need something to fill your time," I said.

She chuckled, sitting down on the edge of the bed. "That will do."

"I'll go talk to Mrs. Hopper about your meals. I'll make sure she prepares them with all the ingredients you need," Dominic said and left the room.

Mom giggled, shaking her head. "He can be too protective sometimes."

I sat next to her. "He's right. We need to do better from now on. You and the baby are what's most important now."

She gave me a nod and caressed her stomach. "Dr. Patal prescribed me meds, and we're going to do more checkups from now on." She placed her hand on my cheek. "I'm also worried about you. You were frightened, weren't you?"

I lowered my gaze. "When I saw you faint . . . I was afraid of the worst."

She sighed. "Oh, sweetie." She pushed a strand of my hair off my face, then caressed my forehead. "I'm so sorry for worrying you."

"No, don't say that. There's nothing to be sorry for. I just don't want to lose you, you know?" I felt as though I might start crying, and I had to take deep breaths so she wouldn't see just how upset I really was.

"You won't lose me. I promise you that." She wrapped her fingers around my hand. "Everything is going to be alright."

I nodded, staring at her engagement ring that glittered in the daylight.

"How's Carter?"

I dipped my chin to my chest. "He was downstairs when you arrived, but as you can see, he's avoiding you. Supposedly, he didn't want to upset you, but if that's true, he should at least have the guts to come here and apologize."

She exhaled a long breath and rubbed her ring absentmindedly. "We really should postpone the wedding."

I shot her a panicked look. "No. Absolutely not."

"But how can we go through with it when it's this bad?"

"Mom, please. How much longer will you postpone your happiness? How much longer until you start living your life?"

She gnawed at her lip, her eyes cutting down. "That's the thing. I'm not that selfless. In truth, I'm selfish."

My stomach stirred with something I didn't want to acknowledge. I grabbed her hand. "You're not. So, stop thinking that way and just enjoy yourself. I want that day to be the best day of your life. Okay?"

She gave me a tight-lipped smile and stood up. "I think I'll go take a shower. Let's talk later."

"Okay. I'll see you later, then."

I kissed her cheek and went downstairs. The look on her face when I left her knotted something inside me, and it frustrated me that I couldn't help her.

"We can't go on like this anymore," I heard Dominic say. I halted.

The door of Dominic's office was ajar, and I tiptoed to it to peer inside. Carter was sitting in the chair across from Dominic's desk. Dominic was standing with his back to him, looking out the window.

"I didn't mean for it to happen." Carter's voice was level, but for a moment there, I thought I caught a trace of remorse.

"That doesn't matter. Maybe I can forgive you for raising your hand at me, but—"

Carter slammed his hand against Dominic's desk. "You hit me!"

"*But,*" Dominic continued as though there'd been no interruption. "I'll never forgive you for putting the baby at risk."

Carter went still, and I could swear he made a choking sound.

"I've been trying to reason with you all this time. I've been giving you so many chances, but I see now I've been too lenient with you."

From where I stood, I could see Carter's face clearly, so when the look of hurt crossed his face before he cloaked it with another mask of cold indifference, I felt the earlier knot inside me tighten.

He gave a bitter smile. "So, what are you going to do? Give

me a curfew? Take my phone away? Make me stay in my room
for days?"

"No, Carter. If you act like that in her presence again, I'm
going to have you move out."

It felt as though time stopped. The only sound I could hear
was the frantic beating of my own heart, and I looked at my fingers clutching the door. They were white.

"You can't do that." This time there was no mistaking the
pain in his voice.

"I can, Carter. Until you're eighteen, I'm responsible for you,
and I'll even send you out of state if I have to."

I squeezed my eyes closed tightly.

"You can't be serious."

I bit the inside of my cheek at the amount of pain in his words.
The betrayal and loneliness he must feel. The realization that he
didn't have anyone by his side. And although he'd made his bed, I
didn't want this for him.

"I'm very serious. It hurts me to say it, but I will do it if you
step over the line one more time. So, think carefully about what
you're going to do from now on."

The room went so silent you could hear a pin drop. I didn't
breathe as I waited for Carter's reply.

"I hate you," Carter gritted out through his teeth, and I winced
at the force of his sentiment.

No, don't say that. My heart split open. I feared we'd reached
the point of no return.

"You don't know what you're saying," Dominic said.

I couldn't listen to this anymore. I raced up the stairs and to
the attic, slamming the door shut behind me. I didn't see how this
family would ever recover from this.

His relationship with my mom had improved once. How was
it possible that it couldn't improve now? Were his lost memories
that integral for their relationship? Had his memory loss shaped
him into a version of himself who could never get close to Mom?

Had his memory loss shaped him into a person who would always be ruled by hate?

I slid down the door to the floor and wrapped my arms around my knees. I didn't get up for a long time.

"You and Carter had sex?" Summer asked, her eyes wide. The opening credits of *Shall We Dance* were paused on the screen.

As soon as I called her and told her about Mom fainting and yesterday's argument between Carter and Dominic, she'd dropped everything and came over to my house. She brought two packs of gummy bears—my only comfort food—and two packs of Lay's chips—her comfort food. We talked about Mom's life as a single mother and everything she had to go through now because of Carter as I made us Long Island iced teas and popcorn.

We'd settled into the sectional sofa in the living room for a movie marathon, but it was then that I'd heard Carter welcome Prescott and Jackson, and their loud voices and laughter had drifted down the hall from the game room ever since. It was distracting, but what was even more distracting was waiting to see Carter. Each time I heard him, something tightened more in my stomach, and I felt as though I would explode with need, never mind that I was trying to move on.

"Yes," I replied to Summer's question and glanced at the doorway, holding my breath as I waited to see if he would show up. He didn't. I didn't like how that disappointed me.

"How did it happen?"

I took another sip. "I came home from the hospital, all shaken up. He followed me up to the attic. We argued, and then it just happened." I sighed. "It's so confusing, Sum. At one point, it looked like he really cared. Like, there's a part of him that's so in love with me. He felt like the old Carter."

"Maybe he really does care. Why would he have sex with you if he didn't?"

"I don't hate you."

My stomach stirred at the memory of those words.

"I don't know. I just know I can't get over how he treats Mom. If he insists on hurting her . . ." I shook my head. "Then there would be no chance of anything ever happening between us again."

"Do you want it to? Happen again, I mean?"

More than anything. "Not when things are like this. He's going too far, Sum." I grabbed a handful of popcorn and stuffed it into my mouth.

She gave me a mischievous look. "How was it?"

I closed my eyes at the memory of his smooth lips and deft hands. I smiled, or I tried to, with my mouth full of popcorn. "It was like it was our first time but also it wasn't."

"How so?"

"There was anticipation like it was our first time, but at the same time, it was like before. Like we already knew each other so well. Do you get what I mean?"

She chuckled, her gaze dropping. "Don't ask me. I'm a virgin."

I examined her closely. Summer had never had a boyfriend. She'd never admitted it out loud, but I was almost 100 percent sure her low self-esteem wasn't the only culprit for it.

"What about you, Sum? Any guy who might change that in the near future?"

She started fiddling with her fingers. She always fiddled with her fingers when something upset her. "Not likely."

The guys' laughter came from the game room once again, and I caught how raspy Jackson's laughter was. His laugh sounded unused, as though he rarely laughed.

Summer's eyes always got these sparkles in them when she heard him laugh. It was as if she was soaking in the sound, letting it wrap around her and nurse her own fantasies, and the same thing happened now. She wasn't even blinking as she waited it out.

"I know how much Jackson means to you, but you've got to

let him go. I do get that it's hard—I mean, look at me and Carter—but it feels like you're only spiraling down as time passes."

She stared at her hands, her gaze clouding. "It's hard when I have to keep seeing him."

"Tell me about it."

"And I really want to like someone else, but he was my best friend, Zo. He was my hero, my world. It's like he ruined me for all other guys."

"What if you make up one day?"

She scoffed. "Unlikely."

"Hypothetically speaking. Would you hook up with him?"

The question triggered a flash of sorrow in her gaze. She dug her teeth into her lip, taking a long breath through her nose.

"Even if he ever wanted to be with me, his mother wouldn't allow it. She's always been clear about who Jackson can settle with, and the daughter of the help is not on that list."

"Is his mom that much of a bitch?"

"A bitch? She could freeze you over with just one look! She's determined that Jackson should live by her rules."

"She sounds like a nightmare."

"She's even worse. It's like Jackson's her lapdog and can't do anything on his own."

"What did you say just now?"

Summer froze as I snapped my gaze to the side, finding Jackson in the doorway. How long had he been standing there?

Summer's face went pale, then so red you could practically feel heat radiating off it. "I-I-I didn't mean—"

He stepped inside. "What gives you the right to talk about me behind my back?"

She stood up, pressing her hands against her thighs. "I'm sorry."

I'd never seen him this pissed off. Jackson never looked out of control. He never looked as if he cared either. He was like a block of ice, just existing in this life. It was one of the reasons why he was so popular in the modeling industry. All his photo shoots contained that statue-like, unsmiling look that forced you to wonder what was underneath. So, seeing his face twisted with rage—seeing real emotions beneath his icy veneer—had me staring at him in shock.

Just how bad had their falling out been?

Prescott popped inside. "There you are," he slurred at Jackson, unknowingly helping to dissolve the tension in the room. He nodded at me. "What are you watching?"

"*Shall We Dance*," I said.

He twisted his lips. "Not my cup of tea."

"What? Dance or romance?"

"Both."

"Strange, considering your last TV role was all about a teenage romance with the girl next door, and you were pretty convincing." I sniggered. The audience had been ecstatic over the chemistry between him and his co-star. Google Trends showed an increase in searches for whether they were actually a couple.

"A job is a job." He slumped onto the sofa next to Summer.

"Why do you sound like you regret ever taking that role?"

"Because being a teenage heartthrob is not what I signed up for. They're all only interested in who I fuck or what mess I get into." His phone started buzzing, and he frowned at it when he pulled it out. "Speaking of a mess, it's my manager again." He returned his phone to his pocket.

I arched my brow. "You're not going to answer that?"

"I don't want to listen to more shouting. He's been grilling me for days about my DUI. Tabloids are having a field day."

Prescott had been caught driving drunk last week, and unlike the first few times it had happened, his manager wasn't able to bribe the cops before the news spread. Social media was all about it these days.

"Here's a solution for you—how about you stop driving drunk?"

He flashed me a smile that didn't reach his eyes, hinting at some serious underlying issue. "Where's the fun in that? So. How about we watch *Die Hard*?"

My brows arched. "You want to watch a movie with us?"

He shrugged. "Why not? I've had enough of pool and ping-pong for today. What about you, Jax?"

Jackson didn't move a muscle as he stared at Summer. "Whatev. I don't care."

Summer stiffened, her fingers digging into her palms as Jackson sat in the armchair farthest away from the sofa.

"Isn't Carter going to be pissed because you want to watch a movie with us?" I asked.

"Why am I going to be pissed when I'll be watching the movie too?" the guy in question asked, entering the room. My heart went to my throat as our eyes connected.

Heat flared to life deep within me, and I was left almost breathless at the force of his presence. He didn't even have to do anything for me to salivate over him. The lines of his face and muscles had never looked more sculpted, and his body in a black T-shirt and sweatpants had never looked more attractive. My gaze followed him as he dropped down in the armchair by the sofa, his hand reaching to push the fallen locks of his hair off his forehead.

His eyes were glazed like Prescott's, making me wonder how many drinks he'd had. It brought me back to his argument with Dominic in his office. Was this him trying to drink away that argument?

He took the remote and changed the movie.

"What are you doing? We're watching *Shall We Dance*."

"Not anymore."

"Excuse me?"

"We're going to watch *Die Hard*."

"No. We're not going to watch *Die Hard*."

"Yes, we are. Isn't that right, guys?"

Prescott's head bobbed. Jackson looked as though he couldn't care less what he would do not only for the next two hours but also for the rest of his life.

SHATTERED MEMORIES | 251

I gaped at Carter. What was he doing? Since when did he want us to watch a movie together? And why did that thought bring an unwelcome heat to my chest?

"You can't just march in here and decide on a movie," I hissed at him.

He gave me a flat stare. "Majority rules."

"Then Summer and I will leave."

I moved to stand up, but Prescott reached out to stop me. "Come on. It will be fun. And Carter won't say a thing to you, isn't that right, buddy?"

Carter locked eyes with me, then looked down the length of my body. My heart stuttered in my chest, each inch of me burning in the wake of his gaze.

He abruptly looked away, shifting in the armchair.

I couldn't find the words. I didn't know whether I should yell at him or just give up and take Summer with me. It felt impossible for me to act as if it was just normal for us to watch a movie together. What made it worse was not knowing if he would act like this if he were sober, and it bothered me how much I wanted that answer to be affirmative.

I grabbed the bowl from Summer's lap, even though there was still some popcorn left. "I'm going to refill this."

I marched into the kitchen, my heart pounding in the rhythm of my steps. I dropped the bowl on the counter and closed my eyes, taking in a deep breath.

Steps came from behind me, and I snapped my eyes open, recognizing who they belonged to.

"I don't know what you think you're doing, but you can't just intrude on my girls' night with Summer."

Carter leaned against the counter next to me, crossing his arms and legs as he trapped me with his gaze. His eyes were the color of grass at sunset, darkening shade by shade.

"It was either that or going to a party."

"You should've chosen the latter."

"Yeah, I'm sure you'd be happy if I was there and chicks were falling all over me."

My mouth parted, my stomach twisting with possessiveness. I hated how much I didn't want him to be with other girls even though he had the complete freedom and right to do just that.

"You've got some nerve to come here and say that to me."

"Why not? It's the truth."

Anger flared in my chest. What was he trying to accomplish here?

"You're drunk." I put the popcorn in the microwave and set the timer.

"So?"

"So you're not making much sense."

He leaned toward me, his breath caressing my face. "Really now? Then why are you looking at me like you want to hop on my dick again?"

My cheeks, my face, my whole body flushed, and I accidentally caught the edge of the bowl with my hand as I turned fully to look at him. The bowl clattered on the counter.

"That was a mistake."

A muscle twitched in his cheek. "Yet you had no problem getting the most out of it."

I winced, drawing a step back. "Let's just pretend it never happened, okay?"

His lips twisted with displeasure, but he didn't say anything. He moved to the fridge and pulled out a bottle of beer, and I grimaced as he took a swig.

"You're drinking too much. Are you sure you want to risk your liver for cheap distraction?"

"If it helps deal with this shitty reality, yes."

A sense of weight settled in my stomach, and I heard Dominic's words in my head.

"If you act like that in her presence again, I'm going to have you move out. Until you're eighteen, I'm responsible for you, and I'll even send you out of state if I have to."

I closed my eyes briefly against the surge of pain and fear for Carter. I guessed he had another reason to drink now.

"That's just temporary relief, Carter. It won't solve a thing."

"That's the only way I know."

"You could go to counseling. It could help you."

He turned to look at me, a strange expression crossing over his face. His gaze skated over me, making my every hair stand at attention. "The guys told me I stopped drinking soon after you and I got together." He looked at my lips then back up into my eyes. "I also stopped having nightmares."

My eyes widened at the sudden switch in topic. The memories rushed back to me, taunting me with better times.

"You had some once in a while."

"I sense a 'but' in there."

I ran my hand down the side of my neck. "But then you'd sneak into my bed and hold me tight against you. It helped you sleep better."

His eyes smoldered, but he said, "It sounds like I was dependent on you."

I snorted. Typical of him to assume the worst about our past. "Believe me, Carter, you were anything but dependent on me."

I wanted to ask him if he was having nightmares again. Not being able to hear him scream in his sleep didn't mean he wasn't having them, all the more now with everything happening with Dominic. But I couldn't ask him that.

The popcorn was done, and I was glad to have something to shift my attention to. I opened the microwave and poured the popcorn in the bowl, wondering why he was still standing here. Wondering what he wanted.

I poured the salt over the popcorn and headed out, feeling his gaze on me every inch of the way.

I started the movie without waiting for Carter to return, adamant on keeping my attention solely on the screen.

The opening credits finished just as Carter dropped back into the armchair. Thankfully, the guys' commentary filled the room, allowing me to forget all about the drama and the conversation I'd just had with Carter. It was just like old times, and even though I'd been in the mood for a dance movie, I had a good time watching the action unfold and commenting on the plot with Prescott and Jackson, realizing how much I missed these two. We'd used to spend a lot of time together when I was with Carter, and we'd always had fun. It was nice to have that back, even temporarily.

Only later, when I thought back to those two hours when we watched the movie, did I realize Carter hadn't paid as much attention to the movie as the rest of us. His gaze had been mostly on me, observing me covertly like he was too consumed by me to stop. And it only took me further away from solving the mystery of what was going on in that head of his now.

CHAPTER TWENTY-FIVE

THE BASKETBALL SEASON WAS STARTING IN A WEEK, AND OUR first season game was against East Creek High. The cheer coach almost ran my squad into the ground, and as the captain, I was expected to give 200 percent. I increased my hours in the gym to be in tip-top shape, and with all the wedding planning and fittings for my bridesmaid dress, school assignments and work, I had no time for anything else.

At nights, right before sleep would overtake me, I allowed my mind to go back to the sex with Carter. I allowed myself to think about him not hating me. It was hard to believe that, but there was definitely something different about Carter these days. I'd thought that after the movie night, he'd go back to ignoring my existence, but I'd been wrong.

I often caught him looking at me, and a couple times, he surprised me by asking me where we kept some things around the house or why some place that had been open two years ago was out of business now. There was still a clear distance between us, though. And he still hadn't apologized to Mom.

Mom was doing much better, and instead of going to work, she brought her work home. Of course, Dominic and I supervised her, making sure she didn't overtax herself. Seeing how much there was to organize even with a wedding planner at your beck and call, it was madness. I'd never thought there were so many things to plan, up to the details such as your wedding band, caterer, or guest seating charts. It had taken Mom days just to decide whether their guest invitations were going to be beige or white with gold, glittery detail. She and Dominic had decided to hold the ceremony at our house, and Mrs. Gibson's assistants kept coming and going to make sure everything would run smoothly for the wedding in eight days' time.

Mom and I spent the whole morning on last-minute dress alterations, and by the time we were done, we were both tuckered out. Mom went to take a nap and I headed to the attic to curl up with a book.

But my plan was thwarted as I arrived and discovered Carter already there. My feet came to an abrupt stop. Two things shocked me:

One—he was here in the attic. In our place.

Two—he was drawing on the whiteboard.

I hadn't seen him draw since the accident. He hadn't shown any interest in getting back to architecture.

"You're drawing," I said in a tone of surprise. His hand stopped.

He caught his lip between his teeth, dropping his hand. "Apparently."

It occurred to me I should leave and return when he was not here, but there was something in his expression that had me doing the opposite. I closed the door and took a seat on the windowsill. I hugged a pillow to my chest, remaining silent.

"I don't remember ever drawing anything, but when I took up this marker, I started to draw without conscious thought."

"And how does it feel to draw again?"

"Strange."

"Why strange?"

"It feels new, but it also feels right. Like how everything's supposed to be."

I sucked in a quick breath. That was exactly what he'd told Nora about me.

I played with the ends of the pillow. "Would you like to keep drawing?"

His fingers tightened around the marker. "Maybe. I don't know. These are all my books, I assume." He motioned at the pile of architecture books beneath the whiteboard.

"Yes. And *Made for Efficiency* is your favorite."

He picked it up and flipped through it, stopping at the images of residential homes positioned against the clear skies and greenery. They belonged to different architecture styles, each described with a bubble of text to its side. He dropped the book back to the pile.

"That's the last book you read before your accident." I pointed at the book still open on the carpet.

He gave it a long look. I couldn't tell what his thoughts were.

"Why did I agree to join Dominic's firm?"

I blinked fast, surprised by the question. I didn't miss he'd called his dad by his name.

He turned to look at me, waiting for my reply.

I wasn't sure whether to say anything or not. He wouldn't like the answer.

"You and Dominic patched things up, so you wanted to give him a chance. Give his firm a chance."

"Why would I ever do that? I don't see myself ever wanting to join his firm, truce or not."

"Dominic has started an accessible-housing program. He followed your suggestion that we should focus on not only providing more houses that accommodate for people with disabilities but also on making those houses affordable for them. So, he suggested that you be in charge of that program, and you agreed, but only once you had an established career. You wanted to have success on your own."

He stared at his books. His hands balled on his thighs. "I used to hate him so much. And now, with the way things are . . ."

I felt my heart ache. "With the way things are?" I prompted him to continue.

The expression on his face went stony. "As I said, I don't see myself ever joining his firm."

My heart gave a jump. I felt as though I had to be careful asking the next question. "How do you see yourself, then?"

"I don't know, but I know I won't let him decide for me."

"He cares about you, Carter."

His lips twisted into a cruel smile. "Really? Since the accident, he's never showed he cared about me or my condition, for that matter. He just demanded that I get back to *his* version of normal. And you saw what happened the other day between us. After that, he took me to his office and he—" He stopped, as though realizing what he was about to confess to me. His fists clenched harder.

I felt a pang deep in my chest. "I overheard your conversation in his office. I know he gave you an ultimatum."

He sliced me with a glare. "What? You had no right to eavesdrop."

"I was worried, Carter. After your fight, I was worried that might happen."

His eyes narrowed. *Shit.* That was the wrong thing to say.

"What do you mean?"

I bit my lip, disconnecting my gaze from his. "Nothing."

He stood up. "No, tell me."

I tugged at the tassel hanging off the pillow, keeping my eyes on it. "After you drove off on the day of their engagement, he said if he couldn't reason with you, he'd tell you to move out."

"So, he's planned it the whole time?"

"That's not it."

He took a step toward me, his eyes two hot coals of fury. "And you knew? You were all in on it together?" He raised his voice.

Something cut through me at the look of betrayal on his face. I dropped the pillow, getting up. "Don't say it like we're all your enemies and it was all a ploy to hurt you. I don't want you to move out. I told him so. But as horrible as he is for even considering that alternative, I can't entirely blame him, Carter. He's all about Mom and their baby these days. He can't let anything happen to them."

"Something already happened to my mom! She's *dead*. But he never gave a shit. Not about her and not about me."

This again? I crossed the distance between us, inhaling a sharp breath through my nose. "You're one to talk! You don't give a shit about anyone but yourself. Because Carter Reese, always the martyr. Because only *you* have problems. *You* always have it worse than anyone else. My mom is *pregnant*, and instead of making sure she isn't stressed out, you go on and act completely out of control. You made everything worse for her, and you didn't even apologize! What if something happened to the baby? What if something happened to her? Have you ever thought about that?"

He just watched me, his breath coming in and out of his nose audibly. I'd hoped for at least some clarification, but of course he wouldn't tell me anything, let alone admit his fault. Why did I even bother?

I moved for the door, but his hand shot out to grab my arm, stopping me. He pulled me around to look at him. "Don't go."

"Let go of me." I tried to yank my arm free, but he didn't give. "Carter, let me go."

"I've thought about it."

"What?"

"I've thought about that day. I've thought about it a lot."

I ground my teeth together, looking to the side. "Good for you."

"I told you, I don't want her or the baby hurt. I don't want to make things worse for her."

"I'm not the person who should hear that. You should at least have the decency to clear that up with her."

His fingers tightened around my arm and pulled me closer to him. I felt butterflies in my belly, despite myself.

"I don't know how," he said quietly. "I've been furious with her for so long, I don't know now how *not* to be furious."

My fingers twitched, and I wanted nothing more than to hug him. Protect him.

I closed my eyes, lowering my head. "I get that you're wronged. If I were in your shoes, I would've felt the same. And I wish, I really wish your parents could've gotten along. I wish your mom was alive. I wish you didn't have to see your dad with another woman, especially not so soon after your mom's death. But you can't keep tearing us down. That won't take your pain away. It won't bring your mom back to life or make things right. It will only prolong this circle of suffering, where no one wins."

He turned his head to the side, blinking rapidly. His eyes grew red.

Something inside me crumbled, and I had to fist my hand so I wouldn't put it on his cheek.

"Maybe Dominic isn't a perfect parent, but he loves you. He doesn't want you gone. But you have to meet him halfway. You have to try to at least tolerate us. That's the only way this family can function."

A tear slipped down his cheek, and he released me, turning his back to me as he reached with his hand to brush the tear away.

Carter never cried. The first and only time I'd seen him cry was on his mom's birthday more than a year and a half ago, so him crying now meant he was falling apart at the seams.

"You say that he loves me, but I don't feel it. When he looks at me, all I see is I'm a nuisance to him. An afterthought."

Another part of me crumbled, and I couldn't take it any longer. How could I stay immune to him when he was suffering? I hated him for the way he treated me and my mom but seeing him like this was killing me.

I placed my hand on his shoulder. "Please don't cry."

The muscles beneath my hand bunched. He went still, not even breathing for a moment.

"Don't pity me."

"I don't pity you."

He didn't move for the better part of a minute, and I debated with myself whether I'd made a colossal mistake by touching him. Just as I started retracting my hand, he dropped his hand on mine and kept it on his shoulder.

My breath lodged in my throat. The sensation of his hand holding mine had my pulse rampaging.

"I've felt lost for so long. I've felt alone. But all this time there's been a part of me that hoped he would tell me he loved me and he was sorry for all the pain he's caused." A shudder ran through him. "At the end of the day, it's not about your mom or even you. It's about him. It's always been about him and his selfishness."

I closed my eyes, feeling as though I could cry too. My chest was throbbing with pain. To know that he was allowing me to witness this, that he was opening up to me . . .

"I'm sorry, Carter. I'm so sorry."

His hand tightened around mine, and I felt his deep intake of breath. I couldn't see his face or hear him, but I was sure he was crying, and I didn't move to look at him, allowing him this privacy.

Witnessing this rare moment of his vulnerability ruptured something in my heart. When Carter was hurt, I was hurt too. When Carter felt lost, I felt lost too, and I wanted nothing more than to help him heal. Help *us* heal.

But we weren't together. And he wasn't mine anymore to take care of.

I pulled my hand out from under his, stepping back. At that, he hurried to wipe his face with both hands, his back expanding with a deep breath.

"I should leave you alone."

I side-stepped him, but I didn't make it far. His hand grabbed mine, and he pulled me back. The soft look in his eyes made my heart bounce in my chest.

"You're helping me again."

I looked down, my gaze landing on his chest. It was all sinewy muscle and taut perfection. His scent was overpowering, and I barely restrained myself from taking a deep inhale of it.

"No matter what I say, you're there."

My gaze dropped to my feet. "Of course I am. I can't just stand by when you're hurting."

He placed his finger under my chin and tilted it up. "Of course you can't," he whispered with a smile. He drew me closer to him, and I could feel my whole body heating up.

"What are you doing?"

His gaze shifted between my eyes. "Do you still want to pretend the other day here never happened?"

I sucked in my cheeks, my heart bouncing in my chest as he took the only remaining step separating us and palmed my neck, his thumb skidding over my jaw. I shuddered with longing, my eyes fluttering closed against my will as he moved his hand to the back of my neck, then down my shoulders. Slowly, with only the tips of his fingers, he slid his hands down my arms to my wrists. I got goosebumps all over.

Why was he doing this? He wasn't drunk this time, so I couldn't blame this behavior on alcohol. "Why are you doing this, Carter?"

He brought his lips close to my neck, close enough to taunt me with the promise of a kiss. His nose skimmed over the spot under my ear, and I had to swallow back a moan. "Because you're looking at me with those fucking eyes that beg for my attention, and instead of pushing you away, all I can think about is how I want to get you naked again."

My heart started thrashing like crazy against my chest. The need for him pumped hard through me, and I wanted nothing more than to yield to it. For him to mark my skin with his lips and make me fall apart with pleasure. If I leaned just an inch closer to him, his lips would be on my skin.

And I almost did just that. Because I still hung on his every word, and my body still sought nourishment in his. Because it was so easy for him to make me desperate for him.

But he couldn't just act like this on a whim, as though he hadn't pushed me away so many times.

I didn't know what was going on with him now, and that was reason enough for me not to drop my guard.

"Apologize to my mom," was all I said, and without sparing him a glance, I broke away from him and left the attic.

CHAPTER TWENTY-SIX

ONLY ONCE I HAD SOME DISTANCE FROM HIM, I COULD RELEASE the breath I'd been holding. I went over every second of our encounter, storing away the look in his eyes and the tone of his voice. His words. His touches.

What was happening with him? Why now? He'd been so determined to keep me at a distance, so why was he acting as if he couldn't resist me? What did he want from me?

The thoughts and questions haunted me even at school, and I was so lost in them, I saw Nora approach me only after she almost had me cornered in the locker room before the practice.

"Can we talk?" she asked.

"Okay."

We dressed into our uniforms, and I followed her to the gym. It was still empty, and I could see she'd counted on that.

We sat on the bleachers. I didn't say anything, waiting for her to speak first.

"I don't think you're good for Carter."

I blinked rapidly. Say what?

"I think everything happens for a reason, and him forgetting your relationship says something, don't you think?"

"Are you for real?"

She didn't even flinch, meeting my gaze straight on. "You two started off as enemies. Carter didn't tell me much, but he told me enough to see there's bad blood between you two. Your mom had an affair with his dad, right?"

"Not that it's any of your business, but, no," I hissed.

She just blinked innocently.

Why did she have to look so calm? That pissed me off even more.

"You don't have to be on the defensive. I'm not judging. I'm just stating the facts."

"I think you should check your facts."

"Alright. Even so, you two didn't get along. I don't believe hate is a healthy grounding for a long-term relationship."

"What are you trying to say?"

"I'm trying to say that his amnesia is the universe's sign that you two shouldn't be together."

What bullshit was this girl spewing out?

I jumped to my feet. "I'm done listening to this."

She stood up too and caught my shoulder to stop me. "Look, I could really make him happy. With me, he doesn't have to deal with constant negativity. He doesn't need to be reminded of his mom's death, and I think he won't be able to forget about it if he's always by your side."

I shrugged off her hand. "You have some nerve saying all this. First of all, I don't think you get to decide how he feels. Second, why are you talking to me about it? Carter and I aren't even together. You should talk to him."

"Because right now, he doesn't even know how he feels. You have him all confused, and I think you're using that to get him back."

"Funny, since it sounds like that's exactly what *you* are doing."

She frowned, finally showing some resemblance of anger. "You don't know me, Zoe. I really like Carter. And I want to help him deal with his demons. He has no clue who he's supposed to be after losing two years of his life. He needs a fresh start. And if you really love him, you'd give him a chance to be with someone else. Someone who could give him that."

I got in her face, taking advantage of the few inches of height I had on her. "As I said, you should talk to Carter. It's his decision to make who he's going to be with. Not yours or mine."

I wasn't going to mention that I was done trying to get him to be with me. If she wanted to think I was still her rival, let her.

The girls started coming in, along with the coach. Dismissing Nora, I started for where Trisha and Amalie were standing.

"You won't make him happy," she said after me. "And you know it."

I didn't even dignify that with an answer.

"You know, when you said you wanted to get some fresh air, I didn't think it meant you wanted to come to the cemetery," I said to Mom, looking at Anastacia's grave. I'd only visited this grave with Carter, so it felt strange to come with Mom.

"I wanted to pay my respects."

I hugged myself in my jacket when the wind picked up. My gaze bounced nervously around us.

Cemeteries always creeped me out. The headstones, moss, crows, and the general sense of death always made for this cold feeling that slithered into me the moment I stepped foot in a cemetery. They made me think about dying. They made me think about Dad.

I hadn't been to my dad's grave in a long time.

I'd come here to visit Anastacia with Carter twice—for her birthday and the anniversary of her death. He hadn't talked much other than to say how he felt most connected with her when he was by her grave. How it helped him remember some things about her that might have been forgotten due to day-to-day things.

Whenever I'd visited Dad's grave in my hometown, I felt like I couldn't have been more distanced from him. His grave was a reminder that he wasn't here anymore, and that all I had left of him were memories. Weak, scarce memories that only added to the pain that had been ingrained in me my whole life.

His grave reminded me of what I'd always tried to suppress— that I'd been deeply unhappy and lonely my whole life. Carter had been the only one to put a bandage on the wound and make it hurt less.

There were fresh lilies by Anastacia's grave, which could only mean Carter had been here recently. Carter always brought his mom lilies; they had been her favorite. Mom lowered a bouquet of white chrysanthemums next to the lilies and knelt down. I knelt beside her.

Her gaze lingered on the pink flowers. "Anastacia died more than two and a half years ago, but for him, it must be like it happened too recently."

"Yeah." I still vividly remembered his nightmares. How lonely he'd been. How he'd dealt with grief and loneliness on his own.

"I remember him that first year," Mom said. "He was a wreck." She smiled at me. "Until you got together."

"And now we're history."

She took my hand in hers. "You still love him."

"Love him? I can't stop thinking about him. It's like I'm obsessed or something. You told me I'd find someone else and forget about Carter, but it feels like it's only getting worse. I'm trying my best to move on, but it's hard considering how it all just . . . it all just ended. One moment we were madly in love, and the next . . . he doesn't love me anymore."

"If it's any comfort, I think he does love you."

"No, he doesn't."

"There's something about the way he looks at you that says differently. Besides, there's still a possibility that he'll recover his memory."

"I don't think that will happen anymore. It's been almost three months already. And if he does, would anything change? Not that it matters unless he changes his attitude toward us and treats you better."

She cradled her stomach over her jacket, her eyes fixed on Anastacia's headstone. They turned glassy. I tilted my head as the lines of her cheekbones sharpened.

"Is everything okay?"

She didn't look at me. "I've been thinking a lot about some stuff lately."

"What stuff?"

"Our life before I met Dominic. Our life after I met Dominic. Anastacia."

My spine grew rigid. "What about her?"

"How she died. That car crash . . . it's horrible."

My pulse quickened. I licked my lips. "It's all in the past. There's no point in dwelling on it now."

"Isn't there, though?"

Her eyes remained glazed over, and the feelings I'd been suppressing all this time came back to me. I'd hoped they'd tail off if I didn't give them the time of day, but Mom hadn't been the same ever since Dominic proposed her, and it was getting harder to ignore it.

I pushed the uncomfortable thoughts aside and wrapped my hand around hers. "You just focus on Dominic and the baby, okay? The wedding is in just a few days. Happiness, remember?"

"Happiness," she muttered. She met my gaze. "What about yours?"

"What about it?"

"You keep talking about my happiness, but you don't fight for yours."

"Is this about Carter?"

"No, this is about dancing."

I tore my gaze and hand off her. I fisted my other hand on my thigh.

"Dancing makes you happy, honey. It's your passion."

"We talked about this, Mom."

"We did, but you always refuse to listen. I don't want you miserable, and you're going to be if you keep chasing this unclear goal of having a stable job. You seem ready to spend your whole life doing something you don't even like, but I'm not sure you're really aware of the consequences."

"You think those consequences outweigh the consequences of failing as a dancer?"

"Dancing can also be a viable career."

I shook my head. "It can be, but you know how I feel about it. It doesn't make sense to start something that will most likely push me right back into poverty. The dance industry isn't all roses and rainbows. Some of them are starving and homeless . . . I don't need to join their ranks."

"You don't have to see everything so black and white."

"I'm realistic."

"No, you're afraid."

That forced my mouth shut.

She pushed a lock of my hair behind my ear. "This is because of your dad, isn't it?"

I closed my eyes, swallowing hard. My most painful memory mixed with my happiest one—the memory of him dying and the memory of him watching me dance in my yellow polka-dot dress while telling me, *"My sweet daughter is going to be the best dancer in the world. And I'm always going to be in the audience watching her and clapping the loudest."*

Before I knew it, tears rushed out from beneath my lashes. I gulped for air, shaking my head against the memories.

"It's okay, honey. It's okay." Mom pulled me against her and wrapped her arms tightly around me, holding me as I sobbed. I didn't know where all these tears and the pain were coming from. I just knew they felt endless.

"He always loved to watch me dance," I said through sobs. "He said I was going to be the best dancer in the world." I clutched her sleeve. "And then he died."

"Oh, honey." Her arms held me tighter. "That's why you think nothing is for certain and want security so much. A safe life choice that won't just be you surviving, but also won't break your heart."

"And how can I not? If I lost him that easily, how can I believe that something bad isn't going to happen again? How can I be optimistic and expect a positive outcome when it's so easy to lose something so precious to you? Just look at me and Carter. Time and again I'm proven that nothing is for certain. My heart has already been broken. If I commit myself to dancing, failing would—it would . . ." I choked on a sob.

"Oh, honey." She drew me away only to brush the tears from my face. I couldn't meet her concerned gaze, and she framed my chin with her fingers to make me look at her. "Please look at me." I did. "If what you say is true, that you're predestined to fail, why did you fight for Carter, then? Why did you try to get him back?"

I opened my mouth to answer, but then I realized I had no reply to that.

"It's because even with all the pain that may come with it, love is something uniquely pure. It's not something to be taken lightly or brushed away. It's something we're privileged to experience, and there's no greater joy, whether it's loving someone or loving doing something."

She wiped the last tears off my face. I took out a tissue from my bag and blew my nose. I stayed quiet.

"Life is hard, Zoe. It comes with disappointments and pain in all its varieties. It's unpredictable and never linear. Whatever you do, there will be setbacks at one point or another."

"That doesn't sound optimistic at all."

"But," she continued as if I hadn't said anything, "the end goal is what matters. So, when you feel like you're failing, pick yourself up and continue. In the end, it has to amount to something good."

"So, you're saying I need to have faith that everything is going to be okay."

"I'm saying that you need to believe in yourself. You can't control others or life. You're only in control of your actions. And as long as you're doing the best you can, you can't fail."

The wind propelled a few orange leaves off the giant oak above us, and I watched them twirl slowly down. They made their first and last dance before they made contact with the ground, coming to their eternal rest.

Everything was finite. Everything had an expiration date. Could I take such a huge risk? Could I really be that fearless?

Mom caressed my cheek with the backs of her fingers, bringing my attention back to her. "We can't bring your dad back, but we can make sure to live as happily as possible. That's what he would've wanted, right? He would've wanted his little princess to do what she loves."

Another wave of pain shot through me, and I knew she was right. Dad would've wanted that. That was his dream. For me to follow my dreams and be happy. That had always been his dream.

I thought about that dance studio and how it had made me feel to see those people dancing. How, sometimes, right before I fell asleep, I let myself imagine what it would be like to perform. To come up with my own dances that would be replicated in perfect, fluid harmony. To be one with the music, with the sounds, the rhythm. To be irrevocably happy.

I'd given up on that so long ago, it felt strange letting myself consider this. It felt strange giving a place to hope even though I was well aware how everything could change in a split second. How I could easily fail and struggle like Mom for the rest of my life.

"I just wish happiness for you, honey. Nothing would make me happier."

I could feel more tears coming, and I took a deep breath before they could come out. "I know, Mom. And I'm sorry for worrying you."

"No, don't say that. You're just a little stubborn, but that doesn't make me love you any less."

I returned her grin. "I love you, too."

"So? Will you promise me to at least try? Will you join that dance studio?"

I wasn't sure this was a good decision at all. But as I thought about applying and dancing with the others in that studio, a feeling of excitement took root in my chest. It felt full of possibility.

"Yes. Yes, I will."

The sun shone high in the sky when we reached home, emitting warmth that made up for the chilly wind.

Mom was in a better mood after I agreed to give dancing a try, and there was a bounce to her step as we entered the house. Her face was glowing happily.

I reached for my phone and held it out to take a picture of her. "Mom, smile."

She turned around, and when she saw I was going to take her picture, she took off her jacket and turned to the side, cradling her bump. She beamed at me.

I snapped a photo. "Your bump shows even more when you stand like that."

"Mm-hmm. It's growing more and more." She sounded excited. "Let me see it."

She crossed to me and looked at the photo, her eyes growing soft. "Sometimes, I can't believe there's actually life in there."

"Yeah. It's incredible."

Carter cleared his throat, and Mom and I turned to look at him. He stood by the stairs, observing us with an expression I couldn't read.

"I want to talk to you," he said to Mom, and my jaw almost dropped.

"Why?" I asked with my chin up.

"Can we talk?" he asked Mom, ignoring me.

"No," I replied for her. "I won't let you upset her—"

Mom placed her hand on my shoulder. "It's okay, Zoe. I'd love to, Carter."

He shifted on his feet, motioning with his head in the direction of the kitchen. "Kitchen?"

"Okay."

I moved to follow them, but Carter gave me a decisive look over his shoulder. "I want to talk with her alone."

What the . . .? "You really think I'd let you be alone with her? Not after—"

"Zoe." Mom's voice came out sharper this time. "Why don't you go to your room while we talk?"

I halted. I didn't know what Carter's deal was now, and I didn't like it.

"Fine," I grumbled, waiting for them to leave. But neither of them moved until I did.

Throwing daggers at Carter, I started climbing the stairs. "You better treat her right."

He didn't respond, watching me climb with a blank expression. I heard them move only after I reached the second floor, and I stopped.

There was no way I'd leave her alone with him. Making sure to make as little noise as possible, I tiptoed back downstairs and to the kitchen, listening to their voices.

"What did you want to talk with me about?"

I peeked around the wall and found Carter pacing the kitchen while Mom observed him, perched up on a stool. He ran his hands through his hair and turned in my direction. I jerked behind the wall before he spotted me.

"I wanted to apologize."

Whoa. He'd actually listened to me?

I had to peer around the wall again. Mom was wearing a shocked expression, and it was clear she didn't know what to say.

"I won't pretend I approve of you as Dad's fiancée. I'm not happy about it, and I don't think I'll ever be okay with you becoming a member of this family. But I have nothing against your baby. And I don't want you to worry about me making this situation worse for you two. I'm sorry for the way I acted. It put the baby at risk, and I regret that."

My heart was thumping so hard it felt as though it would

burst through my chest. He was apologizing. He was trying to make things right.

Despite myself, my chest filled with love, and it was almost overwhelming.

Mom still watched him in disbelief, and twice, she opened her mouth to say something only to close it.

"I don't know what to say. Where is this coming from?"

Carter arched his brow at her, folding his arms over his chest. "Does it matter?"

"No. I appreciate it. I really do. But what happened that day was my fault. I hadn't been taking good care of myself. I can't blame that on you."

"But my attitude didn't help. And I don't want to put the baby at risk. So, you don't have to be afraid of me. Just make sure the baby is healthy and strong."

Mom's eyes misted. "Oh, Carter. Thank you. This means so much."

He nodded. "Just one more thing."

"Yes?"

His eyes sharpened. "Don't take any more things from my mom. Her special places, her special things, don't mess with them. Show at least some respect."

My nostrils flared, and I decided to march into the kitchen and attack him, but when I peered around to see her reaction, I was frozen to the spot. She wore such an expression of guilt that it was almost palpable.

"I won't take anything. That's a promise." Her voice faltered. "Good."

He moved to leave the kitchen, so I darted toward the back of the house before he saw me, my heart thudding against my rib cage.

I felt angry at Carter for that last jab, but when I finally stopped by the pool, I realized I was smiling.

This was far from perfect, but Carter was finally, in a way, easing up on Mom. I didn't know how long this would last, but I could finally breathe more easily after weeks of quiet suffocation.

CHAPTER TWENTY-SEVEN

AFTER CARTER'S CONVERSATION WITH MOM, I'D SPENT THE rest of the day dazed. Things had taken an unexpected turn, and I still found it hard to believe they'd reached a kind of truce.

Was it because of me? Did my words influence him to change his mind about the way he treated Mom? Was something inside him changing despite his amnesia and the circumstances between us?

Whatever it was, it had affixed a smile upon my face, and that along with what Mom had told me at the cemetery almost made me dance on my way to the dance studio. Latin music flowed sensually from the speakers, and I felt drawn to it. There were a few couples dancing together inside under the mixture of red and blue lights. Their bodies moved like a river, back and forth, back and forth, relying on the sounds of an acoustic guitar to guide them.

I didn't know how long I stayed there just watching them. I just knew that I could move freely only after they stopped and I was released from the pull of the music and their dance.

There was a notice on the door stating they were taking new dancers, and it was almost as if I could hear my mom's voice in my head telling me it was a sign I should do this.

Taking a deep breath, I finally made the decision. I was going to give dancing a try.

I opened the door to this new world and stepped inside.

The sun was low on the horizon when I left the studio, and the sky was bathed in purple, orange, and blue. A gigantic smile pulled at my lips. I would attend my first practice next week, and I felt like dancing and jumping with joy all at once.

I didn't know what would come out of this—if anything would come out of it at all—but I'd made the first step, and that was a big deal. I felt as if something monumental had just happened here, and it helped me feel stronger and more sure of myself.

I deserved a mocha to celebrate.

I still had a smile on my face when I came out of the coffee shop with my mocha in hand and almost collided with Carter.

"Carter," I breathed out as I stopped short, my heart speeding up at the sight of him. My eyes took a dive down his body, cataloguing his black jeans, black hoodie, and Air Jordans. He looked so sexy.

His own eyes roamed over me, and I felt warm all over. His perusal stopped on my lingering smile. "You look happy."

"That's because I *am* happy. This is my celebratory drink." I motioned with my mocha.

"Did something happen?"

"Something happened, yeah. What are you doing here?"

He glanced to the side, pushing his hands into his pockets. "Did you come here in your car?" So, he was evading my question.

"Yes."

"Want to drive me home?"

I gave him a look under my lashes. Huh? "Sure. This way."

I kept glancing at him as we walked to the parking lot in silence, my stomach doing backflips. I couldn't tell what was happening with him. I got so nervous, I couldn't finish my mocha, so I tossed it in the garbage bin before I took my keys out.

As he opened the door to climb in, I remembered the first time he got into my car and what he'd said then. A laugh escaped me.

He gave me a confused look. "What's funny?"

I sat down and put on my seat belt. "I just remembered what you said when you got in my car for the first time."

He turned with his whole body to look at me. "What did I say?"

"You told me I better drive like a granny unless I wanted to kill someone. Namely, us." Another laugh burst out of me. "You didn't trust my driving skills."

"If that video on your phone is any proof of it, I more than trusted your skills."

"Yeah." I chuckled. "But it took you some time. So, in case you're worrying now, know that you're safe."

He continued to watch me as I started the car and pulled out of the lot, and I started feeling overly self-conscious. My cheeks warmed, and I had to swallow a couple of times because my throat felt too dry.

"Why do you keep staring at me?"

He abruptly looked away, crossing his arms over his chest.

My heart accelerated. When he was this close to me, I couldn't help noticing how intoxicating his scent was or how beautiful his side profile was. Streetlights illuminated his features, playing with shadows to enhance them, giving him a more striking appearance.

"So will you tell me what's the happy occasion?" he asked. "Or is that top secret?"

I chuckled. "It's not a secret. There's a dance studio near that coffee shop. I've just joined it, and it's a pretty big deal for me."

"Why did you sign up only now? I thought it was a done deal, seeing how much you love dancing."

My fingers tightened around the steering wheel. "Because I didn't think dancing was in the cards for me. But Mom convinced me to give it a shot. To chase my dreams. So here I am. Chasing my dreams." I took the turn toward our neighborhood. "Now it's your turn. What were you doing there?" I repeated my earlier question. "Or 'is that top secret'?" I joked.

He stayed quiet. I thought he would deny me the answer again, but then he said, "I went to see the counselor."

If he told me he'd been to Mars, it would be less shocking than this. "You did?"

He nodded. What did this mean? Why had he decided to give counseling a try now?

I couldn't help feeling it was related to me, and I only felt more confused.

"It's surprising considering you were so adamant not to go to counseling."

"Well, I did," he bit out. "Do you have to make such a big deal of it?" I couldn't be sure in the dim light of the car, but his cheeks seemed tinted pink.

My heart kicked hard. It obviously took a lot for him to tell me this, and I didn't want him to feel vulnerable.

"I'm glad you're giving it a try," I said in a soft voice.

His scowl melted away. "Don't you think it's pointless?"

"I don't think it's pointless. I think you need any help you can get. How was it?"

He sighed. "She asked me how I coped with my amnesia and how it felt losing one part of my life. She wanted to know if I was behind in my classes and if I could function normally, whatever normal is." He sighed. "She said it would get easier in time."

"Do you believe her?"

"No." His Adam's apple moved as he swallowed. "I'm, like, supposed to accept my memory loss and move on, but I feel more frustrated the longer I'm like this."

"Why?"

"Because I *need* those memories."

I stopped breathing, and my stomach fluttered when he turned to meet my gaze. He didn't say it, but I wondered if part of the reason for that had something to do with me.

We reached home, and I parked beside Dominic's car. I looked back on the change in Carter's recent behavior and how he treated me, and I couldn't help wondering if his feelings were coming back. The thought brought strong flutters to my belly.

My teeth gnawed at my lower lip. "I wanted to thank you for apologizing to my mom. That means a lot to her."

He turned his head to meet my gaze. "I figured."

His scent blanketed me, and my chest rose on a quick breath. It was even more intoxicating when he was this close to me. "What made you apologize to her?"

"What you said. I should've apologized to her and let her know I admitted my mistake. It was the right thing to do."

So it *did* have something to do with me, in a way. I didn't know if I was happy because of that or because he'd realized the right thing to do. Most likely both.

"Does this mean you forgive her for the past?"

He looked away. "No."

"Can you at least try?"

"It still hurts, Zoe. Her presence in Dad's life, my mom's death . . . it hurts too much."

I felt an ache deep in my chest. "You still haven't gotten over your mom's death." It wasn't a question but a statement.

His eyes glittered with darkness. "When my mom died, life as I knew it was over." His hands balled on his thighs. "Nothing made sense, and I felt so angry. I felt the world owed me for taking my mom away from me. It's made me into a different person."

He hadn't talked much about his grief or how devastating her death had been for him when we'd been together, and it meant all the more to me that he was sharing his feelings now. "And how do you feel now?"

He frowned, looking at the sky through his window. "It's hard to say. A lot of things happened. I met you, then I got amnesia, losing two years of my life . . . that's a lot to take in." He shifted his eyes back to me and gave me a long look. He didn't stop at my face. He took in my neck, waist, thighs . . .

My heart constricted.

"You said I told you a lot about my mom. What did I tell you?"

I stared at my hands. "You told me she had an artistic soul. She was very emotional. She used to spend days in her studio working on her sculptures, and you could often hear her hum around the house, making it livelier." I chuckled. "She loved cuddling with you and taking you for walks. She taught you how to ride a bicycle and swim. You often went to her studio to play with clay and make figurines while she worked."

With my every word, I could feel more pain radiating from him, and I stopped. I didn't want to tell him that all of that ended when Dominic started pulling away from her and she began withdrawing into herself. She lost her confidence and happiness, turning into a shell of the person she'd been. He didn't need that reminder.

"She sounded like an amazing woman," I concluded.

"She was." His voice was rough, and he cleared his throat. "I often imagine talking with her."

"What do you tell her?"

"How everything feels more complicated now than it felt two years ago. How I'm afraid I've turned into someone she wouldn't be proud of. How alone I feel."

His pain was seeping into me, and I felt my heart contracting under a wave of emotions. There was longing, and grief, and the need to be there for him, to show him he wasn't alone. To show him how much I understood him.

I thought back to the cemetery and my conversation with Mom about Dad. I wanted him to know about him. I *needed* him to know.

The first time I'd told him about Dad, he held me in his arms while he stroked my hair and assured me he would never let me feel alone again. The memory brought a dull ache to my chest. "I understand you," I whispered. "More than you know."

I returned my eyes to him and almost melted under the intensity of his gaze. It would never stop fascinating me how fierce and expressive his eyes could be—how they made me feel more important.

"You remember that my dad died when I was six?"

"Yes. Dominic mentioned it when you moved in."

"I saw him die."

I heard his breath catch. "What?"

"Yes. We were watching a cartoon together, and we were laughing." I lowered my gaze, my heart beating to a dull rhythm in my chest. "One moment, he stood up to bring us more snacks. The next, he was clutching his chest and stumbling to the ground. He died of a heart attack right on the spot." I sucked in a deep breath through my teeth. "And it pretty much marked me."

"I'm sorry." His voice was hardly audible.

I bit the inside of my cheek. "So am I."

"How did it mark you?"

I looked up at the sky. "You asked me why I joined that dance studio just now. That's why. I never had the courage to pursue my dream because I never believed anything would come out of it. Ever since Dad died, I've kept waiting for the world to collapse on me. Because if life was so cruel as to take him away from me, how could I trust it wouldn't fuck me up again? And time and again, it did fuck me up. With my dad, with my difficult childhood, with you. When I lost you—" I released a shuddering breath. "It felt like I lost myself."

I finally willed myself to meet his gaze, and what I found there made my heart go into overdrive. His eyes were swallowing me up. Suddenly, all I could think about was how close we were to each other. He radiated warmth that poured into my every pore.

"Did I make your pain go away when we were together?" he whispered.

My stomach jolted. "Always."

His eyes bounced from my lips to my eyes, all over my face. "I wish I could remember us."

My breath faltered. I blinked twice, as if he were a mirage and would disappear any second now. I looked at him for several seconds, waiting for something to happen that would prove to me his words were a joke or not real, but he didn't take them back. He didn't look as though he wanted to take them back.

I thought back to his recent behavior and how he was letting me in bit by bit. How I didn't feel the same distance between us as these past few months, and despite my resolution to stay away from him, I could feel hope starting to rise in me again. Hope that his feelings were really coming back.

"What's going on, Carter? You were dead set on pushing me away, but you've been acting so different recently. Why?"

He pushed his hand through his hair. "I keep thinking about that night when you said you were done. I felt—I felt like shit then. It was what I wanted, but it didn't feel right at all."

"But why?"

"I don't know. There's just something about you that draws me in. I feel different when I'm with you."

"Different?"

He squeezed his fists, looking away. "It doesn't matter."

"It does matter, Carter. And I think it's high time you're honest with me."

He expelled a loud breath. His forehead bunched. "Whenever I'm next to you, I feel *something*. It's like you're familiar. Your nearness, your smell, everything you do. I don't remember us together, but my body always reacts to you." He brought his gaze back to mine. "And when we slept together, I felt it. The connection between us. It only made it harder for me to get you out of my head."

My heart was pounding too hard in my chest now. I was right. He'd really felt it. He'd felt that connection that couldn't be ignored no matter how much we wanted to do so. But what did that connection amount to in the end if we were surrounded by walls and hate? If it was so hard for us to be together?

"Then why have you been trying to push me away all this time?"

"Because I didn't trust you. I didn't trust myself. How could I when I woke up one day without knowing who the fuck I've been for the past two years? I didn't know what was right or wrong, or how to deal with anything. How to deal with the fact that I'd been in a relationship—in love—with someone I considered my enemy. So, my most natural response was to drive you away."

"And now you trust me?"

His gaze roamed across my face, desperately searching for something. "I don't know. Sometimes, I feel like I do." His gaze stopped on my lips. "Sometimes, I feel like you're the only one I can trust."

Something changed in the air, and I could feel my whole body reacting to it. His eyes took on the darkest shade of jade. I could hardly breathe as longing dug its claws into me.

"Remember your last note?" His gaze had never left my mouth.

"What about it?"

"You mentioned in it that I'm doing a lot of things the same way I did as before my accident."

I sucked in a breath.

"I wonder if I'm doing this the same too." He shifted to me over the console, seizing my gasp with his lips. His tongue pushed inside my mouth, suffusing me with searing pleasure that nurtured and seduced. My hands reached out to him of their own accord, following an urge to haul him to me and let him have his way with me. And for a second, I gave in to it. But I needed more than pleasure. I needed him to be in this for the long haul.

I pushed my hand against his chest, breaking the kiss. "The thing is, I don't trust you, Carter. I don't trust that you're not going to hurt me. So, until you can prove to me that you won't hurt me again, you don't deserve this."

His forehead creased with a frown. He opened his mouth to reply, but he didn't get a chance because Mom called out from the doorstep, "Zoe?"

I froze, then twisted my head in the direction of her voice.

"I heard you arrive minutes ago. Why aren't you coming in?"

Dominic's car was hiding us from her view, so she couldn't

see Carter was with me in my car, and all my muscles loosened. If she'd seen us kissing, it would've been more than awkward.

I stepped out. "Hi." I waved, hoping I didn't look as flustered as I felt.

"Is everything alright?" She moved toward me, then halted when she saw Carter emerging from my car. Her eyes doubled in size. "Carter?" She took one long look at us, and I could practically see the cogs working in her brain. "What are you two doing together?"

"We happened to meet downtown. He didn't have a ride home, so he asked me for one."

Mom's eyes narrowed at me. "You sound strange. And you look flushed. Why do you look flushed?"

I glanced at Carter. "Why don't you go on inside?"

"Sure." He looked me up and down, reminding me of his kiss in the car. Now I was sure Mom could see exactly what was going through my head.

Mom waited for him to enter the house before she gestured for me to explain.

"We're not together, it that's what you think."

"I didn't say anything."

"I just did him a favor, that's all."

"And you're sure nothing else happened?"

I looked down at my shoes. "Nothing." Except that we'd slept together, but that was beside the point now.

"So, you're getting along again?"

"It's difficult to say." I couldn't tell if he wanted us to be together. He obviously wanted to sleep with me, but was that enough to pave the way for more?

"He said some things . . . some things that make me feel like his feelings for me are changing. So, maybe we're going in the right direction."

I thought she would be glad for me, but for some reason, there was something sad in her expression. She crossed her arms and covered her elbows with her hands.

"Mom? Is everything okay?"

She gave me a close-mouthed smile. "It's nothing. Just pre-wedding jitters."

I moved in to hug her. "There's no need to be nervous. Everything will be just fine." I kissed her cheek. "You're going to be the most beautiful bride, you know that?"

She chuckled, but it sounded a little empty. "I'd better be, with as much money as Dominic is spending on my dress and stylists."

"You being beautiful has nothing to do with the dress and makeup, and you know it. You'll be less nervous once the ceremony's done. You'll see."

She nodded and let me usher her toward the house. I didn't ask, but it bugged me that she was growing less and less excited about the wedding.

"Carter isn't going to spoil it, you know that, right?" I said in case she was worried about that. "I'm going to make sure of it."

"I know. He's making good on his promise. He hasn't said one cruel word to me since he apologized."

"There you go. So, try to relax and think how in just a few days, you'll be Mrs. Reese."

My words didn't produce the reaction I wanted. Instead, she withdrew into herself and left me to wonder if these were really pre-wedding jitters or if there was something more to it.

CHAPTER TWENTY-EIGHT

THE DAY OF OUR FIRST GAME AGAINST EAST CREEK HIGH HAD finally arrived, and the school buzzed with activity. There was nothing more sensational for Silver Raven students than playing against our biggest rival team, and today was no different. Our school was decorated in our colors, and there were school banners, balloons, and flags in every corner. The glass display case with our trophies was illuminated brightly in the center of the hall for visitors.

Summer and I were just passing it when Jacob entered the lobby, his duffel bag hanging off his shoulder. He smiled at me when he spotted me.

"He keeps asking me about you," Summer whispered to me out of the corner of her mouth. "He still hopes he has a chance."

A couple of girls watched him walk over to us, and I had to wonder why he was so fixated on me. He always had a line of girls after him. He was popular, handsome, and he had excellent grades. Plus, there was his best friend.

"I just don't understand why. He could have any girl. And there's this one girl that's already pining after him."

She arched her brows at me in question.

"Tara," I mouthed.

"Oh boy, you noticed that too?"

Jacob was already within earshot, so I didn't get to answer her. He looked me up and down.

"Hey, Zoe. Cuz."

Summer tipped an invisible hat at him.

"Hyped-up about the game?" I asked him.

He flashed me his perfect, straight teeth. "Very. We're going to crush them."

"Do it," Summer said. "Because I can't stand seeing their posts saying how they're going to wipe the floor with us."

"Do you think our team is ready?" I asked.

"You saw us practice. We're good. Better than the last year. And Carter . . ." He glanced away, shifting on his feet.

"What about Carter?"

"He's back in the game. He's good. Really good." He sounded strangled, as though it took him a lot of effort to admit anything positive about Carter.

"So, your coach is satisfied with his performance?"

"He says he's playing even better than last season."

My lips wanted to curve into a smile, but the way Jacob's face darkened told me that wouldn't be a good idea.

"We should go so we aren't late," I said and started toward the gym.

"I've been meaning to talk to you," Jacob told me. "I was thinking we could hang out again."

I met Summer's gaze.

"Jacob, I—"

"As friends, of course," he added when he saw my expression.

Nothing in the way he was looking at me said he wanted us to do anything as friends, and I wasn't sure if me hanging out with him would be giving him false hope.

"Maybe. With the season starting and Mom's wedding, I don't have much time these days."

His chin dropped. "I see."

"You see what?"

"You're avoiding me."

I frowned, stopping at the locker room. "Jacob, that's—"

"And this is where I leave you," Summer said, tucking her hair behind her ear. "Go get 'em." She raised her fist and darted off as though she couldn't leave quickly enough.

"I get it. I do," Jacob said. "What I did was not cool. But I don't want that to mess things up between us. I'll always be your friend." He raised his hands in the air. "Zero expectations, I swear."

I shuffled my feet, then smiled. "Okay."

"Okay?"

"After Mom's wedding, maybe we can go grab something to eat, or something."

He flashed me a grin. "Yes. You won't regret it."

I chuckled. "Now go get ready and make sure you crush them."

He winked at me. "With pleasure."

Sometime later, my squad and I entered the gym, and I took a moment to just soak everything in. The bleachers were packed, with so many faces and colors stacked together in a rainbow mass, and it felt as though the whole town had come to watch the game. All eyes were on us. The girls beside me straightened, basking in the attention. I smiled at the audience by default and shook my pom-poms.

It was showtime.

We clapped and chanted as we made our way around the court, and the audience clapped with us. There were a few whistles as we passed close to a group of guys from East Creek High sitting in the first row. My heart pumped harder at the crescendo of excitement in the air, culminating when our team entered the gym and all eyes zoomed in on them.

Carter's eyes connected with mine at once, as if there was no one else here but us two. His gait was smooth, confident, so unlike these last three months—so like it was before his accident. I couldn't stop looking at those massive shoulders peeking out from his black tank jersey. The sinew of his arms and taut planes. The strong hands, deft in providing both comfort and pleasure.

The team passed us, and Carter stopped in front of me, giving me a once-over. His pupils dilated.

My face and chest flushed, and I almost forgot where we were and that we weren't alone. After the other night, I hadn't seen him much, so I was nowhere closer to knowing where we were headed, but it excited me that he didn't try to hide his attraction to me.

Nora, of course, noticed, and her face became like a shrunken pickle.

She inched closer to me to attract his attention, almost stepping on my foot in the process. She couldn't have been more obvious if she tried. He didn't look at her even once.

"Good luck," I told him. "Not that you need it, because you're going to win."

"Nice to know you're that confident in my skills," he said cockily.

I bit into my cheek. "Don't flatter yourself. I meant the whole team."

He leaned closer to me until his lips were next to my ear. "Liar."

Goosebumps erupted all over my arms, and I had to swallow a moan. He was acting so different, and I didn't know what the rules of the game were anymore. I didn't know what to expect from him next.

I could feel cameras on us, and I found a couple of girls filming our exchange. When I returned my gaze to Carter, he'd joined his teammates, looking completely unaffected by what he'd just done. The same couldn't be said for Nora. Her eyes drilled into me, and I sensed it was time to remind her of some stuff.

I leaned toward her. "Focus on the choreography. This is an important game, and we can't mess it up. Got it? I need to know I can count on everyone to do their job right."

She stared daggers at me, and I was startled at the animosity in her gaze. "What makes you think I'll be the one messing it up?

You're the one who can't take your eyes off him like a pathetic loser."

I couldn't find words for a second. This was the first time she'd attacked me, and it caught me by surprise.

One gaze at Kim and Jenna confirmed that they'd heard her and were pleased as punch with this turn of events. They had probably even coached her on how to adjust her attitude.

"Wow. I didn't think you had it in you to be so rude."

"I don't like you, Zoe, and we all know you don't like me either. So, forgive me if I'm not that concerned about hurting your feelings."

"You haven't hurt my feelings. Don't flatter yourself."

East Creek High's team entered the gym, and my lip curled involuntarily when I spotted Brandon at the front. I'd never felt more than today that we needed a win. We needed to kick their asses.

He smirked at me, then shifted his gaze to Nora, and she all but shrank behind Kim and Jenna.

I didn't like what I saw in his gaze. It was possessiveness mixed with danger, and I couldn't begin to fathom why he was so fixated on her. She didn't want anything to do with him, but he obviously wasn't done with her, and I didn't like the implications of that.

He passed by Carter, and I held my breath as he stopped to look at him. "We're going to win," he told Carter in a low voice. "If not, there will be consequences."

Carter squared his shoulders, facing Brandon with his feet wide apart and arms folded over his chest. "Save your empty threats for someone who cares. Get ready to lose."

Brandon snarled, taking a menacing step toward him, and a few of Carter's teammates stepped in.

"Where do you think you're going?" Dawson asked.

"Mead!" his coach called to him. "Over here! Now."

Brandon's face darkened with something that gave me the creeps. He gave Carter one last glare before he took his spot with his coach and team.

The game started soon after, and I made sure to avoid looking at Brandon, focusing on Carter out on the court. The crowd was in a trance, and we all chanted, "Go, Ravens, Go," fueling our team. Our guys kept scoring three-pointers, with Carter scoring the most. Everyone was chanting Carter's name, and my chest swelled with pride as I watched him play one of his best games ever.

Brandon, on the other hand, was getting more reckless. His plays were getting more aggressive, which in turn, caused him to miss more. After Carter stole the ball from an East Creek player and rushed to the hoop, Brandon cut in front of him and shoved him backward.

The ref called a foul. Boos filled the gym.

Carter got in Brandon's face. "You're asking for it."

Brandon pushed against his shoulders. "And what are you going to do about it?"

Carter shoved him back, the tendons in his neck bulging out. "You want me to teach you another lesson? Is that it?"

"Hey, hey, hey! Stop!" the coach yelled as our team swarmed Brandon to help Carter. Brandon's teammates rushed forward too.

It took a whole minute for the ref and coaches to separate our teams, the constant booing of the crowd getting louder. Carter didn't take his eyes off Brandon as they each returned to their positions, and I half expected them to jump at each other again.

I was worried that our team would lose focus after this, but it only made them more determined to bring East Creek High to their knees. The fourth quarter was a breeze for them, and we took East Creek down by thirty points. The whole crowd went wild.

We screamed and leaped, swinging our pom-poms. Amalie and Trisha met for a kiss, while Denise and I high-fived each other, both of us wearing matching grins. I'd never felt prouder of our team and Carter. I couldn't keep my gaze away from him as his teammates flocked to him and raised him onto their shoulders. Even Jacob looked satisfied with him, for once.

Carter looked straight at me, and it felt as if time slowed. He looked so happy, opposite to how he'd appeared these last few months, and I felt so happy for him. I couldn't stop smiling as the team came forward and lowered him back to the ground, our gazes never leaving one another. I wanted to go hug him.

But I'd barely finished that thought when Nora rushed to him with a squeal and hugged him herself.

He stumbled a step back, his arms hanging wide at his sides in surprise. He needed a second to return her hug, his gaze darting my way. I felt a bout of possessiveness that almost made me physically sick.

I tore my gaze away from them only to find Brandon standing all alone on the court, showing no inclination of following his teammates off the court. His attention was fixed on Carter and Nora. Even from here I could feel the hatred oozing from him, and the force of it made me stagger back.

An alarm rang in my head when he moved his eyes to me.

I didn't give him the pleasure of showing him the fear on my face, turning my back on him as though he had no effect on me.

But even long after, his look played over and over in my head.

That wasn't just a simple expression of anger or disappointment.

It was a warning. For the first time, I had a bad feeling—that his threats weren't empty and there would actually be consequences.

For his look was a promise of retaliation.

CHAPTER TWENTY-NINE

I T TOOK ME A WHILE BEFORE I COULD EXTRICATE MYSELF FROM my squad. They insisted I come to Strider's after-game party, but I turned them down because I had to fill in for a co-worker at Bellezza. She was sick, and there was no one else to replace her, which was fine by me because I needed something to distract me from how Nora had clung to Carter when they left the school together earlier. The long, parting gaze he gave me as I got into my car imprinted itself in my mind and nursed my own longing, and I knew there was no way I wanted to spend the entire evening watching them together.

Luckily, Bellezza was busy enough to keep me occupied. But as I rushed back and forth from one table to another, my feet started to ache, and it was bad timing. I needed them pain-free for the whole day of walking in high heels at the wedding tomorrow. Plus, my arm muscles were quivering from all the exertion during our cheer routine earlier.

I was just contemplating whether I'd be able to pull off the entire shift when Brandon came in, his feral smirk in place beneath the bill of his cap.

A shiver coursed down my spine. That creepy feeling from

earlier returned with a vengeance, and I had to give myself a quick pep talk that we were in public place, and whatever he planned to do, he wouldn't be able to pull it off here.

I raised my chin high as he stopped in front of me. I flexed my fingers around my tray.

"You aren't out celebrating somewhere with those mother-fuckers? Shame."

"What are you doing here?"

He sat at the bar. "Is that how you greet a customer, Pom-Pom?"

I almost grimaced. I'd have to pass him each time I went to and from the kitchen.

"What do you want to order, then? Come on, I'm here to work, not chitchat with you."

His grin fell. "You never learn." He took out his Zippo and flipped the lid off, then on, twice, his eyes boring into me. "It's like you want me to punish you."

I put my hands on my hips, my chest rising with my quickening breaths. "You should leave."

"I think I'll stay. Give me a soda."

I arched my brows at that, but I didn't comment, moving to grab his soda from the fridge. Just as I turned around, I saw him slide off his stool and head for the restroom. I released a sigh of relief. At least I wouldn't have to see him or talk to him more than necessary.

One of the guests on the other side of the room raised his hand to attract my attention, and I headed to him. I'd just reached him when the whole place went dark, and I froze—a momentary reaction to the abrupt darkness. A few gasps erupted around me.

I swallowed hard and willed myself to function. There was enough light coming in the windows from the streetlights and cus-tomers were beginning to turn on the flashlights on their phones.

Taking deep breaths, I turned to address everyone. "Everything is fine. We seem to have lost power, that's all."

My coworker, Katrina, stopped beside me. I could just barely make out her features, courtesy of the lampposts outside.

"What do you think is going on?" she asked me.

"I'm about to ask Mr. Dellucci."

Turning on my phone's flashlight, I steeled myself against more darkness and went to find him, but he came from the back just then, carrying a flashlight.

"Dear customers, we apologize for the inconvenience," he said loud enough for everyone to hear him. "Please have some patience while we determine the cause and how long it will last. You're free to finish your meals in the meantime."

"Mr. Dellucci, what's happening?" I asked him quietly so only he and Katrina could hear me.

"I'm on my way to the fuse box to find out. Stay here, and if someone wants to leave, don't charge them."

Katrina and I nodded, and he left.

Just then, I smelled it. *Smoke.*

I spun around and yelped. Fiery flames were rapidly spreading from the bar area, swallowing everything in their way.

"Fire!" someone shouted.

Within seconds, the place morphed into a flurry of screams, shouts, and people racing to get to the exit. I waited for the sprinklers to activate, but they didn't.

I raised my hands in the air, my heart pounding against the urge to bolt out of there. "Everyone, calm down! Please form a single line and allow the children to evacuate first."

Smoke started filling the room, and through it, I saw Brandon's grin directed at me as he stood near a wall, as if he was just an observer, completely unperturbed by the fire. The sprinklers still weren't working. What the heck?

"Zoe, why are you just standing there? We have to get all these people out!" Katrina told me.

"You stay here and direct them out," I told her. "I'm going to check if there's anyone in the restrooms."

The fire licked too close to the hallway leading to the restrooms, and I had an uneasy feeling that I wouldn't be able to return that way if the flames spread this fast. That I would be trapped. But I pushed on and rushed into the guys' restroom. It was empty. Just as I rushed into the girls' restroom and confirmed all the stalls were empty there as well, Brandon filled the doorway, blocking the exit.

"Brandon?" The fire raging off to the side illuminated one side of his face, making a stark contrast to the side of his face that was in the dark. He looked like a demon, the glint in his eyes creating sheer terror in my veins.

"There's just something fascinating about fire, wouldn't you agree? How it can destroy everything in a second. How merciless it is," he said in a conversational tone, flicking his Zippo on and off. My eyes zoned in on it. The implications created a bone-deep fear.

"You set this place on fire?"

His ringing laughter made my heart twist painfully in my chest. "I warned you. But you didn't listen. You think you're all better than us because you won. Because you have everything. Money, popularity. A fucking *future*. But you're not winning now. Reese isn't winning now. Tell me, how does it feel to be on the losing side, Pom-Pom?"

I could sense that the fire was now closer, and my heart pounded frantically against my rib cage. "Brandon, we have to get out of here. You have to move." I started walking for the door, but he continued to block it. The way he looked at me told me he had no intention of letting me out.

"Brandon. Please!" Smoke was spreading fast, and it was getting harder to breathe.

"Reese made it out of the first fire in one piece, but you won't be so lucky."

My eyes widened. Like an avalanche, all the pieces of the puzzle fell into place and became clear in one perfect second. "It was *you*. That fire wasn't just some accident. *You* set that restaurant on fire."

He grinned. "It seemed like a good plan. Nora dumped me, and when I saw her there that night, I knew what I had to do. Reese showing up was an unexpected bonus. But this, tonight? That's what he gets for thinking he's better than me. For being so fucking greedy. For messing around with *my* girl." His grin widened, becoming demonic. "He messes with my girl? I'll mess with his." And with that, he pulled the key out of the lock and locked me in.

"Brandon! No, Brandon!" I screamed, pouncing at the door. I pounded at it with my fists, panic constricting my lungs. "Brandon, let me out! Brandon!"

The smoke was even thicker now, and I started coughing, my eyes welling with tears. Desperation sat heavy in my stomach as I rained blows on the door.

"Help! Can anyone hear me? I'm trapped in here. Anyone, please!"

The only response was the popping of the fire, and I gripped my chest, panic and smoke forcing me to take quick breaths. There was no window or a way for me to break through the door.

I was going to die. The shitshow that was my life was continuing to the very end. I couldn't escape from here, and by the time anyone noticed I hadn't evacuated with the others . . .

Carter. I'd never see Carter again. And Mom was going to lose me. She was going to be devastated.

I slumped against the wall, crying and coughing. Memories swarmed my mind, and I sobbed as I thought about Carter's kisses and hands upon me. I conjured fantasies about him coming to save me as a last-ditch effort not to give in to panic.

Seconds later, I thought I actually heard his voice. I realized I was losing it already.

"Zoe? Zoe, are you in there?"

I snapped my head toward the door. I was hallucinating. That must be it.

"Zoe!"

"Carter?"

No, I wasn't hallucinating. I jumped to my feet and hit the door with the side of my fist repeatedly. "Carter! Carter, I'm here!"

"Step back! I'm going to break in!"

I had enough time to take a couple of steps backwards before he kicked the door open. The fire had almost devoured the whole hallway behind him, but just seeing him, his strong and powerful form, had me almost overwhelmed with relief.

"Carter!" I rushed into his embrace as his arms spread out to wrap around me. My body was a shaking leaf against him.

"We need to go. *Now.*" He half-dragged me out of the restroom.

I couldn't get enough air in my lungs. The fire was so close to us it would become unbearable in seconds. It was so hot, and I could barely see where we were going. All I could do as Carter navigated through the fire was not slow him down.

Something cracked a moment before one of the beams detached from the ceiling, and it was happening right above us. I had only a split second to think how history was cruelly repeating itself before Carter had us out of its way at the last possible moment, sending us to the ground.

He turned on his knees to look at me, grabbing my shoulders. "Are you okay?"

I nodded, blinking to confirm he was actually unharmed.

"We have to move faster. Come on." Taking my hand in his, he helped me to my feet and pulled me after him, and after what felt like an hour but could be only seconds, we made it to the center of the room. There was only a narrow passage available for us to pass now, and at the end of it was the exit.

The desire for freedom had me pushing forward faster, past the unbearable heat, and we finally made it out, running into the fresh night air. I propped my hands on my knees, gulping for it.

Carter grabbed my cheeks, making me look at him. "Are you okay? Hurt anywhere?"

I placed my hands over his. "No. You?"

He shook his head and yanked me into his embrace. "You're okay. You're okay, you're okay." The relief in his tone made my heart swell with love.

He'd just saved me. I could've died. *We* could've died, but he'd risked his life to get me out, and I hadn't thought it was possible to love him more, but in this moment, I did. I'd never loved him more than now.

I wrapped my arms around him tightly. I needed his warmth and closeness. I needed him to hold me just like he had before his amnesia, like we hadn't been separated at all. Like he'd never stopped loving me.

I wanted to keep holding him forever, but Mr. Dellucci's voice rang out, "Thank God!" He rushed toward us as fast as his old legs could take him. "You're alive. *Grazie a Dio!*"

Carter and I separated just in time for Mr. Dellucci to pull me into his embrace.

"When I saw you weren't with Katrina, that you were missing . . . *Dio mio!* I aged ten years worrying about you."

I smiled as he murmured over and over again how worried he'd been, succumbing to more tears. I'd been shaking all this time, and my throat was sore. A crowd had gathered around us. The ambulance sirens came from the distance, growing louder and louder.

Fire had completely engulfed Bellezza, and my stomach lurched as I separated from Mr. Dellucci. The sight brought fresh tears to my eyes. Mr. Dellucci's decades of hard work, pride, and passion was gone. So easily.

Anger blazed through me. This was all Brandon's doing. I wanted him to pay. I wanted him to rot in jail for everything he'd done. I did a sweep of the area, but I was unable to find him anywhere. *Figures.*

This was exactly how Nora had been trapped in that previous fire. To think that it happened again, that it was some sick, twisted retribution . . . Carter had come out a hero once again, but how many times he would get away before his luck expired?

"It seems as though you're destined to rescue girls from fires." I coughed.

He smiled, taking off his jacket and putting it on me. "I'm getting better at it. No injury this time."

I laughed, and after everything, it was cathartic. I needed a way to release all these pent-up emotions inside me. To breathe more freely. To stop thinking about death and pain.

The fire truck parked across the sidewalk, and firefighters rushed out. Almost at the same time, an ambulance pulled up, and Mr. Dellucci ushered us over to it to get checked out. One EMT had us sit on a bench as he took our vitals, and the other examined us for any injuries. Thanks to Carter, though, other than smoke inhalation, I wasn't hurt. The EMTs told me to come to the hospital for a more thorough checkup if I kept coughing or had trouble breathing.

The police had arrived in the meantime, and Carter went to talk with one of them, who was coincidentally one of Dominic's friends. I overheard Carter making the officer promise not to call Dominic because he was getting married tomorrow and Carter didn't want anything to spoil his day. Carter assured the officer we would let Dominic know in person after the wedding. As I watched Carter talk, I felt as if I was in a dream and would wake up at any second. Because it was hard to make sense of this Carter after all those weeks of hate and quarreling.

The police officers questioned us, and Carter's face went dark when I said I suspected Brandon of doing it, describing the events leading up to and during the fire. I'd thought Brandon had gone to the restroom, but he must've gone to the basement across from it and messed with the fuse box and sprinkler system. In the darkness, no one could see him start the fire. I also mentioned his confession about the previous fire. Carter didn't say anything, but the way his body shook with tension was a clear enough sign that he was furious.

Only once the officers were out of earshot did he speak. "I'm going to kill that son of a bitch."

"No, you won't. He's trouble. The police can handle him."

"You can't expect me to just sit here and do nothing. He could've *killed* you. He *tried* to kill you."

"And he can kill *you* if you try to do something."

"I'm not afraid of him."

"I know, but that doesn't make him any less dangerous. He's clearly nuts. Who knows what he could do next?"

He didn't argue with me, but he didn't look convinced either, and I suspected he would do something anyway.

Once the officers said we were good to go, Carter reached his hand out to me. "Come on."

I stood from the bench and let him lead me to his car parked in the nearby parking lot. My brows went up.

"You drove here?"

"Yeah. I don't see any reason not to when I feel completely fine. Plus, I got tired of relying on others to drive me everywhere."

"What are you even doing here? Weren't you supposed to be at Strider's party? And how did you know I was here?"

"I wanted to see you, so I left the party. One of your squad mates, Denise, told me you were working tonight."

"You wanted to see me?"

"It was boring there without you. I waited for you to show up, but you didn't."

"But why?"

He took my hands and tugged me to him. "Do you really need to ask?"

My eyes shifted between his again and again. There was affection in his eyes. Affection, and concern, and also desire. So much desire my chest threatened to cave in.

"I was worried that history would repeat itself. And that this time you would die," I whispered.

His gaze devoured me as he leaned against the side of his car and pulled me between his legs, and I let him all too eagerly. "I was worried that *you* would die. When I saw that restaurant on fire and you weren't among the evacuated . . . I almost lost my mind right there." He shook his head. "If you had died . . ." The crack in his voice made my heart clench in my chest.

Something in my chest twisted and untwisted as emotions coursed through me. The fear of this night—the fear of these past few months—bubbled to the surface and urged me to get closer to him, to forget about everything negative and just hold him.

He cupped my cheeks with his hands. "I almost lost you. I can't lose you."

My heart was thudding so hard I was certain he could hear it. "You don't even have me, Carter."

"I know I don't deserve you, you said so yourself. But I want to do better. I was so stupid for not allowing you in, for all the shit I put you through. I'm so sorry. Only you can make me happy. Everything's fucked up, but when I'm with you . . . none of that matters. I promise you, if you give me a chance, we can start again with a clean slate."

"So, what does this mean? You want to get back with me?"

His eyes glimmered with emotion. "What do you think?"

I couldn't speak. I could hardly even breathe. All the emotions twirled and swirled inside me, and it was a perfect storm. The past few months had been a mixture of nightmares and hope and deep sadness, but not anymore. Tonight, I finally had my answer. The way he looked at me, the way he held me . . . against all odds, Carter had found his way to me again. He'd risked his life for me, and after everything, I wanted to cry, but happy tears. Tears of joy that I had him again. That despite all my doubts, worries, and previous disappointments, *yes*, he was mine.

"What about Nora?"

"What about her? She's just a friend. I don't feel anything for her. How about you? Do you like Jacob?"

"No."

His face split with a grin. "You have no idea how happy that makes me." He leaned his forehead against mine, and my breath stuttered at his nearness. "So? Do I have you? Are you mine, baby?"

I curled my arms around his neck, playing with the ends of his hair. "Yes. I'm yours. Always have been."

He captured my lips with his. His tongue darted out to coax my lips apart and slipped inside, tending to this all-encompassing need within me. This kiss was different from all our previous kisses. It was a kiss of new beginnings and promises, a kiss of the past and present coming together.

I gripped his hoodie and pressed closer to him. He stopped to look at me, and his gaze slid over my face as if he wanted to memorize each inch of me.

He smiled. "You're beautiful."

"I just came out of a fire. I'm not sure that I look so good."

"You're beautiful," he repeated. He raised my arm and pulled up the sleeve of his jacket enough to reveal my tattoo. Looking up at me, he placed an open-mouthed kiss over my throbbing artery.

"Carter," I said on a shaky breath.

"Now I understand why I loved kissing you here." He ran his lips across the heart of my bird over and over, causing my pulse to speed up. "It's so addictive."

This time, his name came out as a moan.

At that, his eyes flashed with need, and he moved in to kiss me again. Our mouths met halfway and melted together, our hands rediscovering each other's bodies. Nothing mattered but feeling more, having more.

"I need to be inside you. Right now," he said roughly, and before I could make sense of what was happening, he had me tucked into the passenger seat and we were on our way out of the parking lot.

"Where are we going?"

"Where I can have you."

His words lit the fuse that was my desire, and during the whole ride, my body was throbbing with the urge to feel all of him. He followed a small road that took us out of town and then parked by the woods, turning off the engine. There was nothing around us for miles.

Carter didn't say anything as he turned toward me, his eyes animalistic and his face strained with desire. He crushed his lips on mine. In a split second, he had his hands all over me, and my body arched against him like a string pulled tight. The overload of sensations had me delirious. His lips were tailored for me, existing to brand pleasure into me with their kisses. His hands were instruments of sweet torture.

I returned the kiss with more ardor.

Without interrupting the kiss, he grabbed my waist and yanked me onto his lap so that I was straddling him. My arms wrapped around his neck as his tongue stroked mine. The kiss verged on wild, almost as if we both needed to drown in each other—to just *feel*.

His lips dove for my neck and left a trail of kisses along my skin. I slid my hands across the broad expanse of his back. His muscles were quivering, betraying the intensity of his desire, and I loved how easily I could make him lose control.

He took his jacket off me and hiked up my shirt. My core clenched at the look in his eyes as they landed on my heaving breasts. It was as though I was his buffet, and this was his last meal.

He shoved my bra up and claimed my nipple with his warm mouth.

"Carter," I moaned.

"You taste so good. So sweet."

He was tormenting me with his tongue and his teeth and his lips, and it was too much. I tilted my hips toward him, silently pleading with him to relieve the pressure quickly building between my thighs. He complied, grabbing my hips to push me against his hard-on, and the contact sent a zap of pleasure through me.

"Yes. Just like that." I pressed my lips to his, and his mouth opened as a welcome, his tongue slipping out, seeking my taste, my heat.

He moaned into my mouth and ground me against him harder. We were both panting, both desperate for more, and I couldn't wait any longer.

I raised myself to my knees and peeled off my jeans, one foot, then another, bumping against the steering wheel in my rush. Carter took a condom out of his back pocket and pulled his jeans down enough to free his erection. He didn't wait for me to take off my underwear. In seconds, he had the condom on and was shoving my panties aside, driving himself deep into me, right to the hilt.

"Yes," I hissed.

His eyes were burning as he watched me, and my heart swelled in my chest at the familiarity of it. He'd always sought my gaze when he was inside me, always deepening our connection, and to have him do that now . . . it was everything. It was more intoxicating than ever. It propelled me toward my release, and after only a few seconds, I was coming so hard I could barely remember my name.

"So beautiful," he rasped out. "You're so fucking beautiful."

He didn't stop. He didn't hold back as he thrust into me, his fingers digging into my hips almost to the point of bruising. It was as if he wanted to mark me. To remind me that he possessed me. That no one could ever make me fully surrender except him.

He brought his hand between us and rubbed me, and the sensations were too much. He never disconnected our gazes, plunging into me deeper and deeper, and then his lips were on mine and we were climaxing together, everything within me yielding to this complex guy who owned my heart. I never wanted this to end.

He held me in his embrace even after the last aftershock had passed, even long after our breathing had returned to normal. His arms were wound around me in a promise of forever.

And I wanted to cry with joy because, recovered memories or not, my Carter was back. And the world didn't feel so bleak anymore, filling with possibilities and unbridled joy.

CHAPTER THIRTY

T HE NEXT MORNING, I WOKE UP TO CARTER'S ARM HOLDING me tightly against his body, my back to him, his breath warm on my neck. I wiggled onto my other side to watch him sleep.

I couldn't believe we were back together. After we'd returned home, part of me expected him to go his own way, but he grabbed my hand and took me to his room, where we'd spent the entire night. We showered together in his bathroom (not before he took me once more against the shower wall) and crashed in his bed, physically and emotionally exhausted after the events of the previous night.

I raised my hand to trace his features, marveling in the feel of his skin against mine. I ran my finger across the stubble darkening his jaw and smiled, because I'd missed waking up by his side and watching his face first thing in the morning. I was finally able to touch him however I wanted and wherever I wanted, and I planned to make the most of it. I had a lot to make up for.

He opened his eyes and smiled. "Good morning," he croaked out.

I smiled back. "Good morning, sleepyhead. Did you sleep well?"

He scrunched up his nose. "Sleep well? You were snoring the whole time."

My lips widened into a grin. He was just like before. "And you're lying."

"Oh yeah? Do you want me to record you next time to prove it?"

I sucked in a breath, my heart giving a hard kick against my ribcage. He said the exact same thing as he'd written in a text on the day of his accident.

I was getting more pieces of him back.

This time, I had a different response for him. "I'm looking forward to it."

My face must be revealing everything, because he grew serious and tightened his arms around me. That brought me flush against him, and my eyes rounded when I felt his arousal pressed against my thigh.

"Carter," I said on an exhale.

His hand pushed inside the waistband of my shorts all the way to my butt and squeezed. In an instant, he spun us around, ending up on his back with me straddling him. "Is this real?" he asked me, his hands roaming up and down my hips as if he couldn't get enough of me. "You're not going to disappear?"

Supporting my hands against his steel-hard pecs, I moved my pelvis against him, making him moan. "I think that's the question I should ask you."

"Not a chance." He brought his hand to the back of my head and pulled me down for a kiss, his tongue coming out to greet mine. I sighed into his mouth, losing myself in the heat of it.

He started to pull down my shorts, but then I remembered I was supposed to get ready for the ceremony.

"Carter, we can't. I have to go get ready. I can't be late."

He tilted his hips against me, threatening to smash my resolve into nothing. "Just a quickie."

He was already reaching for the hem of his boxers, but one look at the clock on his nightstand told me I was definitely going to be late if I indulged him.

"Later." I jumped off him, and he groaned, running his hands down his face.

"You're killing me."

He's not the only one. I wanted him so badly.

"We'll continue this later, I promise." Before I could change my mind, I left his room and made a quick detour to my bathroom to wash my face and brush my teeth before I went to search for Mom.

The house was decorated with arrangements of white flowers, and their soft, fragrant scent permeated the air. There were people everywhere, from the decorators to the waiters and photographers, all getting ready for the main event. The living room had been cleared out to make space for the dais and chairs for the guests. A live band was setting up their equipment in the corner of the room.

The rush of activity amped up my excitement. I couldn't wait for Mom and Dominic to finally take that step.

Mrs. Hopper told me Mom was in her bedroom with the hairdressers, so I headed there.

"There you are," Mom said when I entered the bedroom. She was already stationed at her vanity table, and two hairdressers on either side of her were working on her curls.

"Am I late?" I slumped down on her bed.

"Not at all. As soon as they're done with me, you're next."

"Cool." I made myself cozy on the bed, leaning against my elbows. "This is it. You're getting married. Are you excited?"

She nodded, making it a point not to look at me. I studied her face, noting the dark circles under her eyes, and I wondered if that was her anemia again. We'd made sure she ate well and rested enough. Her last blood tests had come out good.

"Did you sleep well?"

"So-so. Pre-wedding jitters, as you know."

I angled my head. Something wasn't adding up, but I didn't want to pressure her. This was her big moment, and today she needed positive energy only.

Once Mom's hair was done, they ushered me into her chair and pulled my hair into an elegant bun, topping it off with a glittering butterfly hairpin on the side of my head. Soon after, Summer arrived, and she worked her magic on our faces. Mom had opted for light makeup, while I asked for a cut crease with eye shadows that matched my teal bridesmaid dress. Summer made sure to record a video so she could use it for TikTok and as part of her portfolio.

Once we were done up and dressed, Mom and I stopped in front of the mirror to look at each other.

My eyes watered, and I thanked Summer for the waterproof mascara. Mom was wearing a white Oscar de La Renta ballgown with a low-cut neckline that hugged her breasts and flared out at her waist. It was all made of lace with elaborate flower detail.

"Mom, you're gorgeous. Wait until Dominic sees you. You're going to knock him out."

For the first time today, she gave me a real smile, and her own eyes filled with moisture. She grasped my hand and made me spin around. "And look at you. My baby girl looks like a princess."

My dress swished around me. It was a princess line dress that reached my mid-calves.

"You're beautiful, honey," she said, choked up.

"Aww, Mom. No crying today. Okay?"

"I know. It's just that I've always wanted to see you in a dress like this. Always hoped I could afford it one day."

"You're having your dreams come true one by one."

Her expression turned unreadable as she glanced at her dress. "This is a good thing, right? Getting married to Dominic?"

I smothered the frown that wanted out. "Yes, Mom. Both you and Dominic deserve all the happiness in the world."

"How does it feel to build happiness on someone else's unhappiness?" she muttered into her chin.

"What?"

She flashed her pearly whites at me. "Nothing."

A knock came at the door, and Mrs. Gibson peered in. "Good morning! How are we doing today?"

"Great," Mom said, her smile fixed on her face.

"I wanted to do a run-through of the ceremony with you one more time."

I took that as a cue for me and Summer to leave.

"I'll be downstairs if you need me," I said and took Summer with me.

I didn't know what to make of Mom's state of mind. I guessed it was normal for brides to be super emotional and moody on their wedding day, plus Mom was pregnant. But I'd hoped she would be happier, not just go through the motions expected of her with no excitement to follow.

The house had filled with guests, and I went to greet the maid of honor and the rest of Mom's bridesmaids before I joined Summer again in the foyer.

"Your mom looks gorgeous," Summer said. "But a little sad."

"That's what's bothering me. It's not normal to be sad on your wedding day, right?"

"Nope."

"I have no idea what's going on with her. She says it's pre-wedding jitters, but I don't know. Something's not right."

She licked her lips. "I didn't want to mention it in front of your mom, but I heard about Bellezza on the way here. You were working there last night, right?"

"Yes. It was Brandon Mead. He set the place on fire."

"What?"

I recounted the events that led to the fire, mentioning our previous encounters, his connection to Nora, and also the first fire he'd caused.

Summer paled. "He's totally crazy!"

"Yeah. And now he's gunning for Carter." A feeling of concern flickered in my stomach. I hoped the cops would find Brandon before he got someone killed.

"He got away with the first fire, but he can't get away with this one."

"I hope you're right. Anyway, something good came out of it after all."

"What do you mean?"

"Brandon trapped me in the restroom, but then Carter came and helped me escape. We barely made it out of there, Sum." My stomach clenched at the thought that I could've lost Carter for good. "After that, we talked, and long story short, we're back together."

"Wow. Just wow." Her mouth remained open. "Talk about lots of surprises in just one night. So, we have more than one reason to celebrate today, right?" She grinned.

I nodded, lifting my gaze as a figure appeared in my periphery. It was Carter, standing on the top step and looking at me in a way that made my body temperature skyrocket. He was dressed in a dark suit, and his hair was styled back, which accentuated his sharp cheekbones and chiseled jaw. He was absolutely delectable, and the best thing—I got to kiss him whenever I wanted again.

His smile matched mine as he came down, and if I'd thought he would play it cool in front of Summer, I was all wrong, because he closed the distance between us and palmed the back of my head. Without a word, he pressed his lips to mine.

His kiss sent heat all the way down to my toes, and my arms snaked around him to pull him closer to me. His kisses felt equal parts new and familiar, and the contradiction had me swaying on my feet. I got to explore this side of Carter—the one who was getting to know me and falling for me all over again. It made me heady.

For a split second, I wondered if he really wouldn't get his old memories back. We were making new memories, but I wished he didn't have a gap. I wished he could remember our first kiss, our first time together, all our firsts. I didn't want to be the only one who remembered them.

He pulled away from me, and I felt a flicker of satisfaction in my chest when I saw his eyes were glazed. "You're gorgeous in that dress."

"So are you in that suit. You belong on a catwalk."

He chuckled. "I'll leave the catwalks to Jackson. Those are his thing."

Summer shifted her weight at the mention of Jackson, which made Carter finally look at her. "Hi."

"Hi to you too. I'm glad to see you two have patched things up."

Carter grinned. "So it seems." He pulled out his phone and turned me so that we were both looking into the camera, then snaked his arm around my shoulder. "Smile for the camera."

I smiled, then chuckled when he left a kiss on my cheek in time to capture it. His eyes were sparkling as he studied the photo, and I leaned my head against his shoulder to observe the picture, feeling something warm deep in my chest. It wasn't our first photo together, but it was the first he remembered, and I saw it meant something to him.

"We look good together," he said quietly.

I kissed his cheek. "Yes, we do."

Dominic came from the back, fixing his tie. His face lit up when he saw me, and he nodded at me in approval.

"You look beautiful, Zoe." His expression turned wary as he looked at Carter. It was clear he didn't trust Carter not to make a scene and ruin the wedding.

At this, Carter took my hand in his, and Dominic's brows scrunched up.

"You two are back together?"

Carter raised his chin. "Yes. Do you have a problem with that?"

Dominic's lips pressed together. "If you're not going to treat her well, then, yes, I do have a problem."

"He's treating me well, Dominic," I said. "We're okay now."

I could see he didn't believe that, but he didn't press the matter. "We'll talk about this later."

"We're starting," Mrs. Gibson said, popping her head out from the living room, and we followed her inside.

The band started playing a classical piece. I gave Carter a quick kiss and went to join the bridesmaids. A hush settled over the room when Mom showed up at the doorway, a large bouquet of white roses in her hands. She walked down the aisle between the rows of chairs, the train of her dress sweeping along behind her. At one point, the sunlight came down right on Mom's hair, making a halo that transformed the sight into one of those from a fairytale. This was Mom's fairytale coming true, and my heart fluttered in my chest with happiness for her.

Dominic stood still as he watched Mom walk toward him, and the look of love on his face made my heart contract.

I looked behind her to where Carter was sitting beside Summer. He winked at me, and I found myself melting. It still felt unreal that we were back together. That we'd been given another chance. I was so eager to hold him in my arms again, to explore his every sensitive spot and show him mine, as though I'd lose the chance if I didn't do it as soon as possible. I had to tamp down the urge, reminding myself that we had all the time in the world to explore each other again.

The ceremony was short but memorable, and I never felt happier for Mom than now. Dominic kept giving her glances filled with adoration, and the anxiety that had been etched on her face earlier faded away.

A wave of relief washed over me, not only for that smile on her face but also for the fact that Dominic was the best man there was for her. She was in good hands. And now Dominic was truly my family. They shared a kiss, and I could just feel the love radiating from them, warming the room and bringing smiles to all our faces. It was one of the sweetest things I'd ever seen.

After that, it was a blur as we took family photos, then Mom and Dominic went from one guest to another. Glasses of champagne made the rounds. We moved to the dining room, and the meal was served, but I could hardly eat with all the excitement of the day. Carter didn't take his gaze off me the whole time, and as we sat next to each other, it was a struggle not to kiss or touch one another, our hands straying under the table to touch on more than one occasion. Summer kept giving us amused glances, until at one point she told us to get a room.

She wasn't the only one staring. Mom couldn't seem to stop looking between me and Carter, and the relaxed look on her face right after the ceremony gradually shifted to unease with each passing hour—just like the other night when she saw me and Carter together. But why? I had to get to the bottom of this after the wedding was over.

Before long, it was time for Mom and Dominic's first dance, but Mom had gone to use the bathroom and had yet to return.

"I'm going to get her," I said to Dominic and stood up. I brushed my hand across Carter's. "I'll be right back."

His smoldering gaze held mine and followed me as I made my way across the room. It was full of promise, and I shivered with anticipation.

Mom wasn't in any of the bathrooms downstairs, so I headed to her bedroom. Only it turned out the bathroom in her bedroom was empty too. Where was she?

Just as I stepped out of the bedroom, I noticed that the door of the nursery had been left wide open. It was always closed, which could mean only one thing.

I frowned. What was she doing in there now?

My heels clicked on the marble floor as I approached the room. I found her cradling her belly as she stood in profile by the window. The sun was dropping closer to the horizon, the darkening sky casting deep shadows over her face. She was lost in thought.

I looked around the room. There was a fresh coat of yellow paint, Mom's favorite color. She said yellow always made her happy, and she wanted that color for the nursery. There were rainbows and clouds painted on one wall, right above the custom-made crib Dominic had shipped in from Europe. A few boxes with furniture and baby gear sat unopened in one corner of the room.

"Mom? You okay?"

Her lips pressed together as she took a deep breath through her nose. My pulse quickened as I stepped closer to her. Only now I noticed her hands were squeezed into tight fists.

"Mom, you're scaring me. Did something happen?"

She turned to look at me. Her eyes were rimmed with red.

"My selfishness."

She'd spoken so quietly, I thought I imagined her saying those words at first.

"What do you mean?"

Her dress swished across the floor as she moved to the armchair taking up one corner of the room. She lowered herself into it and placed her hand over her stomach, his fingers scrunching up the material of her dress.

"I thought I'd be able to get over it. Dom assured me time and again we were doing nothing wrong. But now I'm not so sure."

"You're not so sure about what?"

"That this wedding wasn't a mistake."

A cold feeling slithered through my chest. I rushed over to her and dropped to my knees on the floor in front of her, taking her hands in mine. "Don't say that, Mom. This marriage is the best decision you've ever made."

"Is it?" She shook her head over and over again. "You don't know everything, Zoe. I've been trying to suppress the past for so long, but I finally realized I can't. I can't pretend the past didn't happen or that it doesn't matter. I can't hide things from you anymore. And when I see you together with Carter . . . it only emphasizes that feeling."

"What are you saying? What feeling?"

"The feeling that I'm letting Carter down."

"But why?"

She untwined her hands from mine. "Carter was right all along. I lied to you. Dominic and I had an affair."

My mouth went dry. "What?"

"Dominic was cheating on Anastacia."

The thudding of my heart grew loud, and for a few seconds, it was all I could hear. That feeling I'd been ignoring all this time returned with a vengeance, and I couldn't hide from it anymore. It was true. Mom had been Dominic's lover.

I'd said to Carter once that we were all human and made mistakes but knowing that Mom had actually chosen to have an affair left a bitter taste in my mouth. For me, Mom was incapable of making such mistakes—of making selfish choices. I'd always considered her incapable of crossing that line. To know she wasn't as perfect as I'd always considered her to be undid something within me.

"Dominic and I have been together since a couple of months before Anastacia's death. At that time, it felt like it was impossible not to fall for him." She smiled, her eyes unfocused with the memories unfolding in her head. "I fell for him the moment I saw him arrive at that company where I was working as a cleaner. Coincidentally, I spilled disinfectant all over his pants, but he was so nice and understanding about it. From there, we hit it off, and every time he came, he looked for me to talk to me. Before long, I was head over heels for him.

"He was everything I ever wanted, Zoe. For the first time, I felt irrevocably happy and safe. I finally had someone to lean on, someone to talk to when I went through tough times. Everything felt perfect with him . . . except, he was married."

I swallowed twice. My hands were cold and shaking.

"I wish I could say I wanted to stop seeing Dom when I found out about her. But, no, I didn't leave him. And even worse—I asked him to leave her."

Judging by how things had gone down, Dominic had not agreed to do so. "Why didn't he leave her?"

"Because her mental health was declining, and it never felt like a good time to break the news to her." Moisture appeared in her eyes. "She was suffering because she knew. She knew all along about me and Dominic."

"But how?"

"She caught us together once."

So that was how Carter was so sure they'd had an affair. His mom had known it for a fact, and she must've told him about it.

I didn't know what to say. As I looked at her and listened to her confess all of this, it felt as though I was looking at a person I didn't know. A stranger. I didn't want to judge; I wanted to understand her, but it was hard, knowing that, yes, she'd built her happiness on someone else's unhappiness, as Carter had said.

She buried her face in her hands. "That's not all."

I felt a lash of fear deep inside me. There was more?

"Dominic and I have been hiding it for so long . . . too long. But it's eating me alive, and it tarnishes the happiness I feel with Dominic. It tarnishes what Dominic and I have, and I thought—*hoped*—things would change once I became his wife, but they only got worse. Because our life together came at a cost. A huge cost."

"What is it, Mom?" My voice was raspy, echoing the dread that coiled in my stomach. I didn't want to hear more things that would show her in a bad light, but I needed to know.

Her gaze was locked on her hands, as if she couldn't look at me while revealing this secret to me. "Anastacia didn't die in an accident. There wasn't any truck driver involved. She deliberately drove her car into a tree at full speed, trying to kill herself because she couldn't live without Dom anymore. She'd admitted as much in the note she left for Dom before she did it."

The bitter taste of acid filled my throat. Her face was now wet with tears rolling down her cheeks, her voice becoming throatier with regret and shame.

"And the worst part—the thing I'll never be able to forgive myself for—is that she came to me after she wrote that note. It was the first time she came directly to me to beg me to leave her husband alone. She said she hadn't felt stable for a long time and she needed Dominic more than anything. She told me she would kill herself if I didn't let him go. It was her last attempt to get him back."

She squeezed her eyes shut, her tears soaking the skin above the neckline of her dress. She was shaking hard.

"You have no idea how I wish I could say I didn't believe her, that I considered it a bluff out of desperation to get her husband back. But I knew it wasn't a bluff, and I . . . I didn't do anything to help her. I refused to leave Dominic." She sobbed hard, her hands twisting her dress so tightly it was bound to leave permanent creases. "She looked shaken when she got behind the wheel of her car, and I didn't even try to stop her. She died after that."

The silence in the room ran deep, and I wasn't even sure I was breathing. My chest was expanding with shock, pain, and disbelief, and I wanted to turn the clock back to the time before I found this out. No, even further—before Carter's mom got into that car and drove herself to her death.

"I'm responsible for her death, Zoe. I stole her husband from her and refused to let him go, and I didn't think twice about taking her place in this house after she died. Because I was too selfish. Because I wanted a better life for myself and you. And my life has been a personal hell ever since."

A guttural sound came from the door, and Mom and I snapped our heads toward it.

No.

Carter was standing in the doorway, gripping the doorjamb with a ferocity that stole my breath. His face was all hatred and fury, and I'd never seen him more dangerous-looking than now. *He heard everything.*

"You fucking bitch," he said through his teeth, his whole body trembling with barely restrained rage that threatened to snap at any moment. "You piece of shit."

Mom stood up, her arm shaking as she supported herself against the armrest. "Carter, I—"

"You killed her. It's all your fault."

Mom pressed a hand against her mouth, a sob tearing out of her. "I'm sorry, Carter. I'm so sorry for everything."

"You're *sorry*? You stole her husband from her and when she begged you to leave him alone, you fucking ignored her! You let her die! You're a murderer!"

Mom swayed, her face too pale under her makeup.

"Mom. Take it easy." I rushed over to catch her, slinging my arm around her waist. She was shaking so hard it was unnatural.

"No, I'm fine." She pulled away from me, taking a deep breath through her nose as more tears made their way down her face.

I felt my own tears breaking loose. I was gutted to see Mom and Carter like this. The hurt in Carter's eyes reached the deepest parts of me, and I wished I could say something that would make this right. But nothing could make this right. Nothing would bring his mom back. Mom was absolutely wrong here, but I couldn't let him tear into her.

"Carter, don't. I know you're upset, and you have every right to be, but whatever you do, keep in mind her condition. We mustn't upset her."

He sliced me with his glare. "Don't fucking defend her."

"I'm not. But she's clearly sorry and suffering because of her mistakes."

His eyes darkened with even more rage. "*Mistakes?* She intentionally allowed Mom to kill herself. That's not a mistake!"

I winced, my stomach filling with lead.

"I regret it, Carter," Mom said, her voice unrecognizable under the weight of her guilt. "I regret destroying your family. I regret ever laying my eyes on your dad. I regret all of it." She wiped her nose with the back of her hand. "I don't deserve your forgiveness. I just hope that we can get past this one day."

His eyes widened, filling with hatred that knew no end. "*Get past this?*" He looked between Mom and me, his face turning to stone, and a terrible fear spread through my chest. This was affecting so much more than his relationship with Mom and Dominic. This was affecting *us* as well, and I feared that from now on, there would be no more love in his eyes reserved for me. Only hate.

Fear propelled me closer to him. "Carter."

"I'm out of here." He pivoted on his heel and disappeared out the door.

I rushed into the hallway. "Wait! Carter, where are you going?"
I grabbed his sleeve, but he shoved my hand away.

"Don't touch me!" His teeth were bared, his breathing coming
out in harsh gusts. He was looking at me as though I was his enemy.

And the fear in me doubled.

"Carter, does this affect us?"

He raised his brows. "You think we can be together after this?
Think again."

Searing pain speared my chest, and I had to clench my hand
against my mouth so I wouldn't cry out. I couldn't lose him just
when we'd found each other again. I couldn't bear seeing him look
at me with hate again.

"Please, Carter, reconsider. You're making a mistake. This has
nothing to do with us. You can't let their past define us."

"Nothing to do with us? This has everything to do with us! I
can't look at you and not remember how much my mom suffered
because of your mom. How I lost my mom because of *her*. How
fucked up your mother was to want to be with another woman's
man to *that* extent."

Mom released a sob behind me as anger that he'd spoken
about her so cruelly took me over.

"If my mom's fucked up, your mom's even more fucked up
to commit suicide." The moment the words were out, I regretted
them, pressing my hand against my mouth as if that would somehow erase them.

He went deadly still. I thought I'd already seen the worst from
him—that he would never look at me with a hate that cut through
every part of my being—but I was wrong. Because the way he
stared at me . . . he stared at me as though he couldn't bear to look
at me a second longer, and I knew that I'd just destroyed whatever
hope existed that we could get over this.

"Now I know why I forgot being with you in the first place.
Because we're not meant to be. Because I deserve better than a
bitch like you."

I almost doubled over with pain. *No.*

Nora's words returned to torment me. *"His amnesia is the universe's sign that you two shouldn't be together."*

No, that couldn't be true. It just couldn't.

He gave a sardonic smile. "And to think that I made the same mistake again. But I got the message loud and clear. You won't get close to me ever again." He directed a glare at Mom. "Since I'm turning eighteen in three days, I'll find someplace else to live and then I won't have to see your face again."

All my muscles froze. This couldn't be happening.

"Carter, no." Mom passed me, going after him. "Don't do that. We can talk this through. *Please.*" She tried to grab his arm as he reached the stairs, but he shoved her hand away.

"Stay away from me! I'm done talking, and I'm done putting up with your bullshit." He went down the stairs.

"You can't leave! Don't leave because of me. This is your home."

He didn't listen to her, already making his way across the foyer.

"Please, Carter. Don't do this!" She rushed after him, reaching for the banister as she took a step down the stairs.

In a second that slowed to a crawl, her foot caught on the train of her dress, and I could only watch in horror as she launched forward, unable to grab for purchase. All sound ceased to exist as she tumbled down the stairs, coming to a halt at the bottom, face down.

It took a second after that for sound to come back—a second for me to break through the paralysis of sheer terror.

And then I was rushing down the stairs, screaming.

"Mom! Mom, are you okay?" I skidded to my knees hard enough to leave scrapes, but I didn't feel anything. She slowly curled into herself, her hands clutching her stomach as she cried out in pain. She squeezed her eyes shut.

I grabbed her shoulders. "Mom, talk to me."

She screamed, "My baby. Oh God, it hurts!"

Dominic and Mrs. Hopper were among the first to rush out of the dining room. Their shouts drowned out Mom's cries.

"Erika!" Dominic ran over and dropped to his knees next to her, placing his hand over Mom's. "What happened?"

"She fell down the stairs," I said.

"My stomach," Mom said through clenched teeth. "It hurts so much. I can't lose my baby. Dom, please help. I can't lose my baby."

The baby. My lungs ceased to work as a new fear paralyzed me. This couldn't be good. She'd hit her stomach directly, and what were the chances that the baby was okay? Mom was already in a fragile condition and now . . . No, no, no.

"You won't lose it. I won't let that happen," Dominic said, holding her hand pressed to his chest.

"But it hurts so much. Why does it hurt so much?" She cried out and exhaled another breath through her teeth.

"We need to call an ambulance," I said. I didn't have my phone with me, so I frantically looked around for someone who could call 911.

"I'm on it," Mrs. Hopper said, her phone already pressed against her ear.

"Oh God," Mom released in a panicky voice.

My heart jumped in my chest. "What is it, Mom?"

"There's something wet. I feel something wet between my legs. It can't be blood. It can't be."

My chest collapsed with a fear unlike anything I'd felt before, and once more time slowed down as I grasped the meaning of what she was saying. My hands went cold, my mind becoming foggy.

"Please, don't let it be blood," she sobbed, clutching both Dominic's hand and her stomach. "Please, don't. No."

I felt dissociated as I rose to my feet. This wasn't happening. She couldn't be losing the baby. This was too much.

My gaze roamed across the foyer aimlessly and unseeingly, across the mash of faces gathered around us, until it caught Carter's. He stood near the door, observing the scene with wide eyes.

Blood rushed to my ears, and fury and hate broke me out of my stupor.

"Are you happy now? You're getting what you wanted, Carter."

He jerked, his expression twisting with hurt.

I didn't let the fear I saw in his eyes stop me as I made my way to him. "This is all your fault. I told you your actions have consequences, but you didn't care. And now she's losing her baby. All because of you."

Someone gasped behind me, but I couldn't care less about the scene I was making. Dominic might've said something, but it fell on deaf ears, because all my attention was focused on the guy who had just annihilated my heart. Who had finally made me despise him. I should've never gotten back together with him.

"You're the worst, Carter. You're vile, cruel, and you have no heart. I can't stand to look at you a second longer. So, you better leave and stay as far the hell away from us as possible. Because the next time you get near my mom, I'll rip your eyes out."

He just watched me, his chest rising and falling fast, his eyes two pools of great pain—all the memories of us, all the time we'd spent together, colliding, imploding into nothing.

Slowly, as if his hate built layer upon a layer, his eyes hardened, and then so did the rest of his face. The wall that he'd built up when he heard Mom's confession was now reinforced with thorns, never to be demolished again. We were done for good.

He spun around and walked out of the house, and it felt as if he was walking out of my life as well.

And as I watched him leave and time gradually returned to normal as EMTs rushed into the house and gathered around Mom, I felt as if the cold quickly overtaking me was here to stay forever.

You couldn't build happiness on someone else's unhappiness. You also couldn't build beautiful memories on ugly ones. Memories could nurture your soul or break it apart, and mine were corrosive shards that could never piece me together again. They were proof of a past that was too dark to give root to any light.

The night Carter lost his memories, he'd said that we belonged to each other and that would never change. He was so wrong.

In the end, the good memories didn't matter. They couldn't, not when they were fickle and deceptive, turning to ashes and a weapon of bitter pain when all there existed was hate. They couldn't, not when all the moments we'd shared—the laughter, the conversations, the fun times—weighed nothing compared to the ghosts of the past. Compared to toxicity and hate. Compared to darkness.

Maybe there was truth to what Nora and Carter had said. Maybe Carter and I weren't meant to be together and his amnesia was life telling us just that.

And maybe the only thing we'd ever have wasn't some soul-mate bullshit I started believing in the moment we had our first kiss.

But just the shattered memories of us.

ACKNOWLEDGMENTS

This story has come a long way since I got the initial idea of a guy forgetting ever loving a girl and remembering only hating her almost three years earlier. I stopped working on it at the time as I focused on my other projects, but at the beginning of 2022, the story called to me, and I just knew I had to finish it. After a major overhaul and new ideas added to the mix, *Shattered Memories* was finally born.

One of my favorite parts of the writing process is that each new story makes me feel like I started an exciting journey to places I've never seen before and impacts me in its own way. The angst and constant push-pull between Zoe and Carter kept me on the edge of my seat and made my heart flutter the whole time, and I enjoyed writing their scenes a lot. I can only hope you enjoyed the first part of their story as well.

There are many people who make the writing process easier for me, who make me remember why I'm writing and make it feel more fulfilling, and I want to start by thanking all the bloggers, bookstagrammers, booktokers, and reviewers who take time out of their day to read, review, and talk about my books, helping more people discover them. You're an integral part of every author's journey, and I highly appreciate all your effort and time.

Clare, thank you so much for always being so supportive and for your immense help. What would I do without you?

Catreena, I can't thank you enough for all your posts and edits and for always supporting me. I appreciate you so much. You're the best!

Special thanks go to Casey, who always cheers on me and is simply amazing <3

Kat, you always stick with me and are so supportive. Thank you for everything!

To Jo and the rest of the Give Me Books PR team—thank

you for your amazing work and dedication. It's always a pleasure working with you.

To my editor Emily—thank you for your great work and extraordinary attention to detail. Your feedback is always so helpful.

To Stacey from Champagne Book Design—I'm in love with your designs. Thank you for making my books look so pretty.

Huge thanks to my beta readers, Aniko, Dalilah, and Rachel—your feedback is so important, and my stories wouldn't be what they are without it. <3

To my ARC team—I can never thank you enough for your dedication and enthusiasm. Thank you for helping my books reach more people. You're the best team ever!

To my Facebook reader group Vera's Evil Bunnies—your enthusiasm always encourages me and puts a smile on my face. I appreciate all of you so much <3

To my dear readers—thank you for giving my books a chance and for your immense support. You always fuel my motivation and remind me to push forward. You make a difference.

And finally, to Rasa—my biggest supporter, my pillar of strength, my twinkling star. My best memories are with you, and I'll cherish them forever. Thank you for always giving me a reason to smile.

ABOUT THE AUTHOR

Vera Hollins writes emotional, dark, and angsty love stories that deal with heartbreak, mental and social issues, and finding light in darkness.

She's been writing since she was nine, and before she knew it, it became her passion and life. She particularly likes coffee, bunnies, angsty romance, and anti-heroes. When she's not writing, you can find her reading, plotting her next book with as many twists as possible, and watching YouTube.

Read more at www.verahollins.com.

Printed in Great Britain
by Amazon